I loved everything about this book. It is a fast-paced mystery, superbly plotted, and kept me guessing right until the end. Despite the murders, it is light hearted, easy to read, and perfect escapism. Sixties atmosphere oozes from the pages to enrich the whole reading experience. An absolute corker of a book.
Wendy Storer *Book Blog*

Headline Murder is a fun read with humour throughout – a literary version of *Heartbeat* but with a journalist lead, Brighton setting and more laughs. The strong supporting cast of colleagues, locals and feisty girlfriend help the story drive along nicely. An engaging and entertaining mystery.
Crime Thriller Hound

I found the novel a highly enjoyable and well-crafted read, with a host of engaging characters. It's a very good choice if you need a break from the darker recesses of *noir* or the modern world.
Mrs Peabody Investigates

I thoroughly enjoyed this newspaper caper set in the early 1960s. There's corruption, red herrings and the brief appearance of an insulting budgerigar. It read like a breath of fresh air and I can't wait for the next one.
Little Bookness Lane

By the end of page one, I knew I liked Colin Crampton and author Peter Bartram's breezy writing style. The author gives the readers much to enjoy both in the setting and characters as the story unfolds. Readers will immediately take to the protagonist, Colin Crampton, and will be eagerly awaiting his next investi-

gation.
Over My Dead Body

...a little reminiscent of [Raymond] Chandler...
Bookwitch

The book provides a pleasant saunter through a bygone age of yellowed newspaper clippings, public telephone boxes and a Britain still coming to terms with its post-war legacy. This mystery offers an enjoyable but mild mixture of English eccentricity, wry humour, social commentary and misdeeds.
Crime Fiction Lover

A lot of fun. There's a light touch to proceedings, as you'd expect from the use of the word "cozy" on the blurb on the back. So, an enjoyable entry into what I hope will be a long series. Highly Recommended.
In Search of the Classic Crime Mystery Novel

Headline Murder is a rather fun and well-written cozy mystery set in 1960s Brighton. Recommended for those who want a lighter crime read, with a genuine 1960s Brighton vibe.
Northern Crime

A skilfully constructed mystery that plays fair with the reader and holds the reader's rapt attention from first page to last. Very highly recommended and certain to be an enduringly popular addition to community library mystery/suspense collections.
Carl Logan, Midwest Book Review

Superbly crafted and breezy as a stroll along the pier, this Brighton-based murder mystery is a delight. *Headline Murder* is the real deal, giving a wonderful insight into local journalism and capturing the swinging sixties to perfection. Bring on the next

Crampton Chronicle.
Peter Lovesey, award-winning crime mystery writer

The story is a real 'whodunit' in the classic mould. The characters and the city of Brighton leap off the page newly minted but feeling like old friends. And don't worry if you don't remember the sixties because you weren't even born then There is none of the clunky scene-setting that so many writers find so necessary. Crampton takes you back effortlessly.
M. J. Trow, acclaimed author of 40 crime mystery novels

Headline Murder is an amiable romp through the shady back streets of 1960s Brighton. Its central character, the breezy journalist Colin Crampton, is very engaging and I look forward to his next investigation.
Simon Brett, award-winning crime writer

Stop Press Murder

A Crampton of the Chronicle Mystery

Stop Press Murder

A Crampton of the Chronicle Mystery

Peter Bartram

Winchester, UK
Washington, USA

First published by Roundfire Books, 2016
Roundfire Books is an imprint of John Hunt Publishing Ltd., Laurel House, Station Approach,
Alresford, Hants, SO24 9JH, UK
office1@jhpbooks.net
www.johnhuntpublishing.com
www.roundfire-books.com

For distributor details and how to order please visit the 'Ordering' section on our website.

Text copyright: Peter Bartram 2015

ISBN: 978 1 78535 440 3
Library of Congress Control Number: 2016931754

This book is a work of fiction and all the characters, events and places, except for those clearly
of public record, are imaginary and any resemblance to persons living or dead is unintentional
and coincidental.

Design: Stuart Davies

Printed and bound by CPI Group (UK) Ltd, Croydon, CR0 4YY, UK

We operate a distinctive and ethical publishing philosophy in all
areas of our business, from our global network of authors to
production and worldwide distribution.

Also by Peter Bartram in the
Crampton of the Chronicle mystery series:

Headline Murder

Prologue

It was the morning of the first of June 1963 when the man in the blue blazer, cavalry-twill trousers and brown brogues crept into the amusement arcade for his final reconnaissance.

The arcade on Brighton's Palace Pier hadn't yet attracted any punters. Later, the man knew, the place would be crowded as the suckers lost their money on the one-armed bandits and roll-a-penny machines.

He slipped behind one of the metal pillars which hold up the vaulted ceiling and glanced around.

At the far end of the arcade the brute of a caretaker prodded a long-handled broom viciously at a pile of litter. In the change booth, the fussy old dear fretted over the crossword in last night's *Evening Chronicle*. As usual. Neither of them would take any notice.

The man swallowed nervously.

He crept out from the shadow of the pillar and crossed to the wall where the What the Butler Saw machines stood in a row. He stopped in front of one. He realised he was panting for breath. He inhaled deeply to steady himself.

There was no doubt about his choice of machine. There never was. He already carried some pennies in his left hand. He noticed they had become slightly damp. No matter. He slipped one into the machine's slot, clamped his eyes over the viewer and cranked the handle that started the film playing.

Like most silent movies, the film starts with a title card.

The card has been lettered by a calligrapher with a fine hand.

The title reads: *Milady's Bath Night*.

The film cuts to the first scene.

A young woman reclines in a bath brimming with soap bubbles. Only her neck and head are above water. Her fair hair is pinned up in looping curls.

The film is old and grainy. It flickers with scratch marks. Black acid spots flash like ink blots. Despite this, it is easy to see the woman is beautiful. She has high cheekbones, a strong chin and eyes that seem just a little too big for her face. The eyes are heavily lined with mascara and dance with challenge. They say: *If you dare me, I'll double dare you.*

The woman lowers her head and looks up at the camera with a devilish smile. She scoops a handful of the bubbles, purses her lips in a kissing moue and blows the bubbles at the camera. Then she throws back her head, so the curls bounce on her head, and laughs.

Her eyes shift from the lens to something behind the camera. Somebody, probably the cameraman, is speaking to her. In film-speak, she is "taking direction". She gives a tiny nod. She moves in the bath and sets up a tidal wave of bubbles. Some spill over the rim.

Then she starts to rise. Her breasts are the first part of her body to break the surface. It is like watching a pair of porpoises leaping for joy.

Then the scene cuts to an intertitle: *"This towel is so fluffy."*

Same fine calligraphy.

In the next shot, the woman is in close-up. She is out of the bath and holding the towel to her left cheek. She has taken the pins out of her hair. It cascades in thick curls around her shoulders. She smoulders at the camera from the corner of her eyes.

She has the satisfied look of a woman who has enjoyed the heady scent of the soap and made good use of the loofah.

The scene cuts to a full-length shot. The woman has wrapped the towel around herself, over one shoulder, like a toga. In ancient Rome, she'd have caused a riot in the Forum. Then she turns sideways, looks back at the camera and tosses her head in a come-with-me gesture.

Another carefully lettered intertitle flickers: "*I must be ready for my beau.*"

In close up, the woman is looking at herself in a mirror. Her eyes widen imperceptibly. She gives a haughty toss of her head. She is happy with what she sees. She puts down the mirror and picks up a perfume bottle. She turns full on to the camera in half shot and sprays perfume behind each ear.

Then she glances at her breasts. The nipples turn slightly upwards. It's as though the porpoises are waiting for someone to throw them a fish. She winks and sprays perfume between her breasts.

The scene cuts to a half-length shot. The woman is wearing nothing but the perfume. She is standing, head bowed, hands behind her back, like a bound girl at a slave auction. But not for long. She shrugs her shoulders as if to say: "That's enough of that."

She turns to the right and begins to raise her left arm.

And at that point the film abruptly ends.

The man stamped his brown brogues. He drew back from the machine and cursed softly. He glanced around the arcade. The caretaker was loading litter into a basket. The change-giver was prodding a pencil in frustration at her newspaper.

The man took another of his pennies, slipped it into the slot, lowered his eyes to the viewer – and started to crank the handle.

Chapter 1

The mystery of *Milady's Bath Night* began with a riddle and ended with a tragedy.

I was sitting at my desk in the newsroom at the Brighton *Evening Chronicle*, weighing up the pros and cons of putting brown sauce on my breakfast bacon sandwich, when my telephone rang.

I lifted the receiver and said: "Colin Crampton, crime correspondent."

A man's voice with a deep rustic drawl, which reminded me of haystacks and summer meadows, said: "If I mentioned the word 'bunch' what would be the first thing that came into your mind?"

I said: "Roses, as in 'bunch of'. Red for the love of your life. Yellow to welcome home a long-lost friend. White for your grandmother's coffin."

"You're not even close. Try again."

"Girls' hair – as in 'tied in bunches'. Tidy when she's ten. Tempting when she's twenty."

"That doesn't count. I said 'bunch', singular."

"In that case, I can offer you a bunch of fives. As in the fingers in a fist – to give you a smack in the mouth."

Haystack voice said: "Tsk. It doesn't pay to get tetchy with a police officer."

The man offering me advice – and possibly a story – was Ted Wilson. He was a detective inspector in Brighton Police Force. And one of the few 'tecs I trusted in the town. The rest of them spent more time looking for the main chance than for clues. Put it this way: if they were drinking in the same pub you wouldn't leave your loose change on the bar.

I said: "What have you got for me? Am I going to be yelling 'Hold the front page'?"

He said: "Possibly. It's certainly bad news."

"The best kind."

"You're a cynical bastard. When I have to deliver the hard word most people don't want to know. They'd rather shoot the messenger."

I said: "If journalists shot the messenger they'd have to go out and find their own stories."

He said: "You won't have any difficulty finding this one. There's been a killing on Palace Pier."

I laughed. "Don't tell me someone finally landed the jackpot on that one-armed bandit in the amusement arcade."

"This wasn't a three-cherries-in-a-row kind of killing. It's a blood-on-the-floor job."

I reached for my notebook. Flicked it open. Grabbed a pencil.

"You mean murder?" I asked.

"Yes."

"When did this happen?"

"Some time last night after the pier closed. But it wasn't discovered until this morning. And there's a bizarre touch."

"Which is?"

"The body was discovered in the coconut shy."

"And hence your riddle about 'bunch'. You were thinking of the song *I've Got a Lovely Bunch of Coconuts*."

"Yes."

"As sung by Danny Kaye. And played endlessly on the Billy Cotton Band Show."

Wilson chuckled. "I'd say, 'Give the man a coconut', if it wasn't in bad taste."

"Why's that?"

"The victim was killed by a blow to the head with one."

I scribbled a shorthand note. "Male or female?" I asked.

"Coconuts don't have a sex."

"The victim."

"Male, I gather."

"Why, 'I gather'?"

Wilson said: "I wish I knew more. But I've been frozen out of this case. Tomkins has taken it."

That wasn't good news. Detective Superintendent Alec Tomkins hadn't liked me since I'd run a story about a cigarette-smuggling ring he'd arrested. The three smugglers had been acquitted at Lewes Assizes when the defence pointed out that the police were unable to account for all the contraband ciggies they claimed they'd seized.

I'd written that Tomkins' case had "gone up in smoke". He'd accused me of insinuating the lads at the cop shop had been treating themselves to duty-free drags from the evidence. Tomkins had blustered about a writ for libel. But the chief constable made it clear he wasn't funding a lengthy court case out of the police budget.

Instead, Tomkins settled for nurturing a life-long hatred of me.

"That explains why I didn't know about it," I said.

"There's more," Wilson said. "I've just heard that Tomkins tipped off Houghton more than an hour ago."

That was worse news. Jim Houghton was my opposite number on the *Evening Argus*, the other paper in town. By now, he'd be at the scene of the crime with Tomkins. The two would be laughing themselves silly over the right royal stuffing they were giving me.

I said: "Thanks for the tip-off, Ted."

"Sorry I couldn't do it earlier. Needed to get out of the office to make this call. You'll know why."

The phone went dead.

I replaced the receiver with mixed feelings.

What Ted told me was enough for two paragraphs for the Midday Special edition's "news in brief". But Houghton would have a front-page lead in the *Argus*.

As soon as my news editor Frank Figgis saw the midday *Argus*, he'd want to know why I'd been scooped. He wouldn't be interested in hearing that Houghton had been given an inside track by Tomkins.

Figgis wouldn't sack me. It would be worse than that. He'd think up some creative revenge – like making me sit through endless meetings of the crime-prevention committee at the Town Hall.

Or he'd book me as the guest speaker on the "ethics of the press" at the Women's Institute in an inaccessible Sussex village.

Or he'd make me interview a retired police-dog handler with bad breath and dandruff.

Or the dog.

To avoid any of those horrors, I had to find an angle on the story that outpaced the *Argus* in time for our Afternoon Extra edition. That meant I had three hours to turn the story around.

I grabbed my notebook and headed for the door.

The bacon sandwich would have to wait.

Chapter 2

I barged through the newsroom's swing doors, clattered down the stairs and charged out into the street.

An *Evening Argus* delivery van sped round the corner. It was on its way back to the print works after collecting yesterday's returns. It missed me by inches. The driver was the one with the pork-pie face and tattoo of Diana Dors on his right forearm. He took his hands off the steering wheel, held his nose and pulled an imaginary chain. I couldn't be bothered to semaphore an insolent reply. Anyway, Diana would have thought of something even filthier.

I was too busy pondering the trouble a murder can cause a reporter when he's not first on the scene. (For the victim, of course, it's the other way round).

It would have made Tomkins' day to give Houghton a head start on the story so that I would look bad. He was probably hugging himself with delight. So I'd need to find a way of catching up on the lead Houghton would already have built.

He'd have been first to interview the police. First to view the murder scene, if the cops let him in. And if they wouldn't, Houghton wasn't averse to slipping the duty officer a fiver. For tickets to the policeman's ball, of course. In his time, Houghton had bought enough dance tickets to pack out the Saturday-night hop at the Corn Exchange.

Houghton would have been first to get the name of the deceased. First to visit their nearest and dearest and pick up the tearful quotes. First to beg a photograph of their sadly departed. (Or quietly pocket one from the mantelpiece if they were too distressed to dig out the family photo album).

I'd be limping along a couple of hours later, after everyone had got it off their chest and thought they wouldn't be bothered again. First time was a duty, second time an intrusion.

So the police would be skimpy with their answers. They'd think twice about letting me see the murder scene. Even if I bought a trumpet and promised to play the mambo at their ball.

The nearest and dearest would be over the shock and into deep grieving so they wouldn't want to talk. And I wouldn't get anywhere near the mantelpiece – even to snatch the last picture, which is usually the family dog.

By the time I reached the seafront, I'd worked up a sweat. It was one of those June days that fool you into thinking you're going to have a good summer. The sun was out and a few cotton-wool jobs were scudding across the sky. A light breeze wafted in from the south-east and gave the summer bunting along the prom a gentle work-out. The tide was up and waves broke with a rhythmic splosh on the pebbles.

A Tamplin's beer lorry, rattling with empties, drove by on its way to the Kemp Town brewery. I let it pass, then hurried across the road to the pier's forecourt. A crowd of rubberneckers had gathered around the pier entrance. They jostled and whispered to one another and pointed at things I couldn't see. I pushed my way through and found a couple of police squad cars parked up by the turnstiles. A flimsy blue tape – "Police line: keep out" – had been strung between Hamburger Heaven and the Popcorn Palace. I ducked under the tape and strode up to a constable who'd been posted to keep out people like me.

He was a copper I hadn't seen before. He was leaning on the railings next to the ticket office. I walked over, pulled out my press card and said: "If you let me through I might buy you some candyfloss later."

He sniffed and said: "You wouldn't feel like candyfloss if you'd seen what we've seen."

"Bad business?" I asked.

"Especially for the stiff."

"Anyone I knew?"

He jerked his thumb towards the seaward end of the pier.

"They're all down there. Any more questions, ask Detective Superintendent Tomkins. He don't approve of the likes of me talking to the likes of you."

"Then we'll keep this *tête-à-tête* our little secret."

I gave him a conspiratorial wink, pushed through the turnstile and hurried towards the far end of the pier.

Normally, the place would be crowded on a day like this. There'd be young lads with tattoos on their arms eyeing up pretty girls in Capri pants. There'd be old blokes with knotted handkerchiefs on their heads, snoozing in deckchairs. There'd be a barrel organ blasting out *I Do Like to be Beside the Seaside*. There'd be seagulls squabbling over discarded chip wrappers. The sea air would be cut by the vinegar sharpness of cockles and whelks.

But the place was deserted. It felt a bit eerie, like a party where the host has forgotten to invite the guests. The shutters had been pulled down over the hoop-la stall. A hastily scrawled note in the window of the fortune-teller's booth read: "Closed due to unforeseen circumstances."

The coconut shy was towards the seaward end of the pier facing the theatre. It was a rectangular space about fifteen-feet deep. It was surrounded on three sides with heavy netting so that wooden balls which the punters flung vainly at the coconuts didn't bounce off and brain some hapless passer-by. The cops had rigged up a tarpaulin over the front of the shy so that nobody could view the grisly scene inside.

I spotted Tomkins at once. He was a tall man with a thatch of black hair which he combed straight back from his forehead. He had bushy eyebrows and a prominent nose like an eagle's beak.

There was no sighting of Jim Houghton. But I already knew he'd had an hour's start on me. He'd have interviewed Tomkins, then dictated his copy for the *Argus* midday edition from the phone box outside the pier. Even now, the comps would be setting his piece in type and the subs would be dreaming up a sensational headline.

I frowned. I had some serious work to do if I was to catch up with the *Argus* on this story. So I strode towards Tomkins. He was busy barking out orders to a couple of uniformed plods. As I approached, he looked my way. Recognition clouded his eyes. The muscles around his mouth tightened. But I didn't think I'd be greeted like an old buddy.

I gave him what I hoped might be a disarming grin and lied: "Good to see Brighton's finest on a big case."

He frowned and said: "Chuck it. You're as irritated to see me as I am to see you. You can save your nasty little falsehoods for the *Chronicle*. That's where you usually print them."

"A simple seeker after truth – that's me," I said.

"And I'm father confessor to the Pope," he said.

"I'll quote you on that. Should give our readers a laugh. Might even raise a smile down at the section house. Alternatively, you can tell me what's really going on."

Tomkins scowled. "I can't tell you much, and I'm too busy for a long interview but I'll answer three questions."

I pointed at the coconut shy and said: "I take it the victim is in there. Who is it?"

"Fred Snout, the pier's night-watchman."

"And how was he killed?"

"Bludgeoned with a blunt instrument."

"The blunt instrument being?"

Tomkins looked embarrassed. "A coconut."

"Since when has a coconut been a blunt instrument?"

"That's a fourth question."

"Treat it as my bonus query and I'll vanish like smoke up a chimney."

"Don't you get me started on smoke."

"I'll take that as a 'no comment'."

"Take it any way you like. I haven't got any more time to waste on you." Tomkins turned away and stomped off behind the tarpaulin. I could hear his muffled voice as he began barking out more orders.

I wasn't going to get any more out of him but at least I had the outline of the story. I glanced at my watch. It was five past ten. I'd missed the deadline for the Midday Special although I still had twenty minutes to get something into the fudge. But if the *Argus* ran a splash and we only had a paragraph in the stop press, it would look as though we weren't on top of the story. Much better, I thought, to wait for the Afternoon Extra and run with a fresh angle the *Argus* hadn't covered. I suspected Frank Figgis, the news editor, wouldn't agree. But he was going to be on my back like a sackful of seaweed whatever I did.

So I hung around by the coconut shy watching the comings and goings. After a couple of minutes, a middle-aged man emerged from behind the tarpaulin. He had greying hair which flopped over his forehead. He was dressed in a sports jacket with leather patches on the elbows. I recognised him as the doctor the cops sometimes called in when a drunk took sick in the cells. I thought his name was Barrett. His shoulders sagged and his face was grey. He'd have had grimmer work today.

He took out a packet of cheroots, shook one out and lit up.

I ambled over and gave him the kind of weary nod that professionals share when they're on the same distasteful work.

I carefully avoided mentioning I was a reporter and said: "Brained by a coconut, Superintendent Tomkins tells me."

"You've spoken to Tomkins?" He sounded surprised.

"He's briefed me on the essentials," I said.

"He doesn't normally say much."

"That's right. Usually leaves it to the hired help, eh?" I flashed him the kind of weary grin that suggested we were all in it together.

Barrett exhaled a long stream of cheroot smoke and relaxed a little. "Meaning me, I suppose?"

"I guess he must," I said. "Just wondering what you've seen in there."

"Well, it wasn't a lovely bunch of coconuts, I can tell you."

"How could you kill a man with a coconut?" I asked.

"From the victim's point of view, I'd say it was an unlucky blow. He'd been hit in the side of the head – that area just behind the eye but in front of the ear. It's called the pterion – it's where four parts in the skull join, so it's the weakest spot. Doesn't need much force with something hard to cause a severe fracture and drive bone fragments into the brain. Then it's goodnight Vienna."

I nodded. "No sign of the weapon in there, I suppose?"

"Can't really think of a coconut as a weapon. But, no. Would be easy to toss it off the pier into the sea."

"Any idea about who could have done it?" I asked.

"I'd guess somebody fit and active from the force of the wound. I found fragments of coconut hair embedded in the flesh. Must have been a random killing. My guess is the murderer was discovered and grabbed the first thing that came to hand."

"Who found him?"

"Pier manager Reginald Chapman – on his early-morning round. He's in his office now, fretting about the money he's losing while the pier is closed."

"Sounds like a charmer," I said.

Barrett took a final puff on his cheroot, pinched it out between his fingers and flung the dog-end into the sea.

Behind the tarpaulin, I could hear Tomkins yelling something. It was time for a tactical retreat. I didn't want him to see me interrogating Barrett. He'd bawl out the good doctor and that would make him less talkative in future.

So I swiftly said: "Well, must get on." I turned and headed back down the pier.

Barrett had filled in some of the gaps in the story. But I needed background so, as I walked down the pier, I kept an eye open for any members of staff who might be able to tell me more about Fred Snout. Perhaps somebody might even have a theory about what was behind this killing. But the place was deserted.

I walked on thinking hard how I could catch up with the lead Houghton had on the story. With a murder story, you need to answer four questions – who was murdered, how they were murdered, why they were murdered, and who did it? Both Houghton and I had answers to the first two of those questions. I was sure Houghton hadn't cracked the last two. If I could get a lead on them first, I would be able to out-scoop him.

I was musing on this as I came around the corner by the amusement arcade and almost cannoned into a large man. He was kneeling down fumbling with a heavy bunch of keys. He was unlocking the door of the arcade.

He looked up. He had a fleshy face, a bulbous nose and a faint scar about an inch long which ran along the line of his jaw just below his right ear. He had heavy arms, a broad chest and four-pint beer belly. He was wearing blue overalls.

He narrowed his eyes, decided I didn't represent a threat and said: "You here about the trouble?"

I said: "Yes. Bad business."

"The worst."

"Know much about it?"

His fat fingers fumbled the keys as he searched for the one he needed. "Only that she's gone."

I said: "Don't you mean 'he's gone'?"

"You're thinking of Fred." He shook his head. "Yes, that's bad. But I wasn't thinking of Fred."

"Then who?"

"I was talking about Marie Richmond. She's disappeared – and I blame that Fred Snout."

I glanced down the pier towards the turnstiles.

A couple of uniformed cops pushed through and headed our way. The last thing I needed now was a pair of plods telling me to move along.

So I said: "Why don't we go in?"

The Key Man said: "That's what I've been trying to do."

He selected a large mortise key, unlocked the door and we stepped inside the arcade.

It was dark but the Key Man flicked a couple of switches and fluorescent light flooded the place.

He said: "Sent you from the office, did they?"

I thought about that for a moment. Decided there'd be no harm playing along with the conversation to see where it led.

So I said: "It's good to get out of the office once in a while."

The Key Man seemed satisfied with the answer. "Come to view the damage, I suppose. Insurance claim, is it?"

"Could be," I said. "By the way, I forgot to ask your name."

"Tom Belcher," he said.

"Trevor Hardcastle," I said.

We shook hands.

Tom said: "I'm the superintendent caretaker for the amusement arcade. So I handle the maintenance of these machines." He waved his arm expansively around the place. "Classics some of these. Have you seen the hangman's noose? Fiendishly clever. I tell you, this ain't an amusement arcade – it's a slice of engineering history."

I couldn't tell where this was leading. So I said: "And Marie Richmond – does she work here as well?"

"In a manner of speaking, she did. In spirit at least."

"You'll have to explain that."

Tom pointed to the other side of the arcade. "Miss Richmond was the star of one our finest films."

Tom had indicated a row of What the Butler Saw machines lined up against the arcade's wall. Each consisted of a metal cylinder with an eyepiece viewer. The contraption was mounted on metal legs. The machines showed short films, normally of young women in some kind of trouble with their clothes. The trouble being that they didn't have them on.

"You mean the What the Butler Saw machines?" I said.

"I don't like the expression. It makes their art seem cheap," he said. "Their inventor – Herman Casler, an American gentleman, but he couldn't help that – called them mutoscopes. Strange name. Never known why he chose it."

"I expect it's because the muto bit comes from mutare, a Latin verb meaning 'to change'."

Tom nodded. "That makes sense. The pictures in the machine change as you turn the handle."

He was right. Each machine held a kind of flip-book of pictures which you looked at through the viewer. You cranked a handle to make the flip-book pages turn and created a jerky moving image usually of the half-naked woman struggling with her clothing difficulty. It was a bit like watching a peep show through a periscope.

But we were straying from the point. I said: "And what has happened to Marie Richmond's pictures?"

"Someone has nicked them."

"Stolen?"

"That's what I said. Half-inched."

"Pinched?"

"You've got it."

We crossed the arcade and Tom stopped in front of one of the machines. A playbill in a frame on top of the machine announced it was showing *Milady's Bath Night*. The others had similar titles on their playbills. The machine to the left featured *Lucy Loses Her Inhibitions*.

I said: "Why would anyone want to steal the pictures from a What... mutoscope?"

Tom tapped the side of his nose. "When you look at these through the viewer, the machine never gets to show you the last few pictures. Something to do with the way the mechanism has worn down over the years. Now, with *Milady*, the film ends at a particularly interesting moment." He nudged me in the ribs.

"I've heard it say that if you could see the last few pictures, they would be very revealing. Know what I mean?"

He nudged me again.

"So you think the machine has been emptied just so that a member of the dirty-mac brigade can drool over the pictures he couldn't see," I said.

Tom winked. "I don't miss much. Can't afford to here. Morning before the pictures went missing – that was three days ago – there was a bloke in. Saw him watch it three times in a row. Thought it was going to need more pennies from the change booth the way he was going. Anyway, he sloped off out of it. Haven't seen him since."

"And do you think he stole the pictures?"

"Don't see how he could. Last I saw of him, he was walking towards the exit."

"Do you know who he was?"

"Never seen him in here before."

"What did he look like?"

"Tall, well dressed in an old-fashioned sort of way. Not the sort we normally get hunched over the mutoscopes."

I inspected the *Milady's Bath Night* mutoscope more closely. "This doesn't look damaged," I said. "How could someone steal the pictures? They're locked inside."

"You open a hinged door round the back to remove them. There's a key, but you can do it with a pair of pliers. If you know how."

"Do many know how?"

"Not many."

I thought about that for a minute and then asked: "When did the pictures disappear?"

"Two nights ago."

"And why do you blame Fred Snout. The late Fred Snout."

Tom looked away. Standard reaction for someone with a guilty conscience. "He's the night-watchman. Supposed to keep

17

the place safe at night. But it's common knowledge he used to make his-self a cup of cocoa, drink it and then fall asleep in one of the deckchairs."

"Not last night," I said.

Tom shrugged.

"No, not last night. I'm sorry about that. And I didn't mean what I said when we had that row."

"You had a row?"

"Morning after the theft. Right royal barney it was. You could hear us as far down the pier as the helter-skelter."

"Hard words were spoken?"

"Yeah, well, I said Fred was a past-it old lump of uselessness. Blamed him for the theft. Said I'd kill him if it happened again." Tom shrugged. "Heat of the moment. I didn't mean it. And I didn't kill him. Of course."

I studied him for a moment. He was a big man who'd hold his own in a fight. The muscles in his arms had turned to fat. Yet they would still pack some force if they wielded a coconut as an offensive weapon. But for all his bluster, he was easily cowed. Besides, he had a real passion for these arcade machines – especially, it seemed, the mutoscopes.

No, I didn't think Tom had killed Fred.

But had the person who'd stolen *Milady's Bath Night*? Had the killer returned to the pier again? Was it Fred's bad luck that he wasn't asleep in a deckchair after his night-time cocoa? And had his uncustomary wakefulness led to a confrontation – and a smashed skull?

I said: "Do you suppose the theft could be connected to Fred Snout's murder?"

Tom said: "How could it? Happened two nights earlier."

"Have you mentioned the theft to the police?"

"Naw. The big boss said not to."

"The big boss being?"

"Reginald Chapman."

"The pier's manager," I said.

"Yes."

"Did he say why he wanted to keep the police out of it?"

"Naw. But he don't fool me. Doesn't want Brighton Council's Watch Committee sniffing round the mutoscopes. Afraid some of the pictures might be a bit too fruity for the old duchesses on the committee."

I wondered whether Chapman hadn't wanted the police involved because he knew there was more to the theft than met the eye – and that Chapman knew what it was. But I was just building a theory – and a theory without any supporting evidence at that. At least Tom had given me a new angle on the story – one Houghton wouldn't have discovered.

That, at least, might redeem some of my reputation with Figgis.

I said: "Thanks for your help, Tom. I hope you get the pictures back."

He didn't look hopeful. "Me, too. Somehow the place doesn't seem the same without *Milady*. I wish I knew where she'd gone."

It was the same thought in my mind as I hurried towards the pier's exit.

Chapter 3

I arrived back at the *Chronicle* ten minutes later to find it buzzing with deadline fever.

The pier murder was the talk of the newsroom. I heard my name mentioned a couple of times as I pushed through the swing doors. I made straight for my desk to a chorus of unwanted comments from colleagues.

"Frank Figgis has been looking for you," said Phil Bailey.

The old buzzard would have heard about the murder. He'd be fuming that I hadn't filed any copy for the Midday Special. Not even a par for the stop press.

"He's been rummaging around your desk," said Paul Goodbody.

"He's madder than that time he dropped a new packet of Woodbines down the lavvy," said Sally Martin.

I reached my desk and slumped onto my chair.

Susan Wheatcroft leaned over with a sympathetic smile. "If he sacks you, honeybunch, can I have your luncheon vouchers?"

Well, really. Where would we be without supportive colleagues?

I'd made a decision on my walk back from the pier. I needed a way to leap ahead of Jim Houghton on the story. He thought he'd scooped me. But he didn't know about the theft of Marie Richmond's pictures. I had a hunch that must be linked to the murder. The fact Reginald Chapman, the pier manager, didn't want the police to know about it, raised questions. Even suspicions. So I decided I'd link the two crimes – the murder and the theft – in my story and then work to make the link stand up in follow-ups. If it all went right, it was a strategy that would make Houghton look like a stumblebum. If it went wrong... I would think about that when the time came.

So I rolled copy paper into my old Remington typewriter and

pounded out: "The killing of Palace Pier's night-watchman Fred Snout could be linked to the theft of saucy pictures from a What the Butler Saw machine in the amusement arcade."

I was about to start on the second paragraph when I realised the newsroom had fallen silent. I looked up. Frank Figgis was stomping towards my desk with a face like a winter weather front.

Figgis was a short man with a wizened face which looked as though it had been made out of ancient leather. He had hard little brown marbles for eyes. He walked with a kind of jaunty bounce on account of his red braces were usually adjusted one notch too tight.

He clumped up to my desk, nodded at the copy paper in my Remington and said: "I hope that's your resignation you're typing."

"'Fraid not. I've forgotten whether you spell 'quit' with a K or a Q."

"You also seem to have forgotten how to file breaking stories."

"Not forgotten. Read this."

I rolled the folio out of the Remington and handed it to Figgis.

A nervous twitch in his cheek pulsed as he read it.

He said: "This changes nothing. Follow me." He turned and marched back across the newsroom towards his office.

I stood up and tagged along behind feeling a bit like Sidney Carton heading for the guillotine.

As I passed Sally Martin's desk she leaned over and whispered: "Good luck."

I felt she spoilt the gesture by crossing herself like a penitent priest as she said it.

Back in his office, Figgis sat down behind his desk, reached for his fags and lit up.

He said: "The *Argus* will be splashing at midday with the

biggest crime story in Brighton for a year. And we don't even have a par for the stop press. I've sacked reporters for less. Give me one good reason why I should spare you the chop."

Figgis hadn't invited me to sit, so I made a bit of performance of pulling out the guest chair and getting myself comfortable.

I said: "Because I'm about to break a story that will make the *Argus*'s coverage look as dull as a dimwit's diary. You've seen the first par of my story – death by coconut linked with a sexy siren's naughty pictures. Only the coconut was shy. It's a combination that will sell papers in thousands."

Figgis read my intro again and scratched his chin. "This sounds speculative to me," he said. "I don't want us to climb out on a limb which some smart-arse at the *Argus* will saw off."

"That's why I've written it in the conditional tense," I said.

"Clever grammar doesn't count for much when you're wrong."

"I don't think I am. Call it intuition."

"When you stand in the witness box defending a libel action, some clever-dick lawyer will be asking you for evidence, not intuition."

"Give me time and I can find it. The evidence, that is."

Figgis had a thoughtful drag on his ciggie. "And the police don't know about this theft?" he asked.

"Chapman, the pier manager, didn't want it reported. Some guff about not wanting the council's Watch Committee reviewing the naughty pictures in the other machines."

"And you think that wasn't the real reason?"

"Those machines have been there since Charlie Chaplin's time. Besides, I suspect most of the Watch Committee members have had a sneaky thrill themselves when they thought nobody was looking."

"And all this will be in your copy for the Afternoon Extra?" Figgis said.

"Every golden word. Plus the snippets Detective

Superintendent Tomkins threw me."

"Tomkins won't like it."

"Since when has it been our mission to bring pleasure into the unsuper Super's life?"

"True."

"Besides, Chapman won't be grinning like a goon, either," I said. "He could have to answer some tough questions from Tomkins about why he didn't report the theft."

"That's an angle we need to keep an eye on," Figgis said.

"So, shall I follow up the lead?" I asked.

"Can I stop you?"

I smiled. "Probably not."

I stood up and started for the door.

Figgis said: "Just a moment. There's another matter."

I turned and tried out my wide-eyed innocent look. "Other matter?"

Figgis wasn't going to let me off that lightly. He'd made it plain he hadn't liked the fact that I'd not filed copy for the Midday Special stop press. Now there'd be a price to pay. No doubt he had one of his pieces of creative revenge in store.

I sat down again.

Figgis leant across the desk, dropped his voice and said: "Keep this to yourself for now. We've had a tip from Dickie Waterford that a big national story's going to break tomorrow."

Waterford was the paper's political correspondent. We saw little of him in Brighton. He spent most of his time schmoozing politicians around Westminster. No wonder he ran up a weekly bar bill on expenses that would have kept me in G and Ts for a year.

I said: "I cover crime. It's more honest than politics."

Figgis said: "If what we hear is correct, there may not be much difference between the two. The whisper is that Jack Profumo is going to resign."

"You mean the Minister of War who's caught in the scandal

with call girls?"

Figgis nodded.

This sounded like the kind of political yarn I could get interested in. Rumours had been running in the nationals for weeks. Despite having a name that sounded like an air freshener, Profumo was a toff straight out of society's top drawer. He had a good-looking wife who'd been a bit-part actress in her day. But Profumo himself couldn't resist acting the goat with a string of strumpets, one of whom had also been dallying with the naval attaché at the Russian Embassy. Anchors aweigh, and all that. Profumo had stood up in the House of Commons and said the rumour about him and the girls was a lie. Now, if Waterford's tip was correct, the naughty war minister was ready to hoist the white flag of surrender.

Figgis said: "Seems Profumo lied to the House of Commons about his affair. That's why he's got to go."

"Not the fact he's cheated on his wife," I said.

"When you're in politics, cheating is second nature."

I said: "So when he made his call to arms at the party conference, he had the wrong arms in mind."

"Trouble is, we'll have to splash on this. I hate running with a national story on the front page without a local twist. That's why I want a backgrounder – we need a Sussex angle to the story."

"Anything in mind?" I asked.

"Harold Macmillan has a house at Birch Grove, near Horsted Keynes. As Prime Minister, he'll have to handle the crisis. Let's use the PM's residence as the local angle. Perhaps Profumo visited there. Or maybe Macmillan will be retreating there to decide how to handle the crisis."

So this was Figgis's revenge. He wanted me to manufacture a non-existent angle for a national story which every other paper would have anyway.

"Sounds thin to me," I said.

"Not the way you handle it, I'm sure," Figgis said. "There

must be some other local peg you can find."

I nodded thoughtfully. Smiled helpfully. "Trouble is, I won't have time – given that I've got a big running story in the pier murder," I said. "There are several angles I need to follow on that story. It'll keep me busy for at least a couple of days."

"Perhaps I should put somebody else on the Snout story," he said. "Somebody who knows how to file copy for the stop press on time."

Figgis had me cornered and he knew it. I furrowed my brow to make it look as though I was giving the matter some deep thought. "As it happens," I said, "I think I may be able to fit in both jobs."

"I thought you would," Figgis said. "We don't want you making an ignominious exit like old Profumo."

I was now under pressure to write the murder story for the Afternoon Extra and have the backgrounder ready to roll when the Profumo story broke. I glanced at my watch: five to eleven. The copy deadline was twelve-thirty. So I headed straight for the morgue – the paper's library where thousands of press cuttings were filed.

Figgis had out-manoeuvred me but there was no point in getting angry about it. Journalism is a bit like war – but without guns or medals. Sometimes you make a tactical retreat so you can plan a new advance.

So I breezed into the morgue with a cheery cry of "Morning, ladies."

Henrietta Houndstooth, the paper's librarian who ran the morgue, looked up from a file she was studying, frowned and said: "What are you so cheerful about? We'd heard a rumour you were about to be fired."

Nothing much escaped Henrietta. She had more ears than a field of corn.

I said: "As Mark Twain might have put it, reports of my firing have been greatly exaggerated."

At a large table in the centre of the room, the Clipping Cousins stopped squabbling over the last toffee in a paper bag.

Elsie said: "That's a relief."

Mabel said: "You won't be on the streets."

Freda said: "Would you like the last toffee to celebrate?"

The other two glared at her.

I said: "Perhaps another time. I'm on deadline."

The Clipping Cousins were a trio of middle-aged matrons who were related more by a love of gossip than by blood. They spent their days cutting and filing press cuttings and chattering among themselves. They'd helped me on many a story.

I turned to Henrietta. "I've got to write a backgrounder on the Profumo affair."

She said: "He's not a Sussex Member of Parliament so I don't think we have a file on him."

I said: "I thought so, but Macmillan has a Sussex home and I'll use that as the peg for my story."

"So you want the file on Birch Grove. Give me a minute."

Henrietta disappeared through the door into the filing stacks. I waited.

Elsie looked up from her cuttings and said: "That Profumo is no gentleman."

Mabel said: "Cavorting with those common women."

Freda said: "And him being a big knob, too."

The other two stared at Freda and her cheeks coloured.

"I think a big knob was the cause of his problems," Mabel said.

Henrietta came back into the room carrying a thick buff file. She handed it to me. "Everything you could ever want to know about Birch Grove," she said.

I opened the file and flicked through the cuttings. There were more than fifty. I said: "Figgis wanted a cuttings job and he's going to get it."

Henrietta said: "Have you journalists no shame?"

I said: "We save it for the editorials. But there's another story where I need your help."

"The murder on the pier?" Henrietta said.

"I thought you would've heard about that. But you might not have heard about a strange incident a couple of nights ago." I told her about the theft of the What the Butler Saw film.

"I'm sure we've never clipped cuttings about those machines," Henrietta said.

"I thought so. But you may have cuttings about one of the actresses that appeared in the stolen one – Marie Richmond."

"Who?"

Henrietta had stiffened before she answered. She had a ruddy complexion from healthy walks on the Downs. But I could have sworn she'd turned a shade paler.

"Richmond," I said. "Marie Richmond."

Henrietta fiddled with the brooch – a sort of flower arrangement – on her tweed jacket. "I'll take a look," she said. "Wait here."

She hurried through the door into the filing stacks.

For want of something to lighten the atmosphere, I waved the Birch Grove file at the Cousins and said: "This should keep me busy."

Elsie said: "That Profumo is a dirty dog."

Mabel said: "An alley cat, if you ask me."

Freda said: "I'd call him an old goat to his face."

I said: "You make him sound like a one-man menagerie."

The Cousins started to squabble over which term of abuse most suited Profumo. I flipped through the file. Minutes passed. I glanced at my watch.

Something wasn't right. Henrietta had been startled when I'd mentioned Marie Richmond. But I didn't know why.

Quietly, I left the Clipping Cousins scissoring their way through old newspapers and crept into the filing stacks. The place was a maze of dusty corridors lit by flickering forty-watt bulbs. The air smelt musty with damp paper dust. Stick a few hieroglyphics on the wall and you could imagine you were creeping into some long-lost Pharaoh's tomb.

As Henrietta was looking for a file on Marie Richmond, she'd be in the corridor with the letter R files. I stumbled along searching for it. I tried one or two of the corridors but couldn't see Henrietta. I stood still and listened. The sounds of the outside world somehow became muted inside the file archive. It was like a parallel universe. As though the presence of so many old press cuttings acted like a kind of time machine dragging you back to the past.

I strained my ears but heard only the sound of silence.

Then I heard a sniffle.

And next a woman's sob.

Not the kind of little sniff you might hear if somebody had forgotten her birthday. No, this was a deep visceral wail of grief. The kind that comes from someone who realises that a deep love has been lost for ever and will never return.

I crept forward and peered around a stack of cabinets. Henrietta was standing by an open drawer in the P to R corridor. She had a buff file, aged with dust, in her hands. She was turning over the clippings in it – and tears were streaming down her face.

Her misery was so profound I didn't know what to do.

My first instinct was to hurry forward and comfort her. To embrace her and give her a shoulder to cry on. To ask her what had caused her grief. But I checked myself. Henrietta was a private woman. She never talked about her personal life. Never displayed powerful emotions. She would hate having to explain what had upset her. Hate anybody even knowing about her sorrow. The horror of that would live with her long after the grief had passed.

I stepped back silently – out of sight.

I wasn't sure what to do next. Questions were running round

my mind like ferrets at a fanciers' meet. What was the file Henrietta was holding? Was it something to do with Marie Richmond? And why had it reduced her to tears? I had no answers. And, for the time being at least, Henrietta was the very last person to ask.

I tiptoed quietly out of the filing stacks back into the clippings room and picked up the Birch Grove file. The Clipping Cousins, for once, were absorbed in their newspapers.

I headed back to the newsroom with much on my mind.

Chapter 4

I was so deep in thought about Henrietta when I stepped into the newsroom, I crashed straight into Sidney Pinker on his way out.

"My dear boy, there's no need to be so rough with me," Pinker said. "At least not here." He arched his left eyebrow and made it wiggle like a caterpillar.

Pinker was the paper's theatre critic. He spent most of his time lounging in an end-of-row seat in the Theatre Royal stalls sneering at the latest drawing-room comedy. He had an aquiline face, cat-like eyes and an extravagant bouffant haircut. He was wearing a white jacket and pink slacks. He'd tied a flowery cravat around his neck in a raffish way so that its ends trailed over his collar.

I said: "Spare a minute, Sidney."

He gave me the kind of lingering look that made me feel I needed to wash my hands and said: "For you, a whole hour. But not just now, dear boy. Busy, busy, busy."

I said: "It's urgent – just one question. Do you know anything about a silent-movie actress called Marie Richmond?"

The cat's eyes shot me a sly glance. He grinned, gave me a playful chuck under the chin and said: "Who's a naughty boy then?"

I said: "Save the Gay Hussar act for your fan club. I'm on two deadlines and need some information."

Sidney pursed his lips. "Trade for trade," he said.

Pinker had a reputation for never giving a little unless he got a little.

So I said: "What is it?"

He reached into his pocket and pulled out a couple of tickets. "Hippodrome tomorrow night. Another variety music hall. How I hate them. Those speciality acts bore me rigid. If I have to watch another young man in tights juggling with his balls… I think I'd rather die."

He did that eyebrow thing again.

"And you want me to see the show and write a crit?" I said.

"I prefer the term 'notice', dear boy. But, yes. Seven pars should do it."

"I don't know…"

"We always get two tickets. You can take a friend. If you have one."

I shrugged. I needed Pinker's help and he knew I'd have to pay the price. "I'll write your notice," I said. "So what can you tell me about Marie Richmond?"

"Not more than you could find in a brief history of Britain's silent-movie industry. But an old friend of mine acted with Miss Richmond. He's also something of a walking encyclopaedia on the days of the silver screen. Toupée Terry. That is to say, Terry Montague. A former thespian himself. Although it's been many a long year since he last trod the boards. Laid on them – well, that's altogether another story."

"Does he live in Brighton?" I asked.

"Near Fiveways. Although I can only think of four." Pinker winked.

I ignored it and said: "And you can get me in to see this Toupée?"

Pinker held up his hands in mock horror. "You must never call him that, dear boy. Not unless you want to witness the hissiest little hissy fit in theatre-land. Artistic temperament, you know. But, yes, I can persuade him to see you – as long as I don't have to sit through another soprano murdering *I Dreamt I Dwelt in Marble Halls* at the Hippodrome."

I took the tickets. "And, Sidney, this is urgent. I need to see Terry today."

"Consider it done, dear boy."

Back at my desk, I pulled the battered Remington towards me

and hammered out the story about the pier murder.

I used the intro I'd shown to Figgis. I had little hard information to go on, so it was a question of planting the few known facts among some artful speculation and colourful background. The piece made 14 pars, enough for a splash in the Afternoon Extra, which would please Figgis. I called for Cedric, the copy boy, and gave him the folios to take to the subs.

"Another of your scoops, Mr Crampton?" he said. Cedric was an 18-year-old who'd been copy boy for three years. In the office, he was as respectful as a Buckingham Palace flunky. Out of it, I'd heard, he was a Jack-the-Lad with a reputation as a bird puller at Sherry's on a Saturday night. I couldn't see it, myself. He had an untidy mop of brown hair, freckles on his cheeks and a gap between his two front teeth that Terry Thomas would envy. He'd been angling for promotion to junior reporter for months, but Figgis wouldn't hear of it.

"This is a big one," I said.

"Anything I can do to help, Mr Crampton, just let me know."

For a moment, I thought about asking him to write the Profumo backgrounder, but Figgis would be mad if he found out. And he'd sack Cedric rather than me.

So I said: "I'll bear it in mind, Cedric."

He bustled off and I turned to the backgrounder. I rifled through the file on Birch Grove I'd retrieved from the morgue. There were plenty of cuttings about Macmillan entertaining distinguished guests at the house, but no mention of Profumo. It looked as though the former war minister had never been near the place. Certainly not on a visit that was recorded in the public prints. So my backgrounder was going to have to be written from the wrists.

I rolled copy paper into the Remington and typed: "Prime Minister Harold Macmillan will return to his Birch Grove home this weekend to consider the fall-out from the political crisis caused by the disgrace of former war minister John Profumo.

"Mr Macmillan has used the house, near Horsted Keynes, to entertain political figures such as President John F. Kennedy and General de Gaulle. But Mr Profumo can expect no welcome there in the future following his lies to the House of Commons about his liaison with call girls.

"As the Prime Minister breathes the clean Sussex air, he will be hoping no more government ministers embarrass the government with sex scandals."

I pounded on in the same vein for ten more paragraphs. As I rolled the last folio out of the typewriter, Pinker slid alongside my desk.

He leant over and whispered: "Terry will see you this afternoon at three." He handed me a slip of paper with an address on it.

"Remember," he said, "no mention of hairpieces."

The man with the flame-red toupée opened the door on the chain, peered nervously up and down the street, and whispered: "Did Sidney send you?"

I leaned closer and said: "Codename Pinker."

He nodded: "You can't be too careful."

I pointed at the door chain and said: "Do I need a password to gain entry?"

He said: "No, just common civility."

To emphasise his point, he shut the door. I stood on the doorstep, suitably contrite, promising myself that I would mend my manners while I listened to him wrestling the chain free from the clasp.

I was outside a two-storey terraced house. A short path of black and white chequered tiles led up to the front door. It had peeling scarlet paint and a brass door knocker with a polished lion's head.

The chain stopped rattling and the door opened again. Terry was backlit by the dim light of the hallway. He was tall and slim and stood in a teapot pose with an elbow sticking out and a hand resting on his left hip. At a guess, I put him at seventy, but he looked like the kind of man who took pride in his appearance so he could have been older. He was wearing a blue-velvet smoking jacket over a pink shirt with fawn slacks. He had tied a red cravat with white polka dots around his neck. He smelt of Eau de Cologne.

He asked: "Are you Colin Crampton?"

I said: "That's what my *Chronicle* byline says – so it must be true."

He said: "Can you prove it?"

I pulled out my press card and handed it to him. He held it up close to his nose. I guessed that old age had made him short-sighted but he was too vain to wear glasses.

He said: "You're a newspaperman, like dear Sidney Pinker."

I said: "A newspaperman, yes, but not like Sidney Pinker. I'm crime correspondent of the *Evening Chronicle*. Is that a problem?"

He said: "Not for me. Although it's the theatre critics I usually dealt with in the old days."

"So I gather."

He said: "Sorry about the secret-service performance. People like me get a lot of attention. Not all of it welcome."

He stood aside and waved me in.

I said: "Pleased to meet you, Mr Montague." We shook hands. His skin felt dry and fragile like old parchment.

"Call me, Terry," he said. "But only Terry."

I couldn't resist a brief glance at the peruke. It was made of thick hair dyed a red so brilliant it would make a pillar box look dowdy. It was combed into a centre parting and perched on his head, barely reaching his ears.

Minding my manners, I forced myself not to stare and lowered my eyes to his face which was lined but still handsome. He had blue-grey eyes and the kind of chiselled profile that used to look good on theatre playbills. It wasn't difficult to imagine him as one of the leading matinee idols of his time, strutting and fretting his hour upon the stage. From his fussy manner, I had the impression he'd have been particularly good at the fretting bit.

He turned, sashayed off down the hall and said: "Walk this way. If you can do that without descending into obvious tomfoolery."

He led me into a small sitting room furnished with a sofa covered with a deep-red velvet material that matched his wig – he'd be neatly colour co-ordinated when he sat down – and a couple of basket chairs. The walls were covered with photographs of him in character roles he'd played. I spotted one of him as Hamlet, holding Yorick's skull, and another wearing a crown and brandishing a sword – perhaps urging his followers "Once more unto the breach, dear friends, once more; Or close the wall up with our English dead".

Montague saw me studying the pictures. "The glories of my past." He shrugged. "Actors have an irresistible urge to surround themselves with their former triumphs. Especially when the applause has died away."

Before he became too maudlin, I asked: "Have you really trodden the boards for the last time?"

"I won't be making a comeback." He made it sound like a death sentence. Then he brightened: "But it's another actor you want to talk about."

I said: "Marie Richmond."

He glanced around the room at his pictures and pointed at a faded photo in sepia tints just above the sofa. It showed a perfectly groomed couple – he with slicked back hair, she with a kiss curl on her forehead – staring into each other's eyes.

"We knew each other well in the old days," he said. "She was Gwendolen Fairfax to my Jack Worthing when we played *The Importance of Being Earnest* at the Theatre Royal. But the part was a little too prim for her liking. Not wild enough." He sniggered at his joke and flapped his hand in a self-deprecating way as though expecting a round of applause. "Besides, she soon found her metier was the silent movies. Especially the risqué ones. She was known in Edwardian times as the *Femme Fatale* of Fulham, you know. Although in those days she actually lived in a small villa on the smart side of Turnham Green."

I said: "I suppose the Temptress of Turnham Green doesn't have such a ring, does it?"

"Not as bill matter," he said. "Anyway, Sidney didn't explain why you wanted to talk about Miss Richmond, but I presume this sudden interest is in connection with her obituary."

"Why should I want to write her obituary?"

"Because Marie Richmond died six days ago."

Toupée Terry said: "Mr Crampton, you look as though you need a stiff sherry and a chair. And not necessarily in that order."

I slumped into one of the basket chairs.

Terry bustled over to the sideboard and poured the drinks. He handed me a glass.

"Under the circumstances, I hardly think it would be appropriate to propose cheers," he said.

I took the glass and emptied it in a couple of gulps. I hadn't realised that, until six days ago, Marie had been alive. I'd broken one of the golden rules of journalism: never make assumptions. Because she was a figure from the past, I'd thought she must've been dead. But now that I considered it, there was no reason why she should have died. If she'd been in her twenties in the Edwardian years, she'd have been in her sixties now. There was certainly no reason why she should have dropped off her perch. But, until now, nobody had said that Marie was dead. Not Tom Belcher in the amusement arcade. Not Sidney Pinker. Not even Frank Figgis.

Presumably, they didn't know. And if they didn't know, neither did Jim Houghton. Especially as he'd not heard about the theft of *Milady's Bath Night*.

But I was now more certain than ever that the theft and Fred Snout's killing were connected. It couldn't just be a coincidence that Marie died, her film was stolen, and the man supposed to keep it safe was murdered.

I just didn't believe in coincidences – random events seemingly unconnected. When you dig deeper, you find the logical links. And it's the journalists who find those connections first who land the scoops.

Terry was sitting on the sofa sipping his sherry through pursed lips.

I asked: "How did Marie Richmond die?"

Terry placed his glass carefully on a lace doily on a side table. "Tragically. As befitted her career."

"How tragically?"

"She was hit by a van while crossing the road."

"And died in the street?"

"No, she was gravely injured. She was rushed to the Royal Sussex County hospital and lingered for a couple of hours. Semi-conscious, I understand. But the injuries were too serious. She was gathered."

His gaze drifted up to the ceiling as if expecting to see her attended by a couple of angels.

My thoughts were closer to earth. I couldn't understand why we hadn't picked up Marie's death on the paper.

I said: "Every day we collect names of people who've died in local hospitals and check them against names held in our press-clippings files. We're looking to see if anyone is sufficiently well known to warrant an obituary in the paper. We obviously haven't seen the name Marie Richmond."

"You wouldn't have done. You see, Marie Richmond was her stage name. But she reverted to her birth name many years ago."

"Which was?"

"Sybil Clackett."

"I can see why she'd want to change it," I said. "But not why she'd want to go back to it."

Terry stood up, moved to the sideboard, collected the sherry bottle and poured me a refill.

"I can see this is going to take a little time," he said.

I pulled out my notebook.

Terry returned to the sofa, took another sip of sherry and said: "Marie was born in 1885. It seems an age ago. Queen Victoria on the throne. Mr Gladstone Prime Minister. The first motor car frightening horses on the streets of London. Marie was one of twins. Identical twins. The other was called Venetia. It must have been a difficult birth. The mother died. Tragic, of course, but not unusual in those days. Especially with twins. In any event, the infants were left in their father's untender care."

"Untender? He was violent towards them."

"Worse than that. Disinterested. The odd clip round the ear at least demonstrates a sense of engagement. The girls got nothing. Their father, Webster Clackett, was a draper. I say draper but, in reality, he was what we'd call today a tycoon. At least, a would-be tycoon. He'd started with a single shop in the Mile End Road and by the time the good-old Queen was cold in her grave, he had twenty or more all over London. Meanwhile, the girls had been brought up by a succession of nursemaids and governesses."

"So they were well looked after."

"In a material sense, yes. In a spiritual sense... Well, they never knew a mother's love and viewed their father from a distance. Perhaps that was just as well. It turned out that Clackett knew more about ribbons and pin cushions than big business. He over-reached himself and went bankrupt. Couldn't stand the shame and hanged himself from a roof beam in one of his stock rooms. Used a silk stocking to do the job. Five shillings a pair, too."

I took a pull at my sherry. "That must have shocked the girls."

"The fact he used a stocking?"

"No, that he killed himself."

"It certainly shocked Venetia who discovered him. Marie was off touring the provinces in a risqué review – *A Flash of My Frillies* – vulgar title, vulgar performance, no doubt. Anyway, from what I gather, the event deeply impressed itself on Venetia and she never completely recovered from the shock."

"When was this?" I asked.

"Edward the Seventh had been on the throne for some years. I think it was around 1908."

"Which would have made Venetia and Marie both twenty-three at the time."

Terry cocked his head to one side while he pondered the arithmetic. "Yes."

"You said they were identical twins – did they pursue the same aims in life?" I asked.

"They were identical in looks – both great beauties. It was said no one could tell them apart, right through their childhood and teenage years. Even their father. But, then, he rarely saw them, anyway. But by the time they were growing up into young women, I think they realised they wanted different things out of life."

"So Sybil turned into Marie and became an actress?" I said.

"And became the toast of London. She mixed with the highest in society. And when I say the highest, I mean the very peak."

"She loved the high life?"

"That was the paradox. She treated it with a kind of cool detachment. She could take it or leave it. It was her sister Venetia who craved acceptance into the upper reaches of the aristocracy. Marie's cavalier attitude to aristocrats amused them at first but became tiresome after a time. Besides, Marie's first love was acting – or at least appearing, which is not quite the same thing. And not the basis of lasting success."

"So her career didn't prosper?"

"For many years it did. She must have appeared in fifty or

more silent movies, mostly the kind that would be avoided by respectable people – at least, when anybody else was looking. I recall her first big break was in a salacious production of *Salome*. There was a disgusting scene with the decapitated John the Baptist. I suppose, at least, it gave her a head start." He sniggered at his joke.

"I always thought Edwardian films were prim and proper," I said.

"That's what they would like you to believe. But there was a *demi-monde* world of silent movies – and Marie was the star of it. Her Nell Gwynne apparently caused a run on oranges in Covent Garden. I don't think anyone had realised such a simple fruit could have such varied possibilities."

"So why didn't the career last?"

"She married a coal owner from Nottingham – Bulstrode by name, I recall. It wasn't long before a son, Clarence, came along and, well... I think she realised how much she'd missed a mother's love and wanted to spend as much time with her own child as she could. Besides, she now had a wealthy husband. So, for many years, she turned down engagements.

"But Mr Bulstrode died shortly after the general strike in 1926. Didn't leave her much, either. The strike had ruined him, I suppose. Marie needed to earn money to sustain the lifestyle she'd become accustomed to and tried a comeback. But, by then, her youthful charms were fading and other silent-movie stars had eclipsed her. And the talkies weren't far away. She never took to them. Finally, she quit acting and retired to Brighton. That would be in 1935. I remember it because I was in the West End in a revival of *London Assurance* at the time. We saw each other once or twice after she moved to Brighton, but I formed the impression she wasn't interested in staying in touch with her old friends from the theatrical world. Something had changed inside her. She even reverted to her birth name – although I believe Clarence retained his father's moniker. All very confusing for a simple thespian such as myself."

"So she died as Sybil Clackett?"

"Yes. *La commedia è finita*."

He picked up his glass, stared at the bottom, realised it was empty. He put it back on the table.

I said: "What happened to Venetia, the sister who wanted to be an aristocrat?"

"Ah, there we enter a different world. No smell of the grease-paint, roar of the crowd for Venetia. She married into a titled family. I was touring as Hastings in *She Stoops to Conquer*, so that would make it 1910. She is now the Marchioness of Piddinghoe. Dowager Marchioness, I should say, because her husband died during the war."

"And so the present Marquess must be her son?" I said.

"Yes. I believe he's something in the government."

"He's the Under-secretary of State for Farming Affairs," I said.

"I don't know what that means," Terry said.

"I think it means he's more interested in pigs than people. But getting back to Marie, how did she react to having a sister in the aristocracy?"

"The two sisters had been as thick as thieves but after Venetia's wedding they drifted apart," Terry said.

"*Noblesse* not obliged, then."

"More than that. After Marie moved to Brighton, the two were estranged. I don't know why. I expect you know the Piddinghoe's stately home is just outside Lewes. Perhaps Venetia thought that, by moving to Brighton, Marie was getting too close for comfort. After all, by then the stardust had faded. But there was still the shadow of notoriety."

Terry stood up, crossed the room, straightened a photo frame that was slightly crooked. He turned back to me: "If you're not writing Marie's obituary, why the interest?"

I told him about the theft of *Milady's Bath Night*.

"Why should anyone want to steal it?" he asked.

"That's what I'm trying to find out."

"Perhaps a memento hunter, now that she's dead?"

It was possible, I suppose. Collectors of memorabilia often have an irrational passion for their subject. But they don't usually commit murder.

I said: "You've been most helpful, Terry."

He puffed himself up as though preparing to take a bow. "Is there anything else you'd like to ask me?"

I glanced at the red wig. Thought about it. Shook my head.

Even as an investigative reporter, there are some questions you don't ask.

Chapter 5

I left Toupée Terry's at quarter to four puzzling over a new problem.

I'd mentioned Marie Richmond in my story for the *Chronicle*'s Afternoon Extra. I had fifteen minutes before deadline for the Night Final. I could phone in an update. The news that Marie had died only six days ago would give the story a new and compelling angle. But if the *Chronicle* ran the story, Jim Houghton and every other hack in town would have the same lead. This was my chance to leap ahead of Houghton and I was damned if I was going to throw it away too soon.

I decided I'd keep the information to myself until I knew more. When you're trying to beat the competition, it's much better to leave them standing at the starting gate.

My meeting with Terry had also convinced me I had unfinished business with Henrietta Houndstooth. I wondered whether Henrietta's grief in the morgue was connected to Marie Richmond's death. If Henrietta had known about Marie's death why hadn't she mentioned it to me? Or if the first she'd heard of it was when I'd asked for Marie's file, why had the tears flowed?

I needed some answers and, after what Terry had told me, I was determined that Henrietta was going to provide them. Tears or not.

But when I arrived back at the morgue, I discovered that Henrietta had gone home early.

"She had a splitting migraine," Elsie said.

"We said she should lie down," Mabel said.

"In a darkened room," Freda added.

"It's the best way," I said.

I gave them a re-assuring smile and said: "I'll just check on something in the morgue."

I wanted to see whether I could find the file that had caused Henrietta such distress. I stepped into the filing stacks and took a moment to orientate myself. I moved down the corridor which housed the bound copies of the newspaper and passed the shelves with the foreign-language dictionaries. I was sure Henrietta had been in the corridor which held the files from P to R. That made sense if she was looking for Richmond, Marie.

I found the place towards the back of the stacks. I tried to remember where Henrietta stood when she was looking at the file. Had I seen any filing-cabinet drawer open? No. But the chances were she'd taken the file from the drawer holding Richmond. I moved down the corridor looking at the labels on the front of the drawers. If I was right, the file would be in the one labelled Ricardo-Roberts.

I opened the drawer and rifled through the buff files. There were two Richmonds – Richmond, Walter, a major from Peacehaven who'd won the Military Cross and Richmond ice-hockey team which had played Brighton Tigers. No Richmond, Marie. I closed the drawer.

Of course, I couldn't be certain that Henrietta had been looking at Marie Richmond's file. But if she had, there seemed only two explanations as to why it was no longer there. Perhaps she had put it back in the wrong drawer. Henrietta had been deeply upset but I didn't think even that would cause her to make a mistake. Or she'd taken the file home with her. And the migraine was a ruse to get it out of the office as soon as possible.

There was only one way to find out whether I was right.

Henrietta lived in a large first-floor flat overlooking the playing fields of Brighton College.

A small flight of steps led up to an old oak door. I plodded up the steps holding a large bunch of carnations and a bottle of gin. I wasn't yet sure whether they'd turn out to be peace offerings or bribes. I pressed the bell firmly three times and waited.

I was about to press again when the door opened. Henrietta was wearing a quilted dressing gown over grey corduroy trousers.

She said: "I was expecting you. Elsie telephoned and said you'd been poking around in the morgue."

I said: "Reporters research – they don't poke. At least, this one doesn't."

I handed Henrietta the flowers.

"The Victorians believed that carnations brought you good luck," I said. "They were wrong about so many things, but they had to be right about something. Let's hope it's this."

Henrietta tried a smile. "Thank you."

I stepped into the hallway and followed Henrietta up the stairs. There was one of those mosaic pattern carpets which look as though they've been made to use up oddments of left-over wool. The place smelt of furniture polish.

Henrietta led the way into a spacious sitting room. It was comfortably furnished with four sagging armchairs worn down over the years by ample posteriors. The sun streamed in through open windows and made the regency stripe wallpaper shine. I could hear the clunk of leather on willow coming from a cricket match on the college's playing field.

Henrietta gestured me towards one of the chairs. She was composed but her eyes were still puffy from crying.

She said: "I can offer you tea or coffee."

I held up the gin. "I think our discussion calls for something stronger."

"I thought it might."

Henrietta took the bottle and disappeared into the kitchen. She returned with two glasses well-iced, fizzing with tonic and garnished with a slice of lemon.

She handed one to me. "I'm not sure what we should drink to."

"How about confusion to our enemies?" I said.

"But who are our enemies?"

"Let's concentrate on the confusion first."

I took a good pull at the gin. Henrietta sat in the chair opposite and sipped her drink.

I said: "I'm confused why a file from the morgue should have upset you so much."

"You saw me crying?"

"Yes."

"I hoped you wouldn't."

"I didn't want to intrude on private grief."

"I thought that's what you journalists did best."

I held my tongue. Took another pull at my gin. Henrietta took a guilty sip of hers.

She said: "I'm sorry. You didn't deserve that."

I said: "I'm chasing a story. It could be a big one. I don't want to make you part of it. But I need to know what was in that file."

Henrietta rose and headed for the kitchen. "We're going to need more gin."

She returned with the bottle, topped up our glasses and sat down.

"It was a shock coming across a file with such a personal memory in it. For all those years I've worked in the morgue, I never realised it was there."

I said: "I think you better start at the beginning."

She said: "You thought I was looking in the Marie Richmond file. I wasn't. There isn't a Marie Richmond file."

"Then which file upset you?"

"It was the Piddinghoe file. The Marquess and Marchioness of Piddinghoe."

Me and my assumptions. Not the Richmond file after all. But I hadn't known about the Piddinghoe connection until I'd visited Toupée Terry.

I said: "There was something in the file that set off your tears."

Henrietta took a sip of gin. "Yes."

"Something about the Piddinghoes?"

"Something about my mother."

Now I took a sip of gin.

"Your mother knew the Marchioness of Piddinghoe?"

"Yes. She was her lady's maid."

"A servant? … I'm sorry. I didn't mean to put that so bluntly."

Henrietta's lips twitched into a thin smile. "Yes, a servant. Few people know that these days, but those that find out usually react the same way. Surprise. I know I don't speak or act like the daughter of a mere servant."

"'Mere' was not a word I used."

"Thank you at least for that."

"But something happened while your mother was the Marchioness's lady's maid. Something that still distresses you."

"I've not talked about it for years. But I know only too well it's no use trying to keep secrets from you."

"I'll take that as a compliment."

"Your choice."

"What happened?" I said. "Why did a file make you cry?"

"Because it brought back the full horror of my childhood."

I paused a moment to absorb that information.

Through the open window came a raucous cry of "How's that?"

I said: "I realise that it's painful, but could you tell me what happened?"

Henrietta shrugged. "It'll feel like walking on my parents' graves, but very well. Both my father, Robert, and mother, Susan, worked for the Piddinghoes. Owned by them, it often felt like. They say the Middle Ages ended in the fifteenth century. In Piddinghoe, it was still going strong in the nineteen-thirties and I doubt that even the war has laid it to rest."

"You had to tug your forelock?"

"As a girl of eleven I had a fringe, but not a forelock. Even if I had, I wouldn't have tugged it for anyone. Certainly not the

Piddinghoes."

"It all sounds a bit feudal."

"It felt like it. My father was a land worker on the estate. We lived in a tied cottage. Ate food from the Piddinghoe's farm. Relied on money, paid as a pittance by the Marquess. We might as well have been serfs."

"But that wasn't what made you cry?"

"No. It was the summer of 1935 when the first blow fell. My father was driving a tractor, harrowing a field. He'd been told by the farm manager to harrow as close to the field's edge as possible. Apparently, the estate manager had mentioned that the Marquess was complaining about the low yield from some of the fields. He wanted every square foot growing crops. But that greed caused a tragedy. My father, desperate to satisfy his bosses, drove the tractor too close to the ditch at the east edge of Yeoman's Field. It toppled over. He fell under it and was killed instantly."

"I'm sorry."

Henrietta flapped her hand. "Many said they were. Even the Marchioness. Although her sympathy didn't extend to attending the funeral. My mother and I were naturally devastated. For weeks, Mama looked like a ghost. I don't know how she carried on. She must have felt bitterness and resentment, but she never showed it. Perhaps so many years in service had trained her to mask her own emotions when she was serving others. But somehow she continued to mend the Marchioness's clothes and brush her hair."

"It must've been a difficult time for you also. You were old enough to understand what had happened."

"At first, it felt as though my heart had been emptied out and that it would never fill with love again. But, somehow – I don't know how – Mama found the strength to ease my despair. And as summer turned to winter, I felt that, despite the loss of my father, there might be better days ahead. I remember the death of the old

King in January 1936 lifted me up in a strange kind of way."

"That would be George the Fifth," I said.

"Yes. It wasn't so much his death as the accession of Edward the Eighth. He was younger, seemed more modern, talked like ordinary people. I felt he might be the emblem of a better future. But that was before the second blow fell – the one that ruined my life and made the tears flow in the morgue today."

I reached for the bottle and topped up Henrietta's glass. She took a generous pull and slumped back in her chair.

"Do you want to go on?" I said.

"I need to tell you everything now," she said.

"Take your time."

"A couple of weeks after the old king died – it would have been early February – something very unusual happened. Mama rarely talked in detail about what went on up at the big house, but she came in one evening truly a-buzz. Marie Richmond and the Marchioness had been estranged for years. Well, one Monday morning, while she was dressing, the Marchioness turned to Mama and said, 'My sister is coming to tea this afternoon. See that it's served in the blue drawing room promptly at three.' I remember that Mama was so excited about this news, she seemed more like her old self while she was telling me. Mama knew about Marie Richmond's scandalous career in silent films."

"So were Venetia and Marie making up – an outbreak of sisterly love?" I said.

"Nothing like that. Apparently, the two were alone in the drawing room for twenty minutes. Mama said she just happened to be in the hall when Marie left. Venetia hadn't bothered to wave her off. According to Mama, Marie stomped off with a face like a thunderstorm. The meeting hadn't cheered Venetia either. When Mama went to help her dress for dinner, she was more sharp-tempered than usual. But Mama said she thought Lady Piddinghoe was worrying about something."

"But she never said what?"

"No. And shortly after we had our own things to worry about. A winter storm must have dislodged some of the slates on our cottage. The roof started to leak. Just a little thing at first – but it ended in the worst tragedy of my life."

Henrietta took a pull at her gin.

"It led to the death of my mother."

I put down my glass.

I'd drunk two large gins, but I felt sober.

"Henrietta, if I'd have known…"

"You would have still asked me. I'm not a colleague now. I'm a subject in a story. That's true, isn't it?"

"Yes."

"I work for a newspaper, Colin. It would be hypocritical of me to take my salary and not approve of the things newspaper people do to make their crust – even when it cuts so close to the quick. So ask your questions."

I opened my notebook and pulled a pen from the inside pocket of my jacket.

"How did your mother die?" I asked.

"You need to know the background," Henrietta said. "Mama was a bag of nerves when she went to tell the Marchioness about the leaky roof. The Piddinghoes never liked spending money – at least, not on their servants. But, it turned out, Lady Piddinghoe was remarkably unfussed by it. In fact, she insisted that the estate manager engage builders to repair the roof. Said it was the least the family could do for a trusted retainer who'd given so much service. I remember Mama coming back from the meeting puzzled by the sudden change of attitude. 'Has she found God?' she said.

"That's as maybe, but she – or rather the estate manager – certainly had trouble finding builders to undertake the work. It was April and nearly Easter before they started. It was a firm from Lewes and, like most builders, they found more things

50

wrong and it all turned into a bigger job than we expected. They ended up erecting scaffolding in the back yard and rigged up a pulley-and-rope arrangement to haul the new slates up on to the roof."

"And you watched all this happening?"

"I found it fascinating," Henrietta said. "So did Lady Piddinghoe, apparently. She prowled around the cottage inspecting the new slates, testing the scaffolding and generally behaving like a site foreman. It was completely out of character. And for a time, I wondered whether she'd taken a shine to one of the labourers. There was one, a handsome young lad, who may have fancied his chances. And I've heard that aristocratic ladies can develop a passion for such men."

"I believe it's known as the *Lady Chatterley's Lover* syndrome," I said.

Henrietta frowned. "In any event, Lady Piddinghoe seemed to be taking a more kindly attitude towards us, at least. Perhaps she'd felt some pangs of guilt about the accident which killed Father. But I don't know."

"So what went wrong?"

"It was only the second day that the builders were working on the roof – they were still erecting the scaffolding. It's engraved in my mind – the Tuesday of Holy Week. Mama came back from the big house with a frown of her forehead as deep as Devil's Dyke. She hardly said a word as she prepared my tea – I pressed her to tell me what was wrong. But all she would say is that she'd seen a photograph she wished she hadn't. In the end, I crept up to my bedroom and tried to read my book. But I cried myself to sleep that night."

"And you never found out what it was your mother saw?"

"She never told me. But the following day I asked Tommy Troughton, who was the son of one of the footmen. He said the goings-on had been the talk of the house among the servants. It turned out that Marie had come to tea a second time. I guess

Mama must have known about that but perhaps not until shortly beforehand. But the scandal was that the two – that's Marie and Lady Piddinghoe – had had a tremendous row in the blue drawing room which ended with Lady Piddinghoe throwing the sugar bowl at Marie who tossed the teapot at the Marchioness."

"That's no way to treat Earl Grey," I said.

"By all accounts, it wasn't a matter for levity, I can assure you. The teapot caught Lady Piddinghoe on the temple and laid her out. Tommy told me that the talk among the servants was that my Mama had been first into the room after the row. According to Tommy, she found Marie looking down at her sister on the floor. After that, Marie stormed from the room, left the house and was never seen again. Apparently, Mama organised for Lady Piddinghoe to be taken up to bed and the room cleared up."

"Was Lady Piddinghoe seriously injured?"

"It seems not. Tommy told me that she regained consciousness within a few moments and that my Mama had stayed with her for nearly an hour. I would have taken this all as an exciting story had I not been worried about the effect it had on Mama. For the rest of the week, she was clearly worried. She wouldn't talk about it. In fact, she hardly said a word. And then the worst happened."

I leant forwarded and topped up Henrietta's glass. She took a strengthening sip.

"On Good Friday, we always went to the Stations of the Cross service at the parish church. The whole village would be there – and the family from the big house. But on this Friday, Mama said she would be staying behind because she had a migraine. She had taken some tablets and was going to rest. So I went to the service with the Troughtons. And they brought me back to the cottage. A good deed which haunted them for the rest of their lives."

"Because Susan was dead?"

Henrietta swallowed hard. Tears welled in her eyes. But she was determined not to cry.

"Yes," she said. "But it was worse. We found Mama hanging

from the pulley arrangement on the scaffolding at the back of the cottage."

"She'd committed suicide?"

"That was the coroner's verdict."

"Which you don't agree with?"

Henrietta shrugged. "I know Mama had been worried but I don't believe she'd have left me alone. No matter how desperate she was, she simply wasn't that selfish to put herself before me. And, even if she was so desperate that she felt there was no other way, I'm sure she would have left me a note. Something to explain. To say how much she loved me."

"And it was a report of the coroner's inquest you found this morning in the morgue," I said.

Henrietta nodded. "It was the shock of finding it after all these years. Of course, when I first came to the *Chronicle*, I looked in the morgue for anything about Mama's or Father's deaths."

"But found nothing filed under Houndstooth."

"No. The report of the coroner's inquest had been filed under Piddinghoe. I'd have never done that."

"Sloppy work," I said. "And what have you done with it?"

Henrietta looked towards the open window. There was a crack as ball hit bat and a cry of "Catch it!"

She turned back to me. "I've refiled it," she said.

I sat for a moment trying to digest the story. I looked at Henrietta. She'd been tense when I'd arrived. Now her face had relaxed as if telling the story had been a kind of catharsis.

I said: "That was a terrible thing to happen to an eleven-year-old child. What happened to you?"

"For a few months, the Troughtons looked after me. But that plainly couldn't last for ever. And then in mid-August, one day when I was strolling down a footpath towards the River Ouse, I came across the Marchioness. She'd been out walking by herself. We got to talking and Lady Piddinghoe told me that they – I assume she meant Lord Piddinghoe and herself – had decided to send me to a boarding school. I'd had so many unpleasant surprises in my life I don't think I reacted much. I still didn't really care what happened to me. So that September, I started a new life."

"Where did Lady Piddinghoe send you?"

"To a public school in Brighton. St Mary's Hall."

I'd heard about it. It had been set up in the nineteenth century as a seminary for the refined daughters of impoverished clergymen. By the nineteen-thirties, I'd heard, there was a shortage of impoverished clergymen – or it may have been of refined daughters – and they were letting in anyone who could pay the hefty fees.

"Posh school," I said.

"It changed me as a person," Henrietta said. "It's why people can't believe I'm the daughter of servants."

"Did you ever ask Venetia whether she had a theory about why your mother committed suicide?" I asked.

"No," she said.

"Why was that?"

"Because I still cannot believe that Mama would have killed herself – no matter how depressed she was."

"Depressed people do irrational things," I said.

"Not Mama," Henrietta said.

"Did you ever ask Lady Piddinghoe why she sent you to St Mary's Hall?"

"No. She is not the kind of person you question about her motives."

"Did you ever get the chance to ask Marie what her row with Venetia had been about?"

"No."

"And I'm assuming you'd not have asked Venetia because you'd have realised that she'd have dismissed any enquiry without a thought."

"Correct."

A child – even one as strong-willed at Henrietta – would never have confronted such a formidable figure as the Marchioness of Piddinghoe.

"So Lady Piddinghoe has some serious questions to answer," I said. "It's about time someone asked them."

Henrietta looked at me pityingly. "In that case," she said. "I think you better have another large gin."

Chapter 6

Piddinghoe was a tiny village not so much lost as mislaid in time.

It occupied a sleepy fold of the Downs, midway between Lewes and Newhaven. A sunken street of whitewashed and flint-napped cottages straggled down a narrow lane that hadn't changed for two hundred years. It was the kind of place where you half expected to see a yokel sucking a straw and leaning on a five-barred gate. Or a milkmaid labouring home with pails of milk suspended from a yoke around her shoulders.

I drove my car – a white MGB I'd bought a year ago with a legacy from a generous uncle – into the village and switched off the engine. I needed a moment to think.

After I'd left Henrietta, I'd rung Piddinghoe Grange from a call box and asked to speak to the Marchioness. A man with the kind of high-pitched upper-class whine I'd always imagined for Lord Snooty in *The Beano* had told me her ladyship was not receiving callers. I told him I was a journalist planning to write a story about the sad death of Marie Richmond, *née* Sybil Clackett and would very much like to speak her twin sister, the former Venetia Clackett. That got the Marchioness on the line. In a voice about as warm as the polar ice-cap she'd told me she could spare me ten minutes before cocktails. Not during, I noted. I suspected I was about to be offered the bum's rush rather than a martini (whether shaken or stirred).

The Grange, the stately seat of the Piddinghoes since the seventeenth century, was situated a mile away from the village down a winding track with high hedges towering on either side. The road suddenly emerged into a flat plain with views towards the river Ouse. And there was the Grange, a gothic nightmare of towers, turrets, high chimneys and mullioned windows.

I pulled up outside two wrought-iron gates, firmly closed,

which blocked the entrance to the main driveway to the house. Evidently, the Piddinghoes didn't believe in rolling out the red carpet for visitors. So I drove on and turned into a cart track at the side of the grounds. I found an entrance into what looked like a stable yard, drove in, parked by a loose box and climbed out of the car.

On the other side of the yard was the wall of a large barn. A heap of old farm machinery had been piled up against it. I used my profound knowledge of agriculture to identify a thing with blades, a thing with rollers and a thing with prongs. All of it was rusty and some of the bits had fallen off. This was a farm where not a lot of cutting, rolling or pronging went on.

As I quietly crossed the yard, I heard voices coming from inside the barn.

"How many shot today, Hardmann?" said a fruity voice.

"Twenty-two," said a voice with coarser vowels.

"Usual form?"

"All laid out on the trestle and waiting for your inspection, my lord."

My lord? So the voice with a mouthful of plums was Lord Piddinghoe.

I crept closer to the old farm machinery to listen.

There's an art to eavesdropping – a skill you acquire almost without trying in journalism. The trick is to get close enough to earwig the conversation while providing yourself with a credible excuse for being there if you're caught.

So I stooped down to tie my shoelace. To be strictly accurate, I untied my shoelace first, so that I could start to tie it if anyone came around the corner from the barn and wanted to know what I was doing.

"All ready for the butcher's boy, are they?" Piddinghoe said.

"They're as good as hanging in old Dundard's window."

"Yes, well the blighter hasn't paid me for the last lot yet. If he holds out any longer, the rabbits won't be the only things hanging in his window."

Hardmann chuckled.

"We may need to add debt collecting to your duties, Hardmann."

"It will be a pleasure, my lord."

"Just as long as my old ducky, the dowager, doesn't find out about our little pocket-money scheme."

"I'll be discreet when I hand you the payment."

"Damned woman was complaining about the amount I spend on brandy again last night. I mean to say, a fellow's got to have a hobby."

"Yes, my lord."

"Just because the woman gave birth to me, she thinks she can behave like my mother."

"She is your mother, my lord."

"Well, that's no excuse. She ought to get over it."

"Yes, my lord."

"I suppose I better take a look at those rabbits. You go and find out what's happened to the blasted butcher's boy."

There was movement in the barn. I retied my shoelace, stood up and turned the corner just as Piddinghoe and Hardmann stepped out of the door.

Piddinghoe was a short man with a florid face, hooded eyes, and a walrus moustache which badly needed a trim. He had a beaky nose and the kind of thick lips that do a lot of sneering. He was wearing plus fours and a hacking jacket made out of some thick hairy tweed which looked as though it could just as easily have been turned into a stair carpet. A monocle swung from a thin leather strap around his neck.

He strode over to a trestle that had been set up outside the barn. Two rows of rabbits were laid out on it. He started to count them.

Hardmann stood to attention beside the table. He was taller than Piddinghoe with a thin whippy body that moved easily. He had the kind of brown wrinkled face which comes from spending a lot of time out in all weathers. He was wearing grey army fatigues and a brown beret with a military badge I didn't recognise.

"What's this?" Piddinghoe pointed at one of the rabbits. "Hardmann, this blighter's still twitching. You must have only winged it. See to it at once."

"Immediately, my lord."

Hardmann picked up a large stone flint from the side of the barn. He crossed to the table and picked out the rabbit. His arm moved like a blur as he crashed the flint onto the bunny's head.

He turned to Piddinghoe and grinned. "Ready for the butcher's window, my lord."

Piddinghoe turned. He spotted me and said: "You the butcher's boy come for the rabbits?"

"I'm after different game," I said.

"What's the fellow talking about?" Piddinghoe asked Hardmann.

"No idea, my lord. But he's not the butcher's boy. He ain't wearing an apron. And there's no blood on his shoes."

"I'm here by appointment. To see the Dowager Marchioness."

Piddinghoe shot Hardmann a worried glance.

"Then why didn't you come in the main gate? Shouldn't be skulking around my barn like a poacher on the prowl."

"The main gates were closed. Probably because the drive to the front of the house is full of potholes."

Piddinghoe shrugged. "See what you mean." He turned to Hardmann. "Take the fellow round to the main entrance. Make sure Pinchbeck deals with him. And get those front gates opened. Can't have unwelcome visitors weaselling round the back way."

Hardmann crossed the yard. "Follow me," he said.

I fell in behind. When I looked back, Piddinghoe was counting his rabbits again.

The Lord Snooty I'd spoken to on the telephone turned out to be the butler Pinchbeck.

He showed me into a large drawing room.

"Her ladyship will be with you presently," he said. "If you would care to be seated." He made it sound more like a punishment than an invitation.

I sank into a deep armchair that almost swallowed me whole and had a good look round. The walls were covered with blue wallpaper and hung with portraits. There was a guy in a white tie with a waxed moustache and row of medals. There was a bloke in a naval uniform with a telescope in his hand. There was a big-game hunter type with a rifle over his shoulder.

But all of these faded into the background compared with the portrait above the fireplace. It showed a young woman in a three-quarter pose. The artist had cleverly caught how her strength of character accentuated her beauty. Her head was held high, her neck slender, her eyes haughty, her smile just a brush-stroke short of condescending. She was dressed in a white ball-gown. Her left hand was resting lightly on her right breast, her fingers slender and straight. And on the ring finger a stunning engagement ring. The ring was a gold hexagon set with diamond clusters in four of the sides and emeralds in the other two. The clusters surrounded a huge diamond at the centre. I stood up, walked over and peered closer at the signature at the bottom of the painting: Orpen. William Orpen had been the portraitist of choice for Edwardian society.

I was admiring the painting when I heard a door open behind me. I turned and Venetia, Dowager Marchioness of Piddinghoe strode into the room.

"I see you are studying your quarry, Mr Crampton."

Many years had rolled by – and two world wars – since Orpen had caught the haughty young woman showing off her engagement ring. But the woman who now faced me was still beautiful. True, her skin was now criss-crossed with a fine tracery of lines, rather like the tiny cracks on old porcelain. But her high cheekbones and strong chin meant she would retain a regal beauty until the day she went to her coffin.

I said: "I rarely have such elegant quarry in my sights."

Venetia nodded to acknowledge the compliment. "I posed three days for Mr Orpen. Sir William, as he later became."

"It sounds very trying," I said.

She gestured towards the chairs and we sat.

"Not as trying as unwanted interviews with reporters," she said.

I was going to have to watch my step with this sharp-tongued ladyship.

So I said: "May I convey the *Chronicle's* sympathy for the sad loss of your sister?"

She narrowed her eyes. "Spare the crocodile tears. I always do. You're here to see what dirt you can dig up."

"Marie Richmond was a celebrated film star and actress of the early part of this century. It is only natural that we should want to record her passing in our columns."

"And you propose to do that by dragging my name in the mud."

"There will be no mud and no dragging," I said. "Not by me. I'd just like to ask a few questions."

Venetia sighed. "Very well. But you realise that I haven't seen my sister for a good many years."

I said: "Why was that? After all, you lived not far from one another."

"I expect you've already dug up the fact from some gossip-monger that we'd fallen out."

"Would you care to tell me why?"

"No, I would not."

"When did you last see your sister?"

"Before the war."

"Were you in contact in any other ways – letter or telephone, for instance?"

"No."

"What did you think about her career as an actress?"

"My views are not for publication?"

Tight-lipped didn't even begin to describe her ladyship. I'd had more information from speak-your-weight machines. It was time to see whether I could provoke an indiscretion.

"What did you feel about your twin sister appearing in a film called *Milady's Bath Night* showing in a What the Butler Saw machine on Palace Pier?"

"My sister made her own decisions without reference to me."

"Did you know that the film had been stolen from the pier in the last few days?"

"I trust there is no suggestion in the question that I had anything to do with that."

"Certainly not. I just wondered what you thought about the fact."

"It is beneath my consideration."

"Before the war, your lady's maid Susan Houndstooth killed herself. You paid to have her daughter Henrietta educated. Why was that?"

"I do not seek praise for any act of charity I may have given. Nor any publicity for it, Mr Crampton."

"But does that mean you felt an obligation of some kind to the Houndstooth family."

"It means, Mr Crampton, that I have no further time to answer your impertinent questions."

She rose from her chair. I glanced around to see if I could spot anything that would give me a peg to keep the conversation going. A large portrait of an old gent dressed in the full fig of a peer of the realm – red-velvet cloak, ermine collar, coronet – hung by itself at the far end of the room. If the wall lights were any guide, it had once been one of three, but the other two had been removed.

I pointed at the picture and said: "Is that distinguished gentleman a former Marquess of Piddinghoe."

Venetia turned, relaxed slightly. "It is my late husband's father – my father-in-law. He was a great politician in Mr Disraeli's government. You may, if you wish, see a statue of him in Victoria Gardens in Brighton."

"And those words along the bottom of the picture?" I asked.

"*Cave latet anguis in herba*. The family's motto."

My schoolboy Latin was up to that. "Beware the snake in the grass," I said. "A curious motto."

For the first time, Venetia smiled. "But not for a family that has always had to be watchful of the dangers around it."

"Like intrusive reporters?" I said.

The ghost of a smile crossed Venetia's face. "And now if you'll excuse me," she said.

We crossed to the door. Outside, Lord Snooty hovered – waiting to see me safely off the premises. I glanced back as I walked along the path to my car. He was staring after me. He looked pleased.

No doubt congratulating himself that another snake had been safely repelled.

The light was fading on a perfect June evening when I reversed the MGB into its parking slot in the Mews behind my lodgings.

I'd done some hard thinking on the drive back to Brighton through the Sussex countryside. I hadn't expected the red carpet treatment at Piddinghoe Grange but Venetia would have made an ice maiden seem cuddly. Families fall out. Often death brings reconciliation. But Venetia didn't strike me as the forgiving type. There weren't going to be any tears around Marie's grave from her.

But there was an even darker thought chasing through my mind. Could Marie, even in death, be a snake in the grass that posed a danger to the Piddinghoe escutcheon? Venetia hadn't shown any surprise about the existence of *Milady's Bath Night* when I mentioned it. But when news of Marie's death hit the nationals, they'd be hunting for pictures of the dead actress. For the tabloids, the saucier, the better.

Milady's Bath Night, once an obscure recreation for sad old men and spotty schoolboys, could become a national sensation. It could be featured by *Pathé News* in the cinemas. Selected clips might even be shown on television news. There were newspapers and magazines that would be eager to print the best nude shots. As Marie's identical twin, Venetia would be mortified. Wherever she went, she'd be the object of pointing fingers and whispered back-of-the-hand comments.

I sat in the car and imagined what the Marquess would do to protect his mother. He wouldn't seek to buy the film from the pier's owners. That would only draw attention to its value. Instead, with aristocratic arrogance, he'd decide to steal it. He'd give the job to Hardmann. The fellow seemed to have no qualms about obeying his lordship's orders. Hardmann would hide up on the pier after it closed to the public at ten o'clock. Then, when it was dark, he would creep to the amusement arcade and remove the film. And, I reasoned, the plan would have worked just as his lordship said it would.

Except that Hardmann made one mistake.

He stole the film from inside the machine but forgot to take the revealing photo of Marie in the playbill above it. His lordship would order him back for a second attack. After all, what could go wrong? The raid had worked the first time. But on this occasion, something did go wrong. Hardmann must have been discovered in his hiding place in the coconut shy by Fred Snout. There was a struggle and Snout died.

I had watched Hardmann despatch a rabbit with a stone – and not flinch.

Would he have any qualms about killing a night-watchman with a coconut? Especially if his own freedom was at stake. Not to mention the good name of the Piddinghoes.

I was tired. It was a question I'd try to answer tomorrow.

I levered myself out of the car, locked it and walked round to the street. I occupied the top-floor rooms in a five-storey house in Regency Square, an address which didn't quite live up to its billing. But the place suited me, as long as I could avoid Beatrice Gribble, the landlady – known to her tenants (but always behind her back) as the Widow.

I climbed the steps to the front door, inserted the key silently in the lock and crept into the crepuscular gloom of the Widow's hallway. My luck had run out. She'd just come out of the kitchen and spotted me at once.

She said: "Mr Crampton, I need to have words with you."

I said: "Animadvert and persiflage are nice words, Mrs Gribble. Have them with my compliments."

I headed for the stairs. The Widow hurried up the hall and cornered me by the hat stand.

She said: "Just a moment, if you please. What about these phone calls?"

I frowned. "Which phone calls?"

"The ones I've had today. Two of them. Picked up the receiver and nobody speaks. Just some breathing." She moved closer. "Heavy breathing."

"Don't look at me. I've been so busy I've hardly had time to breathe at all."

"I know it's not you. I'd recognise your breathing anywhere. This is new breathing. Dirty breathing. I suppose it's one of your so-called contacts from the criminal world."

Ever since the Widow had discovered I was crime correspondent on the *Chronicle*, she'd convinced herself I spent my days getting chummy with former jailbirds and crooks on the run from the law.

But I was too tired to get into a barney with her now. So to get her off my back, I said: "The calls could've been for you."

"Then why didn't he speak when I answered?"

"He was too shy"

"Too shy?"

"Secret admirers often are," I said.

"A secret admirer. Are you seriously saying I have a secret admirer?"

I could see the cogs turn a couple of times in her brain. The idea was just outrageous enough to appeal to the Widow's economy-sized vanity.

"What about Mr Evans, the butcher?" I said.

I'd remembered he'd included an extra string of sausages in the Widow's order the previous week. They would have been put in by mistake, but it was a useful piece of supporting evidence to get the Widow thinking.

I said: "Remember the sausages? A love token of his undeclared passion."

The Widow thought about that and said: "I'd rather have had a nice piece of brisket."

"But he sent the thing most dear to him."

She cocked her head to one side and said: "I suppose that makes sense. Do you think I ought to say anything when I next call in at the shop?"

"I wouldn't at this stage. Unrequited love needs time to declare itself. Best not to rush things."

The Widow nodded. "You're right. But next time, I'll buy extra lamb chops."

She bustled off to her parlour. I headed for the stairs. If only I'd known this wasn't going to be the last I'd hear of the Widow's phone calls, I'd have taken them much more seriously.

Chapter 7

The following morning, I made sure I reached the newsroom well ahead of Figgis.

He'd be angry that I hadn't provided an update on the Snout murder for the previous evening's Night Final. I reckoned that if I could make more progress on my own leads before he cornered me, I'd be able to smooth him over with the promise of a really juicy exclusive. But I wasn't yet sure what it would be.

I checked a stack of routine messages on my desk. There was a note that the daily police press conference would be half an hour earlier than usual at nine o'clock. I checked my watch. Ten past eight. That left time for a quick breakfast at Marcello's. I headed for the door.

Marcello's was always crowded early as office workers stoked up on the caffeine they'd need to get them through the morning.

A fug of tobacco smoke and burnt toast hung in the air. On the jukebox Brian Poole and The Tremeloes belted out *Do You Love Me?*

I walked up to the counter.

Ruby, Marcello's paid help, was frying bacon on a griddle.

I said: "Coffee and slap a rasher or two of that bacon in a sandwich. Plenty of sauce."

"I thought you already had enough," she said.

"Careful, or I'll put your tip in the Lifeboat box."

She grinned as she fixed the sandwich and coffee. I took the plate and cup. Made my way to the only free table at the back.

I flipped open my notebook and studied my notes from the previous day's interviews. Decided they weren't going to tell me any more than I already knew. Took a bite of my sandwich.

A young woman came in, walked up to the counter and ordered a coffee. She had a slim figure and short blonde hair cut in a bob. She was dressed for the office in a pale-grey jacket and pencil skirt.

Ruby handed her the coffee in a glass cup and saucer. The young woman turned and looked around the café. She was searching for a free table. Saw they were all taken. Her eyes darted from side to side. Nervous. She'd have to share a table. But it was embarrassing having to ask the people already there. Mortifying if they said no.

I watched. She moved a little to her right. Then to her left. Indecision. She looked at one table with two office girls. Thought about it. They'd be having a private conversation. About clothes. Or hair styles. Or men. Better to choose a table with only one person who might actually welcome company.

Her gaze travelled around the room. Landed on me. I smiled. Just enough to say: 'Please allow me to help you out of your predicament'. Not enough to suggest: 'Sit here and I'll have your knickers off within the hour'.

She walked over. "Would you mind if one joined you?"

She had a voice that could have landed her a job reading the news on the BBC Home Service.

"One would be delighted," I said.

She laughed. "I'm sorry. I didn't mean to sound pompous."

I smiled: "You didn't."

She sat opposite. Put her coffee on the table. Fiddled with her handbag and said in a voice that was more Light Programme: "Is it always as crowded as this?"

"At this time. It'll empty out later. Your first time, presumably?"

"Yes. I'm new in town. Finding my way around."

"Not easy in a place like this."

"Especially when you're hunting for a job."

"Anything in mind?"

She rummaged in her handbag. Brought out a cutting from the *Chronicle*'s Sits Vacs pages.

"I saw this advertisement a couple of days ago." She handed it across the table.

The Kayser Bondor knicker factory in Portslade wanted to hire a shorthand typist. Hours nine to five-thirty. Pay six pounds fifteen shillings a week.

"I've got an interview this morning at the job agency." She sipped her coffee. Spilt a little as she replaced the cup in the saucer.

She grinned. "Nervous," she said.

"Only natural," I said.

We fell silent. I munched on my bacon sandwich. She sipped her coffee. A little ran down the outside of the cup. She rummaged in her handbag again and pulled out a card.

She said: "I don't suppose you know where this place is?" She handed the card to me.

It was an appointment card from the Buckle Job Agency, Ship Street, Brighton. Miss Fanny Archer was to attend an interview at ten o'clock.

"It's not far from here," I said.

"Could you give me directions?"

"I can do better than that."

The *Chronicle* published pocket street maps of central Brighton which it gave away as promotional gifts. I usually had a couple on me. I shoved my hand in my jacket pocket and pulled one out.

And the Hippodrome tickets which Sidney Pinker had given me yesterday fluttered to the ground. I'd forgotten I had them.

Fanny bent down and picked them up. Handed them across to me.

"You're a theatregoer," she said. "I love a good play, too."

"This is more variety theatre," I said.

"Still fun, though." She put on her posh voice. "One hasn't been able to get into the social life of the town yet."

I grinned. "Then, perhaps, one can help. I'm Colin, by the

way. Colin Crampton."

"You can, Colin?"

"Would you like to join me at the Hippodrome this evening?"

"Well, that's a lovely invitation, but isn't the other ticket spoken for?"

"It will be if you say 'yes'."

Fanny smiled. "In that case, yes."

I said: "The show starts at seven-forty-five. So let's meet outside the theatre in Middle Street at seven-fifteen."

I handed over the map. "You'll find Middle Street and Ship Street on there."

I glanced at my watch. "And now, I've got to go."

"Anywhere interesting?"

"Let's just say I'm hoping the police will be helping me with my enquiries. I'll tell you more this evening."

I left Fanny smiling. When I looked back she was drinking the last of her coffee with a steady hand. Her nerves had evidently vanished.

I had a lurking suspicion that I would be in for a difficult time at the police press conference.

My story in last night's *Chronicle* which linked the Fred Snout killing to the theft of *Milady's Bath Night* wouldn't have pleased Tomkins. He'd have stormed round to Palace Pier to demand why Reginald Chapman, the pier manager, hadn't told him about the film's disappearance. I could just see Tomkins quivering with anger as he threatened Chapman with withholding vital information from the police. I'd not mentioned Tom Belcher, the source of my exclusive, in the piece so both Tomkins and Chapman wouldn't know how I'd ferreted out the scoop. As long as Tom kept his mouth shut. He'd struck me as the type who would.

Then there was Jim Houghton. He'd be fuming that he'd not discovered the film theft himself. My story which spelt out a clear motive for the murder made a racier read than his own plodding piece which said the police were "baffled". So what? Brighton police spent most of their life in a state of blissful bafflement.

By the time I reached the briefing room at the cop shop, it was already crowded. This story hadn't just attracted the locals, but a good turn-out of journos from the nationals. There was a lively buzz of conversation and the sort of carnival atmosphere you get when crime correspondents are on to a good murder.

I noticed that Houghton was sitting in the front row, so I took a seat at the back. But he'd seen me enter, made his way towards me and slumped down on the next chair. He looked more tired than usual and there was a small shaving cut on his chin. He'd done his best to cover it with a sliver of tissue paper.

He leaned over towards me and said: "Would you like a tip from an old pro?"

I said: "If it's for the two-thirty at Kempton Park, fire away."

He ignored that and said: "Don't fly kites you can't keep aloft."

I said: "I gave up flying kites when I was fourteen."

He frowned: "You know very well what I mean. That story you wrote in last night's *Chronicle* about the naughty film – *Milady's Bath Mat...*"

"*Night*."

"If you insist. There's no way you'll stand up that theft as a motive for the killing and you'll end up looking like a fool. Just a friendly word from a crime reporter who's been at the game since the Trunk Murders."

I said: "Thanks, Jim. I'll swap a word of advice from a young pro. Never try to provoke a journalist into revealing his sources by suggesting that he hasn't got any. He might think you're getting desperate."

"Cocky young bastard." Houghton levered himself up. "You'll come a cropper on this story – and sooner than you think." He limped back to his seat in the front row.

The door at the side of the room opened and Tomkins trooped in flanked by a couple of uniformed plods. Tomkins took a little time to seat himself at the top table and arrange his papers. He looked over his beaky nose at the assembled company with the satisfied smirk of a man who's always wanted to be the centre of attention. He caught my eye at the back of the room and curled his lip in a sneer.

He picked up his papers, cleared his throat and said: "I am going to read a short statement and will then take questions."

He put on a pair of spectacles and read: "We have now confirmed that the body of the person found in the coconut shy on Palace Pier yesterday morning is that of Frederick Tinkerman Snout, aged fifty-three, of Ewart Street, Brighton. Mr Snout had been employed as the night-watchman on the pier since 1952."

One of the national journalists said: "Was there ever any doubt about his identity?"

Tomkins gave him a look that would have melted marble and growled: "I've said I will take questions at the end."

He adjusted his specs and read on: "Mr Snout leaves a widow, Mary, and two grown-up children. The family have requested privacy at this difficult time."

I thought: some hope. The best Tomkins could have done to keep the press pack off their back was to stay mum about Snout's family background.

Tomkins continued: "Mr Snout died from a severe blow to the pterion region of the skull which drove fragments of bone into the brain and caused a fatal haematoma. Police officers have searched the premises but have not located the murder weapon which we believe to be a coconut."

There were a few sniggers at this. Black humour is never far below the surface in a murder story.

Tomkins cleared his throat ominously and went on: "I can categorically reject the theory, propounded in certain quarters, that the murder was linked to the theft of a What the Butler Saw machine film from the pier two nights earlier. I strongly deprecate the publication of this irresponsible newspaper specu-lation which can only hinder the task of apprehending the real criminal."

Tomkins put down his paper, removed his spectacles and looked around the room. "I will now take questions."

I was fired up and on my feet before anyone else could speak. "Superintendent Tomkins, can you tell us why you've been able to rule out a link to the theft?"

Tomkins leaned back complacently: "Our enquiries have failed to establish any connection between the two crimes."

"What kind of enquiries?"

"Confidential enquiries?"

"Have you interviewed Reginald Chapman, the pier manager and asked him why he didn't report the theft?"

"Mr Chapman provided an acceptable explanation?"

"Which was?"

"Confidential – like our other enquiries in this case?"

I said: "How can you be one hundred per cent certain that the person who stole *Milady's Bath Night* hadn't returned to the pier a second night to steal something else?"

"The *modus operandi* of the coconut-shy killing was different."

"In what ways?"

"That's confidential at present."

I said: "The truth of the matter is that you don't know whether you're looking for one person or two. So you can't say anything certain about the *modus operandi* used on both crimes. For all the progress you've made, you might as well have been interviewing the skeletons in the pier's ghost train."

That raised a laugh from the other journalists. Tomkins blustered something about "an outrageous comment" but I'd heard enough. It was plain Tomkins was making no progress in the investigation. He had no suspect in his sights and couldn't produce any convincing motive for poor Snout's killing. There'd be other questions but Tomkins would answer with the same waffle. If any of the hacks tried to pin him down, he'd hide behind the comfort blanket of confidentiality. I stood up and pushed my way out of the conference room.

I stomped down the corridor, shoved through the door and clattered down the steps into the street.

And came up hard.

I wasn't thinking.

I leaned on the wall outside the cop shop and thought about why Tomkins had called a press conference when he'd not made any progress in his investigation and had no hard news to offer a roomful of cynical hacks.

There was only one reason – to rubbish my story in last night's *Chronicle*. The only possible story to come out of the conference was that Tomkins didn't think Snout's murder was linked to the *Milady's Bath Night* theft. The other journalists would head back to their offices and make that the lead of the pieces they wrote. Tomkins had been cleverer than I'd given him credit for. Instead of being out in front with others trying to catch up – I'd be isolated.

Crampton against the world.

I couldn't see Figgis being happy about that. And when Figgis wasn't happy there was no telling what he might do. I could see him taking me off the story. And I wasn't prepared to let that happen.

So I crossed the road to a telephone box, went in and dialled a number. From the box, I looked up at the window in the police station where I expected the phone to be answered. It rang three times and then a voice said: "Brighton CID. Ted Wilson speaking."

I said: "Ted, I need to speak to you."

"I'm busy."

"Too busy for a large scotch?"

"Too busy even to sniff the bottle."

I said: "We need to speak about the Snout murder."

"I've told you – that's Tomkins' case."

"Don't I know it. I've just been listening to the risible description of his fumbling investigation at the press conference. I need to know what's really happening."

"Tomkins is playing this one close to his chest. There's not much I can tell you."

"Which suggests there is something." I needed to force Ted's hand. "I'm in the phone box over the road, I'll come straight over and we'll talk."

"Are you crazy?"

"Our usual rendezvous then. In fifteen minutes."

"Make it half an hour. But don't expect me to have anything useful to say."

The phone went dead. I replaced the receiver and looked at myself in the phone-box mirror. I didn't look as ashamed as I thought I should.

Prinny's Pleasure was my rendezvous of choice for clandestine meetings with contacts.

It was a run-down boozer in a narrow road in the North Laine part of Brighton. The place had a front door with peeling red paint and frosted-glass windows thick with dust. A pub sign board hanging from a rusting bracket squeaked as it swung in the wind. The sign board featured a portrait of Mrs Fitzherbert wearing a bouffant wig and low-cut gown. She had a beauty spot painted on her right breast. Or it could have been a pigeon dropping.

It was a pub which punters looking for a friendly pint and a tasty snack had learnt to avoid. Which suited Ted and me just fine.

I went in and walked up to the bar. The bar contained an ashtray full of dog-ends and a plate with a bloater-paste sandwich. A tabby cat sniffed the sandwich suspiciously, climbed on top of it, lay down and went to sleep.

Jeff, the landlord, was already dozing on a stool behind the bar. His head rested on the cash register. His lank hair flopped over the keys. He was wearing baggy jeans and a stained tee-shirt with a picture of Lonnie Donegan and the words: "Does your chewing gum lose its flavour on the bedpost overnight?"

I rapped loudly on the bar and shouted, "Service."

Jeff awoke with a start. He slipped sideways onto the cash register and accidently rang up two shillings and nine pence.

He looked confused and said: "Look what you've made me do. Now my till will be out when I cash up."

I said: "Just under-ring orders until you've made up the money. At your level of trade, you should do that by the end of the year."

He said: "Who needs a smart-arse like you in their bar?"

I said: "A publican who would otherwise have no customers. Now give me a gin and tonic with…"

"I know, one ice cube and two slices of lemon."

"And you can add a large scotch to the order. I'm expecting a guest."

I took the drinks to the corner table at the back of the bar. I'd just taken a couple of pulls at the G and T when Ted opened the pub door. He glanced around and slipped quickly inside.

He walked over to my table, sat down and said: "This isn't what I expected to be doing when I joined the force."

I pushed the scotch towards him and said: "It beats helping old ladies across the road."

Ted picked up the glass and took a healthy swig.

I said: "I guess you heard Tomkins had lined up a ritual humiliation of me for the press conference this morning."

He said: "Word in the canteen was that you went down fighting."

"My fellow hacks enjoyed the sport. The trouble is that's all they've got to write about now. And as they didn't break the story, they'll rubbish mine. So my theory that *Milady's Bath Night* theft is linked to Snout's killing is looking about as flat as that sandwich over there."

The cat stirred itself, turned round and went back to sleep.

Ted took another swig of his scotch and said: "So get a new theory."

"There are two problems with that."

"Which are?"

"First, I think I'm right. For years, there are no night-time crimes on Palace Pier. And then there are two in the space of a couple of days."

Ted shrugged. "Coincidence happens."

"Which brings me to my second problem. I think you believe the two incidents are connected."

"What makes you say that?"

"Because you're a better 'tec that Tomkins. Because you would've at least put in some footwork to find whether the two crimes were linked."

"Thanks for the vote of confidence."

Ted drained his glass. I signalled to Jeff to bring us refills.

I said: "What I can't understand is why Tomkins was so quick to dismiss my theory that the theft and the murder were linked. He wouldn't have read my piece until he picked up the *Chronicle* late yesterday afternoon. But already by this morning he's rubbishing it."

"No mystery there. It didn't fit the story he'd already told his favourite hack."

"You mean Houghton?"

Ted nodded. "Trouble with Tomkins is that his mind is about as flexible as an iron bar. That's fine when you're on the right track. Not so good when the investigation is going nowhere and you need new ideas."

"And is Tomkins' investigation going nowhere?"

"No comment."

Jeff arrived with the drinks. I handed him a ten-bob note and told him to take one for himself and a saucer of milk for the cat. He shuffled off.

I said to Ted: "You can do better than that."

Ted took a pull at his drink. "This is strictly off the record."

"As always."

"Sooner or later, Tomkins will have to consider a link with the theft. It stands to reason. He can't ignore it for ever. He shouldn't have brushed it aside from the start. I wouldn't have."

"That's what I thought," I said. I swirled the G and T in my glass, then took a gulp. I stood up: "Let's keep in touch on this one."

Ted stared into his scotch. "Can I stop you?"

I turned to leave, walked past the bar. Jeff was leaning on the beer pumps. The cat was sleeping on the sandwich.

I pointed and said: "That's not fit for human consumption."

Jeff smirked. "Who's ever heard of anyone eating a cat, anyway?"

Chapter 8

I hurried back to the office.

My detour to Prinny's Pleasure meant I'd cut it fine to write up copy for the Midday Special. Figgis would be prowling the newsroom wondering why I hadn't returned immediately after the police press conference.

But, as it turned out, he wasn't. As I walked into New Road, I saw him come out of Charlie's. He spotted me at once and marched over with a face like an undertaker who's lost his corpse.

He said: "Charlie has sold out of Woodbines. Can you believe that?"

I said: "Easily."

Charlie's was a lock-up tobacconist a couple of minutes' walk from the *Chronicle*'s front door. The place featured a window display with an old meerschaum pipe, a collection of novelty ashtrays – star item: a lavatory with the seat up – and a nicotine-stained sign which read "Smoker's requisites". The apostrophe was in the wrong place. Or perhaps not. Figgis was the only person I'd ever seen go in there.

Figgis said: "Until Charlie restocks, I'll have to get by on Weights. They make me cough."

I said: "You won't be missing out on your daily exercise, then."

We were walking through the Royal Pavilion gardens on our way back to the office.

Figgis said: "The dearth of Woodies is not the only bad news I've had in the past hour."

I said: "'When sorrows come, they come not single spies – but in battalions.'"

"That's as maybe, but word reaches me that you took a hammering from Tomkins at the morning police briefing." He gave me a crafty sideways glance.

"I gave as good as I got."

"I don't doubt it. When it comes to verbal fisticuffs, a cocky bastard like you is more than a match for an old dullard like Tomkins."

"Thanks for the testimony," I said.

Figgis took out a packet of his new Weights and started to fumble with the packaging.

"The problem we face on the Snout murder is that we're running a different line from the other rags," he said.

"In the news business, we call that an exclusive," I said.

"Not if it's exclusively wrong," Figgis said. He fumbled with his fag packet and complained: "The trouble with trying a new brand is that you can never open them so easily."

Figgis tugged viciously at the packet and the cellophane wrapper came away in his hand.

"There's a simple way out of that," I said.

"You think you can open a packet of gaspers more easily than someone like me who's been smoking them since I was a nipper?"

"I was talking about the story," I said.

"I see."

"The simple way out of our dilemma is to make sure our story stands up. I've got a police source that contradicts Tomkins' theory."

"I think this is the way to do it," Figgis said.

"To use my anonymous police source?"

"I was talking about how to open the packet." Figgis tugged at a flap at the top. The contents shot out and landed on the ground. Cigarettes were rolling around all over the path. "Now look what you've made me do."

Figgis stooped to retrieve them.

I said: "Tomkins' case is a bit like those fags – all over the place. I'm going back to the office. I've got copy to write."

He said: "While I scrabble around like a tramp looking for

dog-ends."

"Be positive. If anyone asks, you can say you're a Weight lifter."

I left him shaking the water off a cigarette that had rolled into a puddle.

Back in the newsroom, I headed for my desk and rolled copy paper into the ancient Remington.

For a couple of seconds I sat with my hands poised over the keys. Then I slumped back in my chair and looked around the room. Phil Bailey had his phone wedged between his shoulder and his neck while he scribbled notes. Sally Martin cursed as she untangled the jammed keys of her typewriter. Susan Wheatcroft checked share prices on the Press Association teleprinter. Fourteen minutes to deadline. Everyone had a story. I wasn't sure what mine was.

The police press conference had left me out on a limb and skating on thin ice. And I didn't care how many metaphors I mixed because I was up a gum tree. From the start, I'd given the Snout murder a different spin to the other papers. The dilemma I now faced was whether to back my hunch or row back to the line the other papers were taking. There was no doubt that every other rag would make Tomkins' statement that the theft of *Milady's Bath Night* had nothing to do with the murder the lead in their stories.

Cedric, the copy boy, sloped up to my desk. "Any copy for the subs, Mr Crampton?" He glanced at the newsroom clock. "Thirteen minutes to deadline."

I said: "Come back in ten minutes."

"Right you are." He shuffled over to Sally Martin's desk.

I came to a decision. Some people say that when you're in a hole, the first thing you have to do is stop digging. I say dig on, you may find gold.

I pulled the Remington towards me and typed: "Police may

investigate whether the murder of Palace Pier night-watchman Fred Snout was linked to the theft of saucy pictures from a What the Butler Saw machine.

"Superintendent Alec Tomkins, heading the case, told a press conference he believed there was no connection between the two crimes. But a senior source in Brighton Police said detectives would have to consider a possible link if the current enquiries lead nowhere."

Ted Wilson wasn't going to thank me for quoting our off-the-record conversation in Prinny's Pleasure. But I hadn't named him and, if asked where I'd got the information – as Tomkins certainly would – I would take pleasure in telling him: "That's confidential."

I added another half-dozen paragraphs recounting the basic facts of the story, rolled the final folio out of my typewriter and waved the pages at Cedric.

He hurried over and took the copy. "Another scoop, Mr Crampton?"

I winked. "You read it in the *Chronicle* first."

A little bravado does no harm from time to time, but it rarely solves problems.

And my problem was how to make my story stand up. I'd have to come up with some convincing evidence that the theft was linked to the murder or Figgis would insist I drop it. The trouble was every way I turned, I hit a dead-end. Tom Belcher in the Palace Pier amusement arcade wouldn't be keen on talking to me again. I'd not mentioned his name, but if he'd read last night's *Chronicle*, he'd guess that the information must have come from him. He'd worry that Reginald Chapman, the pier's manager, would finger him as the source. Not that Chapman could prove anything.

Toupée Terry had come across with some useful background information, but he evidently didn't know enough about Marie Richmond's later life to be much help. If my previous encounter was anything to go by, Lord Piddinghoe and Venetia would brush aside any further questions as though I was a surly peasant looking for a hand-out. Ted Wilson would treat Prinny's Pleasure like a leper colony when he discovered I'd used him as my anonymous source. And Tomkins was no doubt savouring a cop-shop cuppa while he congratulated himself for rubbishing my story.

So the question I had to answer was: who hadn't I interviewed who might provide new information that would make my story stand up?

And there was one figure in this drama that everyone had overlooked.

I walked into the morgue.

Henrietta was standing by the cuttings table talking to the Clipping Cousins. She looked more cheerful than when I'd left her yesterday.

Elsie saw me first and said: "This morning we clipped that story you wrote in yesterday's paper about the murder."

"And we've been wondering about something ever since," said Mabel.

"Why are those machines called What the Butler Saw?" Freda asked.

Henrietta said: "I expect Mr Crampton has more important things to do than answer your questions."

I said: "I do need to speak to you, Henrietta, but the ladies have posed an interesting question. And there's a scandalous answer."

"Do tell," said Elsie.

"Out with it," said Mabel.

"Spill the beans," said Freda.

"It all dates back to a sensational court case in 1886. Lord Colin Campbell, a son of the Duke of Argyll, and his wife Gertrude wanted to divorce each other. It had all turned very nasty. They were at each other's throats. Each accused the other of having several affairs.

"According to Campbell, the beautiful Gertrude had been carrying on with Captain Eyre Shaw, the head of London's fire brigade. Gertrude denied she and Shaw had been doing anything naughty when he'd called at her home. But the butler had been watching them through the keyhole and the court case all hinged on how much he could see of what they were doing. Newspapers used the phrase 'what the butler saw' and it entered everyday speech."

"But what we want to know is what did the butler see?" said Elsie.

"Did it involve his fireman's helmet?" said Mabel.

"Or his chopper?" said Freda.

"Really!" exclaimed Elsie and Mabel together.

Freda blushed.

I said to Henrietta: "I knew I shouldn't have started that."

"So what did you actually want to see me about?"

"I'm afraid it's about Marie Richmond again."

Henrietta crossed to her chair and sat. I perched on the edge of her desk.

"I've been thinking about people I haven't yet interviewed for this story and I remembered that somebody mentioned Marie had a son."

Henrietta nodded. "That's right. He was born in the Edwardian years – I think towards the end of the King's reign."

"And do you have a file on him?"

"I'm afraid not. But I can tell you his name was Clarence and there were rumours he was a strange boy."

"In what way?"

"Well, from what I heard, Marie kept him very much cloistered – away from other children. I don't know why. Perhaps she was just possessive. Sometimes promiscuous people can be like that. Nothing matters to them and then when something – or someone – does, they have to keep them all to themselves. By all accounts, her marriage was one of convenience on both sides. So without a husband to love, perhaps Clarence was all she had."

I thought about that for a moment.

"So did Clarence turn into a classic mummy's boy?"

"I don't know for sure," Henrietta said. "From what I've heard, he's always lived with his mother – so her sudden death must've been a terrible blow to him."

"From what you say, it sounds as though Clarence may have been the victim of his mother's possessiveness."

Henrietta cocked her head to one side while she considered that. "It's possible," she said. "But I don't know. After all, I've never met either of them."

I thanked Henrietta for her help and headed back to the newsroom.

Phil Bailey was at his desk laughing at something. Phil had a great sense of humour, which was just as well. He wrote most of the obituaries for the paper. Which meant that he collected each day from local hospitals the names and addresses of people who died.

I walked over and said: "Anything you can share, Phil?"

He chuckled. "Just trying to write an obit about a bloke who's going to be cremated."

"Why is that funny?"

"Because his name is Graves. So they'll be cremating Graves!"

I smiled indulgently. Obit writers develop a quirky sense of black humour.

I said: "Do you have the hospital death list from a week ago. I need to find the address of a Sybil Clackett."

"It's on my spike. Help yourself. Anything I should know about?"

I wagged a friendly finger at him. "This is my story, Phil. Keep out."

He grinned. I rummaged through the papers on his spike.

Found the page. Made a note of the address.

"Let me know if you get another funny obit," I said. "I could do with a laugh."

From what Henrietta had told me, I didn't think I was going to get many from Clarence.

Chapter 9

I decided to make a short detour on my way to see Clarence.

I wanted to view the statue of the first Marquess of Piddinghoe in Victoria Gardens. During our frosty interview, Venetia had urged me to take a look-see the next time I was in the area. It was about the only piece of information she'd volunteered. I wondered why. Perhaps it was just a way of putting me in my place. If so, she hadn't succeeded.

I vaguely recalled the story of the first Marquess from grammar-school history lessons.

When Disraeli decided to buy shares in the Suez Canal in 1875, Piddinghoe – then a belted earl and Under-secretary of State for African Affairs – had been the minister despatched to meet the Khedive of Egypt and negotiate the price. Piddinghoe was a lame-brain who'd impressed Disraeli less by his forensic intellect – he didn't have one – and more by the flamboyance of the cravats he wore. The Khedive, on the other hand, had the diplomatic skills of a man used to juggling the conflicting demands of a wife and considerable train of mistresses.

When the Khedive said he wanted two million pounds for his shares, the dim-witted Piddinghoe cheerily exclaimed: "A bargain at twice the price." The wily old Egyptian grabbed his hand and said: "I agree. Let's shake on it." So the price became four million pounds. Piddinghoe later claimed that at the crucial hand-grabbing moment, he'd been distracted by an asp doing a theatening sideways shimmy across the floor towards his feet. But Disraeli couldn't pretend the purchase was anything less than a diplomatic triumph. So he talked up the deal and raised Piddinghoe to the rank of marquess.

Politics!

I ask you!

Victoria Gardens was a tranquil haven of trees and grass

sandwiched between two main roads choked with traffic roaring into Brighton. Sun dappled through the trees. Birds twittered. A nanny pushed a pram and made coochie-coo faces to the infant inside. A tramp wearing a patched overcoat tied together with string shuffled along hunting for dog-ends. An old girl, head slumped on her chest, dozed on a park bench.

I'd passed the statue many times without ever giving it a second glance. Now I stared up at it more closely. The Marquess had been carved out of the kind of grey stone often used for the more sombre kind of tombstone. He was wearing a Victorian frock coat and trousers with creases sharp enough to slice bread. The sculptor had posed him looking straight ahead, mouth slightly open as though addressing a public meeting. His right arm was crooked so his hand rested on his hip. It made the old aristocrat look as camp as a row of tents. But, I was forgetting, he'd been mates with Disraeli.

The statue was mounted on a plinth, about five-feet high and crafted out of the same grey stone. A brass plaque was fixed onto the front of the plinth. The plaque was engraved in the kind of flowing script you often see on wedding invitations. Except the engraver had added an extra fancy whirl on each S. I guess his aim was to make it seem important. The inscription read:

Montmorency Philibert Hugo Mountebank
 First Marquess of Piddinghoe, 1838-1912
 Under-secretary of State for African Affairs 1874-1875
 Unveiled by Edward Deane, Mayor of Brighton
 24 April 1936
 Cave latet anguis in herba

Beware the snake in the grass. I wondered whether the asp had given Montmorency the idea for the family motto. Or perhaps it was the way the cunning Khedive had tricked him. Whatever the truth, the passing years had not treated him well. His head had become a favoured perch for pigeons. His hair was encrusted with their guano. Dead leaves lodged in the folds of his frock coat. Someone had stuck lumps of chewing gum on his shoes so they looked like pom-poms. On the plinth, a lovelorn swain had scrawled romantic graffiti: "Reg loves Carol: True." The brass plaque had turned green with age. The inscription had weathered with mould. One of the screws fixing it to the plinth had come loose.

So this was the father-in-law that Venetia had been so keen I should see. I strolled round the statue a couple of times while I sorted out the family tree in my mind. Venetia's husband Algernon had been Montmorency's son. Charles was Montmorency's grandson. Marie had been Venetia's sister which made Clarence Charles's cousin. Twins Venetia and Marie had started life as equal as any two human beings could ever be. Yet now Venetia's son Charles lived on a country estate and was a respected member of the government while Marie's Clarence eked out a pointless existence in a flat off the Lewes Road.

Family rifts had been fashioned from far less.

I gave the statue a last look. Another pigeon landed on Montmorency's head. I hurried on my way before he suffered a fresh indignity.

Clarence's flat turned out to be on the ground floor of a large Victorian house converted into apartments.

The house would have been a grand residence in its day, with a dozen servants who would have scurried around in the rooms below stairs. There was a small porch and a front door with an Arts and Crafts-style window of red and green glass in a floral pattern. Eight doorbells had name-plates neatly attached to them. Number two read: Sybil Clackett.

I pressed it.

A dog barked.

Nobody came.

I wondered whether Clarence was still at home. There was no reason why he should be. After all, his mother had died only five days earlier. Perhaps he was at the funeral director's arranging the burial. Or with the vicar choosing the hymns for the service. Or the solicitor reading through Marie's last will and testament in the hope that she'd left him enough to pay his bills.

I pressed the bell again.

The dog yapped furiously.

Footsteps hurried up the hall. The front door opened.

A heavyset man with a round face of fleshy cheeks, small mouth and prominent ears stared at me. What little was left of his fair hair straggled over his collar. The buttons of a deep-red waistcoat strained over a paunchy belly.

I said: "Clarence Bulstrode?"

He said: "And you are?"

"Colin Crampton, *Evening Chronicle*." I rummaged in my jacket pocket, pulled out a card and handed it to him.

He glanced at it, pulled his lips back in a grimace which revealed yellowing teeth and handed it back to me.

He said: "What business have you here?"

Not a promising start. But grief often comes out as truculence. So I inclined my head in what I hoped he would take as a respectful pose and said: "On the paper we were all so sorry to hear about the sudden death of your mother."

He frowned.

The dog let out a fortissimo howl that would've done the Hound of the Baskervilles proud.

Clarence glanced nervously over his shoulder.

I ploughed on. "Many of our readers will recall your mother as the movie star Marie Richmond. We'd like to give them a last opportunity to remember her life by writing an obituary."

The dog snarled. Angry now.

Clarence jumped. "Damn that animal. 'I loathe people who keep dogs. They are cowards who haven't got the guts to bite people themselves.' I agree with Strindberg."

"The Swedish playwright?" I asked.

Clarence nodded.

"Not your dog then?" I said.

"Belongs to the old witch in flat one. Wretched beast barks all day. Vicious brute, too. You better come in before she lets it out."

I hurried through the door into a narrow hallway. The place had cheap lino on the floor and fading paint in institutional green on the walls.

I reached behind me to close the front door. As I did so, a door to my left opened and a black-and-tan Alsatian raced out. It bounded towards Clarence, jumped up and pinned him against the wall with its paws on his chest.

Clarence waved his arms furiously. "Get it away from me. Get off," he screamed.

A middle-aged woman followed the dog through the door. Her auburn hair was tied back in a bun. She carried a leash.

"Rufus, here, boy," she shouted. "You know Mr Bulstrode doesn't want to play."

"Keep your animal away from me, Mrs McConachie," Clarence yelled.

His forehead shone with sweat.

"He only wants to be friendly," she said.

"Well, I don't."

The dog jumped down and circled the small hallway.

Clarence edged away from the wall and hurried towards his own door.

I winked at Mrs McConachie. "Love me, love my dog? Don't bet on it." I followed Clarence.

His hands were shaking. He fumbled for a moment with two keys, a Yale and a mortise.

We went inside and Clarence relocked the doors and shot two bolts. He saw me watching the performance.

"We liked to be secure," he explained.

"Can't be too careful," I said.

"That's what my Mumsie always said. She had these locks put on the doors years ago, before the war. Bars on the window to the back kitchen, too. We've never been burgled."

Clarence led the way into a large sitting room with a bay window which looked over the street. There was a Victorian fireplace with embossed green tiles round the hearth. An old chaise longue stood on a small Wilton rug. A pair of armchairs had been arranged in the bay so whoever was sitting in them could look out into the street.

Clarence gestured towards the chairs and we sat.

He frowned. "Do you have trouble with dogs?"

"Only when they limp in last at Hove greyhound stadium," I said.

The frown wrinkled into what might have been a smile. Came out more as a snarl.

"Seriously, this must be a difficult time for you," I said. "But I know our readers would love to hear more about your mother's fascinating life."

"You surprise me. They've shown no interest for the past quarter century or more. As Mr Wilde put it: 'There is only one thing in the world that is worse than being talked about, and that is not being talked about.' And for as many years as I can remember, my late mother fell into the latter category."

Clarence was clearly a dab hand with the dictionary of quotations so I said: "It's not only old men who forget. The young ones never knew – but they ought to hear what it was like in the great days of the silent cinema."

Clarence leaned back in his chair. His face relaxed a bit.

"I suppose you're right. Even though Mumsie had long retired, I suppose I owe it to her memory to help her take one last bow."

I took out my notebook.

"Did she talk about her career much in later life?"

"Not often, but sometimes she'd reminisce, usually when a picture of her appeared in the paper. They still did from time to time. Until a few years ago. Occasionally, a clip of one her old films would be shown on television, perhaps as part of a documentary on the silent cinema. It would prompt a memory or two. And sometimes it would bring a small-but-welcome royalty cheque."

"I suppose money must have been tight after she retired."

"Mumsie once told me that a society belle she'd known in her heyday had told her that thrift and adventure never went hand-in-hand. It was advice she took to heart. She'd had as many adventures as she could, until the money ran out."

"And that was after your father died."

"Some years after, when we moved to Brighton. To this flat."

"But did she have no income?"

"A white envelope arrived every month – with a cheque. She'd become worried if it was late. I believe it was an annuity from one of the studios she'd made films for. But Mumsie never bothered me with details."

Outside in the street, the dog barked. I glanced out of the window. Rufus was pulling on a lead, taking Mrs McConachie for a walk.

Good news for Clarence.

But there was bad news for me.

Further down the road, a familiar figure in a crusty suit limped towards the house. So Jim Houghton was on Clarence's trail, too.

The crafty old devil had told me there was nothing in my story about the theft of *Milady's Bath Night*. But he was leaving nothing to chance. I wasn't going to let Houghton near Clarence.

So I switched my attention back to him, turned on a smile and said: "In this difficult time, I expect you find it a struggle to make a meal. There's a good pub I know near here – shall we continue our talk over lunch? My treat."

Clarence looked confused. "I don't know…"

"They do an excellent steak-and-kidney pie."

"Very well. I suppose so."

I folded up my notebook, put it my pocket and stood up. "But we'll need to hurry as the place is very popular at lunchtime."

"I'll get my jacket."

Clarence returned struggling into a worn blazer that had seen better days.

"Let's go out of the back door," I said. "That way we can avoid the dog."

I was sure Clarence hadn't seen Mrs McConachie take Rufus for his walkies.

"Will we need my car?" Clarence asked.

"No, it's just a short walk. Your car can take the day off."

"So we won't need the clever little minx." He grinned showing some yellow teeth. I think he was trying to signal that he'd told a joke.

We went into the kitchen. The place had been turned into a fortress with bars on the windows – the legacy of Marie's security paranoia. Clarence fumbled about drawing back two heavy bolts on the back door. Then he rummaged around with his keys looking for the one he needed. I hustled him along, expecting Houghton to arrive at the front door at any moment. Finally, Clarence turned the key. He opened the door and stepped outside. I swiftly followed.

I heard the front doorbell ring as I closed it behind me.

The Rising Moon stood at the corner of a couple of side streets just off Lewes Road.

We made our way there through a back alley which led behind a laundry and a builder's yard. I didn't want to run into a frustrated Houghton stomping back down the road after he'd discovered Clarence wasn't at home.

The Rising Moon was several steps up the hospitality scale

from Prinny's Pleasure. Which wasn't saying much. The place had tables topped with oak-patterned Formica and upright chairs upholstered in *faux* red leather. A dedicated boozer nursed a pint at the bar. A young couple held hands discreetly under the table and whispered into each other's ears. A blowsy matron in a blue Crimplene suit sipped a schooner of sherry and flipped the pages of *The Lady*.

I turned to Clarence: "Place seems to have become less popular since I was last here. Why don't you take a seat on that table over in the corner and I'll get the lunch and drinks."

He scowled. "Whisky. No ice."

I walked over to the bar. A middle-aged bloke with chubby chops wearing a tight tee-shirt and jeans folded up his *Morning Advertiser* and said: "What's yours?"

I said: "Is the steak-and-kidney pie on today?"

"It's off."

"Since when?"

"Nineteen-fifty-seven."

"What other delights are on the lunch menu?"

Chubby chops scratched his chin. "Crisps. Salt and vinegar flavour."

"How about rustling up some sandwiches?"

"Cost you."

"Last of the big spenders, that's me."

"Ham or fish paste?"

"Make it four rounds of ham. And don't spare the mustard."

I ordered the drinks and carried them over to the table. Put the large scotch down in front of Clarence.

"Do you like ham sandwiches?" I asked him.

"I can take them or leave them."

"Today, you'll be taking them. Apparently, the Kate and Sidney is off."

Clarence shrugged. Picked up his glass. Took a generous swig of scotch. Let out a deep sigh. Relaxed a little.

"Hit the spot?" I asked.

"Just about."

I said: "One thing that puzzles me is why your mother reverted to her maiden name when she retired."

Clarence took another pull at his whisky. "I think she realised that when she'd been Marie Richmond, she'd always been playing a part. When she stopped being her in the films, she wanted to stop being her in real life."

"And what did you think about that?"

"'Life's but a walking shadow, a poor player, that struts and frets his hour upon the stage and then is heard no more…'"

We were back in the dictionary of quotations. It was as though the man couldn't think for himself. Relied on other people to provide things for him to say. I was thinking what to make of that when the sandwiches arrived.

Clarence took one. Had a bite. Chewed thoughtfully.

I picked up a sandwich and bit into it. Stale bread. Tasteless ham. Lumpy mustard. I washed it down with a swig of G and T. I signalled to the barman to bring fresh drinks.

Clarence chewed on morosely. Put his sandwich back on the plate.

"I'd rather have had the steak-and-kidney pie," he said.

I nodded. "Me, too."

He drank some whisky. I sensed it was getting to him.

"The accident must have come as a dreadful shock to you," I said.

"Mumsie had gone round the corner to the phone box. She said she had an important call to make. If only she'd not gone. But 'when fate summons, monarchs must obey.' Retired actresses, too."

"And Marie was hit by a car, I understand."

"A baker's van."

The barman arrived with fresh drinks. I handed him a ten-bob note. Told him to keep the change.

"I gather your mother died in the Royal Sussex County hospital," I said.

"An ambulance rushed her there. A neighbour came round to tell me what had happened. I took a taxi straight away. Mumsie was still conscious. Just. A nurse – Trish, I think her name was – said Mumsie had been clinging desperately to consciousness waiting for me to arrive."

"That must've been devastating for you."

"Trish helped me – even though her shift had finished and she was supposed to be at her sister Marjorie's birthday party. She told me my mother had a message for me."

He took a good pull at his fresh whisky.

"What was the message?" I asked.

He frowned. "Private."

"I understand."

Clarence scowled at me. "They were the last words Mumsie ever spoke to me. To me. Not to anyone else. And certainly not to titivate newspaper readers."

"We will respect your privacy," I said.

Clarence sat back. His lips were pursed and eyebrows drawn together. He clenched and unclenched his right hand. He was living on his nerves.

I said: "Had you heard that pictures of a film featuring your mother were stolen from a What the Butler Saw machine on Place Pier four nights ago?"

"And what of it?" he snapped. "Do you think I equate the loss of pictures with the loss of Mumsie. I'd rather lose all the pictures of her in the world if she could still be here. 'Thou art lost and gone for ever…'"

For a horrible moment, I thought he was going to sing *My Darling Clementine*. Instead, his head slumped forward as though he were too upset to continue.

I said: "I guess the theft must have been an awful coincidence."

"Yes. That's what it was. An awful coincidence."

I changed the subject. "I expect you'll observe a period of mourning before resuming your work," I said.

"A period of mourning, certainly. But I don't work."

"You're between jobs?"

"No. Mumsie always said that as we had enough money to live quietly, there was no need for me to seek a career. She made a joke of it – that we could both live in retirement together."

"And you've never felt you wanted to work?"

"No. Whichever career I'd chosen, I'd never have been known for myself – only as my mother's son. If I were accepted, it would be because of my mother. If I were rejected, it would be my fault. I couldn't bear that."

"So a life of ease."

"Living with Mumsie was never a life of ease," he said.

He picked up his glass, drained it. Stood up. "And, now, I've got no more to say to you."

"Not even a quotation?"

"Never mock others' words of wisdom," Clarence said loftily.

I needed to preserve Clarence as a contact. So I said: "Let me give you my card. If you want to get in touch, don't hesitate."

I fished out a card and said: "I'll write my home address on the back so you can contact me at any time."

Clarence took the card. Studied it with a look of distaste on his face. For a moment, I thought he was going to hand it back. But he thrust it into his jacket pocket.

He gestured at the sandwiches and smirked. "I suppose I should thank you for a delicious lunch." He turned and strode out of the pub.

I glared after him. Perhaps there'd be a large doberman pinscher outside hungry for a bite.

But there's never a dog around when you need one.

Chapter 10

Back at the *Chronicle*, I went straight to the newsroom.

But I'd barely had time to roll copy paper into my typewriter before Figgis appeared alongside my desk.

He scowled. "Have you seen this?" He tossed the latest edition of the *Evening Argus* onto my desk.

A screamer headline on the front page read:

PIER MURDER: ARREST SOON

Under it, Jim Houghton's breathless prose informed us that the police were close to nailing Fred Snout's killer. The piece quoted "informed police sources". He meant, of course, Tomkins. The pair were still intent on keeping me in the dark.

Figgis said: "While you're touring the town chasing theories, the opposition is scoring one scoop after another before our very eyes. I don't like it."

"Neither do I," I said. "Can we talk?"

"We are."

"I mean in private."

We trooped through the newsroom and went into Figgis's office. I closed the door carefully behind me.

Figgis sat down behind his desk. The Weights he'd dropped in the Pavilion Gardens were lined up on his windowsill, drying in the sun.

I pointed at them. "If the sun stays out they should be dry soon."

"I'm gasping for a fag."

"Everything comes to those who Weight," I said.

"It's going to take more than one of your cracks to satisfy me, young Crampton. This is the second day running we've been beaten by the *Argus*. People are starting to think I'm news-editing a parish magazine. In fact, I've already had His Holiness on the phone asking why we're not leading on this story."

Gerald Pope – His Holiness behind his back – was the *Evening Chronicle*'s editor. He spent his time penning wordy editorials that nobody read and looking for minute errors in the cricket scores.

"And to ignore a Pope would be a cardinal error," I said.

Figgis harrumphed. "Never mind what His Holiness thinks. It's my opinion you need to worry about. I've given you your head on this because you've proved in the past that your instincts are good. But, now, I'm not so sure. I think we need to take the police line on the murder seriously. Otherwise we're going to be running behind Houghton until the story finally folds."

"In that case, why is Houghton running behind us?" I said.

"What do you mean?"

I told Figgis how I'd seen Houghton heading for Clarence's house.

"At the police station this morning, Houghton was clearly delighted when Tomkins rubbished my theory that Snout's murder was linked to the theft of *Milady's Bath Night*. Yet a few hours later, he's hustling round to interview Marie Richmond's son."

"Classic misdirection," Figgis said. "Experienced journalists do it all the time when they're hoping to put rivals on the wrong scent."

"There's more to it than that," I said. "I mentioned Marie Richmond by name in my piece in last night's paper. What I didn't mention was that many years ago she'd reverted to her maiden name of Sybil Clackett."

"Distinctive."

"Maybe, but you'd need to know enough about Marie to be aware of that. And very few do. Certainly not Houghton, I'll wager. But it gets more mysterious, because Marie's son goes under her married name of Bulstrode. Marie didn't have a telephone. I checked when I interviewed Clarence. And even if Houghton spent hours trawling through the electoral register, he'd only have seen the names of Sybil Clackett and Clarence Bulstrode – and there would've been no way to link them with the late Marie Richmond."

"So you're suggesting that all the while Houghton was dismissing the connection between Snout and *Milady's Bath Night*, he was getting information about it elsewhere?"

"Must have been. And it wouldn't be Superintendent Tomkins – because I'm convinced he really does believe there's no connection between the theft and the murder."

Figgis leaned back in his chair, glanced at the Weights.

We fell silent.

After a moment, I said: "I think there's only one conclusion."

"A snitch?"

"In the newsroom."

Figgis rubbed his forehead.

"Tricky to deal with. Last time we had a snitch, it was one of the subs. Ernie Stebbings. Before you joined the paper. He'd been slipping some of our best stuff to one of the regional television news programmes. Of all the low dirty tricks – television. Our sworn enemy."

"You fired him?"

"Too simple. I discredited him. I fed him a piece of fiction I'd concocted about a gang that were rustling sheep on the Downs and had two hundred of the animals hidden in a barn out Henfield way."

"Great story had it been true."

"I even watched Ernie as he made some excuse to leave the building and scurry to the box over the road to phone the tip-off through. Apparently, the TV people sent a full crew up to film the barn. They weren't pleased when they found it was stacked with straw. Nor was the farmer when the crew started poking around. Ernie resigned a couple of days later. Couldn't stand the strain that the TV people were going to out him. Of course, they never did. Had too many red faces themselves."

"But finding a snitch in the newsroom won't be so easy," I said.

"Thirty-two of you out there – forty-one if you include the sports desk."

"The jock-strap brigade may have the balls to play double agent, but they don't have the brains."

"You may be right. Any thoughts on the culprit?" Figgis asked.

"None. At the moment. I haven't made a secret of what I'm working on. I guess it's common knowledge throughout the newsroom."

"Could be one of the subs – or even the feature writers," Figgis said.

The subs occupied a squalid paper-strewn garret on the top floor. The feature writers had been moved out of the newsroom a couple of years earlier when more general reporters were hired. Now the feature team – the leader writer, gardening editor, theatre critic and other one-subject obsessives – worked in their own room downstairs, next to the advertising department.

"I don't think so," I said. "They don't get to hear the day-to-day gossip in the newsroom."

Figgis stood up, walked over to the windowsill and picked up one of the Weights.

"Still feels too damp," he said.

He went back to his desk and sat down.

"I'll give it some thought. You should, too. Meanwhile, we still haven't decided what we're going to do about the *Argus* lead on this story," he said.

I said: "I don't accept the *Argus* has a lead. At the moment, they're printing what the police tell them, which is fair enough – but it doesn't mean the police are right. This case is a lot more complex than Tomkins realises. My own police insider confirms that."

Figgis nodded. "As we reported in the Midday Special."

"We'd look foolish if we changed direction now – just when it looks as though we may be onto something. Houghton wouldn't be sniffing around Clarence if that wasn't true."

Figgis shrugged. "Very well. I'll give you until tomorrow to come up with some concrete progress or I'll be handing the story over to another reporter. I'll keep His Holiness quiet in the meantime."

I stood up, moved towards the door, turned back to Figgis. "Perhaps you could persuade him to join the Trappists," I said.

I went through the door before Figgis had time to reply.

I strode back into the newsroom and sat down at my desk.

I looked around the room. No one was taking any notice of me. My fellow journos had their heads over typewriters batting out last-minute copy or were bellowing down telephones trying to tease quotes out of contacts who didn't want to talk.

It was hard to believe any of them could be the snitch.

I put the matter out of my mind. The Afternoon Extra deadline was just fifteen minutes away and I had to write a story about my interview with Clarence.

Even making allowances for his grief, I hadn't liked the man. Yet if I was going to pursue the *Milady's Bath Night* angle, I might need his help in the future. So I decided to go easy on him in the story.

I started typing:

"The son of Marie Richmond, the silent-movie star who died following a motor accident on Friday, has spoken of his grief.

"Clarence Bulstrode, 54, was at his mother's bedside in the Royal Sussex County Hospital when she died.

"Mr Bulstrode told the *Chronicle* how his mother had chosen to retire from the silver screen and live a private life in a small flat in Brighton."

I carried on for another twelve pars and wrapped up:

"Police are still puzzled by the theft of a What the Butler Saw film of Marie Richmond three days before her death."

I rolled the last folio out of the typewriter, called for Cedric and handed him the copy.

"Another exclusive, Mr Crampton?" he said.

"Let's hope so," I said.

He shuffled off reading the top folio of the piece.

I sat back and thought about it. As an episode in a running story, it was inconclusive. I'd admit that privately. Even to Figgis. But it kept the story alive. And now I had to find a way to take it forward.

There was one thought that had been hiding at the back of my mind like a rat skulking behind a dustbin. It was about as ugly, too.

I already believed that Fred Snout's killing was linked to the theft of *Milady's Bath Night*. What if Marie Richmond's death was also connected?

It wasn't the kind of question I could raise with Clarence. In his present volatile state it could send him climbing the walls with despair or smashing the furniture with rage. I needed to know more about the accident.

I reached for the telephone and dialled a number.

A voice said: "Wilson."

I said: "Can you talk for a minute?"

"No. I'm busy."

"For how long?"

"Let's say the next twenty years."

I said: "You've seen the *Chronicle* Midday Special."

"Everyone in the station's seen it."

"I understand."

"Including Tomkins."

"Not happy?"

"No one here's happy. Including me." His voice dropped to a whisper. "Especially with that bit about a senior source saying the Snout murder team would eventually have to consider a link with the *Milady's Bath Night* theft. You set me up."

"I didn't mention you by name."

Ted snorted. "Big deal. There aren't that many senior sources in Brighton police station. Tomkins has been eyeing me like I'm some festering jetsam that's been washed up on the beach."

"He can't know for sure that it's you," I said.

"He doesn't have to. In our game, suspicion is enough."

"Ted, I'm sorry about that, but I need your help again. I need more about the motor accident that killed Marie Richmond."

"Forget it. I thought I could trust you. I was wrong."

He replaced the receiver.

I thumped my desk in frustration. Some pencils rolled onto the floor. Ted was the only contact I had in Brighton cop shop. Without his help, I was going to find it near impossible to crack any stories ahead of the *Argus*. Especially this one. I'd have to work out a way to regain his confidence.

But my immediate priority was to discover whether Marie's death was an accident or something more sinister. I remembered that Clarence said he'd been helped by a sympathetic nurse at the hospital. I rummaged in my notebook and found her name. Trish. Perhaps she would know more.

I stuffed my notebook into my pocket and headed for the door.

Pushed through it and ran straight into the person I least wanted to see – Sidney Pinker.

"Really, dear boy, you're so rough with me." He winked. "Not that I'd normally mind, but can't you think of anywhere more intimate than a corridor."

"Haven't got time for your gay banter, Sidney. I have real work to do."

His hand gently held my elbow. "Just before you fly. About the show tonight."

"The music hall at the Hippodrome. Don't worry you'll have your blood money in time for the Midday Special tomorrow."

"My notice?"

"Yes, that too."

"About that, I've got a teensy-wheensy favour to ask."

I brushed his hand off my elbow. "What is it?"

"The features editor, bless his darling pink corduroys, has asked me to do a featurette on one of the acts for the weekend review in Saturday's paper. Obviously, as I won't be there, I must throw myself on your mercy."

"Meaning you want me to write it?"

"You're such an angel. It'll be just three hundred words and I've already arranged for you to do the interview during the interval in tonight's performance."

"And the name of this star performer?"

"Performers, dear boy. Performers. It's an animal act. Professor Pettigrew and his Pixilated Poodles. Woof, woof."

Chapter 11

Sidney Pinker was developing the unwelcome habit of popping up like the demon king in a pantomime.

At least he'd reminded me that I was due at the Hippodrome this evening to write his crit. And I remembered that I had a date with Fanny Archer. So the evening might not be entirely wasted.

But before the fun with Pettigrew's poodles could begin, I needed to find and speak to the saintly nurse Trish who'd consoled Clarence on the day Marie Richmond died.

The Royal Sussex County Hospital was in Eastern Road. It had a gloomy Victorian façade which was about as welcoming as a debtors' prison.

When you stepped through the door, you half expected to see Florence Nightingale doing her rounds with the lamp.

Instead, I ran into a fat commissionaire who eyed me biliously. He had a peaked cap and a uniform with brass buttons that strained round his bulging stomach. He had bushy eyebrows and a whisky nose. He wheezed as he waddled over to me.

He said: "You look too healthy to be in here, my lad."

"I wish I could return the compliment," I said.

"Now, now. A little less cheek. Or I'll send you along to the doc with the rubber gloves and those long tubes."

"Don't let me take your turn," I said. "Meanwhile, can you tell me whether Trish is on duty?"

"Do you mean Trish, the radiographer, Trish who takes the tea trolley round the surgical wards or Trish who works in Accident and Emergency."

"The last one."

"And who might you be?"

"Her brother-in-law."

"That's interesting. I didn't know Trish's sister Marjorie had married."

"Marge and I wanted to keep it quiet," I said. "There's a little one on the way."

I winked at him and headed off towards A&E before he could ask any more questions.

I had a bit of luck when I reached Accident and Emergency.

The place was unusually quiet. But at four o'clock, I suppose it was a bit late for window cleaners who'd fallen off ladders and too early for drunks who'd tripped over their own feet. A solitary old girl sat in the reception area knitting. A young bloke in a brown overall was mopping vigorously at a stain on the floor. The place smelt of disinfectant.

There was a small room off the main reception area. I stuck my head round the door. A young nurse with auburn hair and a single wrinkle on her forehead was washing some metal dishes in a sink.

I said: "If you pass me a tea-towel, I'll dry."

She turned and gave me a quick but searching once-over. Decided I was in no immediate need of medical assistance and smiled. The wrinkle in her forehead crinkled fetchingly.

She said: "Where were you when I was washing up after Sunday lunch?"

I winked. "Not where I should have been when you were serving it."

She nodded towards the dishes. "Actually, these have to be sterilised. And, anyway, you shouldn't be in here."

I said: "I'm looking for Trish."

She said: "Do you mean Trish, the radiographer…"

"I've been through that. It's Trish in Accident and Emergency I need to find."

She smiled again and I thought I could get to like that crinkle in her forehead.

"Looks as though you could be lucky, then. I'm Trish. But if you're from admin looking for someone to do more unpaid overtime or the League of Friends selling raffle tickets, that luck just ran out."

"Nothing like that. I'm looking for information."

She frowned. "I don't think there's any information I can give you."

"Actually, it was the son of a previous patient who suggested I came to see you. Clarence Bulstrode. You may remember his mother Sybil Clackett died here on Friday after a motor accident."

Trish nodded. "I remember. Very sad case."

I put on my serious face. "Do you know what happened?"

"I was told she'd been knocked down by a baker's van. But surely Clarence has told you..."

I cursed myself for asking an unguarded question.

I said: "Clarence has been too distraught to talk about the actual accident. He simply can't bring himself to think about it."

"I can understand that. He became almost hysterical when Sybil passed on."

"Poor Clarence. He's taken it very badly. I was with him earlier today. He's still very depressed but I managed to cheer him up by taking him out to a slap-up lunch."

"That was nice."

I crossed the room. Closed the gap between us. "Well, the point is this. Clarence was able to tell me about his time at the bedside. He remembers his mother was trying to give him a final message before she died. But he was so distraught, he can't remember what it was. Now he's beating himself up because he feels he's missed out on his mother's last words. I thought that if someone here heard what she'd said, I could pass the infor- mation on to him. I think it would help him come to terms with her death. My good deed for the day, really."

Trish stacked the dishes together and dried her hands. "I

didn't hear much, you understand. We're trained not to listen into patients' private conversations. But when you're at the bedside striving to save someone's life, it's impossible not to hear some of what's said."

"Did Sybil say anything to Clarence that sounded as though it might be a last message?" I asked.

"She was slipping rapidly into delirium. Much of what she muttered made little sense. But, shortly before she died, she reached up and stroked Clarence's face. It's sometimes like that. People who are facing death find one last reserve of strength. Her eyes opened and she tried to lift her head off the pillow. There was a kind of urgency in her eyes. Again, I've seen that before. 'Clarrie, my darling, your fortune lies on the pier,' she said. 'Seek and find your fortune on the pier.' Speaking seemed to suck the last strength out of her. She flopped back on the pillow and closed her eyes."

"And she said nothing else?" I asked.

"No. She breathed her last about two minutes later. But I'm surprised Clarence didn't recall her last words. She spoke them so clearly – and with such urgency – even I heard them at the end of the bed."

"Maybe he heard them. But perhaps the trauma made him forget them afterwards. The mind plays tricks with people when they're under so much strain."

Trish nodded. "That's true."

I didn't mention I knew full well that Clarence had heard the message. He'd told me so himself. And he'd said the message was private. Which was fair enough. The last words between a mother and son could well be too intimate to share with strangers. But Marie's words were bizarre. Trish said Marie had spoken them urgently, which suggested she, at least, knew they held some important meaning. Perhaps Clarence knew what it was. But I could make nothing of it.

So I asked Trish: "Did you have any idea what Sybil meant? As someone's final words, they seem very strange."

"No. And I didn't have any time to think about it because minutes later I was called to help the other person injured in the accident."

My eyebrows jumped at that news. There'd been no talk of a second victim.

"I didn't realise anyone else was involved."

"This was nothing serious. A lady who lived nearby – a Hilda Bailey – saw the accident from her window, rushed out to help, fell off the kerb and sprained her ankle. Nothing life threatening, but very painful."

"So just walking wounded," I said.

"More limping wounded as it turned out."

Trish hurried across the room carrying the metal dishes. She stacked them in a steriliser and switched it on.

She said: "Now if you'll excuse me, I've got a bad case of piles."

"From the way you skipped across the room, I'd never have guessed."

"In cubicle seven."

I grinned. "And who said there's no glamour in nursing?"

I slipped out of the room and headed for the exit.

I thought about what Trish had told me as I walked back to my car.

Marie's dying message came just two days before *Milady's Bath Night* was stolen. And four days before Fred Snout's killing. On the face of it, Clarence could be in the frame for both those crimes. He was a strange man, sent spinning close to the edge by his mother's sudden death. But did he have the gumption to organise a theft – let alone the guts to commit a killing?

He wasn't the only suspect in my book. From what I'd seen, Lord Piddinghoe's henchman Hardmann had the gumption and guts to do both. One of the few facts I'd discovered from my interview with Venetia was that her family already knew of her sister's death. All the while *Milady's Bath Night* was a forgotten entertainment on a seaside pier, it posed no threat. But if the tabloids picked up that Marie was Piddinghoe's aunt, they'd be sure to run stories – and pictures – with headlines like "Minister's naughty aunt comes clean" or "Piddinghoe aunty's saucy soap opera". In the moral panic which had gripped Macmillan's government in the wake of the Profumo revelations, the Prime Minister wouldn't wait a second to dump Piddinghoe from the government.

If I accused Clarence to his face, he'd probably flip over the edge and start babbling quotations. And Piddinghoe would have Hardmann dump me out in the street – or somewhere worse. So if I was going to make any progress on the story, I needed more background. Marie's dying words could well have been the incoherent ramblings of a dying woman. But what if there was a fortune on the pier?

All in all, I decided my next move ought to be to track down the witness of the accident – the limping Mrs Bailey. She observed Marie come out of a telephone box. There couldn't be many boxes that Marie would have used and Mrs Bailey would need a direct line of sight to it to see what happened. So with some doorstep work it should be possible to track her down.

I glanced at my watch. It was ten to five. If I hurried and got lucky, I could find and interview Mrs Bailey before I met Fanny at the Hippodrome. I slid into the driving seat of my MGB, revved up the engine and roared off towards Lewes Road.

In the event, I discovered there were two phone boxes which Marie could have used for her call.

So I had to ring fifteen doorbells before I found Mrs Bailey.

She opened the door with her hair in curlers, did a double-take and said: "You're not Rene with the Littlewoods catalogue."

I glanced down, spotted the bandage around her left ankle and said. "Sorry to disappoint, Mrs Bailey."

Her eyebrows lifted as she looked me up and down. She was wearing an apron with blue stripes over a cream blouse and a fawn skirt.

She said: "I don't normally have my curlers in when I answer the door. Especially when it's a young gentleman."

I said: "I hope your ankle is feeling better."

"How did you hear about that?"

"Trish at the Accident and Emergency department briefed me."

"A real saint that girl. Heart of gold."

"Twenty-four carat."

"You a doctor, then?"

"Not exactly. But I'm here because we need a bit more information about the accident."

"Nothing much to say. I tripped off the kerb. Felt my ankle go. Next thing I knew I was lying in the road with a corporation dustcart bearing down on me."

"It must have been very distressing. But, actually, it's the other lady's accident we need to know about. We want to get the full picture. To put her son's mind at rest, you understand."

Mrs Bailey nodded. "If you don't mind the curlers, you better come in."

I said: "Actually, I think they make a contemporary fashion statement."

She preened herself in the hall mirror and said: "Perhaps you're right."

She led me into the kitchen at the back of the house and we sat down at a deal table. A pile of unwashed crocks stood on the draining board. A frying pan with congealed lard festered on the hob.

I said: "I understand you saw the whole accident unfold from your sitting-room window."

"I told the police all this. Didn't they pass the information on?"

"They like to play their cards close to their chest. We sometimes have to ask a second time."

"I don't like to think about it. Quite shook me up."

She stood up, reached into a cupboard and brought out a bottle of gin.

"The doctor said the occasional one would steady my nerves." She poured three fingers into a tooth glass and took a gulp. "Where are my manners? Will you join me?"

"Not while I'm on duty."

She stared into the glass.

I said: "So I gather you saw the lady come out of a telephone box."

Mrs Bailey braced herself with another gulp of the gin. "Yes. She sort of pushed her way out of the box reading a letter. She was shaking her head. I think she may have been crying but I couldn't be sure."

"You didn't see how long she'd been in the box?"

"No."

"But she looked distressed?"

"She just kept looking at the letter and shaking her head. You know, as though she couldn't believe what she was reading."

"So, bad news," I said.

"Must have been, I suppose. Anyway, after a minute or so of this, she fumbles in her coat pocket and pulls out an envelope. By now she's walking to the kerb. She steps off the kerb trying to fold up the letter and stuff it in the envelope."

"Not looking to see whether any traffic was coming?"

"I suppose she can't have done. She just wanders into the road trying to stuff her letter in the envelope. But it was windy and the letter kept blowing around. So she stopped dead, scrunched the letter and shoved it in. Then she stepped forward into the middle of the road. And that's when the van hit her. *Bam!* She went up in the air, over the bonnet. Nothing the driver could have done about it. I just dropped everything and raced out."

"And twisted your ankle falling off the kerb."

Mrs Bailey poured herself another slug of gin and took a gulp.

"That's right. I tried to get up, fell down again and got grease from an oil patch on the road all over my apron. Thought to myself, that's another pinny for the rag-bag. Daft thought under the circumstances."

"So you were lying in the road?"

"Couldn't get up. Looked over towards the old lady. Couldn't even crawl towards her. I was feeling woozy. Thought I might faint. Then something happened which made me pull myself together."

"Go on," I said.

"The wind was still blustery. Must have caught the letter the old woman had been looking at when she came out of the phone box. It started to blow towards me. Well, I thought, can't let that go – it might be important. But I could tell it was going to blow right past me. So I heaved myself up on my elbows and dragged myself into its path. Well, nearly at any rate. Had to reach out my right arm at full stretch to get it. The action sent a jolt of pain right down my leg."

"The leg with the twisted ankle."

Mrs Bailey nodded. "Felt like a red-hot poker being run down my leg. I passed out. By the time, I came-to the ambulance men were loading me onto a stretcher."

"And the letter?"

"No sign. I suppose I must have let go when I fainted. Probably blew away down the street."

I clenched my jaw in frustration.

"So gone for ever?"

"Like my pinny."

Mrs Bailey took another sip of her gin. Her cheeks had turned pink.

"That vanished as well?" I asked.

"I passed out again at the hospital when they lifted me off the stretcher onto a trolley. I suppose they must have taken my pinny off while I was out. Never saw it again. Mind you, by the time I'd been scrambling around in the road trying to get the letter it wasn't fit to wear. Covered with oil, mud, and dog shit. Pardon my French. I suppose they thought it wasn't hygienic enough for a hospital."

"Did they keep you in hospital long?"

"A few hours. I was x-rayed, prodded, bandaged and generally patched up and brought home with a couple of crutches. Not that I've used them. I told the ambulance men to shove them in the coat cupboard under the stairs with the other stuff."

"That's been very helpful. I'll pass on your co-operation to the appropriate authorities." I stood up. "Don't get up. I can see myself out."

I walked back down the narrow hall and out of the door. So Marie's death had been an accident, after all. Mrs Bailey was definite about that. But what was the letter Marie had been reading in the phone box? It was clear the letter had been important. And the fact she'd taken it to the phone box suggested she'd needed to call somebody about the information it contained. It looked as though whoever she'd spoken to had had bad news. At any rate, she'd been preoccupied enough not to see the van bearing down on her.

I walked back to my car thinking about it. And stopped so suddenly a young woman pushing a pram behind nearly ran into me. I grinned an apology and stepped aside.

I wasn't thinking. More to the point, I hadn't been listening. What had Mrs Bailey said about the ambulance men who had brought her home with the crutches? "I told them to shove them in the coat cupboard with the other stuff."

The other stuff.

What other stuff? Could it have included the letter?

I marched back to Mrs Bailey's and rang the doorbell. She

came to the door carrying her glass of gin.

I said: "Sorry to interrupt the pain relief. I forgot to ask if I could check the crutches the ambulance men left in your coat cupboard."

She swayed slightly. Put out a hand to steady herself and said: "Why do you need to check that?"

I said: "The crutches remain hospital property. It's just a question of stock control. Keeps my boss off my back."

She stepped back. "You better take a look. But be quick."

I followed her up the hall. Nodded at her glass. "Looks as though you've got an empty there."

She let out a soft belch. "I'll just have another small one. Call me when you're finished." She limped off to the kitchen.

I opened the coat-cupboard door. The cramped space was filled with the kind stuff you find under the stairs – an old rug, a picture of the Royal Pavilion in a cracked frame, a rusting biscuit tin, a bicycle pump. No coats. The crutches were neatly propped in the corner. A brown paper bag was resting on them. I picked it up, looked inside. And there was the pinny Mrs Bailey said she'd been missing.

But no letter.

I took a quick glance down the hall. I could hear Mrs Bailey shuffling around in the kitchen, no doubt pouring herself a small one. I took the pinny out of the bag and unfolded it. Mrs Bailey has been right. It was covered with street muck and smelt rank. There was a pocket in the front. I felt inside.

My fingers closed around an envelope.

I felt a flush in my neck as my heart beat faster. I took out the envelope, looked at it. It was addressed to Miss Sybil Clackett.

I pictured the scene in my mind. Mrs Bailey was lying unconscious in the road, the envelope clutched in her hand. The ambulance men would have concluded it was hers. They'd have plucked it from her hand and shoved into her pinny's pocket before heaving her body onto the stretcher.

I took another glance down the hall. Mrs Bailey was no doubt administering another dose of the pain-relieving gin. I thrust the envelope into my inside pocket. Closed the cupboard door.

I stepped towards the kitchen just as Mrs Bailey came through the door.

"Look what I've found – your pinny."

She pulled a face. "Did you have to? Now I feel sober again."

I handed her the apron, nodded goodbye and headed towards the door. I tried not to run.

I sat in the MGB and took the envelope out of my pocket.

I ran the envelope through my finger and thumb and felt the quality. It was made out of thick vellum-style paper, in a pale-cream colour and way above the blue Basildon Bond stationery my mum used to write to her sister on. The envelope carried a couple of brown smears which I didn't investigate too closely. No doubt it had picked them up as it blew across the road.

There was a neat slit along the top of the envelope where it had been opened with respect by a sharp knife. The envelope had been addressed in blue ink with a pen which had a thin nib. I'm no graphologist but the handwriting looked like a woman's – and a woman with a strong character.

I pulled out the letter. It was written on the same kind of thick paper and folded twice. I unfolded it.

The paper was headed Piddinghoe Grange. There was an impressive crest with the motto underneath: *Cave latet anguis in herba*. I read:

> *Dear Sister,*
>
> *I am writing with news that is no less disagreeable to me than it will be to you. As you know, for some considerable time now, I have been able to make a modest subvention every month from the personal allowance I receive from the Marquess. I regret that circumstances have arisen which make it impossible for me to continue this*

arrangement. I appreciate that this will cause you no little difficulty but I can assure you that I would not be taking the decision were it not absolutely necessary.

I am only too painfully aware that the circumstances which led to this arrangement have not changed. But they are now far in the past and I beg you to let matters rest. There is nothing either of us can do to change what has been. We can only struggle to survive in what is to come and pray for God's help in doing so.

Please, sister, believe me that my decision is not open to question so that I plead earnestly with you to accept it for what it is — a reluctant choice made in less-than-happy circumstances, but made with unchangeable finality.

Yours ever,

Venetia.

So when Venetia had looked down her nose and told me she'd not been in contact with Marie, she'd been lying through her aristocratic teeth. In the French Revolution, they sent aristos to Madame Guillotine for less than that.

But I was forgetting. In this tale, it was Marie who played the part of Milady. Even if she hadn't managed, like her sister, to become the real thing. I can smell extortion like a rotting haddock. And this notepaper may have had a faint hint of expensive scent, but it reeked with a tale of blackmail.

I suspected Venetia had been paying Marie for years. Henrietta Houndstooth had told me about the row the two sisters had had before the war – the row witnessed by her mother. I wondered whether these payments could have had anything to do with that. After all, Venetia's letter said that the payments started because of something that happened many years ago. But there was no clue what it could be.

I reread the letter. The tone suggested to me that Venetia was ending the arrangement with genuine regret. Perhaps she was in financial difficulty. I had certainly seen evidence of that at the

Grange. Or maybe there was another reason why the payments had to stop. In any event, the letter explained why Marie and Clarence had been able to live a life of modest comfort when they had little apparent income.

Venetia had told Marie that her decision was final. But I doubted Marie would have accepted that. I suspected that was why she was in the telephone box. She'd been to call Venetia and plead for the payments to continue. Or, perhaps, it was to threaten rather than plead. In any event, she was so distracted when she came out of the box, she'd walked straight into the path of the van.

I was feeling hot. I wound down a window. A bus drove by belching out grey exhaust smoke. I coughed.

It surely couldn't be coincidence *Milady's Bath Night* was stolen from the pier a few days after Marie had received the letter. So, could the crimes on the pier be linked to whatever Marie had apparently been blackmailing Venetia about?

I had no answer to that question. And finding one would have to wait.

I had a date at the Hippodrome. And a job to do for Sidney Pinker. I pressed the starter button, put the car into gear, and pulled out into the traffic.

Chapter 12

Crowds were already gathering in Middle Street by the time I arrived at the Hippodrome.

I scanned faces looking for Fanny. I hoped I'd recognise her from our brief meeting earlier in the day. I shoved through a scrum of people pushing their way into the theatre. But I couldn't see her.

Perhaps it was just as well. I was feeling a bit like a pimple-faced teenager on a first date. The truth was that I hadn't been on a proper date since my erstwhile girlfriend Shirley Goldsmith had left me ten months ago to hitchhike to India.

My affair with Shirley had come to a head late one night in Prinny's Pleasure, just after I'd solved the case of Arnold Trumper, the disappeared golf man who left his balls behind.

The story had won me plaudits on the paper. But at Shirley's expense.

She hadn't been happy that I'd stood her up on a date when I went to interview a contact, which helped me crack the story.

Well, to be strictly accurate, it was two dates. The second time I was taking an unscheduled trip to France when I was supposed to be meeting her at Piccadilly Circus for a night on the town in London.

And then there was the time she was arrested by the police while acting as a lookout for me. I was searching the dustbins of a suspect.

I suppose it was inevitable that Shirley would rebel. We'd had one of those arguments that get out of control.

I said that my work was important to me and she needed to understand that.

And she said that I spent more time chasing stories than chasing her.

And I said I was chasing her because I thought I loved her.

And she said she didn't know what to believe, but she needed to understand more about what she wanted out of life, and she'd heard there was this guy in India called the Maharishi Mahesh Yogi who was the fount of all wisdom and could see into your innermost soul.

And I said that sounded like the mental equivalent of rummaging in her knicker drawer.

And she said it was typical of me to make crude jokes about something serious and she needed advice from somebody she could trust to help her understand what she wanted out of life.

And I said why couldn't she write to agony aunt Marje Proops on the *Daily Mirror* like everybody else.

And she said she wasn't baring her soul in a newspaper even though it seemed I didn't care what I wrote in them.

And then we sat silently for twenty minutes, nursing our drinks, and hating ourselves for letting this happen.

And then she said she was going to India and if she missed me she'd come back and if she didn't she wouldn't.

And then she left.

Since then, I'd had two postcards from her.

The first from Jabalpur, India: "Weather hot. Curries hotter."

The second from Istanbul, Turkey: "Rained. Got soaked in the souk. Not a Turkish delight."

But she didn't mention her future plans.

Or whether she missed me.

Or whether she'd be coming back.

I looked up and down the street but there was no sign of Fanny.

Since Shirley had left, my love life disqualified me from entering a monastery but left me well short of being nominated as Stud of the Year. So it wasn't surprising, I told myself, that I was uneasy about the evening ahead.

I was musing on this when a mocking voice in my ear said:

"One is awfully pleased to see you again."

I turned suddenly. Fanny grinned at my surprise.

"One is delighted," I said.

Fanny was wearing a stylish yellow check A-line dress that looked as though it would set a shorthand typist back a good week's wages. Her blonde hair was styled in a bob with a kind of half fringe and for just a split second when I'd turned I'd thought she was Shirley. Perhaps it was just because I'd been thinking about Shirley. But now that I looked at Fanny, I could see a resemblance. If I'd been the introspective type, I'd have started to question my motives for inviting her to the show this evening. But Fanny didn't give me time for that.

She leaned closer and gave me a peck on the cheek. I caught the fragrance of some French perfume, perhaps Chanel No. 5. (Whatever happened to the first four, I wondered).

Fanny said uncertainly: "You were expecting me?"

I grinned. "I've got the two tickets right here. It's great that you came."

I glanced at my watch. "There's fifteen minutes before curtain-up. Shall we have a drink in the bar?"

Fanny nodded. We pushed our way through the crowd into the theatre. We ordered our drinks – vermouth and soda for Fanny, G and T with one ice cube and two slices of lemon for me – and made for a corner of the crush bar.

I raised my glass: "Should I congratulate you?"

"Congratulate?" Fanny's brow furrowed.

"On the interview. You were hoping for a job at the knicker factory."

She grinned. "Of course, as a shorthand-typist. I start next Monday."

We clinked glasses and drank.

I said: "I'm pleased that you could come, but I should've warned you that this isn't a completely social evening for me."

"I don't understand."

"I'm a reporter on the *Evening Chronicle* and I've got to review the show we're going to see."

"You're a critic. So you have the power to make or break actors' careers. That's awesome. And a bit frightening."

"Not really. I'm not the paper's regular theatre critic. That's a vision of loveliness called Sidney Pinker."

Fanny giggled.

"Besides, this isn't straight theatre – it's just music hall," I said. "A serious play with star actors might get half a page in the paper. This will get half a column. But I've also agreed to interview one of the acts. So we'll need to go backstage during the interval."

"Wow! That'll be a first for me. Have you been before?"

"A couple of times. I don't know about the roar of the crowd, but if you've got a sensitive nose, you'll recognise the smell of the greasepaint."

Fanny smiled. "Can't wait. So who will we be rubbing shoulders with backstage? Anyone famous?"

I shrugged. "Apart from Professor Pettigrew and his Pixilated Poodles – I'm interviewing the professor not the poodles – I've been too busy to find out who's on the rest of the bill. Wait here a minute and I'll buy a programme."

I left Fanny nursing her drink and made my way back to the programme sellers in the foyer. I bought a couple of programmes, then hurried back. Walked into the bar and goggled with shock.

Fanny was talking to Jim Houghton of the *Argus*.

I edged into the room. Jim was wearing his trademark baggy grey suit. His hair was longer than usual. It flopped over his forehead. He leaned towards Fanny talking in an animated way with lots of hand movement. She was nodding thoughtfully. Then she said something and Jim laughed.

I walked towards them. Came up behind Jim and said: "Not trying to steal my date off me?"

He whirled round and I thought I caught a glimpse of concern in his eyes. But Jim was too wily an operator to be thrown off his

He grinned. "Saw you talking to this charming young lady a few minutes ago. Just thought I'd come over and introduce myself as your hated rival."

"Mr Houghton…" Fanny began.

"Jim, please."

"Jim was telling me that you're both crime correspondents."

"Both, apparently, with a love of the theatre," I said.

"Mine's pure leisure," Jim said. "I don't do notices on the side."

I glanced at Fanny. She'd obviously been busy while I was buying the programme, regaling Jim with my business at the theatre. Jim may have been an old boy who walked with a limp, but he had a way with him that could tease intimacies out of people he'd just met. So I could hardly blame Fanny for giving the game away.

"Versatility. It's how to get on in journalism, Jim," I said. "And talking of getting on, you'll have to hurry if you want a drink before the show."

Houghton nodded at Fanny: "Nice to have met you."

Fanny smiled. "You, too, Jim."

I was about to say something, but at that moment the two-minute bell rang and we hurried through to take our seats.

The curtain rose on six chorus girls dressed as liberty horses.

They wore white plumes on their heads, piebald leotards and fishnet tights. They kicked their legs up in unison as the band belted out *There's No Business Like Show Business*. That finally segued into a frantic chorus of the *Post Horn Gallop* as they trotted frantically around the stage.

I don't go for girls dressed as horses but I would've normally sat back and let myself enjoy this. Instead, I couldn't shake off the notion that Fanny and Jim hadn't met by chance.

That they knew one another.

125

Jim had rubbished the line I'd taken on the Snout murder story, but he was a man to keep his options open. He'd been caught out before by sticking to one theory and ignoring other possibilities.

I wondered whether Fanny was his plant – a tame spy sent to befriend me and winkle out my own ideas about the case. She'd seemed very eager to get to know me in Marcello's. On the other hand, if Fanny was Jim's stool-pigeon, would he have risked speaking to her in the bar? Perhaps he'd hoped to give her some last-minute instructions before I returned with the programmes. Or perhaps he was playing a cleverer game – thinking that I wouldn't suspect a plot if the pair had pretended to meet for the first time. It was just the kind of double bluff Houghton would cook up.

I still hadn't reached a conclusion when the second act came on stage, a red-nosed comedian with a stock of mother-in-law jokes. "I was talking to a bloke down the pub. He said, 'My mother-in-law's an angel.' I said, 'You're lucky, mate, mine's still alive.'" The audience roared but Fanny looked faintly shocked.

She cheered up when the next act appeared – Professor Pettigrew and his Pixilated Poodles. The professor, an old boy who must have been pushing seventy, strolled onto the stage in front of four little podiums. He whistled and the four poodles – two white, two brown – scampered on stage and jumped on the podiums. I'm not a great fan of animal acts, but the professor had thought up a cute angle. The idea was that the dogs – Peggy, Perdy, Polly and Poppy – were out of control. Every time he ordered them to do something, they'd do the opposite. He shouted: "Come" and they sat and shook their heads. He placed bones on the stage and ordered: "Leave." The dogs rushed forward and gnawed them. He commanded: "Play dead." And they all scampered round in circles.

The climax of the act came when the professor lectured the dogs on the dangers of fire. He pointed to a bucket of water to put out flames. Then he set fire to a hoop and ordered Poppy not to go near it. Instead, she drank from the bucket, charged round the stage and leapt through the burning hoop. Then she turned and leapt back again. The audience applauded wildly.

Fanny whispered in my ear: "I'd love dogs like that. They're so tricksy."

Yes, I thought. And perhaps it takes one to know one.

We'd sat through a blowsy soprano – as Pinker predicted, she sang *I Dreamt I Dwelt in Marble Halls* – a ham-fisted juggler who dropped his Indian clubs, and a final dance routine from the chorus girls, before the lights came up for the interval.

I hurried Fanny out of her seat and we hustled down the aisle to the door which led backstage. We threaded ourselves through the narrow passage beside the wings.

The stage manager was berating the juggler: "You couldn't catch a train."

"The lights made my hands sweaty."

"So do your act in the dark. The audience won't miss much."

We found Professor Pettigrew in a dressing room at the end of a corridor which led to the property store. Not exactly star treatment, but I guess the management wanted to keep the dogs away from the other performers.

Pettigrew sat on a stool in front of a table littered with make-up sticks, cigarette packets and dog biscuits. On stage, he'd looked tall and slim with slicked-back grey hair and pleasantly lined features. But close up, even the heavy make-up couldn't hide the wrinkled forehead, bags under the eyes, sagging flesh around his jaw.

The dogs were lying in identical baskets along the far wall. Three of them stirred as we entered. They looked at us with those half-curious, half-hostile eyes dogs have when they're deciding whether to lick your hand or bite you on the bum. The fourth dog jumped out of its basket, trotted over, sniffed my crotch and decided there was nothing there worth getting excited about.

Pettigrew said: "Meet Poppy. She's the leader of the pack. No doubt about that."

"She's lovely." It was Fanny speaking. She was kneeling on the floor, tickling Poppy behind the ears. Poppy gave Fanny a friendly lick. She laughed with delight.

"I've come for the interview," I said.

"Delighted. But I can't see why the local rag is interested in an old trouper like me."

"Human interest."

"About dogs?"

Pettigrew had a point. Still, animal stories are always popular with readers and I'd promised Pinker I'd deliver three hundred words. So I fished out my notebook and asked the first question.

"Have you always liked dogs?"

"No. Hated the beasts as a child. Ma and Pa kept a wolfhound called *Nebuchadnezzar*. Damned stupid name for any dog."

"Why did you hate it?"

"Brute towered over me as kid. Knocked me down the stairs. Did what it liked. Crapped on the carpet. It was Persian."

"The carpet?"

"The dog. Pa picked it up on war service in the Middle East. That would be the first war – the one to end all wars."

Pettigrew rummaged on the dressing table. Found some dog biscuits. Handed them to Fanny.

"You seem to be getting along with my little treasures. They need a snack during the interval," he said.

Fanny looked like a natural with the animals. They'd all jumped out of their baskets and were crowding round her for the biscuits.

I asked Pettigrew: "So how come a man who hates dogs ended up with a dog act?"

"I dreamed of becoming a ventriloquist but I couldn't stop my lips moving."

"Spoils the effect," I said.

"So I had to find something else and as luck would have it, I was sharing a compartment on a train with a lady from Stow-in-the-Wold. She'd been to see a show a couple of nights earlier where a dog act had been the hit. Well, I had to find something. I couldn't sing, play a musical instrument, tell jokes, juggle or perform conjuring tricks. What else was there? I did hear of one bloke who'd put together an act out of waggling his ears. But I couldn't do that either."

I looked over at the dogs. Fanny had Perdy on her lap. She tickled Polly's tummy. Peggy and Poppy looked up at her with mooneyes and their tongues hanging out.

I asked Pettigrew: "Where did you get the dogs?"

"There's a bit of a story to that. The four were all from the same litter. But originally, I had only three from the breeder – Peggy, Perdy and Polly. The fourth had already been sold to a haberdasher's wife in Walthamstow.

"Well, it soon became clear that the three were missing their sister. They were sullen and listless – not like puppies should be. They didn't respond to anything I tried. So in the end, I teased the haberdasher's address out of the breeder and took the tram to Walthamstow."

"And found Poppy?" I said.

"Not immediately. The wife – a Mrs Slyburn, I remember – would barely speak to me. I had to do a bit of sniffing around and eventually I found Poppy tied up in the back yard of the haberdasher's on a short cord barely long enough to reach her water bowl. Not that there was any water in it. The poor mutt was lapping the drips from a muddy puddle when I saw her.

"A bonfire of rubbish from the shop was shooting flame and filling the yard with smoke. It was like keeping the animal in Hades. You wouldn't do it to a dog. But, of course, they were."

I scribbled some shorthand in my notebook and nodded to Pettigrew to continue.

"Any roads, when Poppy saw me poke my head round the gate she started barking. Strained on her lead to get to me. I reckon I was carrying the scent of the other three about me and she recognised it. Her bark brought the Slyburn woman to the door. She shouted at me to clear off – and then everything seemed to happen at once.

"Poppy slipped her leash, and raced towards me. The Madam Slyburn moved across the yard at an angle to cut her off. Poppy headed for the gate but the bonfire blocked her only means of escape. The fire was red hot, too. It seemed that Slyburn must catch her by the collar and tie her up again. Poppy simply ran for the bonfire and leapt it. She was out of the gate before Slyburn had taken another step. And with me heading after her as fast as I could run."

"Did Mrs Slyburn ever come after you?"

"No. For a start, she didn't know who I was. And I don't expect she'd have wanted it known among her customers that she'd been keeping a dog in those conditions."

"And I suppose that's where you got the idea that a dog could leap through fire in the act?" I asked.

"Never trained an animal to do it before. But Poppy is a true leader – she'll do anything. Courage of a lion. Mind you, she needs a little strengthener before doing the business."

"Of what?"

Pettigrew pointed to a bottle of Sandeman's Tawny Port on the dressing table.

I smiled. "So that bit in the act when she drinks from the bucket before leaping through the fiery hoop – she's drinking port?"

"And lemon. I give it a good dash of lemonade."

I closed my notebook. Looked over at Fanny. She had a couple of the dogs on their hind legs begging for biscuits.

I said to Pettigrew: "Looks like you've got a competitor for your act."

"You let me know if you fancy treading the boards, miss," he said. "At my age, I could use an assistant. What do your legs look like in fishnet tights?"

Fanny frowned. I intervened: "Miss Archer has obtained an important position at the knicker factory," I said.

"Begging your pardon, miss."

We stood up. I shook hands with Pettigrew and told him the article would be in Saturday's paper. Fanny gave the dogs a final pat and ear tickle.

Pettigrew reached for the port.

"Poppy needs a strengthener before her next show?" I asked.

Pettigrew pulled out the cork. "She's not the only one who needs a drop of Dutch courage before going on stage."

The second part of the show raced by.

My mind was only half on the performance. I vaguely remember a witless ventriloquist who had the audience roaring every time his dummy said "bum" and a honky-tonk pianist who had the crowd singing along to old music-hall favourites. The headliner was a comedian best known from his time hosting a television quiz show. He seemed only to get laughs by endlessly repeated his catchphrase: "What a kerfuffle!"

My mind was still on what game Fanny was playing.

So as the curtain came down, after another routine from the chorus girls, I whispered in Fanny's ear: "Let's go for supper."

I guided her backstage again and we left through the stage door.

If, as I suspected, she was Jim Houghton's nark, I didn't want them passing secret signals after the show.

Chapter 13

I led Fanny through the back-doubles to Meeting House Lane.

I planned to grab a quiet table in the Four Aces where I could ask her a few searching questions. I needed to discover exactly what she was up to.

So as we pushed through the restaurant's door, I gave Casey, the proprietor, my usual conspiratorial wink. He'd know it meant we wanted to be as quiet as possible. He led us to an alcove at the back of the ground-floor dining room. A curving red banquette formed a semi-circle around a small table. An electric candelabrum cast a mellow light and illuminated a single painting – a sideways view of a seated elderly lady in a long black dress and a white bonnet.

Fanny raised her eyebrows when she saw it. "What's *Whistler's Mother* doing here?"

"What mothers usually do," I said. "Making sure we don't get up to any mischief."

Fanny giggled.

Casey handed us menus and, while we studied them, I ran through a few opening gambits in my mind. I obviously couldn't accuse Fanny outright of being Houghton's stool-pigeon. She'd deny it, probably storm out and I'd have another unresolved mystery on my hands. As if Fred Snout's killing, the missing *Milady's Bath Night* and Venetia's letter to Marie weren't enough.

Casey took our order – smoked salmon and chicken chasseur for Fanny, pate maison and beef bourguignon for me. I asked him to bring a bottle of Medoc.

Fanny handed her menu back to Casey, turned to me and said: "So, do you bring all your conquests here?"

"I wasn't aware you'd surrendered."

"Let's just say I'm thinking of calling off the sentries."

"I didn't realise there were guards on the gate."

"After your invitation this morning, I thought I'd better be on my watch, especially when you chose the quietest table in the restaurant. Don't think I didn't notice your wink. Regular code, is it?"

"You make me sound like a cross between Casanova and Bluebeard," I said.

"I just sensed that there might be another girl around the corner."

"Female intuition?"

"You could put it down to that. But I'm right, aren't I?"

This wasn't turning out how I'd planned. But, perhaps, if I was frank with Fanny I would lure her into lowering her own defences.

So I said: "There was another girl. Last summer. Her name was Shirley. She came from Australia. She'd been working her way around the world and pitched up in Brighton."

"But it didn't work out?"

"I thought it was going to. There was a time when I thought Shirley did, too. But Shirley had wanderlust. Walkabout she called it. Like the aborigines. Except that she said anyone could do it. As a way of finding their true self."

"And her walkabout took her away from Brighton?"

"Yes. I only hope she finds her true self."

"Perhaps she'll come back," Fanny said.

"Perhaps," I said.

The waitress arrived with the wine and filled our glasses. I raised mine and said: "Here's to your new job at the knicker factory."

Fanny blushed. "I'd forgotten. Of course, my new job in the underworld."

"Don't you mean underwear?"

"Of course. I suppose that must be a Freudian slip." She sipped her wine and replaced the glass awkwardly on the table.

The waitress reappeared with our smoked salmon and pate

maison. We picked up our knives and forks and ate.

I said: "Have they given you a job title in your new position?"

"Not really. I'm very junior."

"I suppose when you're working in a knicker factory, you have to start at the bottom."

Fanny giggled again.

I said: "What will your work involve?"

"Mostly shorthand."

"Pitman's or Gregg's?"

"Yes."

"Both? That's most unusual."

"Sorry, no, only one. The first."

"Pitman's?"

"Yes."

"So what's your speed?"

"Fast enough. I gather I'll be mostly taking down letters – usually replies to customers wanting to know why they haven't got their knickers."

"That must be embarrassing."

Fanny blushed. "I didn't really mean it that way."

"I know."

"Anyway, you sound like you're interviewing me for a job. Tell me about yours."

"Well, I've been crime correspondent of the *Evening Chronicle* for two years."

"A life of crime. Do you meet any criminals?"

"Sometimes. But not when they're working."

"Are you working on any big stories at the moment?" Fanny asked.

"Nothing particular," I lied.

"I think I saw something in last night's paper about a murder on the pier."

"That's right. But I don't think it'll amount to much." I lightly brushed by nose to make sure it wasn't growing too long.

We fell silent. The waitress came in and took away our plates. I poured Fanny some more wine. The waitress returned with the chicken chasseur and beef bourguignon.

I said: "Did you enjoy the show."

Fanny chewed on a piece of chicken. "If I'm honest, some of it. The comedians were crude. But I loved the dogs. And it was a real treat to be able to pet them backstage."

"You seem to have a real way with animals. Do you have a dog of your own?"

"Yes... that is to say, no. My parents have a dog but now I'm living in a flat in Brighton and out all day working, it's not practical."

"Trials of a working girl, eh?"

Fanny shrugged. She cut into her chicken. "This is delicious. The restaurant is quite a find. It's not what it seems from the outside."

No, I thought, nothing is quite what it seems from the outside. But I'd thought of a way to prove whether Fanny was a shorthand typist – or a spy.

Over the coffee, we talked some more about the show – and especially Professor Pettigrew's poodles.

Finally, I said: "I've enjoyed this evening. Could we meet again tomorrow? This time, there won't be any work. Perhaps we could go dancing at Sherry's."

Fanny smiled. "That would be nice. Where shall we meet?"

"How about outside the ice rink in West Street?"

"I think I can remember that."

"Just to be sure I'll write it down for you."

I tore a page out of my notebook and wrote some shorthand. I handed Fanny the page.

"There," I said, pointing at the perfect Pitman's. "Outside the ice rink, West Street."

Fanny read the shorthand: "Outside the ice rink, West Street," she said.

I smiled. Now I knew she'd been lying.

My shorthand had read: "Not the knicker factory in Portslade."

I left the Four Aces without winking at Casey.

Fanny had been sharper than I'd originally given her credit for. I knew she was playing a game, but I wondered whether she knew that I knew. Yet my trick with the shorthand had left me with a further puzzle. I was certain she was no shorthand typist. But if Fanny knew Jim Houghton well enough to act as his informer, the chances were that she would also be a journalist. In which case, she should've had at least a working knowledge of shorthand. I'd enjoyed the supper – for a spy, she made good company – but I felt I was no further forward.

Outside the Four Aces, Fanny leaned forward and kissed my cheek. "Thank you for a fab evening," she said. "I've really enjoyed it."

"My car's only parked in Ship Street. I could give you a lift back to your flat," I said.

"It's right up in Woodingdean – too far out of your way. I can get a bus in North Street."

"Well, if you're sure."

Fanny turned, gave a little wave and headed down the lane. "Until tomorrow evening."

I watched her turn into North Street, then started to walk in the opposite direction towards Ship Street. I took half a dozen steps – and stopped.

Nothing about Fanny made sense. I knew she'd lied to me about being a secretary at Kayser Bondor. Could she also be lying about living in a flat in Woodingdean? I turned round and headed towards North Street.

At the end of Meeting House Lane, I took the precaution of hanging back and peering round the corner towards the bus stop. Fanny was crossing the road towards it. Further up the street I could see a Brighton Corporation number 22 for Woodingdean approaching from the Clock Tower.

Fanny quickened her pace and trotted to the bus stop, stuck out her hand. With grinding gears, the bus pulled into the kerb. I watched as she took a seat downstairs. The bus pulled out into the traffic and headed towards the Old Steine. It was fifty yards down the road before I stepped out of Meeting House Lane. Up towards the Clock Tower, I could see a cab with its light on heading down the road, probably towards the East Street cab rank.

I stepped into the road and hailed it. It pulled over, I yanked open the passenger door and slid in beside the driver.

"Follow that bus," I said.

"It'd be cheaper to catch it," he said. He was a young bloke with a thin face and curly brown hair.

"I want to see where it's going."

"It's the number 22 for Woodingdean. Where do you think it's going – Timbuctoo?"

I said: "Would you like a tip?"

He grinned. "Sure."

"Cut the clever chat and drive."

He frowned, put the cab into gear and we took off down North Street.

The bus was passing through the Steine and heading towards the Lewes Road by the time we caught up with it. I told the cabbie to keep well back. He grunted.

The bus made a couple of stops as it headed north through Grand Parade and into Richmond Place. It pulled in again at The Level. A couple of young men got off. An elderly bloke with a walking stick got on. The bus started to move again. Then Fanny jumped off the platform, looked guiltily up and down the road and dashed into The Level.

The cab had pulled into the side of the road about fifty yards back. I slipped the cabbie ten bob and told him to wait. I scrambled out of the cab and ran into The Level. I caught a glimpse of Fanny hurrying between the trees. I picked up my pace to close the distance between us, but she'd started too far ahead.

She left The Level and walked briskly into Ditchling Road. I reached the edge of The Level, stood behind an oak tree and watched. Fanny was a hundred or more yards north on the far side of the street. She paused under a lamp-post, opened her handbag and searched for something inside. She found what she was looking for and walked on.

Ten yards further on a smart red Aston Martin DB4 – top-of-the-range in sports cars and way more expensive than my own MGB – was parked by the kerb. Fanny had evidently been searching for her car keys. She sprinted round to the driver's door, opened it and slipped inside. Seconds later, the engine roared and the car edged out into the late-evening traffic.

There had been many puzzles during the evening. But of one thing I was sure: Fanny wasn't running an Aston Martin on a shorthand-typist's wages.

I thought about running back to the cab and pursuing the Aston Martin. It would be a step up in the world from following the number 22 to Woodingdean. But there was no way a Brighton taxi could keep pace with a sports car. Even if I could find which direction it was heading.

In any event, by the time I'd returned to our parking spot, I found the cabbie had driven off. Either that, or he was still following the bus to Woodingdean. So I walked back into town, collected my own car and drove back to my flat.

By the time I arrived in Regency Square, I'd thought of a way to unmask the true identity of Miss Fanny Archer.

It was a quarter to midnight when I inserted my key silently in the lock and crept stealthily into the hallway of my lodgings. A light was showing under the door of the Widow's parlour as I tiptoed towards the stairs. I scrupulously avoided the hall table with the glass ornaments that tinkled when you brushed against them.

I was just putting my right foot silently on the first tread of the stair when the Widow's door opened and she said: "It's a good job you make such a racket when you come in or I might have missed you."

"Goodnight, Mrs Gribble," I said.

"Not for me, it isn't."

"You'll feel better after a good night's sleep."

"Unless I get one in the night."

The conversation seemed to be taking a dangerous turn so I said: "You'll need to explain that last remark."

The Widow bustled into the hallway. She was wearing a long pink flannelette dressing gown. Her hair was in curlers.

She said: "I got another one this evening. About half past nine."

"Got what?"

"One of those breathing telephone calls."

I sighed. I'd forgotten the Widow had bearded me about it as I was leaving for the office.

She wagged a finger at me. "And this time I know it's not the butcher."

"With that kind of call you can never be sure."

"That's where you're wrong. Because Mr Evans knows nothing about it."

"You asked him?"

The Widow looked awkwardly at the picture of Holman Hunt's *Light of the World* on the wall as if seeking advice.

"Not directly," she said. "What do you think I am?"

I didn't answer that question. Instead, I said: "Then how do you know?"

"Because when I went in this morning to give him my weekly order, I deliberately paid him a kind compliment to see how he reacted."

If Evans had been on the wrong end of one of the Widow's backhanded compliments, there was no telling what might have happened.

"What did you say?" I asked.

"I said I'd always admired his faggots." Her lips pursed in a moue of disgust. "I won't even tell you what he replied unless you insist."

I looked down, said nothing and studied the stains on the carpet.

"Well, if you insist," she said. "He said, 'I've had no complaints and they deliver the necessary on a good night.' I could tell by his leer that he was being suggestive."

"Perceptive of you."

"And that's not the worst of it. I needed some cooking fat so asked Mr Hodges, quite politely, 'Do you keep dripping?'"

I brushed my hand over my forehead.

The Widow had turned a shade of puce: "And he said, 'Only when the old faggots are working overtime.' I didn't know where to put myself. So I just stormed out of the shop. I shall be placing my weekly meat order elsewhere."

"It's just as well you didn't ask whether he had any sausage meat," I said.

"That's as maybe," the Widow raged. "But I want no more nonsense about shy suitors. And I want to know where these anonymous telephone calls are coming from. At least, I know who they're coming from."

My eyebrows shot up at that. "You do?"

"Yes, he's a filthy pervert called Ivor Colin English."

"How do you know that?"

"Because when the call came this evening, there was the usual breathing sounds on the line and I said, 'Who are you, you disgusting creep?' And he said, 'Ivor Colin English' before I slammed the receiver down."

"He gave his name just like that?"

"No, not like that. He had some kind of accent. I think he was trying to disguise his true identity."

"People who want to disguise their identity don't generally give their name," I said.

"Well," said the Widow, "if I ever catch him he'll know what's what."

I didn't have time to reply to that.

The Widow had already stormed back into her parlour and slammed the door.

Chapter 14

I was first into the newsroom at the *Chronicle* the following morning.

I'd told myself I was going to crack at least some of the mysteries that were still puzzling me. But first I had to write the crit I'd promised Sidney Pinker.

Just as I'd hammered out the final folio on my old Remington, Cedric, the copy boy, strolled into the room. I called him over, handed him the folios and said: "Take this purple prose up to the subs."

Cedric glanced at the copy: "Branching out, are you? Surely this is Mr Pinker's territory."

"And he can keep it, as far as I'm concerned."

"Any developments in your murder, Mr Crampton?"

"It's not actually my murder, Cedric. I'm still breathing. On your way."

Cedric grinned and sloped off across the newsroom.

As he did so, Frank Figgis came out of his office and stomped over to my desk.

He said: "If you spent less time at the theatre, you'd make more progress on the Snout story." He gave a throaty chuckle. It sounded like a rake being dragged over gravel.

"You've heard about my favour for Pinker, then?" I said.

"There's nothing happens in this office I don't hear about."

"But you won't have heard that Venetia, Dowager Marchioness of Piddinghoe, had been paying a monthly honorarium to Marie Richmond until a few days before her death."

Figgis shook a Woodbine out of his packet and lit up. "You interest me greatly, young Crampton."

I told Figgis how Trish – the one in A&E – at the Royal Sussex County hospital had put me on to Mrs Bailey and how I'd found

Marie's letter in the pocket of her pinny.

Figgis sucked on his ciggie. "Strictly speaking, we ought to hand that letter over to Tomkins as part of a continuing murder investigation."

"I don't see it that way," I said. "For a start, Tomkins made it plain that he doesn't believe the theft of *Milady's Bath Night* is connected to Snout's murder. *Ergo*, any correspondence that Marie received from anyone, apart from Snout or any of his suspected killers, is not a material clue. We're pursuing a newspaper story which, in Tomkins' stated opinion, is unrelated to his investigation."

"He won't see it that way if it turns out that we're right." Figgis blew a long stream of smoke across the newsroom.

"In which case, he'll have to explain why he dismissed the connection when the *Chronicle* pointed it out right from the start. His face will be redder than when he lost that cigarette-smuggling case."

"I don't want you riling Tomkins by bringing that up. Just concentrate on putting together a case to link the theft to the killing."

"That's why I plan to see Venetia later today and ask some pointed questions about her payments to Marie."

Figgis stubbed out his fag and searched around for a bin. Couldn't find one so dropped the dog-end on the floor. "Mind you behave in a refined way like me when you're tangling with the aristocracy. They've got friends in high places."

"I won't be tugging my forelock, but I'll make sure that we're well covered with anything I write," I said.

"Speaking of which, I was pleased with that backgrounder you wrote on the Profumo case. I know there's no strong Sussex angle – more's the pity – but at least you gave us a showing in the story."

"Sorry there's not more," I said.

"Well, maybe. But keep a watching brief on that. I'm sure you can fit it in."

"Of course, I'm only working twenty-three hours a day at the moment. There's a whole hour going to waste."

Figgis always ignored sarcasm. Instead, he hitched up his trousers and said: "Anything else?"

I flipped through some papers on my desk to give the impression that I was giving his question serious consideration. I didn't plan to tell him of my suspicions about Fanny yet. I wanted to handle that my own way.

So I looked him the eye and said: "No, nothing."

Figgis stroked his chin. "Hmmm. I think you're hiding something. But I won't press you on that now. You'd only lie and then I couldn't trust you."

He turned and headed off to his office.

"And where would we be without trust," I said to his retreating back.

Shortly after Figgis had returned to his office, Sidney Pinker wafted into the newsroom.

He threaded his way through the desks towards me like a ballet dancer on the run. The cloying aroma of his aftershave reached me ten seconds before he did.

"Just been with the subs, dear boy." He stroked an eyebrow, perhaps to make sure it was still there. "They showed me your notice of last night's show. Very good, I must say. I see I shall have to watch my position here."

"Your seat in the front row of the stalls is safe with me, Sidney. You can keep theatricals. At least with crime you know who's conning whom."

Pinker trilled a little laugh. "Always the old cynic. But, forgive me for reminding you, my bonny lad, but you also promised a featurette for the Saturday supplement."

"Don't worry, Sidney, you'll get your pound of flesh."

"Pound of flesh? After the night I've just had in Kemp Town,

Y

I don't think I could manage any more just yet."

He turned and pranced his way out of the newsroom.

As far as I was concerned, Pinker could wait for his feature on Professor Pettigrew. I had more pressing business. I swept the papers which covered my desk to one side. I'd jotted the Piddinghoes' phone number on my blotter. I wanted to copy it into my notebook as I expected to be out of the office most of the day and I'd need to phone Venetia to question her about the retainer she'd been paying Marie.

But when I'd cleared the detritus of a week's *Chronicles*, office memos and useless press releases to one side, I discovered that somebody had changed the paper in the blotter. Probably the office cleaner. And just as well. It was a bad habit, but all of us in the newsroom tended to use our blotters as handy memo pads when we were making notes on the phone. Mine had been crammed full of jottings.

I spent a couple of minutes looking up the number for Piddinghoe Grange in the phone directory. Then I scooped up my notebook and headed out of the newsroom.

Pinker's aftershave seemed to follow me like a bad memory.

The true identity of Miss Fanny Archer was the most urgent of all the mysteries I had to unravel.

I needed to know for sure whether or not she was a plant spying on me. It had been impossible to follow Fanny's Aston Martin when it had sped off up Ditchling Road. But I had, at least, managed to note the number plate. The CD in the plate was a giveaway that the car had been registered in Brighton.

The registration office was in Brighton Town Hall. It occupied a room in the basement. The Town Hall was a pleasant five-minute stroll from the *Chronicle* through the fringe of the Lanes.

I arrived at the office a couple of minutes after it had opened. As I'd hoped, it was too early for Brighton's new car owners. They'd still be under their bonnets admiring big ends or

145

whatever it was they loved about engines.

The office had a dark wooden counter with a couple of desks behind it. One of them was occupied by a young woman with light-brown hair tied back in a bun. She was wearing a cream blouse and a tweed skirt. Tortoiseshell framed glasses balanced on a prominent nose. She bent studiously over the *Daily Telegraph* crossword. A nameplate on her desk read Miss Delia Walters.

I knocked gently on the counter and said: "Good morning, Miss Walters."

She glanced up with worried eyes. Saw I wasn't one of the bosses come to reprimand her for slacking on the job. Replaced the worry with a resentful frown. From her scholarly appearance, I guessed she'd wanted a job in the public library. But the council's personnel department had handed her the short straw. Boring car registrations, basement office. As revenge she took as little interest in her work as possible.

I said: "Sorry to interrupt you. Bit of a beast is it?"

"Beast?"

"The crossword."

"I can normally solve the *Telegraph*'s in half an hour, but this morning I'm stuck."

"What's the clue?"

"'Possibly vicar's paperwork sin'. Two words. Eight letters, five letters."

I made a bit of a play with scratching my head and said: "While I'm thinking about that, could you help me with another little problem?"

She stood up and came over to the counter, leaned on it and said: "Try me."

"I'm thinking of selling my car but I don't want to buy a new one until the end of the summer. I'd very much like to keep the same registration number. Is there any way I could transfer it, and reserve it for the new vehicle?"

"That's not normal. But I'll see what we can do. What's the

registration number?"

From memory, I reeled off the number on Fanny's Aston Martin.

Delia crossed to a bank of filing cabinets, selected a drawer and yanked it open. I crossed my fingers behind my back hoping this was going to work.

She drew out a card and studied it. Briefly turned it over to see if anything was written on the reverse. Stared at the front again. Furrowed her brow. Scratched her cheek. Gave the edge of the card a speculative flick. Turned to me and said: "Could you repeat the registration number?"

I did so. Nodded to emphasise my certainty.

She looked at the card again. "There's a problem. This car seems to have been registered to a lady."

"There must be some mistake."

"Not according to the card."

"May I see it?"

"Well, it's not strictly…"

"I'd just take a quick confidential peek. It could save a lot of trouble. I'll be out of your way and you can get back to your crossword."

Delia shrugged. "Well, the handwriting shows it's not my mistake."

She passed the card over the counter. I looked at it. Couldn't avoid a sharp intake of breath.

"Something wrong?"

"I've just realised it's my mistake, not yours. I've given you the wrong registration. Mine starts CDJ not CDI. I think."

I handed back the card.

"You think?" she said.

"The best thing for me to do is to bring in the registration documents. Perhaps tomorrow," I said. "In the meantime, that crossword clue: 'Possibly vicar's paperwork sin.'"

Delia glanced back at the newspaper on her desk.

"Clerical error," I said.

She picked up the paper and started to fill it in. I hurried out before she had the chance to ask me anything else.

I had a more urgent clue to follow.

There was no chance that Miss Fanny Archer was Jim Houghton's paid informer.

Because Fanny Archer, aka Lady Frances Mountebank, was the Marquess of Piddinghoe's daughter.

I left the Town Hall with my brain buzzing like a power drill.

I needed time to think, so I walked round to Marcello's. The place was winding down after the breakfast rush. I ordered a coffee and took a seat towards the back.

I'd originally planned to confront Venetia with the letter she'd written to Marie about the payments. But the revelation that Fanny was really a scion of the aristocracy – Venetia's grand-daughter – changed all that. Fanny – or should I now call her Frances? – was a nark all right. She was a posh nark with a whole canteen of silver cutlery in her mouth.

She was Venetia's nark.

That convinced me more than ever that Venetia had much to hide. Perhaps she was worried about me finding out about the payments to Marie. She might have guessed I'd get in touch with Clarence. But, perhaps, there was more.

Venetia didn't know that I'd unmasked her spymaster. Or, rather, spy-mistress. That gave me an advantage. Despite the suspicions I'd had, I'd sensed Fanny and I had made some kind of connection over supper at the Four Aces. So I decided to confront Fanny first. What Fanny told me could put Venetia in a position where she had to reveal what she was hiding.

But if this plan was going to work, I'd need to move fast.

I left my coffee on the table and walked up to the counter. Marcello was busy buttering bread. He looked up and said: "No bacon sandwich this morning?"

I said: "I'd rather have the use of your telephone, if you don't mind."

Marcello shrugged. "Turned you out of the office have they?"

"Not yet. But if I don't get this story right, my days may be numbered."

Marcello grinned. "You better make the call then. Go through to the back. The telephone's just inside the door to the kitchen."

I nodded thanks and walked through. Ruby was over by the sink washing up. I smiled at her, pulled out my notebook and flipped over the pages looking for the Piddinghoes' number. I picked up the phone and dialled. Listened to it ring seven times before someone lifted the receiver.

A voice said: "Piddinghoe Grange. Who is speaking, please?" It was Lord Snooty – Pinchbeck the butler.

I put on a bit of a lisp and said: "Thith ith Rodney, Lady Frances' hairdresser. May I speak to her ladythip, please?"

"I was always given to understand that her ladyship's hair stylist was called Peterkin."

I dropped the lisp. "Peterkin is my partner. At the moment, he is rather engaged with a permanent wave which seems to have become a little too temporary."

"I see. In what connection, did you wish to communicate with Lady Frances?"

"We need to confirm her next appointment. If you could kindly connect me with her ladyship, I will not detain her for more than a moment."

"I regret to inform you that Lady Frances is not available. She is with Herbert."

"She's never mentioned Herbert to Peterkin and me."

"Herbert is the love of her life, if I may use a rather vulgar turn of phrase." Lord Snooty gave an apologetic little cough.

"Perhaps you could say when Lady Frances will be free to take a call."

"That is hard to say. She likes to spend at least two hours a day on top of Herbert."

"Lucky Herbert."

Pinchbeck cleared his throat to signal his disapproval. "I don't care for your insinuation, sir. Herbert is a horse. Lady Frances is hacking across the countryside. I believe towards the Cuckmere River. It is unlikely that she will return until luncheon. Kindly call later."

He replaced the receiver.

I looked across at Ruby. She was drying some cups and saucers.

"You look like a bloke who's just been given the bum's rush," she said. "Not that girl I saw you chatting up yesterday, is it?"

"From what her butler says, she's horsing around."

"If she's got a butler, you stand no chance."

I grinned. "'They also serve who only stand and wait.'"

Ruby pulled a puzzled face. "Don't know what you're talking about."

I headed for the door. "I'll explain it one day."

Outside Marcello's, I glanced at my watch.

If Fanny wasn't due back at Piddinghoe Grange until lunchtime, I had time to attend the regular morning police press conference. It was due in ten minutes. So I hurried back to the police station and sprinted round to the briefing room.

Superintendent Tomkins was just walking in flanked by a couple of his under-strappers. He was wearing a grey suit, spotted blue tie and an insufferable grin.

The room was packed. A seaside murder just before the silly season was like an early Christmas present for the national newspapers – even though they still had the Profumo scandal to feast on. There were enough hacks from the nationals to drink a bar dry. There were rumours that some of them had. But they all looked bright enough. Tomkins made a performance of seating himself, getting comfortable and rummaging through his notes.

He surveyed the assembled faces like a suffragan bishop about to preach the Good Word.

An expectant silence fell over the room. Tomkins said: "I am going to read a statement and then I will take questions."

He put on his glasses, picked up a sheet of paper and read: "This morning, police officers arrested Thomas Archibald Belcher, forty-seven, of Maple Road, Coldean on suspicion of the murder of Frederick Tinkerman Snout in the early hours of June the fourth."

I took the statement down in perfect Pitman's in my notebook. Then wrote a single word in capital letters after it: RUBBISH.

As I'd discovered, Tom Belcher and Fred Snout had had a right royal row after the theft was discovered. Plenty of witnesses would have heard it. And there was no doubt that Belcher blamed Snout's lax attitude to night-time security for the loss of *Milady's Bath Night*. But Belcher's threat to kill Snout was words spoken in anger. He'd no more kill Snout than an old seagull. It seemed to me the pair were like a couple of football fans who support opposing teams in the same city. On the surface, the worst of enemies. Underneath, united in a common love. In their case, the precious seaside pier they worked for.

I realised Tomkins had called for questions. A forest of hands shot up in front of me. Tomkins surveyed the room. He'd be looking for a patsy to ask a simple question.

I decided to play the rude guest who barges to the front of the queue. So I jumped to my feet and said: "Mr Tomkins, how do you explain the fact you've arrested the man responsible for keeping the Palace Pier What the Butler Saw machines safe when you previously said that Fred Snout's murder had nothing to do with the theft of *Milady's Bath Night*?"

There were a few complaints around the room that I'd stepped out of turn. But everyone wanted to hear how Tomkins would wriggle out of that question. So the grumbles died to an expectant silence.

But Tomkins positively crowed. "The arrest of Belcher proves my point. Irresponsible newspaper speculation suggested that the killing was linked to the theft. We know Belcher didn't steal *Milady's Bath Night* but, we say, he did murder Snout. Thus, the two are plainly not linked."

I wasn't letting Tomkins get away with that lazy answer. So I ignored mutterings around the room and asked: "Has Mr Belcher confessed to the killing?"

"We have not yet completed our interviews."

"So the answer is no."

"I am confident we will assemble all the evidence we need for a successful prosecution. And now, perhaps, a question from a more senior journalist." He pointed at Jim Houghton.

I made a quick note of Tomkins' answers to my questions as I heard Houghton ask: "Have you any forensic evidence to link Belcher to the murder?"

Tomkins mumbled: "That is still a focus of our investigation."

In a word, no.

Some of the national journalists jumped in with questions about Tom Belcher's background. They'd be thinking that a man who had a love for What the Butler Saw machines could have an exotic past. Although I'd spent only half an hour with the man, I doubted it. His passion for the machines was largely for the technology they used rather than the content.

I noticed one or two of the nationals trying to sneak out at the back of the room unnoticed. They'd be heading for Belcher's house – hoping to find his wife in. In the next few days, they'd camp out on her doorstep. They'd promise to leave for just one titbit of information or an old photo of Tom. But they never would. Her life was going to be hell until the tabloids found another victim to harass.

As far as I was concerned, I intended to leave them to it. Belcher's arrest was a typical Tomkins tactic designed to grab personal headlines. It was plain from Tomkins' answers that he didn't have enough evidence to nail Belcher for the crime. He was hoping to turn up evidence in the next twenty-four hours. But it wasn't there – and so he'd have to release Belcher without charge. But not before Tom and his missus had been to hell and back, courtesy the gentlemen of the press.

But not this gentleman.

Even so, Tomkins' announcement left me with a problem.

Belcher's arrest was news – and my job was to report it. But I had to find a way to do it which didn't undermine my own theory. Tomkins' move could encourage Figgis to put pressure on me to drop my own line of enquiry. I had to avoid that.

By the time I walked into the *Chronicle* newsroom fifteen minutes later, I'd decided what to do. I'd write a full report of Tomkins' press conference, but I'd use my own questions at the top of the story. I'd make it clear in the first five pars that Tomkins wasn't able to produce a single shred of hard evidence against Belcher. The story should satisfy Figgis while leaving me the option of developing it in my way over the next few days.

At his press conference two days earlier, Tomkins had dismissed out of hand the notion there was any connection between the murder and the theft. Now he was edging towards admitting there was. I decided to check back in my notes of the first press conference to see whether there were any more contradictions I could use in my story. The notes of that were in my previous book.

So I yanked open the top drawer where I kept my old notebooks neatly filed in date order. It's an important discipline for reporters. If you're ever challenged on the accuracy of a story, the evidence of a contemporary shorthand note will generally get you off the hook. It was a rule on the paper that we had to keep old notebooks for at least six months. But my neat piles of books had been disturbed. Someone had been rummaging through them. Person or persons unknown had taken out the most recent book – which also included the notes of my interview with Toupée Terry and Clarence – and rifled through it.

I'd expressed my concern to Frank Figgis that there was a snitch in the office. This was supporting evidence. And it could also be the reason behind the mysterious removal of my old blotter. I used the thing as a handy memo pad. I'd made numerous notes of telephone numbers and addresses on it including Clarence's address. That could explain how Jim Houghton had found Clarence's flat so swiftly.

But who was the snitch? I had my suspicions. Cedric the copy boy had been taking an unusually deep interest in the Snout story. Only this morning, he'd been questioning me about it. Besides, he was the one person in the office, who had a chance to read everyone's copy as he took it up to the subs. And, I recalled, he might also have a motive. A couple of months back he'd tried to persuade Figgis to promote him to junior reporter. But Figgis had told him he wasn't ready yet and had to spend at least another year as copy boy. But I was building a theory out of circumstantial evidence. Before I pointed the finger, I needed some proof.

A snitch who'd been a successful blotter bandit once, might come back a second time. I made a few inconsequential notes on the blotter to make it look used. Then I wrote: "Friday 1.00pm. Bat and Ball public bar. Meet Snout witness."

If the snitch passed on that information, I'd thought of a way to trap him.

Chapter 15

It was twenty minutes shy of midday when I parked the car in a narrow lane just outside Piddinghoe.

I'd been looking forward to getting out of Brighton into the peace of the countryside. But the gruff rumble of agricultural machinery from the other side of a sprawling hedge drowned out the twitter of the birds. No doubt a horny-handed son of the earth was ploughing the fields and scattering the good seed on the land.

I stepped out of the car and looked up the lane. I'd circled the village and Piddinghoe Grange a couple of times trying to work out which way Fanny would return to the house. Lord Snooty had said that she'd hacked off towards the Cuckmere in the east. I'd studied the Ordnance Survey map of Sussex I kept in the car and identified three possible bridleways back. But one skirted north towards Lewes before turning south to Piddinghoe and another passed too close to the busy A27 road. I reckoned Fanny would choose the quietest – the one which passed through uninhabited countryside.

After all, she was a girl with a lot on her mind. She'd been playing double-agent on behalf of her grandmother. Throughout British history, the aristocratic classes had kept the upper hand through a mixture of subterfuge and trickery. It ran through their veins as much as their blue blood. But Fanny didn't strike me as a natural at the dark arts of the double-cross. Perhaps that's why she'd chosen to spend the morning riding across isolated country. Perhaps she needed time by herself to think. Or, perhaps, as Lord Snooty had pointed out, she just liked spending time on top of Herbert.

I'd parked the MGB about a half a mile from the village. I didn't want curious yokels spotting an unfamiliar car and asking awkward questions. I also wanted a spot where I could surprise

Fanny before she saw me. The combination of an ancient oak tree and a bend in the lane meant I'd be able to leap out like Dick Turpin as Fanny appeared. Whether she would stand and deliver remained to be seen. I could drive my MGB fast, but it would be no match for a horse across country. I'd cornered on two wheels, but I'd yet to get the car to jump a hedge.

It turned out Lord Snooty had been correct almost to the minute.

At five to twelve, Fanny clip-clopped round the bend in the lane. Herbert turned out to be a handsome bay. Perhaps not sleek enough to win the Derby but much too posh to pull a milk-float. His flanks glistened with sweat. Fanny had evidently spurred the animal through some hard gallops. Perhaps another sign she had frustrations to work out.

She was dressed in brown jodhpurs, a tight-fitting riding jacket and one of those peaked horse-riding caps that straps under the chin. Her high black riding boots had a shine that I could've seen my face in had I been close enough to look. Fanny saw the car before me. Annoyance clouded her eyes. As though it were a damned cheek for four wheels to intrude where only four legs should go. But that look vanished when I stepped out from behind the oak tree. I caught a flash of fear in her eyes.

I said: "It's a long ride back to Woodingdean. But I suppose you could always tie the horse up to a lamp-post when you get there."

Fanny pursed her lips – glanced anxiously around as though looking for a way to escape. Then she shrugged in a resigned sort of gesture – her way of registering that she'd been rumbled and didn't really care.

She said: "It was the shorthand, wasn't it? You tricked me with the shorthand."

I nodded. "Once I knew you were playing a part, it was just a case of following you. I saw the Aston Martin, took the registration plate and traced you from there."

"But you don't know why I tricked you."

"I think I know some of it."

"And you expect me to tell you the rest?"

"That's why I'm here."

"You don't know the half of it," she said.

I stepped towards the horse. "Then let me tell you the half I do know."

She dismounted, led Herbert forward and looped his rein around the branch of a bush.

I said: "When I saw your grandmother a few days ago, she told me she'd had no contact with her sister for many years."

"And so she hasn't. Do you think I could have lived with Grandmama for so long without knowing where she went and whom she saw? She's the closest friend I've ever had."

"Lady Piddinghoe refused to tell me why she was estranged from her sister." For a moment, I considered telling Fanny that Venetia had been sending Marie money every month for years. But I decided to keep that information in reserve.

Instead I said: "When I spoke to the daughter of one her former servants, I was told the two sisters had broken up after a furious row."

Fanny's eyes blazed with anger. "So you're prying behind my family's back."

"And you were playing Mata Hari without the sequins behind mine."

"You think I don't have good reason, when all you're concerned with is to dig up as much dirt as you can."

I shook my head. "I'm not in the dirt-digging business. Never have been. But I am trying to find the truth. A dead man lies behind my enquiries – and I want to find out how he was murdered and why."

"So now you're a detective."

"No, I'm a journalist. And when I find the truth, I will write about it, no matter what effect it has on the noble escutcheon of the Piddinghoes."

Fanny turned away. Walked over to where Herbert was quietly browsing on some grass. Patted the horse's neck. Whispered something in his ear. She turned back to me. The anger had vanished from her face. "I told Grandmama that no good would come of it."

"You mean spying on me?"

"Yes. But she thought I could gain your confidence, discover what you knew."

"Some kind of damage-limitation exercise?"

Fanny sunk down on a tree stump. The fight had drained out of her. "I suppose so. Although what Grandmama planned to do with any information I discovered I just don't know."

I moved closer. Knelt down beside her. "So why did you agree to do it?"

Fanny took off her riding gloves and rubbed a hand over her face. "My God, I don't know. I must have been mad even to consider a deception like that. But I've been so worried about her. About both of them."

"The Marquess, too?"

"Yes, Daddy. He's seemed so distracted in the past few days. Of course, as a government minister, he's got important problems to deal with. He's always seemed a bit remote. But now it's as though he's withdrawn into himself. He hardly speaks – except to Grandmama and then only when they think I can't hear…"

I'd watched the tension rising inside her. She snivelled but fought to control her tears and keep her voice steady. Generations of breeding in the stiff upper lip were being put to a tough test. But the test failed. The grief she'd bottled up broke loose and she wailed as the emotion inside took over. Her shoulders heaved and her head slumped as she wept. All the arrogance had gone. She crumpled with despair.

I moved closer and put my arm around her shoulders. I said: "There's more isn't there?"

She nodded.

"And it's frightening you."

She nodded again. She pulled a lace-fringed handkerchief from the pocket of her jodhpurs, dried her eyes, blew her nose.

She spoke in a voice thick with tears. "There's something bad that's worrying Daddy and Grandmama. I don't know what it is. But I can tell it's destroying them. And I don't know what to do about it."

I said: "Let's talk."

Her eyes widened. "With a journalist. You think that will help?"

I said: "In journalism, we often see people at their best and at their worst. People accuse us of being cynics. That can happen to you when you only see people at their extremes. You can start to believe that there's nothing in between. But there always is. Perhaps I can help you to see that whatever it is that you think is the worst is not as bad as you imagine."

"And then you'll write about it in your newspaper."

I smiled. "Not this time. This conversation will be on background only. I won't write about what you tell me."

Fanny managed a thin smile. "You promise?"

"I promise." I didn't mention that Frank Figgis always justified breaching a confidence by quoting Jonathan Swift: "Promises and pie-crust are made to be broken."

Me? I still hadn't decided whether I agreed with Swift.

"I think the trouble started three days ago," Fanny said.

We were sitting in the snug bar of the Marquess of Angelsey, a pub in the village of Rodmell, a couple of miles from Piddinghoe Grange. I'd ordered Fanny a large brandy and myself a small G and T. Herbert was drinking his fill from a water trough outside.

I said: "How can you be sure of that?"

"Daddy came down to breakfast in a foul mood that morning.

Shouted at Pinchbeck because there were no devilled kidneys. Spilt his coffee. Then stormed out with his shotgun to shoot rabbits."

I thought about that. Three days ago would have put the outburst on Monday – the day after *Milady's Bath Night* was stolen.

I kept that to myself and asked: "Did your father mention what was on his mind?"

"No. He barely spoke to me or Grandmama. Just munched his toast in silence."

"What did Venetia say about it?"

"She made an excuse for him. Said he had a lot of problems at the ministry."

"Was that likely?"

"Daddy often has government problems to solve. He relishes them. It's what he lives for. I've seen work problems make him tired – but never to lose his temper. And he never shouts at the servants. It's just something one doesn't do."

One made a mental note about the correct form in case one ever hired a butler.

I said: "Do you think that Venetia knows what's worrying your father?"

Fanny's eyes filled with tears again. She took a sip of her brandy. It steadied her.

She said: "That's the worst of it. Mama died shortly after I was born. She was killed in an air raid during the Blitz. So Grandmama became like a surrogate mother to me. As I grew up she was at the centre of my life – much more than Daddy who was always away at a political meeting or something boring like that. I've never had a single secret from Grandmama – not even those silly teenage things like my first boyfriend. And, until now, I didn't think she had any secrets from me."

"I can see that's hard."

"Very hard. I've just felt these past couple days she's started to exclude me from her life."

"And that's why you agreed to be a spy?"

"I thought that if I said yes, perhaps Grandmama would trust me enough to tell me what's worrying Daddy so badly."

"But it's not worked out that way?"

"No. I've just made a fool of myself."

"Not in my eyes," I said.

"That's kind of you." She cupped my hand in hers and gave a gentle squeeze.

I said: "Couldn't you confront your father and grandmother and demand to know what's on their minds?"

Fanny shook her head. "You don't know them. That would just make them even more determined to hide their secret." She picked up her glass and drained her brandy. Looked at me with a new determination in her eyes. "But I do know something," she said.

I took and sip of my G and T and said nothing. Waited for her to decide whether she wanted to tell me. I saw doubt chase across her face. Then she made up her mind.

"Since all this started, I've taken to creeping around the house, hoping to overhear Daddy and Grandmama whispering to one another. I know it's terrible. It's not the sort of thing one was brought up to do."

"Being in journalism, I was brought up to do the reverse," I said. Then wished I hadn't spoken.

Fanny frowned but continued. "This morning's breakfast wasn't as fraught as Wednesday's but I could sense a tension in the air. Finally, Grandmama stood up and said, 'I'm going to speak to cook – she's put too much curry powder in the kedgeree.' That was nonsense. It tasted the same as always. As you know, you only need a small pinch of curry powder - and a small pinch there was."

"My usual breakfast dilemma is how much brown sauce to put in my bacon sandwich," I said.

Fanny sniffed. "A minute later, Daddy got up even before he'd had any marmalade with some excuse about his car coming earlier for him this morning. After he'd left the room, I followed him. He went through the servants' door into the passage that leads to the pantry. I pushed the door ajar and I could hear him talking to Grandmama."

"About what?"

"That's it. I'd missed most the conversation. But I heard Grandmama say, 'Leave it to me, Charlie, I'll make the delivery tonight as instructed.' Daddy said, 'Don't take the Bentley – it's too conspicuous.' Grandmama said, 'I prefer driving the Riley anyway.' I heard Daddy grunt, 'Do it after dark,' and then his footsteps came back up the passage. I let the door swing shut and ran."

I finished my G and T and sat back. "What do you make of that?" I asked.

Fanny turned her head and gazed out of the window for fully a minute. Some unpleasant options must have been running through her mind. They were certainly doing so in mine.

"I don't know what to think," she said at last. "But I'm certain that Daddy's in some kind of trouble. And it must be some sort of trouble that even his position and influence can't remove."

It was trouble, all right. And trouble with a capital B for blackmail. I'd had my suspicions that Lord Piddinghoe had instructed Hardmann to remove *Milady's Bath Night* from the pier. But it was just a theory. Now the theory started to harden in my mind. Suppose Hardmann had been doing the dirty work on the pier on the Marquess's orders. If somebody discovered that, Lord Piddinghoe would be as much in the frame for a black-mailer as Hardmann himself. Perhaps more so – because Piddinghoe was the one with the ancient title and the job in the government. But who would've discovered it? Could someone have seen Hardmann close to Palace Pier? If they did, Hardmann could be hard pressed to explain his presence there. And perhaps the blackmailer had followed the same chain of reasoning as I had. Somehow I had to find a way to follow Venetia when she went to make this mysterious delivery.

I said: "There is a way to get to the bottom of this mystery."

Fanny's lips parted and I barely heard her whispered "How?"

"Follow Venetia and discover what she's delivering and to whom."

"I couldn't do that. I don't know how."

"I do," I said.

Fanny shifted in her seat. "I'm not sure. It's so risky."

"If you let me drive, I will keep the risk to a minimum. We'd be in a car which Venetia doesn't know and won't suspect."

"I hate this. It's as though a lifetime of trust is being cast aside for ever."

"Not for ever. Venetia hasn't trusted you, but you can help rebuild the trust you both cherish. You need to let her know that whatever she's doing, you will understand. But you can't do that, until you do know."

Fanny chewed on her lower lip. Worried at one of the buttons on her riding jacket.

"We can't go on as we are," she said. "Perhaps your plan is the only way."

I said: "Your father said that Venetia would not be leaving until after dark. It won't be fully dark until nearly ten o'clock tonight. So let's meet here at half past nine."

Fanny nodded reluctantly. "Anything else?" she asked.

"Yes. Dress in dark clothes. And don't bring a horse."

Chapter 16

I met Fanny in the Marquess of Anglesey pub just after nine-thirty.

She was in the saloon bar dressed as a super-spy in a pair of designer jeans, black polo-neck sweater and dark-grey jacket. James Bond would have been proud of her. She was nursing the remains of a gin and tonic. She looked like a woman who needed a drink and was determined to have it.

I sat down beside her and pointed at the glass: "Your first?"

"Second."

"Kemosahbee no track big white hunter with stench of juniper berry masking scent."

"If you think I'm playing Lone Ranger to your Tonto, you can think again."

"A man can dream."

"I'm in no mood for your jokes – or your dreams." She took another swig of the G and T.

"Tough up at the Grange?" I said.

"The atmosphere in the house has been terrible this evening. Cook made one of her very best cheese soufflés and Daddy hardly touched it. We could hear cook's ructions in the kitchen even from the small dining room."

I pondered for a moment on the rarefied lives of people who had a choice of dining rooms in which to turn their noses up at a cheese soufflé.

But there were more pressing issues. I said: "We need to find a place to hide the car when Venetia drives through the village."

Fanny downed the remainder of her drink and said. "There's a cart track which leads up on to the Downs. Grandmama will have to pass it to reach the Lewes road. If we park fifty yards up the track, we can see her drive by."

"And suppose she doesn't head for the Lewes road."

"She will. Trust me."

I shrugged. I'd reached the stage in this story when I was wondering whether I could trust anyone.

Of course, Venetia did take the Lewes road.

And at a fair clip. The Riley was bulky for country lanes with a bouncy suspension that wouldn't have shamed a trampoline. But Venetia manoeuvred the car around the bends as though she were negotiating a Silverstone chicane with Stirling Moss. I hung back at least two hundred yards. At times the Riley disappeared around a bend but we could follow its progress by the glow of its powerful headlights above the hedges.

Venetia hurried through Lewes and headed for the road leading north towards Uckfield. She maintained a steady sixty through the town and pushed on towards Crowborough.

"Have you any idea where this delivery is taking place?" I asked Fanny.

"None. I only overheard the tail-end of the conversation in the pantry passage."

"It's possible Venetia doesn't even know her final destination yet. Blackmailers have a way of keeping their victims in the dark as long as possible. It's why too many of them get away with their crime."

"And they come back for more. Isn't that right?"

I glanced to my left and saw Fanny's tense face illuminated by the headlamps on an oncoming car.

"Yes," I said. "Do you have any sense that this is the first time Venetia has made a delivery?"

"It's only been in the last few days that the atmosphere in the house has been so bad. So maybe. But I'm not sure."

I feared Fanny could be wrong. Perhaps the Piddinghoes' financial problems had been worsened by having to make blackmail pay-offs.

At Crowborough, Venetia turned left towards Friars Gate and

within a few minutes we were in the heart of Ashdown Forest. The road narrowed as trees crowded in on both sides. At times, their branches stretched over the road forming a dark canopy. In front, the Riley slowed and I throttled back to avoid closing the distance between us. A quarter of a mile ahead, Venetia pulled into the side of the road just before it curved sharply to the left. I swung the MGB into a track which led into the woods, turned off the engine and lights.

"What now?" Fanny whispered.

"We wait and watch," I said.

We climbed out of the MGB and stepped behind a tree.

"Stay here," I said. "I'm moving forward to get a better view."

"I'm coming with you."

"Two of us will make more noise."

"Then you better stay here. She's my grandmother."

"And we got here in my car."

"That doesn't give you a casting vote."

Fanny's face was pale with tension. I could hardly blame her. We were secretly following the grandmother she'd adored to an assignation where anything could happen. I laid my hand gently on her shoulder.

"We've got this far. Let's not blow it by arguing – or taking impetuous decisions."

Fanny shrugged. "I suppose you're right. But this is a joint enterprise."

"I agree. But we need to plan our next step very carefully. I'm going to do a reconnaissance to see if we can get any closer without being seen. Venetia is less likely to see me if I do it alone."

Fanny nodded reluctantly.

The road ran through a dense part of the forest but there was a narrow grass verge on either side. I crept along it, keeping as close to the trees as possible. Ahead, I could just make out the outline of the Riley. Venetia had switched on the courtesy light, so a faint glow came from inside the car.

About a hundred yards from the car, I slipped into the forest and pushed forward parallel to the road. Brambles snagged on my trousers. Nettles brushed against my hands. Spiders' webs wrapped themselves around my face. Twigs snapped under foot. Bushes rustled as I shoved my way through undergrowth. I probably sounded like a herd of rampaging elephants. I hoped that inside the car Venetia wouldn't hear me. Unless she'd opened the windows.

After a few minutes, the trees thinned. I crept to the edge of the forest and looked back down the road. My trek had brought me out just ahead of the Riley, a little around the left curve of the road. From my vantage point behind a beech tree I could see Venetia's face through the windscreen. She was smoking a cigarette with a kind of nervous energy I'd never seen in her. And the driver's window *was* open.

It had been a risk getting this close but I now knew why she'd stopped at this point. Just across the road from the Riley, around the left-hand bend, was a small layby. There was a red telephone box in the layby. Its lights illuminated the ground around it for about ten yards. I looked up and down the road, but it was deserted. The blackmailer had chosen his spot well.

If this was the spot... I wondered whether Venetia had been lured here so the blackmailer could pass further instructions by phone. I risked a peek at the Riley. Venetia was lighting another cigarette. She shot anxious glances at the phone box.

I listened. A gentle breeze rustled the leaves in the forest's canopy. In the distance, a fox barked. Behind me, something rustled in the leaf cover.

And then the telephone rang.

Its shrill tone cut insistently through the night.

In the car, Venetia stubbed out her cigarette. She opened the Riley's door, clambered out and crossed the road.

She paused at the phone-box door. Took a deep breath, went

inside and seized the receiver.

I saw her body tense as the caller said something. Then she asked a question, nodded and relaxed a little. The caller said something else and she nodded again. Then Venetia asked another question. But the caller had hung up. Venetia rattled the telephone cradle to reconnect the line, but it was dead. She replaced the receiver, visibly braced herself, and pushed her way out of the box.

She crossed the road, went to the passenger-side door of the Riley, opened it and took a package off the seat. It was about a foot long and maybe three inches thick. It was wrapped in what looked like an oilskin and secured with two wraps of string, one at each end.

Venetia crossed the road, walked round to the back of the telephone box and put the package on the ground. She hesitated, looked at the package, then at the telephone inside the box. Her hand reached for the telephone-box door. It hovered by the handle for a few seconds. Then she took a decision. She drew back and straightened her shoulders. She stalked across the road with the same haughty arrogance she'd shown when I'd first met her at Piddinghoe Grange.

She slid into the Riley and seconds later the headlights flared, the engine roared, and the car raced away down the road.

Everything had happened so quickly I hadn't had time to plan my next move. I certainly couldn't follow the Riley. By the time, I'd run back to the MGB, Venetia would be three miles down the road. She would lose me in the maze of byroads and farm tracks which criss-crossed this part of Sussex.

Besides, it looked as though the main business of the evening had been transacted. The package behind the phone box, I assumed, contained the pay-off. Was the blackmailer even now lurking in the woods on the other side of the road waiting for a safe moment to collect? That seemed unlikely. He – or could it be a she? – had clearly pre-arranged for Venetia to come to this spot.

He had made the call to the box from a safe house, perhaps miles away. So now he'd be making his stealthy way to pick up his loot.

The MGB was parked back down the road, round the curve, and out of sight on a farm track. I was reasonably sure, when he finally approached the phone box, the blackmailer would be unaware that Venetia had had company. Perhaps we could nab him in the act. At some point, he'd have to show himself to collect the package. And when he did I had a surprise for him.

Before I'd left the *Chronicle*, I'd paid a call on Freddie Barkworth, the paper's chief photographer. I wanted the loan of a camera. He'd asked me what it was for and I'd told him to snap somebody who didn't want to be pictured. He'd thought about that for a bit and handed me a Nikon F with flash attachment and automatic rangefinder. Perfect for surveillance photography, he'd said. I'd asked him for some advice on using it.

"Simple," said Freddie. "Just press the button – then run like hell if your victim comes after you."

I'd laughed.

Here, in the darkness of Ashdown Forest, it didn't seem so amusing.

I hurried back through the forest the way I'd come. I crunched over twigs. Cursed as brambles snagged me. Fanny was pacing around the car when I came out into the clearing made by the forest track.

"You've been an age. I heard a car drive off," she said.

"Venetia."

"Then why aren't we following?"

"She's made the drop."

"And you did nothing?"

I frowned. "If I'd tried anything, Venetia would have seen me. But I think we have a chance of catching the blackmailer."

Now Fanny's eyes were gleaming with excitement. "How?"

"I have a plan."

I opened the MGB's boot and retrieved the camera.

"Will this work?" Fanny asked.

"I don't know," I said. "But I think it's the best chance we have."

Fanny and I were hiding in the same spot from which I'd spied on Venetia. We'd worked our way through the forest to avoid being seen from the road.

I said: "It seems logical that the blackmailer will come out of the forest on the other side of the road. He'll be able to keep under cover until he reaches the layby. Then he'll be in the open for only ten yards. At that point we rush in a pincer movement – you to the right, me to the left."

Fanny looked doubtful. "He could be violent."

I shrugged. "It's possible but unlikely. Blackmail is the coward's crime."

I glanced around. Part of a broken tree branch was lying on the ground nearby. I picked it up, hefted it in my hand. "Take this. Use it like a cudgel. But not too fiercely. We want him alive to answer questions."

Fanny took the branch and looked at it thoughtfully. "I'll pretend it's a rounders bat and I'm trying for a quick run."

I grinned. "Just don't put his head into the next county."

We nestled down behind the tree like a couple of old tramps settling in for the night.

"We could be in for a long wait," I said.

"Hours or days?" Fanny asked.

"I think hours. He's chosen a quiet spot to pick up his booty but, sooner or later, someone will come to use the telephone and discover the package. He'll want to collect before that happens."

I glanced at my watch. It was quarter past eleven.

"It will help if we hear which direction he comes from," I whispered. "So let's be quiet."

But for the next hour there were few sounds. The breeze continued to rustle the leaves. At midnight, I heard the distant chime of a church clock sounding the hour. Nearby, an owl hooted. Behind me, I heard a rush of wings and a desperate squawk as a small rodent died. A rabbit flushed from the undergrowth dashed across the road. A car flashed by, its tyres fizzing on the rough road surface.

Silence descended again.

We waited.

Minutes passed.

My eyes felt heavy with sleep. My head nodded forward.

Then yards away in the forest a twig snapped.

I sat upright with every muscle tense.

"He's coming," I whispered.

Fanny was leaning heavily on the tree. Her eyes were closed. They opened. Quietly, we stood up.

"I hear nothing," Fanny said.

"Towards the south-east. Rustling among the bushes. He's trying to be quiet, but it's impossible in undergrowth this thick."

Fanny tensed. "Now I hear it." Her hand closed tightly around the makeshift cudgel.

There was a loud shriek. A woodland bird disturbed. Then a bush on the fringe of the forest shook as the blackmailer pushed his way closer.

"Get ready," I said.

We crouched like a pair of sprinters preparing to run the hundred yards dash.

"Now," I said.

A cocker spaniel broke through the foliage and ran towards the phone box. It had a long low muscular body. Its flappy ears trailed along the ground. Its body was black but its head was distinctively patterned. A black patch around the right eye, white around the left. For a few seconds it snuffled around the box, its nose twitching at the smells. Then it lifted the package into its mouth as gently as if it were retrieving a dead partridge.

Fanny and I had stopped – stunned in our tracks. But when the dog snaffled the package we dashed forward. I raised the camera as I ran and pushed the shutter wildly. The flash strobed through the trees. It cast eerie shadows.

But the sudden light spooked the dog. It turned and raced into the forest.

Fanny and I came up hard in the middle of the road.

I looked at Fanny. Her mouth had dropped open. She gaped in disbelief.

"I wasn't expecting that," I said.

"We've been outfoxed," I said.

"It was a dog," Fanny said. She was gawping at the impenetrable blackness of the forest on the other side of the road.

"It won't be coming back," I said.

"That was cunning," Fanny said. "Nobody could catch a dog scrabbling through undergrowth that thick."

"What I want to know is where the blackmailer got it and how he trained it to pull off that scam."

"It couldn't have been a random dog just exercising in the forest." Fanny's tone was halfway between a question and an answer.

I took her arm and guided her back to the side of the road. "No point in us staying here," I said. "We've seen the action for tonight."

We started to walk back to the car.

"We should have collected the package after Grandmama had left it," Fanny said. "We could have looked inside and seen what it was."

"It was a wad of money. Hard cash. The only thing we don't know is how much."

"And now never will."

"We've confirmed that there is a blackmail threat," I said. "But we don't know whether the threat is against Venetia or your father."

"And we don't know why. And probably never will," Fanny

said. I could hear the despair in her voice.

We reached the car. I unlocked the doors and we climbed in.

Fanny turned to me. Her face was bleak. "What do we do now?"

I fiddled with the ignition key for a while. I needed some time to think this through. I'd felt confident that we'd unmask the blackmailer and that – one way or another – I'd find a way to write a front-page story. It wouldn't have pleased the Piddinghoes. It would have made Fanny angrier than a spitting cobra. But my job was to find stories for the paper.

Now I had nothing to write – apart from an inconclusive caper on a dark night in the heart of the countryside. I also had a demoralised Fanny on my hands. I'd got her into this – and now I had a duty to help her find a way out. Besides, I still believed that somewhere in this convoluted trail there was a link between a package grabbed by a gun-dog, the theft of *Milady's Bath Night* and the murder of Fred Snout.

I reached over and laid a hand gently on Fanny's shoulder. "I think you have to tell your father and grandmother what you know and ask for an explanation."

"And destroy the trust between us?"

"Haven't they already damaged that by their actions?"

Fanny nodded. "I suppose so. In a way."

"Besides, how could you live with them now knowing they're keeping a huge secret from you?"

"I couldn't. I'd have to move out."

"But they'd want to know why," I said.

"I'd say I wanted to get a flat in town with friends."

"But they'd know it wasn't the real reason. Because you wouldn't be able to hide your true feelings. If I can see the despair in your face, they'll notice it the instant you walk through the door."

"I know leaving home is not perfect, but it's the only way to preserve some kind of trust."

"You can't build trust on a lie. And that's what you'd be trying to do. It'd be like building a fortress on a sand dune. Sooner or later, the sand would slip away and everything would collapse."

Fanny shook her head. "I simply don't think I can face them alone. Not after what I've seen tonight."

"I could come with you."

"Papa would never agree to see you."

"But your grandmother would. Especially if I tell her that I've discovered she'd set you up to spy on me."

"She wouldn't like that."

"Perhaps not. But it would give you the perfect excuse for having spied on them. You could say that when I discovered what was happening, I threatened to expose you in the *Chronicle* unless you helped me. I could say you let slip you'd heard a compromising conversation and I forced you into tonight's adventure."

Fanny gave a mirthless laugh. "She'd throw you out."

"I don't think so, because she'd be worried I'd write a story based on what I already know. She wouldn't look good – especially the bit about setting her granddaughter to do the dirty work."

"I wish I'd never agreed to it in the first place."

I gave her shoulder a comforting squeeze. "One must remember one is a scion of the aristocracy," I said. "Regrets are for the peasants. Where is that stiff upper lip?"

Fanny managed a thin smile. "Above the quivering lower one," she said.

"They both look good to me," I said. I leant forward and kissed her. For a moment she responded warmly and then we broke apart.

She smiled again, this time more brightly. "I know you meant that like a caring brother," she said.

"Let's go," I said. I turned the key in the ignition, put the car into gear and we took off.

Right now, the last thing I wanted was to be enrolled as an honorary member of the Piddinghoe family.

Chapter 17

There was a lone light burning in the porch when I circled the MGB round the carriage drive at Piddinghoe Grange.

I pulled up next to the Riley Venetia had been driving and looked at Fanny.

"Are you ready for this?" I asked.

Her shoulders shivered. She took a deep breath, composed herself and gave a solitary nod.

We climbed out of the car. I looked at the house. The nooks and crannies of its rambling Jacobean façade cast sinister shadows. A bat detached itself from the ledge of an upper window and flapped languorously into the blackness of the night. It was a setting worthy of a heart-rending melodrama. And perhaps we were going to get one when we went inside.

I took Fanny's hand and we walked up to the door. She let us in with her key.

We stepped into an oak-panelled hallway lit by a small chandelier. The place would have made a funeral parlour seem like the palace of varieties.

Fanny gave me a worried glance and said: "This way."

We walked quickly down a long corridor hung with fading landscapes. There were gaps where some had been removed. Our feet echoed on the bare boards like drum beats. At the end of the corridor a band of light filtered from under a carved oak door.

"They'll be in the blue drawing room rather than the one we use for grand occasions," Fanny said. "It's where the first Marquess collapsed and died. Ever since, it's been a place where the family come to talk about their troubles."

And handy to have more than one drawing room if visitors unexpectedly call, I thought. So embarrassing to show someone in when there's a dead body on the carpet and you've run out of air freshener.

Fanny opened the door and we stepped inside.

It was the same room in which I'd originally met Venetia.

Nothing much had changed. The Orpen portrait of her still hung over the fireplace. The first Marquess cast a disapproving eye over proceedings from his wall at the far end of the room. There was no sign of a snake in the grass. But, perhaps, that was because I'd only just walked into the room.

Venetia was over by the drinks table pouring herself a knock-out measure of scotch.

Lord Piddinghoe, grandson of the bloke on the wall, had his back to the fireplace. He nursed a large brandy snifter and puffed on a thick cigar.

He'd been saying something to Venetia as the door opened but abruptly stopped as Fanny appeared. His expression switched from guilty grin to angry scowl as I walked in behind Fanny. He put down his snifter, removed the cigar from between his lips and said: "Frances, what is this? ..." There was a pause while he searched for a word. Decided he couldn't find anything that matched his contempt for me and continued: "...this, er, newspaperman doing here."

Venetia had frozen, her lips parted in shock. Then she recovered, looked at the half-full glass of scotch she'd poured, picked up the bottle and added an extra measure.

Fanny said: "I've got something important I have to talk to you about."

Piddinghoe advanced across the room. "Then perhaps your, er, acquaintance would withdraw."

"No, Papa, Colin has seen what I've seen and he needs to hear this, too."

Venetia took a generous gulp of the scotch. "It's late, darling. You're missing your beauty sleep. Go to bed and let's talk about this in the morning. Whatever it is, I'm sure it can wait."

"No, Grandmama, it can't wait."

"In that case, I think we all better sit down." Lord Piddinghoe retreated to a wing chair and put his snifter on a side table. Venetia slumped into a deep armchair. Fanny and I perched uneasily on the edge of a brown-leather Chesterfield.

"Now, what seems to be the trouble?" Piddinghoe said.

"Yesterday, Papa, Grandmama asked me to play a deception on Colin. I was to pretend to be a secretary, worm my way into his confidence and find out what he knew about Marie Richmond."

Piddinghoe looked baffled.

Venetia held her head up defiantly.

Fanny continued: "Anyway, one is obviously not cut out for deception and Colin found out what I was doing. I must say he's been awfully sweet and hasn't written anything about it in his newspaper."

"Not yet," I confirmed. I didn't want the family thinking this was an off-the-record session.

"But that's not the only reason I've asked for Colin's help," Fanny said. "I know you've both been worried about something for the last few days."

Piddinghoe and Venetia exchanged anxious glances. Venetia opened her mouth to speak.

"No, don't deny it," Fanny said. "I've seen it in your faces. Heard it in your voices. Even watched it in the way you walk with sagging shoulders and drooping heads. Do you think you can live years with people you love and not recognise every shift in their mood – joy, sadness? And fear?"

"You're talking rot, girl. And not for the first time." Piddinghoe's face disappeared behind smoke from his cigar.

"Don't speak to me like that, Daddy. I'm not a Roedean girl in pigtails any longer. And I know when something's troubling the people I love most."

Piddinghoe waved an apologetic hand. "I'm sorry. Speak your piece – and be done with it."

Fanny stood up, crossed to the fireplace and warmed her hands. She turned to face Piddinghoe and Venetia.

"Well, it's like this," she said. "I knew that something was going to happen this evening. I'd overheard a conversation between you both – something about 'making a delivery'. No, don't bother to deny it. It's true and that's all that matters.

"I've been worried sick about what's going on – and so when Colin penetrated my mask as an amateur spy, I asked him to help. The fact is, Grandmama, we followed you this evening."

Venetia tensed. "Deceitful girl. How could you?"

"How could you recruit me to be your unwilling spy? And without telling me the whole truth."

Piddinghoe said: "So you followed Venetia on her evening drive. Perhaps there's no harm in that."

Fanny turned on her father. "But it wasn't just an evening drive, was it, Daddy?"

He looked away guiltily.

"As I thought, you knew all about it." Fanny was getting into her stride. "Colin and I watched as Grandmama left a package behind a telephone box in Ashdown Forest and saw it collected."

Venetia's hand flew to her mouth. "My God!"

"Not the deity," I said. "Unless He's turned himself into a cocker spaniel."

"It was money in that package, wasn't it? One of you," – Fanny looked from Venetia to Piddinghoe – "is being black-mailed. And I want to know who it is and why."

Fanny had delivered her big speech with enough panache to win an audition at the Old Vic. She crossed the room and sat down on the Chesterfield.

For a full minute, the only sound in the room was the crackle of logs burning in the grate. Then Venetia stood up and crossed the room to the drinks table. She thought about pouring herself more whisky, but changed her mind.

"I'm going to have to tell her, Charles," she said. "I've no choice. I must tell her the full story."

Venetia put her glass down. Returned to her chair empty-handed.

"Apart from me, I believed only three people in the world knew what I'm about to tell you," she said. "And since Marie died, there's only two."

She turned towards Piddinghoe as though expecting him to say something.

For a moment he looked faintly embarrassed. He drank some brandy, belched softly and said: "Of course, I've known."

He turned his gaze on me, narrowed his eyes, nodded dismissively as though I were an errant foxhound that'd strayed into the room. "This not something for the scribbler chappie's ears."

"I'm here at your daughter's invitation," I said. "I received it because she couldn't discover the truth about whatever devious plan it is you've concocted. I'm assuming her invitation still stands."

Fanny nodded.

"Be it on your own head," Piddinghoe said. "But if I see a word of this in print I'll flay you from your head to your arse, like one of my rabbits."

"Most people settle for a letter to the editor," I said.

"Charles!" Venetia sounded like a mother telling off a two-year-old. He subsided in his chair, puffed angrily at his cigar. She turned back to face Fanny and me.

"You know that Marie and I were identical twins," she said. "It was remarkable. As children we'd look in the mirror and revel in it. We could barely tell ourselves apart. Our mother died in childbirth, but our father hired a nursemaid called Agnes – Saggy Aggie – and she loved us like a mother. She'd laugh and say that any baby was perfection and to have two the same made it doubly perfect. She loved dressing us in identical clothes and as our father was a draper, there was no shortage of supply.

"Our father had come from humble beginnings – in trade. But

he aspired to better, to become a member of the upper classes, although I realise that term is despised these days. As we grew older, father hired a governess called Miss Horn. She was as stiff and unbending as her name. We learnt nothing academically useful from her – no literature, no mathematics, certainly no science. But we did learn how enter a room gracefully, how to tell a fish fork from a fruit fork, and how to make small talk to a bishop.

"Both Marie and I hated Miss Horn but as we grew older, I began to realise that some of these social skills were helpful if one wanted to move in the best society and receive invitations to the finest houses. But Marie didn't share my outlook on life. Although we continued to look identical, in the way we approached life, we were as different as a princess from a pauper. As I drifted closer to what I like to think was the best of society, Marie gravitated to the worst."

"You mean she became a criminal?" Fanny sounded incredulous.

Venetia scoffed. "I sometimes wish she had. It was worse than that. Worse for me, at any rate. She took to the halls."

"I don't understand," Fanny said.

"She means Marie became a music-hall performer," I said.

"But I knew that. Then she became an actress and, for a time, a silent-movie star."

"If that's what you want to call it," Venetia said. "Flaunting herself for money, singing those common songs – she was no better than a woman of the streets."

"Grandmama! You're talking about your sister. And she's barely cold in her coffin." Fanny was fired with anger.

Venetia waggled her fingers about in what looked like some kind of apology by hand signal.

"It was so difficult for me trying to make my way in society and meet the right people," she said. "It wouldn't have been so bad if we hadn't been identical twins. But every time a handsome man looked at me, I couldn't help wondering whether he was comparing me with my twin sister who flashed her frillies for the Friday-night crowd at the Stepney music hall. Of course, Marie and I maintained civil relations on the surface – to please our father. He was generous to a fault to both of us."

"Rather too generous," I said. I'd remembered that Toupée Terry had told me he'd gone bankrupt and hanged himself in disgrace.

Venetia scowled. "That came later, Mr Crampton. When we were growing up as young girls, our father's business was prosperous."

I nodded.

"By the time I was into my early twenties, I had been accepted into society," Venetia said. "I spent most of my life either paying calls on London salons or visiting country estates for weekend house parties. It was at one of these that I met Algernon."

"The late Marquess of Piddinghoe," I said.

"Yes. Although he was still the Earl of Kingston in those days. He'd not yet inherited his father's title. I loved him as soon as I saw him. And, I flatter myself, that he loved me, too. That spring should have been the beginning of an idyllic Edwardian romance. But at that same house party – I recall it was the twenty-fourth of April 1908, two days before my twenty-third birthday – something happened which changed my life. It appeared I had attracted the attention of an even more eminent personage."

"How eminent?" I asked.

"As eminent as it is possible to be," Venetia said.

"You mean the King?" Fanny asked.

"Edward the Seventh," Piddinghoe chipped in. "*Rex Imperator.*"

So the stories were true, I thought. The old King had had the bulk of a bison but the libido of a randy old goat.

"If I may continue without interruption," Venetia said testily. "The long and the short of it was that I was approached by one of the King's lords-in-waiting. It was explained to me that the King sought the pleasure of my society and that, if circumstances were propitious, the pleasure could be mutual. The lord-in-waiting's meaning was quite clear to me."

"But you'd fallen in love with Grandpapa," Fanny said.

"I think you'll find that royal rumpy-pumpy takes precedence over true love," I said.

"Mr Crampton!" Venetia exclaimed.

"Vulgar scribbler," Piddinghoe muttered.

Fanny nudged me in the ribs. "Just listen."

I ignored her and said: "What I meant to say – while avoiding the lord-in-waiting's circumlocution – was that a royal request is, in fact, a royal command. To a monarch, an affair of the heart is of no greater matter than a page-boy's curse."

Venetia's lips twisted into a mirthless grin. "Mr Crampton has the essence of the matter. It tore my heart to be unfaithful to my Algy, but I attended upon the royal personage. I hope I won't be confined to the Tower of London if I say that I did not find it a pleasant experience."

"Grandmama, you didn't allow the King to...?"

"Spare us the sordid details." An angry puff rose from Piddinghoe's cigar like a smoke signal.

I said nothing. People don't realise that listening is as important as writing for reporters.

Venetia swallowed hard. "I returned to my own bed late that night – or, to be more exact, early the next morning – a changed woman. I vowed that I would never visit the royal quarters again."

"But a royal invitation is a royal command," I reminded her.

"Indeed, Mr Crampton. And, inevitably, another command came a few days later. I was sick to my stomach at the thought. I considered feigning sickness, but knew I couldn't pull it off. And then I hit upon an idea."

"You persuaded your identical twin sister to take your place,"

I said.

Venetia's mouth dropped open. "You knew?"

"No, I guessed."

"But how?"

"Let's just say we share the same kind of devious mind."

"I hadn't been on good terms with Marie, but I had helped to extricate her from one or two difficult situations which her dissolute life on the stage and in the silent films had led her. I knew by asking this, I would be cashing in my favours with her, but I could think of nothing else. I wasn't even sure she would agree to the deception, although I thought with her complete likeness to me and her acting skills there was a chance she could pull it off."

"But she hadn't lived your lifestyle. How would she know what to talk about?" I asked.

Venetia blushed. "I'd discovered during my first encounter with the royal personage that not a lot of conversation was required. In any event, Marie jumped at the idea. She borrowed my clothes, my perfume and certain other matters which I need not go into, and stepped into the carriage sent for me as though she were Miss Venetia Clackett, shortly to become the Countess of Kingston."

"But Marie did not return in triumph, as far as you were concerned," I said.

"Once again, you are ahead of me, Mr Crampton. When Marie came into my boudoir the following morning, she had that supercilious grin on her face which always made a nervous pulse in my neck beat harder. Her deception had lasted as long as it took to remove her...her undergarments. You see, Marie and I had always believed that we were identical twins. But in one tiny respect we were not. Marie had a mole – a small insignificant mole in a place... Well, let's just say that it was in a place that would not normally be noticed."

"But, of course, King Edward was renowned for having an eye

for such details," I said.

"When Marie told me she'd been discovered, my heart pounded. I could suddenly see my future life collapsing. My position in society, my good name; above all, Algy's love for me – I saw it all falling away like the leaves in autumn. But then Marie grinned again – and I knew it was worse."

"That the King had enjoyed the deception, taken his pleasures and decided that Marie would be worth an encore," I said.

"If you must put it that way. I did not acquaint myself with the details – I couldn't bear to – but I believe Marie's association with the monarch lasted for several months until even her vitality had waned and a certain *ennui* had set in – on the King's part at any rate. But at least I was free of any further encounters."

"But you'd made a Devil's pact with Marie," I said.

"I knew I would have to suffer Marie's taunts and demands for the rest of my life. If the King hadn't discovered the deception, at least Marie and I would have kept the secret between ourselves. But the fact that the King had enjoyed his dalliance meant that others were bound to find out. I could imagine him dining out amongst his intimate circle on the story. It made me shiver just to think about it."

"The secrets of the bedchamber are never so secret," I said.

Piddinghoe grunted. "Especially when there's a News Johnny peering through the keyhole."

"Be quiet," Venetia said. "You're not helping."

"And you believe that someone has now found out about this regal liaison and is blackmailing you?" I asked.

Venetia nodded. She looked as bleak as an aristo in a tumbril with a wonky wheel.

Venetia's story raised a lot of questions. Had the payments she'd been making to Marie been a pay-off for this royal deception? Now that Marie was dead, who was the new black-mailer? And how, after so many years, had Venetia's secret liaison with Edward the Seventh been discovered?

But I didn't ask any of these questions.

I knew for a fact that the story Venetia had spun about having slid between the sheets with the late King was as transparent as the emperor's new clothes.

It was a lie as fat as Edward the Seventh's belly.

Chapter 18

My old form master at school had sometimes accused me of not paying attention in class.

He was wrong about that – as about many things. I paid attention when something of interest was happening. After all, it's just a waste of energy to concentrate on boring things.

And it was because I had paid attention in one history lesson that I knew Venetia had lied about her royal liaison. She'd said that Edward the Seventh had picked her up for a one-night stand at a country house party in England in April 1908. She'd been definite about the date. April the twenty-fourth. Two days before her birthday. But I knew that Edward wasn't in England in April 1908. He'd spent it in Biarritz, the opulent resort on the Atlantic coast of south-west France.

I had this arcane fact stored in one of the dustier corners of my mind because it had cropped up unexpectedly in a history lesson. It was just after lunch one lazy summer's day towards the end of my first year in the sixth form. In April 1908, the Prime Minister, Sir Henry Campbell-Bannerman, died. It's an odd tradition that newly appointed Prime Ministers have to kiss the monarch's hand on accepting office. Odd, but preferable in my opinion to tyrannies where anyone with a government job is expected to kiss the dictator's arse.

At the time, people expected the King to cut short his holiday so that H.H. Asquith, the new Prime Minister, could call at Buck House and give Edward the traditional smacker. But Edward caused a scandal by staying in Biarritz and making Asquith travel to see him. Arthur Lee, our history master, was a strong republican and fulminated entertainingly about it for half the lesson. And, thus, the fact was lodged for ever in the filing cabinet of my mind.

You never know when seemingly useless information is going

to come in handy. The trouble was, although I knew Venetia had lied I wasn't sure what to do about it.

I could have challenged her over the dates. I could have explained it was impossible to have met the King at a house party in England in April 1908. But she'd have just claimed she'd got the date wrong. It was another month – when the King was in England, she'd say. It was a long time ago. How could she be expected to remember every detail? She was an old woman. Her memory was failing.

I could just hear the excuses pouring out of her mouth.

But something had happened between Venetia and Marie. Otherwise, why should she carry on paying the sister she claimed to despise a generous allowance over so many years? Before I tackled Venetia about her big lie, I needed more information. She still didn't know that I knew about her payments to Marie. I decided that when the time came, I'd used that to prize the truth out of her.

Before we'd left I'd considered asking Venetia who she thought the blackmailer was. But she'd only lie about that, too. Besides, I would never be able to put a name to the blackmailer until I knew the real reason why Venetia was leaving packets of readies behind phone boxes in the middle of the night.

These thoughts ran through my mind as I scuffed the gravel on the Piddinghoes' drive, avoided the potholes and negotiated the MGB through the pillars holding the ornamental gates. I glanced at Fanny in the passenger seat and said: "Are you sure you want to come with me?"

She gave the kind of resigned shrug which says: if I had a better option I'd take it but, for now, I'm stuck with you.

She said: "I couldn't spend tonight in the house. Not after what I've just heard. How could Grandmama behave like that. Like a common tart."

"Not common," I said. And not a tart, I could have added. But this wasn't the time to tell Fanny that her beloved granny was telling porkies. Not until I could work out why Venetia was lying.

We raced down the lane towards Newhaven. The headlights threw weird shadows among the trees that lined the road. A rabbit sat frozen on the verge, then scampered into the under-growth. The tyres squealed as I took the tight corner onto the coast road at sixty.

What puzzled me was that Venetia's lie reflected badly on herself and those she loved most. Lord Piddinghoe. And Fanny. There was no doubt that she was being blackmailed. But if you had to explain it, why not concoct a lie which put you in an innocent light? And why invent a lie which involved one of the most prominent public figures of his age?

Which raised another question. Venetia had certainly not tickled the royal winkle. But had Marie? She'd inhabited a corner of the Edwardian *demi-monde*. It was a world Edward had always been drawn towards. Could Marie have polished the royal sceptre? There was no evidence one way or the other. And it just seemed to pile mystery upon mystery.

I pushed the MGB up the hill towards Roedean. The lights of Brighton came into view. In the distance I could see Palace Pier, where it had all started.

A murder, a theft, a blackmailer – and now a lie.

How were they all connected? If I couldn't join the dots, I'd have no story. And Figgis would have me writing filler pars on motorists fined for parking on the pavement.

I slowed as we approached the roundabout at the Old Steine. Fanny said: "Drop me off at the Grand Hotel."

I said: "What for?"

"So I can take a room for the night."

I glanced at my watch. "At two o'clock in the morning."

"The Grand is a five-star hotel. They'll have a night porter."

"Who will be familiar with attractive ladies who turn up in the wee small hours without luggage claiming they want a room for the night."

"What do you mean by that?"

"That the lady in question is expected by a gentleman upstairs who is – how shall we say? – having difficulty in getting to sleep."

"Are you suggesting I could be mistaken for a common prostitute?"

"At the risk of repeating myself, not common."

Fanny put on her poshest voice. "One finds that an unforgiveable thing to say."

"How far is it from Piddinghoe Grange to Brighton seafront?" I said.

"About ten miles."

"It's about fifty years."

"I don't understand."

"The distance between your kind of life and the people around here is measured in time, not distance."

"You're telling me I'm living in the past?" Fanny asked.

"You're living in a world where beautiful young women who turn up at hotels by themselves are sent on their way with a few choice words. Most of them with four letters."

Fanny let out a long sigh. "I can't go back to the Grange now."

I swung the car off the seafront into Regency Square.

"You don't have to. You can sleep on my sofa. It's stuffed with horsehair and the lumps press in all the awkward places, but it's better than the pebbles under the pier."

As it turned out, I slept on the sofa.

But not before another surprise. When we crept up to my room, I found a note in the Widow's handwriting pinned to my door. It read: "A Mr Bolstride called to see you. Didn't say what he wanted."

Mr Bolstride was obviously Clarence Bulstrode. I wondered why he'd called. Perhaps he regretted stalking out on me after our pub lunch. But it was pointless to speculate. And we were both tired.

When Fanny eyed the sofa, she looked so bereft, I offered her my own bed. My trouble, in a nutshell. Just too soft-hearted.

I'd been right about the sofa. It was going to be a sleepless night. After half an hour of tossing and turning, I stood up to stretch myself. I walked over to the window, pulled the curtain to one side and looked out at Regency Square. A solitary cat stalked silently across the grass.

For several minutes I stared at nothing in particular and tried to make some kind of logical sense of the evening's events. But the more I thought about it, the more it became a puzzle.

On the far side of the square, a door opened and a man hurried out. Turned towards Western Road. Broke into a run as he passed a grey Hillman parked by the kerb. Ten seconds later, the Hillman's headlights flared, the car pulled out and drove off in the opposite direction.

I briefly wondered whether the car's occupant was a private detective hired by a suspicious wife to watch a husband playing away from home. But I'd had too many mysteries for one night.

Lumpy or not, I had to get some shuteye on the sofa.

"You know the rules, Mr Crampton."

"Yes, Mrs Gribble."

"And what is rule number one?"

"No women in the rooms."

It was just after seven the following morning. I'd recognised the Widow's imperious rap on the door. I'd shifted uncomfortably on the sofa and groaned something which approximated to "go away". I'd turned over and tried to go back to sleep.

But when the Widow was roused there was no stopping her. She had a pass key to the room – and wasn't afraid to use it. So I'd scrambled off the sofa and opened the door. And that's when she'd fired her accusation.

"Do you have a woman in your room?" she said.

"No."

"But I believe you have."

"Why?"

"Because after you'd come in last night – at an hour I might add when all good people should be abed – I distinctly heard the toilet flushed twice in quick succession. You only flush it once normally."

When it came to sniffing out illicit visitors, the Widow made Sherlock Holmes look like Dopey the Dwarf.

"I repeat, you have a woman in your rooms." She edged forward but I moved to block her way.

"I have a lady," I said.

"Same thing."

"Not at all. A woman is usually missus or miss. A lady is the daughter of an earl or a duke. In my case, a marquess."

"Since when did you know any marquess's daughters?"

"Since he met me." Fanny had stepped out of my bedroom. She was wearing one of my shirts as a makeshift nightshirt – and not much else.

The Widow's eyes goggled. "And who might you be, young madam?"

Fanny stepped forward, smoothed her mussed hair. "One is Lady Frances Mountebank, daughter of the third Marquess of Piddinghoe. And I should like a cup of tea – Assam if you have it – and two slices of lightly buttered wholemeal toast."

A puzzled wrinkle appeared on the Widow's forehead. And then I could swear she dropped the tiniest of curtseys. "I'll see what I can find in my pantry," she said.

She turned for the stairs.

"Lightly buttered," I reminded the Widow's retreating back.

I shut the door. Turned back to Fanny.

"Do you always have that effect on people?" I asked.

Fanny grinned. Fastened an extra button on the shirt. "The

Mrs Gribbles of this world are not difficult to tame if you know how."

"I wasn't thinking of Mrs Gribble," I said. "I was planning on wearing that shirt to the office today. But it looks better on you."

Inevitably, I had to wear the last shirt in my drawer – the one with the frayed collar.

It seemed fitting. After days chasing clues that led nowhere, I was feeling more than a little frayed myself. But I still had to produce some copy for the day's paper.

So I breezed into the newsroom with the confidence of a man about to announce the scoop of the century. I'd invited Fanny to tag along. I was anticipating trouble from Figgis and I felt a touch of aristocratic hauteur might help to put the old boy in his place. But the trouble with Figgis was that he had a healthy disrespect for everyone. And, in any event, after stalking out on her father and grandmother last night, Fanny was feeling some morning-after remorse.

She'd eaten the lightly buttered toast the Widow had provided with dainty nibbles, then announced: "One ought to put in an appearance at the Grange, I suppose. No need to take me. I'll telephone to Pinchbeck and ask him to send Hardmann with the Bentley."

I'd said: "And one has to put in an appearance at the office or one may receive the Grand Order of the Boot."

She'd giggled and said she'd call me when she'd had time to talk to her father and grandmother. I'd given her a brotherly peck on the cheek and told her not to worry.

But I should've been the one told not to worry. When I reached the newsroom, I plonked myself down at my desk and wondered just how I was going to take the murder story forward. It was all very well building up to a great scoop at some time in the future, but I needed to write a story every day.

I picked up the phone and called the duty officer at Brighton police station. He told me that Tom Belcher was still being held for questioning, still denied killing Snout, and that there had been no further developments in the investigation.

I heaved the Remington towards me, rolled copy paper into the machine and typed: "Police have made no further arrests in their hunt for the killer of pier night-watchman Fred Snout.

"Tom Belcher, the pier's amusement-arcade caretaker, has been held for questioning, but he has not yet been charged with any offence.

"This morning, a Brighton-police spokesman admitted there had been no further developments in the hunt for the killer. He said there was, as yet, no forensic evidence to provide a fresh lead."

I rattled on in the same vein for a few more paragraphs. But it was all a non-story. A piece about nothing happening. Like that famous *Times* headline "Small Earthquake in Chile: Not Many People Hurt". I knew Figgis would start sounding off as soon as he saw my copy. But I called Cedric over and gave him the folios to take up to the subs.

"Didn't see much of you yesterday, Mr Crampton," he said.

"I didn't know you missed me when I wasn't here," I said.

Cedric blushed. "Only wondered whether you were anywhere interesting."

"Interesting enough," I said. "Now better get that copy up to the subs before deadline."

Cedric was taking a deep interest in this case. Perhaps it was the lad's natural enthusiasm for bloody murder, mayhem and mystery. Or, perhaps, there was more to it.

But I didn't have time to worry about that. When Mrs Gribble had brought Fanny her lightly buttered toast, she'd pointedly not offered me any. I'd not even had time for my regular bacon sandwich in Marcello's. So I headed to the tea room for a sticky bun – if Susan Wheatcroft hadn't already scoffed the lot.

I had a bit of luck as I pushed through the door. Henrietta

Houndstooth was just coming out with a cup of coffee.

"Could we have a quick word?" I said.

Henrietta glanced back. "The tea room's unoccupied at the moment."

We both hurried inside.

I said: "I'm sorry to have to hark back to your childhood again, but something else has cropped up. It's a delicate matter. Did your mother or father ever pick up any hint of a scandal about Lady Piddinghoe – the Dowager Marchioness?"

"Her sister whipped up more than enough scandal for both of them."

"Yes, I know that Marie was the wild child, but I was wondering whether Venetia might also have had her naughty side – but perhaps kept it better hidden."

"Mama or Father never spoke of anything like that – certainly not in front of me. But, then, you wouldn't expect to talk about such matters in front of a young girl."

"Does that mean they might have known about something but kept quiet about it?"

Henrietta frowned. "To answer your question, I simply don't know. When I was a child, Lady Piddinghoe always seemed severe and upright to me. But, then, perhaps she had hidden depths."

"Perhaps," I said. "There's just too much hidden about this story."

"Don't be afraid to ask, if you need to know more," Henrietta said. She took her coffee and pushed out of the door. I walked over to the tea bar.

Needless to say, Susan Wheatcroft had pillaged the last of the buns.

Chapter 19

I was sitting at a window table in Reg's Café stirring a cup of coffee as thick as sump oil.

I had no intention of drinking it. Reg's wasn't the kind of place you went to eat or drink – unless you had a stomach lined with reinforced steel. But it was just across the road from the Bat and Ball pub. That was where I'd set up the meeting with a fictitious Snout murder-case contact. I'd scrawled the details on my blotter. A trap for the snitch who'd been feeding my stuff to Jim Houghton.

I checked my watch. Five to one. I'd fixed the mythical meeting for one. If Jim was going to gate-crash it, he'd probably leave it a few minutes before strolling into the pub. He'd hope I wouldn't spot him. Then he'd try to take a table in the adjacent alcove so he could earwig the conversation. If he was spotted, he'd pretend he was in the area on another story and had just popped in for a lunchtime pie and a pint.

He'd sit down uninvited at our table. Then he'd scratch his head and pretend to know my informant from somewhere – usually somewhere not quite respectable, such as Lewes prison. This, Houghton hoped, would panic the informant into denying the suggestion and revealing his true identity. With the identity established, Houghton would slide in a piece of slimy flattery and offer to buy the informant a drink. Probably a pint and a whisky chaser to put the poor sap on the back foot in the gratitude stakes. After that, teasing out the sucker's story would be simple.

Game over.

But it wasn't going to happen like that. Because there was no meeting. And if Jim turned up, he was going to get a surprise.

I gave the coffee a couple more stirs to pass the time. Checked my watch. Eight minutes past one. If Houghton was coming he should be here by now. Perhaps he was watching the pub – a recce before committing himself. Wise. I'd have done the same thing.

A greasy net curtain covered the bottom half of Reg's window. I pulled it to one side. No sign of Houghton. Perhaps I'd been wrong. But I didn't think so. He was getting his information from somewhere.

I stirred on irritably.

"You drinking that or just making a hole in the bottom of the mug?" I'd been so intent on watching the Bat and Ball I hadn't noticed Reg sidle up to the table. He wore an apron so stiff with grease it crackled as he walked.

"Wouldn't want it leaking away, would we?" I said. "It might be a fire hazard."

"Cheeky beggar. Don't know why you come in here if you don't appreciate it."

I caught a movement out of the corner of my eye. Across the road, a tall man with thinning hair and a slight limp was pushing his way into the saloon bar of the Bat and Ball.

I turned back to Reg. "How's your customer service?" I asked.

"Best in the town."

"Great. Can I use your phone?"

"Cost you four pence," he said. "And another coffee."

I shrugged. Sometimes you just have to pay the price.

The phone was on Reg's counter. Like everything else, it was covered in a thin film of grease. It looked as though an army of slugs had just crawled over it.

I took out my handkerchief wrapped it round the receiver and picked it up. I dialled a number with the end of my pencil. I heard the ringing tone.

I pictured the scene.

In the Bat and Ball, the barman would be puzzling over why someone was calling the pay phone in the bar. He'd wonder whether he should answer it. Figure it was a wrong number.

Decide not to bother. Then one of the drunks propping up the bar would state the obvious: "Did you know your phone's ringing?" And he'd have no choice. He'd heave up the flap which led out of the bar, stomp over to the other side of the room and grab the receiver.

And then...

A gruff voice in my ear said: "Bat and Ball."

In a Welsh accent straight out of the valleys, I said: "You should have a tall man in the bar, boyo. Thinning hair. Wears a grey suit, worn round the cuffs and elbows. Walks with a limp. Could you get him to the phone?"

"Who wants him?"

"A friend."

"What kind of friend?"

"The kind that gets very angry when he can't speak to the person he needs."

"Wait."

I heard the receiver clumped down on a table.

Silence.

Then some wheezing as the receiver was picked up again.

"Hello." It was Jim Houghton.

I stayed silent. Didn't move. Hardly breathed.

"Hello."

Silence.

"Hello. Can you hear me?"

Silence.

"Is there anybody there?"

Silence.

"Is that you, Sidney?"

Got you!

I replaced the receiver. There was only one Sidney at the *Chronicle*. The fragrant Sidney Pinker. So Sidney, not Cedric, was the snitch. I wondered whether Sidney was doing it for the money or whether Houghton had something on him. Pinker was the kind of man who would have more skeletons than the Bear Road cemetery.

But for the time being, I needed to get away from Reg's. Houghton would have suspected the call was a trap. He'd have me fingered as number-one suspect. It would take him about two minutes to work out I was watching the place from somewhere nearby. A further minute to identity Reg's Café as the most likely vantage point. So I had to be away from the place *tout de suite*.

I dashed for the back door which led to an alley that connected with the neighbouring street.

"You off?" said Reg. "You're moving like a streak of lightning"

I shouted over my shoulder. "After being in here, make that greased lightning."

I was through the door before Reg could reply.

I was in a windowless room with a coffin, a couple of vicious-looking duelling swords and a werewolf's head.

And Sidney Pinker.

"The Theatre Royal is doing *The Duchess of Malfi* next week," he said. "God, those seventeenth-century dresses with their frills and bows are to die for."

We were backstage in the props room at the theatre. A few minutes earlier, I'd bearded Sidney in the stalls bar carousing with a couple of his claque. I'd suggested we'd go backstage where we could be more private. That caused a few arched eyebrows and knowing nudges. But I was beyond that sort of thing by now.

"I appeared in the play once," Sidney said. "I was a pilgrim."

"Not exactly typecast then."

"No, but I could have been a performer."

"But instead you decided to become a snitch," I said.

Sidney flounced across the room and plopped down on a prop basket. "I find that offensive."

"Not nearly as offensive as you copying information off my blotter and passing it to Jim Houghton on the *Argus*."

"Well, really." Sidney crossed his right leg over his left. Decided that wasn't comfortable. Crossed his left leg over his right. "I don't know where you get such ideas. But may I remind you there is a law of slander in this country?"

"Sidney, I'm a crime reporter. I've been threatened with that one more times than you've dallied in the wings with the juvenile lead."

Pinker pouted. "All I'm saying is that you've made a terrible accusation and you don't have a shred of evidence to back it up."

"As it happens, my evidence is the best. Your client squealed on you."

"What? The low…"

"Not deliberately. Jim wouldn't rat out a contact any more than I would."

"So you tricked him. That's low, mean and despicable."

"Get over it, Sidney. When you play with the big boys you must expect to take some knocks."

Pinker licked a finger and ran it over an eyebrow. "If only."

"The question I want answered is: did you do it for money?"

"You have a very commercial mind, young Colin. Of course not."

"So Houghton has something on you?"

Pinker studied a spot on the floor. "It was years ago. When I was up north working on the *Sheffield Star*. It was – how shall I put it – a lapse of taste. In a public lavatory. All a mistake really. Do I have to spell out the details?"

"No. You've told me enough."

Pinker's shoulders slumped. "So what now? Back to the office. Sacked on the spot. Escorted off the premises by that fat commissionaire. My belongings sent on in a cardboard box."

"Not as far as I'm concerned. If it had been money, that would have been different. But you're entitled to protect your own character – although not at my expense or any other *Chronicle* journo."

"So you'll not say anything?"

"Not unless it happens again."

Pinker relaxed. "It's a mercy it's over."

"Not over, Sidney. There is always a price to pay."

Pinker's lips curved up in a sly smile. "You don't mean, young Colin, that…"

"Don't even think about it, Sidney. The price I have in mind is one which will help me on the murder story. I just want your help once – and then it will be over."

"What do I have to do?" His eyes narrowed cunningly.

"Tomorrow, I want you to pass a message to Jim that you've overheard me speaking to Figgis about the Snout murder. I want you to tell him that you didn't hear everything but Horsham was mentioned a few times. Tell him that Figgis has put the compositors on overtime to set late copy for the final edition of the paper. I think that will be enough to panic Houghton and get him out of town for a few hours. He'll head up to Horsham and work his local police contacts trying to find out what I know. Of course, it's nothing."

Pinker shuffled from foot to foot. "I can pass the message but where does that leave me? When Jim realises I've set him up, he'll out my secret."

"You think? Jim moves in the same world as me. It's a world where we hear a lot of confidences from people who have their own dirty little secrets they want kept under wraps. If the word gets around that Houghton is prepared to out a contact's shady past in order to get information, nobody will ever speak to him again."

Pinker nodded glumly. "I suppose you might be right."

"Trust me. Jim's not a snitch."

"I suppose I deserved that."

"Cheer up," I said. I waved a hand around the room at the

weird collection of props. "Are you previewing this show?"

"Yes. It's the opening night on Monday."

"What's with the werewolf?"

"One of the characters – the evil Ferdinand – turns into a werewolf. But after a lot of torture and murder he ends up being killed."

"All good family fun, then?"

Sidney shrugged. I left him slumped on the prop box pondering his future – and the prospect of watching a werewolf getting the chop.

He'd find it a lot simpler than the puzzles I was trying to unravel.

That became painfully clear when I arrived back at the *Chronicle*.

There was a message on my desk: "See me at your earliest convenience. FF."

I walked straight round to Figgis's office, knocked on the door and went in before he could growl "Enter".

I said: "My earliest convenience was the outside privy at my parents' house in Battersea. So I thought you'd rather see me here."

Figgis stubbed out his Woodbine. "I'm in no mood for your cracks. Sit down."

I pulled up the visitor chair.

"Have you seen this?"

He pushed across the midday edition of the *Evening Argus*. A screamer headline across the front page read:

SUSPECT RELEASED: NEW ARREST SOON

Under the headline, Jim Houghton's breathless prose revealed that Tom Belcher had been sent on his way without charge – "insufficient evidence" a grouchy Tomkins grumbled – but that the cops were closing in on a new suspect. Jim had scooped me again.

"They couldn't hold Tom for more than twenty-four hours without charging him," I said.

Figgis said: "I'm less concerned what's happening to Belcher and more concerned about what this is doing to us. I've that pricking behind my ears I get when we're going to be beaten hollow on a big story. The *Argus* beat us on the Snout murder. They beat us on the Belcher arrest. They've beaten us on the Belcher release. And now they're running a piece hinting at further sensational developments."

"Jim is flying a kite," I said. "He's been fed a line by Tomkins. If Jim's story turns out to be correct, I'll dance in a G-string and nipple tassels in the end-of-the-pier revue."

Figgis reached for his ciggies. "It would almost be worth Houghton being right to see that."

"Put your opera glasses away. That show won't happen."

"So is Tomkins any closer to finding Snout's real killer?"

"Tomkins couldn't find his own bum in the bath. Besides, he started off dismissing any connection between the killing and the *Milady's Bath Night* theft. Then he arrested Belcher without evidence. And now he doesn't know what to do."

"And from the smug look on your face, you do, I suppose."

I put on my serious look and said: "This case is like a *mille-feuille*?"

"A what?"

"One of those fancy French cakes with layers of pastry and cream."

"Not as tasty, though."

"The top layer was Snout's murder. We don't yet know who did that – or why. There's no motive. But if we go down to the next level, the *Milady* theft, there is a possible motive. I'd wondered whether Lord Piddinghoe and Venetia could have a reason for removing the pictures because of the embarrassment they'd have if they were reproduced in national newspapers. Marie Richmond being Venetia's twin sister."

"You're surely not suggesting that Lady Piddinghoe killed Fred Snout."

"Of course not. She'd rather chase a fox or shoot a pheasant than mingle with the working classes. But I have wondered whether her son might have engaged in a little freelance activity to save his mama's blushes. Not personally, perhaps, but he has a batman – former army servant – called Hardmann who seems to live up to his name."

"But there's no proof of any of this."

"Not directly. But there are suspicions."

I described how Venetia had been paying a monthly honorarium to Marie. And had now paid off an unknown blackmailer and concocted a cock-and-bull story to explain it.

"And you think the real reason was because she was behind the Snout killing – even if she didn't do the dirty deed herself."

I nodded. "It's a possibility."

Figgis scratched his chin. "Trouble is, all this is speculative. We can't print a word of it – and at the same time the *Argus* is coming as close as it's legally possible to suggesting that Tomkins is about to collar the killer."

"But then the next layer down in the *mille-feuille* is Clarence, Marie's son," I said. "By all accounts, he's a volatile customer at the best of times. But he's plainly distressed by his mother's sudden death. Nothing suspicious in that. But I've discovered that with her dying breath Marie told him that his fortune lay on the pier. But that could have been the ramblings of a dying woman."

"And it could be, of course, that none of this has anything to do with Snout's murder," Figgis said. "It could've been a random ne'er-do-well who'd made his way on to the pier – perhaps looking to pick up the day's takings from some of the kiosks – who ran into Snout."

"Could be," I said. "It's just that my nose is twitching. I think there's more to it. Perhaps—"

But we were interrupted by three loud knocks on Figgis's door.

"Enter."

Cedric's head appeared around the door.

"Call for Mr Crampton at his desk."

"Tell them to switch it through here," Figgis said.

Cedric's head disappeared and the door shut. A minute later Figgis's phone rang.

I lifted the receiver. Fanny's voice said: "We need to see you."

"Trouble at the Grange?" I asked.

"No more than we already have. But when I got back this morning, Daddy and Grandmama said they'd be talking the situation over. They felt they'd treated you a bit roughly yesterday. They want to speak again and tell you a little about the background to all this."

"Is this at your prompting?"

"No. They mentioned it to me as soon as I walked through the door. They've apologised to me as well. Can you be here at seven o'clock? For cocktails."

"Yes."

"No need to dress."

"You mean I can come in the nude?"

"No need to put on a dinner jacket and black tie, peasant."

"Where I come from, men wore flat caps and mufflers at the dinner table."

Fanny giggled. "I'm going out for a hack now," she said. "Feel I need the fresh air, but I'll see you at seven."

"Give my regards to Herbert." I replaced the receiver.

I turned towards Figgis. "Lord Piddinghoe and Venetia want to speak more."

"They'll be trying to hush everything up," he said.

I stood up, opened the door. "Then they've invited the wrong man."

Chapter 20

Lord Snooty, aka Pinchbeck, the butler, looked at me like I was something that had slithered out of a lettuce and said: "I'll announce you."

"Like a train arrival?" I said.

"Like an unwelcome guest," he said.

It looked as though this was going to be an evening when I would need my wits about me.

We were standing in the entrance hall of Piddinghoe Grange, a place that looked as if it could well have been home to the evil Ferdinand from *The Duchess of Malfi*. I wouldn't have been surprised if the werewolf had jumped out from behind one of the oak screens that lined one side of the room. An ancient grand-father clock ticked like a dying heart. The minute hand moved with a clunk. Four minutes past seven.

We trooped down the long corridor hung with landscapes. There were dust stains on the walls where some pictures had been removed. Their title plates remained. I had a quick shufti as we hustled by. I noticed that a couple of paintings by Turner had gone but others by lesser-known artists – Benjamin Haydon and Augustus Egg – remained.

Lord Snooty opened the door and we entered the same drawing room in which I'd heard Venetia's false confession the previous evening.

Pinchbeck came to attention with one hand behind his back and announced: "Mr Colin Crimpton."

Out of the corner of my mouth, I hissed, "Crampton, you dolt".

Then I put on my winning smile and strode across the room. Venetia was perched on the edge of a chaise longue. Piddinghoe lounged in his wing chair close to the fire. Logs crackled in the grate, but the room felt as cold as an empty grave.

Venetia dismissed Pinchbeck with a peremptory wave of her hand. Pinchbeck gave the kind of insolent nod which said, "And you can naff off, too, hagface," and left.

"What we're about to discuss is not a matter for servant's ears," Venetia said.

"Too damned right," Piddinghoe chimed in.

"We'll help ourselves to drinks," Venetia said. "I understand journalists usually like a pint of something called half-and-half."

"Only when it comes with pork scratchings," I said. "I'll settle for a gin and tonic – one ice cube and two slices of lemon."

Venetia crossed to a table with a modest collection of bottles to fix the drinks.

I said: "Will Lady Frances be joining us?"

"She's been riding," Venetia said. "She should be with us shortly."

"Just as well that the girl's out of the way," said Piddinghoe. "Rather delicate matter to mention. Not something to bother Frances's pretty little head with. Money. Rather vulgar."

"Especially when you haven't got any," I said.

Piddinghoe cleared his throat noisily. Reached for a large brandy snifter on a side table. Took a generous pull. "How did you know?" he said.

"The signs are there if you know what to look for. Missing pictures – mostly the best ones – in some of the rooms. Presumably sold. More holes in the carriage drive than an old colander. Rusting machinery out in the stable yard. I could go on."

"Ah!" Piddinghoe took another pull at his brandy.

Venetia gave Piddinghoe a withering look. "I think Mr Crampton may want to understand why our temporarily straitened circumstances may have created the embarrassing situation we're now in," she said.

"Yes, of course. Keep to the point. Can't stand ramblers. Well, it's like this... How shall I put it?"

"You're worried that any breath of scandal would get you sacked from the government," I said.

"In a word, yes. Like poor Jack Profumo. Not that I've been playing the stallion with a stable of young fillies, you understand."

At least I could believe that.

"And you didn't want to lose your government salary on top of your other financial problems."

"Again, you state the case concisely, young fellow."

"I blame myself." Venetia took the floor. "I never realised that a rare and unwilling folly in my youth would resonate down the century in such a cruel way. As soon as the problem arose, I told Charles that I would handle it so that it would have no unpleasant repercussions."

If lying were an Olympic sport, this woman would win gold, I thought. She'd spun an intricate fabrication of lies the previous evening about the reason for leaving money behind the phone box. And now she was suggesting that her motive was to prevent Piddinghoe having to flog off the family silver. I'd had enough. It was time to get at the truth.

So I asked: "Could the blackmail be linked in any way with the payments you'd been making to your sister?"

Venetia's face turned as pale as a ghost's. Her lips parted. Her tongue flicked nervously over them.

"I don't know what you mean," she whispered.

"There is no point in denying it," I said.

"What's the fellow driving at?" Piddinghoe said.

Venetia turned towards him. "Oh, do, for once, be quiet, Charles."

I said: "I've seen the letter you wrote to Marie saying that you would have to discontinue the payments."

"But that letter was private."

"Through a chapter of accidents – which I won't describe now – it came into my hands."

Venetia slumped back on the chaise longue. Brushed a stray strand of hair away from her eyes. For the first time since I'd met her, she looked like an old woman. The flesh on her cheeks sagged. The wrinkles around her neck etched deeper.

She said: "Yes, I'd been paying Marie for years. I must tell you I regret every penny of it. Every penny. But I had no choice. Our…" – she searched for a word – "…adventures with Edward the Seventh meant that no matter how much we grew apart and lived different lives, we would always be yoked together by a common secret. It was a secret that neither of us could afford to whisper – I because of my position in society, Marie because of her career."

I thought of telling Venetia that I knew her story about being a lover of Edward the Seventh was a lie. That it couldn't have happened the way she'd described it the previous evening. But she would either lose her temper or clam up. And, first, I wanted to learn more about her relationship with Marie.

So I held that in reserve and asked: "Surely an affair with Edward the Seventh would have added to Marie's notoriety?"

"Among the common clay, the riff-raff who frequented the music halls, yes. But the upper reaches of her so-called professions – the film-makers and theatre owners – the very people who employed her, had pretentions to society. A breath of scandal among one of their performers would have had society's doors closed to them. Marie was shrewd enough to recognise that."

"And so she stayed silent."

"Yes."

"But not for ever?"

Venetia shook her head wearily. "No."

"And that's when the demands for money began?" I said.

"Yes. It was in 1936. Her career had declined during the nineteen-twenties. But the arrival of the talkies in 1927 finally finished it. Her coarse tones may have wowed the gallery crowd in the music halls but they were too rough for talking pictures."

"So parts were few and far between?"

"Her career was in decline, but not her lifestyle. She spent recklessly until all the money was gone. And then she turned to me."

"And you refused her?"

"Yes. She came to tea and I explained that the expenses of the estate were such that we couldn't afford to keep her in the style to which she'd become accustomed. At first, she seemed to accept that. She left and I thought we'd hear no more about it."

"But she was back a few weeks later? And this time with threats?" I said.

"How do you know that?"

"Damned fellow's been poking his snout into places it's not wanted," Piddinghoe said.

Venetia said: "Be quiet, Charles."

I said: "What were the threats?"

Venetia took a long pull at her drink. "She pointed out that now her career had faded she'd nothing to lose. Indeed, much to gain if she sold her story to one of the Fleet Street scandal-mongering newspapers."

"The tabloids love a royal scandal," I said.

Venetia sniffed. "I fear you may be right, so I had no choice but to take Marie's threats seriously."

"Would that be before or after she threw a teapot at you?"

"After. That meeting ended acrimoniously. But I later communicated with her in writing. I said that provided she undertook not to mention the events to which she'd alluded to a living soul, I would pay her a modest emolument each month."

"And those living souls included Clarence, her son?"

"Most certainly. Even by 1936, it was already clear that he was going to be – how shall I put it? – a loose cannon."

"Did Marie keep her promise?"

"Until last week."

"When you sent the letter saying you couldn't continue to
make the payments?"

"Yes."

"But she didn't accept that?"

"No. She telephoned me. We had a long conversation."

"A row?"

"Yes, I'm afraid a row. She said she'd kept her promise of
silence to the letter over the years but would no longer do so if I
stopped paying her. I was adamant that I would not pay any
more. She said she was going straight back home to tell Clarence
and then call the newspapers. She slammed the phone down."

And stormed out of the telephone box into the path of a
baker's van. Final curtain for Marie. But convenient for Venetia.

Yet not so convenient, because now there was now another
blackmailer on the scene.

I asked: "Do you have any idea who last night's blackmailer
is?"

"No."

I nodded. This time, I sensed Venetia was telling the truth.

Somewhere in the house a telephone rang three times. It was
answered.

I asked Venetia: "How did the latest blackmail threat come?"

"In a typewritten envelope, posted in Brighton. The letter was
also typewritten."

I thought about asking Venetia what the letter said. But she'd
only repeat the lie she'd already told me about her dalliance with
the King.

In any event, I didn't have time to ask anything more because
the door flew open. Pinchbeck rushed in. His white-tie was
askew. His coat-tails billowed out behind him.

"The telephone," he blurted.

"What about the damned instrument?" Piddinghoe said
irritably.

"It's about Lady Frances. She's been kidnapped. She's being

211

held to ransom."

The news brought all of us to our feet.

"What do you mean, man?" Piddinghoe shouted.

Pinchbeck swallowed hard, Took a couple of deep breaths. "The call came from Mr Bulstrode."

"You mean Clarence Bulstrode, Marie Richmond's son?" I asked.

"Yes. He claims he's taken Lady Frances to what he says is a safe place, my lord. He is going to keep her there until you pay him ten thousand pounds so that he can leave the country."

Venetia's hand flew to her mouth. "But she was out riding."

"Did Bulstrode explain why he wanted to leave the country?" I asked.

"No, sir. Just that his lordship should collect the money and stand ready to receive another phone call with delivery instructions."

"I don't understand it," Venetia wailed. "Clarence Bulstrode is Frances's cousin."

As though kidnapping a relative simply wasn't the done thing among the right sort of people.

"Does he know her well?" I asked.

"He's never met her."

I said: "Lady Piddinghoe, when Marie mentioned on the telephone that she'd not told anyone including Clarence, did you believe her?"

"Yes. She'd said that she'd kept her word and expected me to keep mine."

"Could anyone else have found out about all this?" I asked.

"I don't see how," Venetia said. "Even Charles didn't know until a few days ago."

"In the dark. As usual," Piddinghoe complained.

I turned to Pinchbeck. "Are you sure the phone call was from Clarence?" I asked.

"He said so."

"Have you spoken to him before?"

"No."

"So you wouldn't recognise his voice?"

"No. But he told me he was Clarence Bulstrode."

"What was his voice like?"

Pinchbeck pondered for a moment. "Deep, quite cultured, but not the true article. Not like his Lordship's."

That sounded like Bulstrode.

"I assume he didn't say where he was phoning from?"

"No. But it was a call box because I heard the pips before he pressed button A."

I was about to ask Pinchbeck for Clarence's exact words.

But I never got the chance.

Because, at that moment, Fanny walked through the door.

"You all look as though you've just been haunted by a spectre."

Fanny gave a little laugh and made her way to the drinks table.

"My God! It's you!" said Piddinghoe.

"I'm so relieved," said Venetia.

"I...I don't understand," said Pinchbeck.

Frances turned at the drinks table. She was pouring herself a vermouth. "What are you all babbling about?"

"You've not been abducted," said Piddinghoe.

"You're free, my darling," added Venetia.

I said: "Pinchbeck had just given us all a telephone message that you'd be kidnapped."

Fanny's eyes darted from side to side. "What on earth do you mean? I've been hacking with Herbert – over towards Rodmell."

Piddinghoe turned on Pinchbeck. "Is this some kind of practical joke on your part? Because I assure you, it's in very bad taste."

"My lord, it is not..."

"Still, it's all right now." Venetia breathed a sigh of relief.

"But it's not," I said. "Because if Fanny isn't the kidnap victim, someone else is."

For a moment, we all froze. We looked nervously at one another. We tried to read each other's thoughts.

Then I turned to Pinchbeck and said: "What did Clarence say? We need to know his exact words."

Pinchbeck's eyes clouded with anxiety. "It's so difficult to remember," he said. "I was just taken aback."

"Take your time. Think about the voice you heard. The words will come."

He stroked his chin nervously with his bony hand. "I'm trying to recall. He was speaking very quickly. I think he was nervous."

"That figures," I said.

Pinchbeck screwed his eyes shut. Tensed his body. "Clarence said, 'There's no fortune on the pier. Mumsie's let me down. She never did before. I have to go away. Abroad. I need ten thousand pounds. From Lord Piddinghoe. I know he can afford it. But he's a tight old windbag. So I've taken Frances from the house in the square. She will be safe. Get me the money. No tricks and Frances will be safe. I will call again. Remember, 'When in doubt, win then trick.' I will win it."

Pinchbeck's body went limp. Forcing the memory had drained him. He opened his eyes. "I think I've remembered it correctly, my lord."

I thought about that for a moment, then turned to Pinchbeck. "Are you sure Bulstrode said he'd taken Lady Frances from 'the house in the square'?"

Pinchbeck scratched his chin. "Yes, I'm sure. But Mr Bulstrode didn't say which square."

I knew which square. And, suddenly, the murder of Fred Snout and the theft of *Milady's Bath Night* – even the prospect of scooping the *Argus* – didn't seem important after all. I'd been stupid. I'd not listened when I should have listened. I felt my stomach churn. Blood rushed to my head. The room started to revolve before my eyes. I steadied myself by gripping the back of a chair. I focused on the painting above the fireplace. The one by Orpen of Venetia after her engagement. But even that seemed to morph into strange shapes. And I was not looking at Venetia but at Ophelia in Millais's painting. The one where Ophelia is lying dead in a river, floating on her back, garlanded with flowers.

Except the face on the painting was not Ophelia – but one I loved. It felt as though there was a fog behind my eyes.

And then the moment passed. I took a deep breath. The room stopped revolving. The painting above the fireplace was once again Venetia. I let go of the chair.

I stared at Fanny. She saw the fear in my eyes. She said: "It's all become worse, hasn't it?"

I said: "Yes. I need your help. Will you come with me?"

She nodded.

Venetia said: "You can't leave now. I forbid it."

Fanny said: "This is your fault. You and your pathetic secrets."

"Sit down and do as your Grandmama commands," Piddinghoe snapped.

But Fanny was already on the move.

"Stop her, Pinchbeck," Piddinghoe bellowed.

Lord Snooty made a half-hearted attempt to grab Fanny's arm as she passed. But she sold him a dummy that would have done a fly-half proud. We shot out of the drawing room and raced down the corridor towards the front door.

"Now it's personal," I said.

I pushed the MGB up to ninety as we took the coast road from Newhaven to Brighton. The engine whined. The tyres hummed on the road. I swerved to overtake a bus.

"Personal? What do you mean?" Fanny asked.

"I think Bulstrode has snatched Shirley."

"Your girlfriend? I thought you said she'd gone travelling."

"She had. But I think she's returned. Mrs Gribble, my landlady has been getting strange phone calls. I didn't take them seriously. But now I think they were from Shirley calling from overseas – probably somewhere where the phone service is unreliable. Like Turkey. That's where her last postcard came from."

"How can you be sure?"

"The Widow said there were breathing sounds. But I've made calls to the more remote parts of the world and sometimes interference on the line sounds like laboured breathing. And then there was the name which the caller gave the second time. Ivor Colin English."

"Heavy breathers don't give their name," Fanny said.

"That's right. The Widow said the man spoke with an accent. I think he was a telephone operator in some remote town trying unsuccessfully to put Shirley through. I'm certain she'd have been calling to say she was returning to Brighton."

"But what about the name?" Fanny asked.

"I don't think he was giving his name, Ivor Colin English. I think he was saying, 'I've a call in English.' The Widow put the phone down on him before he could get any further."

Fanny twisted sideways to look at me. "And you think Shirley came back to your flat?"

"I'm certain of it. We know that Bulstrode had called to see me yesterday before we arrived back. He's a strange bloke. I'm now wondering whether he was watching the flat and saw us both return."

"But that's terrible," Fanny said.

"After you'd gone to bed, I found I couldn't sleep on the sofa. So I spent some time looking out of the window at the square. There was a little incident – the sort of thing that happens all the time in the middle of Brighton – and then a car drove off. I didn't think much of it at the time, but looking back, I believe the car may have been a Hillman Minx."

"And that's important?"

"I think so. When I met Clarence at his flat, I invited him for lunch in a pub. He asked me whether he'd need to take his car and when I said 'no', he said 'So we won't need the clever little minx.' The bloke is a walking dictionary of quotations and I thought he was making some obscure quote at the time. Now I think it was his oblique way of telling me he owned a Hillman Minx. Remember, this is a seriously weird guy."

As we approached Brighton the traffic became thicker. I kept up the pace. Fanny grabbed the side of her seat as we sashayed through a junction and accelerated up a hill.

"But surely Clarence would realise that Shirley is not me?" Fanny said.

"We don't yet know what's happened. But there is a superficial resemblance between you and Shirley. I noticed it the night we went to the Hippodrome. Besides, Clarence is clearly a man who's gone over the edge. He's not thinking straight. He's just crazy. And crazy people do crazy things."

"But he's lived peacefully all these years. Why should he suddenly turn into a monster?"

"Because his mother died. Suddenly, violently and without warning. He never had time to say a proper goodbye. And because now he's afraid – no, terrified – of a future without her. He relied on her for everything. Not least what little money he has."

I slowed the MGB to fifty as we approached the roundabout at the Old Steine.

"Shouldn't we go to the police?" Fanny asked.

"Not yet. We don't know what we'll find in Regency Square."

Another thought was forming in my mind. If Clarence had kidnapped Shirley, what had he done with the Widow?

We found her in the kitchen.

She was tied to a chair with pieces of old electrical flex and had a large sticking plaster over her mouth. I ripped the plaster off while Fanny worried away at the knots binding her wrists and ankles.

She was into her stride even before the flesh round her mouth had stopped wobbling. She wagged a finger at me: "When Lady Frances has untied my leg, I'm going to kick you."

She felt her mouth where I'd just ripped off the plaster, thought about it for a bit and said: "Ouch! That hurt."

Fanny put on her Roedean head-girl act. "Mrs Gribble, Shirley Goldsmith's welfare is more important than your hurt feelings – or chapped lips." The Widow calmed down a bit.

I knelt down and faced the Widow as Fanny wrestled the final knots free. "We need to know what happened," I said. "You can kick me later. Throw me out on the streets later. Now we have to save Shirley."

The Widow shrugged. "I suppose so. But don't for a minute think I've finished with you."

I said: "Tell us what happened. From the beginning."

The Widow turned to Fanny: "Your Ladyship, would you mind getting me a drink? I think you'll find a bottle of sherry in the right-hand cupboard."

"For medicinal purposes." I nodded at Fanny as she crossed the room. The Widow scowled.

I ignored that and said: "When did Bulstrode arrive?"

The Widow said: "He came back this morning after you and Lady Frances had left. I explained I'd given you his message. We got talking. At the time, he seemed a pleasant man. Cultured. He was always quoting things. I mentioned that I'd had aristocracy staying with me overnight."

"You didn't mention my name?" Fanny asked.

"I'm afraid I may have done." The Widow stared at a point on the far wall. "I may also have said that you would be welcome here as a long-term resident."

Typical! The Widow's snobbery had made everything worse.

Her suggestion would have given Clarence just the incentive he needed to keep a watch on the place in the hope of kidnapping Fanny.

She took the sherry from the cupboard, poured a glass and handed it to the Widow.

I said: "When did Clarence return?"

She said: "It was about an hour ago, shortly after Miss Goldsmith had arrived."

"He just walked in?"

"Of course not. He knocked the door."

"And you answered it."

"Yes."

This was going to take some time.

I said: "What did he say?"

"He asked to speak to Lady Frances. I said she wasn't here. He said he didn't believe me because he'd seen her arrive earlier with a backpack. He said it looked like she was moving in."

"I said that wasn't Lady Frances and he said I was lying and pushed me into the hall. He closed the front door behind him. He was very rough."

"I'm sorry," I said.

"Nothing you could've done about it. Or would," she added.

"Did you tell Clarence that the young woman who'd arrived was Shirley?"

"Didn't get the chance. He clamped his hand over my mouth – yeuk, it was all sweaty – pulled one arm up behind my back and frogmarched me into the kitchen."

"And nobody heard this?"

"The other tenants were out. Besides, as soon as we got into the kitchen, he produced that plaster and put it over my mouth. The beast said he'd hit me with my own rolling pin if I so much as struggled."

"And then he tied you up?"

"Yes."

"Where was Shirley while all this was happening?"

"On the top floor. In your rooms. Waiting for you. She said it would be a nice surprise."

And it would've been. Anger simmered inside me. Hot as the molten lava in a volcano. If Clarence harmed Shirley, the long arm of the law wouldn't be the only hand of retribution reaching out to him.

"So you didn't see what happened to Shirley?"

"Not upstairs. But about three minutes after the beast had gone up the stairs, he came down again pushing Shirley in front of him. He was going to leave by the back door. I assume he'd parked his car in the mews."

Fanny shivered. She slumped on a chair. "That treatment was meant for me," she said in a small voice. She clamped her arms round her body and hugged herself.

"Did Clarence speak?" I asked the Widow.

"The great bully was babbling. Hardly making any sense. But it seemed I shouldn't contact the police. As if I could, trussed up like a chicken. He said that Shirley would be safe as long as I didn't talk."

"I take it Shirley couldn't speak?" I said.

"Could you with an Elastoplast over your cakehole?"

"Did Shirley try to communicate with you in any way?"

The Widow signalled Fanny to pour another sherry. "I was so angry, I was thinking about what I'd do to the monster when I got the chance. He was jabbering away ten to the dozen. Then I realised that Miss Goldsmith was looking frantically around the room. As though she were desperately searching for something."

"What was it?"

"I don't know but eventually her gaze came back to me and she looked hard as though she wanted me to know she had a message. And then she looked right at the cheese grater there on the kitchen table. Then over to the kitchen utensils hanging on those hooks. And finally at the trussing needle which I'd just been using to sew up a chicken breast I'd stuffed with mushrooms. Then she looked back at me. All defiant. And gave two distinct nods."

"Did you take any meaning from that?"

"I think she was in shock. Probably didn't know what she was doing."

I looked at Fanny. "Shirley doesn't shock easily," I said. "She'd be as mad as a wallaby at a dried-up waterhole, but she'd have been scheming to get free."

"But why stare at those things – a cheese grater, kitchen utensils and a trussing needle. It makes no sense."

"Not immediately. But there must be a hidden message there if only we can work it out."

"Let the police do it," the Widow chimed in.

"No." My voice echoed off the kitchen's tiled walls.

The Widow stiffened. "Don't raise your voice in my kitchen."

I said: "Clarence is having a breakdown. The appearance of Mr Plod with helmet and truncheon and blowing his whistle could take him over the edge. And Shirley with him. She must be our first priority."

The Widow shrugged, reached for the sherry and poured herself another.

"Could all those random articles be a clue to where Clarence is taking her?" Fanny asked.

"I don't think so. Clarence may have been in a volatile state, but I don't think he'd give away the most vital piece of information. I think the articles must relate to something Shirley discovered when she was grabbed by Clarence upstairs."

"But that could be anything," Fanny said.

"Not anything. It must be something that Clarence revealed – perhaps that he had no choice about. Something which Shirley thinks is so important she was desperately trying to find a way to tell us. I think she meant us to take the articles as a code."

"You mean we need to re-arrange the letters in each item to

find the message?"

"I'm not sure. Take the first item – cheese grater. There must be dozens of anagrams." I thought for a moment, "Such as 'her geese cart' but it doesn't make any sense."

"What about kitchen utensils?" Fanny asked.

I considered that one. "'Let sunshine tick' doesn't get us anywhere. And I don't think we'll find a clue with the trussing needle." Again, I thought for a few seconds. "'Sentinels urged' is a little more promising – except we don't know which sentinels Shirley was talking about or what they were being urged to do."

"So it's hopeless," Fanny said.

"Perhaps not," I said. "It would be too complicated for Shirley to work out anagrams in the time she had. I think we have to take the initial letters of the items to make a word"

Fanny cocked her head to one side as she thought about that. "Cheese grater, C G, kitchen utensils, K U, trussing needle, T N doesn't make any word I know."

"No," I said. "And if you take the first letters of each of the items, neither does C K T. But remember that right at the end Shirley gave two nods. I think she was trying to tell us that we need to take the first letter of the second word of each item."

Fanny spelt it out. "G. U. N."

"Yes," I said. "Clarence has a gun."

Chapter 21

"The gun explains how Clarence was able to capture Shirley," I said.

We were in my MGB racing across town towards Clarence's apartment. I jumped a red light in the Steine. Pressed my foot on the accelerator. The MGB's exhaust roared. We shot past The Level where I'd followed Fanny two nights ago. Hurtled towards the Lewes Road. Dust from the road flurried in our wake.

I said: "Clarence may be a big man, but Shirley would've put up a doughty fight – but not with a weapon in play. The gun changes everything."

"How would Clarence get a gun?" Fanny asked.

I'd been pondering that myself. "There are a couple of dealers of militaria among the antique shops in The Lanes," I said. "I know there are rumours that one does an under-the-counter trade in firearms for customers who don't plan to show them off in display cabinets. But the cops have never pinned anything on him."

"Doesn't that mean we should call in the police?"

"It's an even stronger reason not to. Superintendent Tomkins is running the case. If he knows firearms are involved, he'll charge in with all guns blazing. Like the death-and-glory brigade. Shirley's death, his glory. I'm not having that."

I glanced at Fanny. Her lips were pressed tight with tension. "The situation seems hopeless," she said.

"Not hopeless. Clarence is crazy but that doesn't necessarily mean he won't listen to us. We may be able to talk him into letting Shirley go."

"But he wants money. Where are we going to get ten thousand pounds?"

I shrugged. "Not from my Post Office account, that's for sure."

We drew up outside Clarence's house three minutes later.

The street was quiet. Long shadows were creeping between the houses. An uneasy twilight was settling over the place. Or perhaps it was just my mood that was uneasy.

We scrambled out of the MGB and hurried up a short path to the front door. I pressed the bell.

"He won't answer," I said. "But we have to make sure."

"What do we do then?"

"We'll ask ourselves in."

"You mean burgle the property?"

"Cracksman Colin and Fingersmith Fanny are on the case," I said.

"You can't be serious?"

"Let's just say we're going to pay an uninvited call."

We'd waited for a minute. As I'd predicted, nobody appeared.

"Let's go round to the back," I said.

We wouldn't be able to force our way through the front door without attracting too much attention. But when I'd taken Clarence out the back way to the pub in order to avoid Jim Houghton's unwanted attentions, I'd noticed that there was a kitchen door which opened into a small yard. I remembered that Clarence had drawn back two heavy bolts on the inside to let us out. But there was something else about the door that made me believe I would be able to find a way in.

We entered the back yard through a tall gate and closed it quietly behind us. The twilight had now turned to dusk and I wished I'd brought a torch. The yard contained a sentry-box shed, an old mangle and a rusting bicycle. I crossed to the shed. The hinges squealed as I opened the door. The inside was covered in dust and heaped with rubbish that had been thrown out of the house over the years. A few tools hung from a small rack.

I took down a sturdy screwdriver and crossed to the backdoor. It was a conventional two-panel job with a pane of frosted glass in the top half and a panel of wood in the bottom.

"You're not planning to take the door off its hinges?" Fanny asked.

I grinned. "They didn't teach elementary carpentry at Roedean, then. That wouldn't be possible. The screws in the hinges are always hidden when the door is closed."

I squatted down on my haunches and prayed that my hunch was right. Some doors have the wooden panel fitted into the framework with a tongue-and-groove joint. There would be no way of removing that kind of panel without taking the framework to pieces. But I'd noticed when I'd been shepherding Clarence away from the advancing Houghton, that this back door was fitted with a cat flap. There was no sign of a moggie – and I guessed it had long gone the way of poor Marie Richmond's career. But for the flap to be fitted, it was likely the bottom panel had been removed – then screwed back in. And what has been screwed in can be screwed out.

In the fast-fading light, I examined the panel while Fanny craned over my shoulder.

I was right. The panel was fixed into the frame with a screw in each corner. With the sturdy screwdriver, I had the panel out within a couple of minutes.

I turned to Fanny: "Normally, I'd say ladies first. But, under the circumstances, I'll lead the way."

She nodded. I stooped down and crawled through the hole in the bottom half of the door. Inside, I turned around and stuck my head out again. "The coast's clear."

Fanny scrambled through and clambered to her feet. "And before you say it, they don't teach housebreaking at Roedean either," she said.

"So not a practical curriculum," I said.

She punched me on the arm. I looked around. We were in the kitchen. A few plates were piled in a drainer by the sink. A saucepan encrusted with dried-up gravy stood on the stove. A small worktop area held a packet of cornflakes, a pot of jam and a lone Oxo cube. The oily stench of rancid fat hung in the air.

I said: "We'll have to risk putting some lights on – otherwise we simply won't be able to see. I think anybody who spots the light will simply assume Clarence has come back. But we'll need to keep our voices down. We don't know how thick these walls are."

We crept into the living room. The only sound was the ticking of a clock in the hall.

"What are we looking for?" asked Fanny.

"Anything that gives us a clue about where Clarence has taken Shirley. He'll be looking for a place where he's confident he'll be private and undisturbed."

"But that could be anywhere," Fanny said. "It's not even like looking for a needle in a haystack – because we don't even know which is the right haystack."

"I'm not so sure. Clarence has limited options. Besides, he's not had much time to prepare – certainly not more than twenty-four hours before he cooked up this scheme. So he'll have to choose somewhere that satisfies his private-and-undisturbed criteria – but which he can get to easily. There won't be many places which fit the bill. Perhaps only one."

Fanny shrugged. "You may be right. But it seems a long shot."

"No matter how long, we have to try. Shirley's life may depend on it."

We started to search the room. It was like taking a journey back into the nineteen-thirties. The place had clearly been Marie Richmond's domain. A chair covered in faded red velvet with a lacy antimacassar was pulled up to the fireplace. A sewing basket, overflowing with a confusion of needles and threads, sat on a small table by the chair. An old copy of the *Chronicle* was propped up against the table. I picked it up. It was dated the day before Marie died.

I'd expected to see photos and mementoes from Marie's acting career. But there were none. It was as though she'd made a deliberate effort to wipe that part of her life from her memory. There was a bookshelf packed with paperbacks – mostly romantic potboilers. I pulled a couple off the shelf. Dust swirled in a little cloud as I flicked through the pages. On one of the shelves were a few photos in cheap frames. Clarence as a young boy, as a teenager with a bicycle. One of Marie looking surprisingly flirty as a pensioner in a bathing suit. And a surprise: a small print of the Orpen picture of Venetia which hung at Piddinghoe Grange. So perhaps Marie had harboured a scintilla of love for her sister despite the animosity between them.

But there was nothing here that would give us the clue we desperately needed.

On the other side of the room, Fanny was rummaging through a cupboard.

"Just glasses and a few bottles. Mostly sherry," she said.

"Let's try the bedrooms," I said.

We crept into the hall. Three doors led off a short corridor. One opened into a bathroom. We ignored it. The second revealed Marie's bedroom. We went in.

The sharp scent of cheap perfume made our nostrils twitch. The dressing table contained a couple of atomiser bottles, a hairbrush and comb, and a small vanity case, which I presumed was for make-up. The bed had been neatly made. It was covered in a bright counterpane that featured sprays of red roses.

The wardrobe was a monster in dark wood with two heavy doors. A full-length mirror had been let into one of the doors. I opened both doors and we peered in. At the height of her fame, Marie had dressed in the finest creations from Worth or Givenchy of Paris. (Or, more often, undressed from them). But the few clothes hanging on the rail looked dowdy and well-worn. This was the wardrobe of a skivvy rather than screen-siren.

"She'd put the world of *haute couture* behind her then," Fanny said.

"You've forgotten – she was living on hand-outs. But what's this?"

At the top of the wardrobe a shelf held a couple of cheap felt hats, a wrap thing like a dead fox, and what looked like a pile of papers. I reached up and hefted it down. It was a fat scrapbook.

I opened it and flipped through a few pages. The book had obviously been compiled as a labour of love. Each cutting was neatly clipped, carefully pasted in and labelled with its date and source of origin. Most of the cuttings had come from the *Sussex Express*, the weekly newspaper published in Lewes. But this wasn't a scrapbook full of headlines about Marie's triumphs on the stage and in the silent movies. Indeed, at first glance, I could see few cuttings about her. Most were about village life in and around Piddinghoe. The cuttings dated from before the war until a couple of years ago. I wondered why Marie wanted to collect cuttings about a place she rarely visited rather than about her own career.

But this was no time to ponder an answer to that question. We had more urgent business.

I said: "This won't help now, but I'm taking it with us. Let's try Clarence's bedroom."

We slipped silently back into the corridor and moved into his room. I flicked on the light switch and surveyed the room.

Clarence had not made his bed. It was strewn with discarded clothes. The dressing table was piled with stuff he'd left behind. I spotted an old shaving kit, a pair of hair brushes, a tin of shoe polish among the junk.

I rummaged among the stuff. And turned up a car logbook for a Hillman Minx.

"He left in a hurry and forgot this," I said.

Fanny began to pick through the clothes on the bed. I moved to the bedside cabinet. The top of it hadn't been dusted in weeks. The footprints of what looked like a couple of picture frames were outlined in the dust.

"He's had some bedside photos here," I said.

Fanny crossed the room and traced the outline of the frames in the dust with her forefinger. "He's taken them with him," she said.

"Possibly. But the room is a shambles. They could be anywhere. He wasn't packing for a holiday. He was scrambling to get out of the flat as fast as possible."

"I don't see how that helps us," Fanny said.

"Two pictures by the bedside. I reckon one of those must be his mother," I said.

"So the second is his father."

"I'm not so sure. Clarence's father died back in the nineteen-twenties. Besides, Clarence is the mummy's boy from hell. I wouldn't be surprised if the second one doesn't have some kind of link to her as well."

"But we'll never know."

"Look at the room," I said. "It's like a tornado has passed through the place. For all we know, the pictures could be under the clothes on the bed, jumbled among that stuff on the dressing table or anywhere."

We started at opposite ends of the room. We rummaged under clothes. Lifted up bedding. Peered down the back of furniture.

I found one of the photo frames five minutes later. It had slipped down behind the bedside cabinet – no doubt accidentally as Clarence rushed to pack his belongings.

"Look at this," I said.

I held out the photo frame to Fanny.

"It's a ship," she said.

"No, it's a houseboat," I said. "People live on them."

The picture showed an ungainly looking craft, a bit like a cross between a cabin cruiser and one of those narrowboats which sail Britain's canals.

"I think this is where Clarence has taken Shirley," I said.

"What makes you think that?"

"It meets his needs – private and undisturbed. But this is the clincher." I pointed at the photo. "You can see the name of the boat painted on the prow."

"*Marie,*" Fanny said.

"He didn't take the picture with him because he'd lost it down the back of the cabinet. It was because he didn't need a reminder of what it looked like. He was planning to be on it."

"So he's stuck on this boat – wherever it is."

"Not necessarily. Houseboats don't normally move from their moorings. But that doesn't mean they can't. After all, how did they get there in the first place?"

"You think he's planning to move?"

"In his present state, he could be thinking of anything. He's probably just mad enough to believe he could sail to safety in this vessel. We need to get to that houseboat before it weighs anchor and disappears out to sea."

"But we don't know where it's moored," Fanny said.

I pointed to something in the background of the photo. "See that bridge? It's the footbridge across the River Adur. The boat is moored at Shoreham-by-Sea. Let's go."

Fanny hung back in the room. She looked anxiously from me to the bed to the dressing table. She said: "Haven't you forgotten something?"

"The gun?"

"Yes. We could be walking into an ambush with an armed maniac. How are we going to defend ourselves?"

"I've had an idea about that," I said.

A wet tongue licked my ear.

"Stop it," I said. "This is neither the time nor the place."

Fanny giggled.

We were in the MGB. We'd just passed Hove Lagoon on the coast road heading towards Shoreham, five miles to the west. I depressed the accelerator and the arrow in the speedo climbed past sixty. The road ahead narrowed. The four steaming chimneys of Southwick power station loomed out of the dark.

The wet tongue foraged in my ear again.

"I said 'stop it'."

"She's just trying to get to know you," Fanny said.

I glanced in the rearview mirror. Poppy, Professor Pettigrew's star poodle, fidgeted around in the jump seat, mouth open, tongue hanging out. She snuffled hopefully around the back of my neck.

"Now I know what people mean by dog days," I said.

"Do you really think that Poppy can help?" Fanny asked.

"The first time I visited Clarence, I discovered he had a phobia about dogs. I don't just mean that he doesn't like them. He's terrified of them. Even the softie of a mutt owned by the old lady across the hall put him in such a fright he nearly had to change his underwear. So, perhaps, Poppy may put him on the defensive and give us an edge. We need it."

It hadn't been easy persuading the professor to part with Poppy for a couple of hours. We'd barged into his dressing room like a couple of stage-door Johnnies just as he'd finished his last performance of the evening. He seemed surprised to see us. I could hardly blame him.

I'd pretended Fanny wanted to give Poppy a run on the beach. A little treat after a hard week treading the boards. Pettigrew didn't seem too keen on the idea. Mumbled something about getting the dogs back to the digs. But, on our previous visit, I'd discovered that it wasn't only the Pixilated Poodles who liked a little drop of port as a strengthener before a show. The professor did, too. Except that he also liked a drop after the show. And probably during it. I'd counted two empty bottles in his waste bin. I'd handed him a fiver to replenish supplies. And Fanny had promised on her Grandmama's life we'd get Poppy back to the digs unharmed. Not perhaps the best choice of life to offer as a promissory note, I'd thought. If it hadn't been for her Grandmama we wouldn't have been here.

But the port and the promises did the trick. And Poppy had trotted happily after Fanny and jumped into the MGB.

We raced passed the Kayser Bondor factory – the one which Fanny had used to spin the yarn about getting a job.

"But, remember, Clarence has a gun," Fanny said.

"That might scare us. But it won't frighten Poppy. You saw what she was like at the Hippodrome show – absolutely fearless. And she really took to you in the dressing room afterwards. The fact she followed you this evening without a backward glance proves it."

She said: "If Marie was relying on money from Grandmama, how come she could afford a houseboat?"

"I'm guessing she's had it for years. It looks old in the photograph. Years ago, back in the nineteen-twenties, Shoreham Beach was a centre for the silent-film industry. Hollywood-by-Sea they used to call it. But without so much sunshine. They even built film studios there. And many actors and actresses had holiday homes. Marie's may have been the houseboat. No doubt she could afford to buy one in those days – and perhaps she just kept it as a memento of better times."

"And now it's a prison for Shirley," Fanny said.

"Yes," I said. I felt my cheeks flush with anger. But I told myself I needed to think clearly if we were to rescue Shirley.

We flashed through a junction lit by sodium lamps. I glanced at Fanny. "What if Shirley isn't on the boat?" she said.

That thought was already haunting me. I'd been so certain my deductions were correct when we'd discovered the photograph in Clarence's bedroom. Now I wasn't so sure.

"I don't know," I said. My voice sounded as bleak as a winter crow's.

But I didn't have time to worry about that. Ahead a road sign read: Shoreham-by-Sea.

"We're nearly there," I said.

I glanced at Fanny again. She was chewing her lower lip.

"We'll be all right," I said. "As Henry the Fifth nearly said, 'Cry havoc and let slip the dog of war.'"

My bravado didn't do much for Fanny.

But Poppy licked my ear.

Chapter 22

I pulled the MGB onto a patch of rough ground close to the River Adur.

I switched off the engine. For a few seconds, Fanny and I sat in silence. We were so tense it felt like an electric current was running between us. Like some kind of magnet had pinioned us to our seats with a magic force.

Then I said: "Let's go."

It broke the spell. We scrambled out of the car. Poppy bounded after us. Fanny attached her lead.

Dusk had turned into night. A three-quarter moon scudded behind thin clouds. It bathed the ground in that kind of pale light you get in the cinema when the usherette is walking backwards down the aisle with a tray of ice creams and they've only half dimmed the lamps before the main feature.

The place was deserted. There was a scattering of houses about hundred yards away to our right. No lights in any of them. In front of us, the river bank rose like a dark shadow. It looked like one of those levees I'd seen them building along the Mississippi in *Pathé* newsreels. A narrow footpath ran along the top of the bank. Behind it, the outlines of houseboats were silhouetted by the moon. Like a ghostly armada ready to sail.

Ten yards to our right another car had parked. Clarence's Hillman Minx. I walked over and put my hand on the bonnet. It was warm. So Clarence wouldn't have been on his boat for more than an hour. That was good. He'd have had too little time to work out a plan. Too little time to harm Shirley. At least, more than he already had.

All the while Clarence believed he'd seized Fanny, Shirley would be safe. After all, Clarence needed a live hostage to exchange for the ten thousand quid he vainly expected to spring from Lord Piddinghoe.

But one scary thought turned my knees to water. What if Clarence did realise he'd made a mistake? That Shirley wasn't Fanny. Given the chance, Shirley had a turn of phrase that could make a trucker sound like Miss Manners. Clarence was a man with low self-esteem. If Shirley let him have it with both barrels, she'd make him feel about as significant as a blob of chewing gum on the pavement. A hostage he thought was Fanny would be an asset all the while ten big ones were in the offing. Without the prospect of a pay-off, Clarence would soon find Shirley was a burden.

And Clarence had the gun.

But the riverbank was silent. No shots. No screams. No cries for help.

Besides, I thought, Clarence was the one with the problem to solve. He had to work out how to collect the ransom money without getting caught. It was a problem that would tax his brain to the full. I imagined him sat in his cabin humming and hawing over one unlikely scheme after another. Perhaps he'd already made his plan. But I didn't think so. Clarence was a man driven by impulses. And this kidnap hadn't been planned far in advance.

Fanny and Poppy joined me by the Hillman. Poppy jumped up on her hind legs looking for a pat. I obliged by ruffling the quiff of fur on her head.

"What now?" Fanny said.

"As old Winston once put it, 'jaw jaw is better than war war'. So I'm hoping it might be possible to talk some sense into Clarence. Perhaps I can persuade him it'll be easier in the long run if he drops his ransom demand and lets Shirley go."

"You think a man with a gun will go for that?"

"I'm not optimistic, but we've got to try. So I think, at first, it's best if you and Poppy stay in the background."

We moved off. Our feet crunched on the gravel as we headed for the footpath. We climbed a flight of wooden steps up to the path. Then we picked our way along it, searching for the *Marie*.

It took us only a couple of minutes to find.

The *Marie* looked much as it had in the photograph we'd seen in Clarence's bedroom. It was moored with its stern tied to the riverbank, the prow pointing into the river. At one time, it had been painted a bilious green. But much of the paint had flaked off and rotting wood showed through. The ropes which held the boat to the riverbank were stained black with age. Even so, the Marie floated well in the water and looked seaworthy. There was an observation cabin towards the stern of the deck and a small wheelhouse further forward. No light showed from either. But light filtered from the curtained portholes of the cabins below deck.

I motioned to Fanny and we crept a few yards closer for a side view of the vessel. As we looked, a shadow passed in front of one of the portholes.

"Well, someone's at home," I whispered. "Let's pay a call."

We moved further along the footpath to a companionway which connected the *Marie* to the land. Years ago, a tall metal gate and some spiky railings had been erected at the landward end. It blocked our way. A heavy chain fastened with a padlock had been wrapped around the gate and the railings.

I said: "I wasn't expecting to be piped aboard, but I didn't think Clarence would've turned the place into a fortress. After all, he thinks nobody knows where he is,"

"Can't we cut through the chain?" Fanny asked.

"I just happen to have left my heavy-duty bolt cutters at home. We'll have to think of something else. Besides, knocking on the front door and waiting politely for it to be answered may not be the best tactic."

A few yards back along the footpath, I'd spotted a small tender tethered to another houseboat. I guessed the owners used the tender as a ferry to cross the river. The houseboat itself was in darkness.

I nudged Fanny and pointed. "We'll borrow that tender, row around to the prow of the *Marie*, and climb aboard."

"You make us sound like a pair of pirates," she said.

"Shiver me timbers," I said.

We clambered down the bank from the footpath towards the river. I heaved on the rope which tethered the tender to the shore and it floated silently towards me. It rocked gently as we climbed aboard and as I lifted Poppy in.

I took the oars, cast off the rope and gently pushed us away from the bank. The oars made a gentle rippling sound as they dipped the water. The words of the old nursery rhyme flashed through my mind: "Row, row, row your boat gently down the stream..."

We coasted towards the *Marie*. I eased silently around the prow.

Hisssssss.

A swan opened its wings like an avenging angel and swooped towards me. It had been slumbering in the lea of the *Marie*.

Hisssssss.

Louder this time. And now its mate joined the attack. Poppy barked and lunged across the tender. Fanny slipped sideways. I dropped the oars. The tender drifted into the side of the *Marie*.

CLUNK!

The sound echoed around the riverbank. A flock of wading birds screeched loudly and took off. Their beating wings sounded like sheets flapping in a gale. I scrabbled for the oars. Grabbed them. Manoeuvred the tender under the prow of the *Marie*. Fanny seized Poppy. Held her muzzle.

The swans hissed again. Turned and glided imperiously down river.

We held our breath.

"Clarence must have heard," I whispered.

Fanny nodded.

I said: "If we've spooked him, our task has just become ten

times harder."

I risked a cautious glance around the side of the prow.

Light from one of the portholes grew brighter. Clarence had pulled back the curtain and was looking out. The light dimmed as the curtain fell back. I guessed he'd do the same on the other side of the boat. But there were no portholes in the prow. I figured he'd put the commotion down to a night-time squabble among river birds.

We waited fully five minutes until silence had returned.

Then I tethered the tender to the side of the *Marie*. By standing up I could just reach the deck rails on the houseboat.

"I'll haul myself up first," I said to Fanny. "Then you hand up Poppy. Finally I'll pull you up."

By the time we were all on board, I felt as though my arms had stretched six inches, and I was breathing like a marathon runner.

I leant towards Fanny and whispered: "You wait here with Poppy. I'll go aft and see if I can find a way into the cabin. If I run into Clarence, I'll try sweet reason. If that doesn't work, we'll unleash Poppy. If you hear a gun shot, jump over the side with Poppy and make for the bank as fast as you can swim. Then call the police."

Fanny gave me the thumbs up. But her hand was shaking.

I tiptoed forward like I was playing a game of grandma's footsteps.

I rounded the corner of the observation cabin and gently tried the handle on the door. It didn't budge. Perhaps I could have shifted it, but only by making enough noise to wake the riverbank – and have Clarence taking pot shots at me from the other side.

Further towards the stern, a hatch closed off a companionway which led to the lower deck. It might prove a way in but would be a riskier proposition. As I came down the stairs, I'd appear feet first. Clarence would see me at least a couple of seconds before I saw him. Plenty of time to get off a couple of shots if he was in a trigger-happy mood.

I crept over and pulled at the metal ring which lifted the hatch. The metal creaked but the hatch stuck solid. If we couldn't find our way in, the only alternative would be to lure Clarence out. But that tactic would remove our element of surprise.

I considered our options as I tiptoed back to the prow.

Fanny crouched in the lea of the wheelhouse with Poppy by her side. She started to speak, but I laid my finger gently on her lips.

"There's no way in aft," I said. "Our only hope now is the wheelhouse. Wait here."

I crept towards the wheelhouse door. It squealed as I opened it. Deep in the folds of my brain, I had a distant memory of once interviewing a captain whose ship had sunk in a storm. He'd told me he'd been able to save two members of the crew from the engine room by bringing them up through a hatch in the wheel-house floor. If his ship had a hatch, perhaps the *Marie* did, too.

I crawled into the wheelhouse on hands and knees like a penitent before the altar. I ran my fingertips across the floor. I was feeling for a latch. Or a hinge. Or a handle. Or a lever. Anything that would indicate there was a hatch to the lower deck. My fingers came away greasy with accumulated slime from years of neglect. I wiped them on my handkerchief and tried again.

This time, my fingers brushed against something sharp.

I moved closer. Felt around the object. It had the shape of a small ring. It was recessed into the floor. Surely it must be the lever which opened a hatch. I tugged on the ring. Nothing moved. I heaved again. Nothing.

I was an idiot. I was kneeling on the hatch trying to yank it up with my own weight pushing it down. I moved position and gently pulled on the ring from the other side. The hatch made a low puff, like a tired old steam engine, as air from below released. I pulled some more and the hatch rose. A finger of yellow light crept out from the gap I'd created. I lifted the hatch a little higher and peered in. It was a small space which looked like a storeroom. A ladder had been fixed to one side of the opening.

I replaced the hatch quietly and edged backwards out of the wheelhouse.

I gestured to Fanny. She tiptoed across the deck carrying Poppy.

"There's a ladder down into a storeroom," I said. "I'll go down first. If it's safe, you can hand Poppy down to me, then follow."

Fanny opened her mouth to speak. Changed her mind. Nodded nervously.

The old hinges of the hatch whined as I opened it fully, and the ladder creaked every time I put my foot on a new rung. But within a couple of minutes we were all in the storeroom.

The place was lit by a single bulb behind an iron grill. The room was heaped with years of junk. There were empty oil cans. Piles of rags. Cracked panes of glass. A box of tools. A rusted fire extinguisher. A bucket of tar. Coils of rope. Metal brackets and fixings. A broken compass. All covered with a thick film of dust. The air was stale and musty.

Fanny put Poppy down. The mutt snuffled happily around.

The storeroom had a single door. It was ajar. It led into a short corridor to the aft of the vessel. There was one door off to the right – presumably to a cabin – and another door at the far end. I guessed that would lead into the day cabin. As we'd approached the *Marie*, I'd noticed that the brighter portholes were towards the stern. It seemed logical to assume that's where Clarence was lurking.

Besides, music blared from behind the far door. Grand opera. A big orchestra and a fat lady were at full volume. Something by Wagner, I thought.

I put my mouth close to Fanny's ear and whispered: "I'm going forward for a recce. Wait here with Poppy. Don't come unless I call you."

Fanny nodded reluctantly.

I pushed the door open and stepped into the corridor. I crept forward, tried the door to my right. It was locked. There was only one reason Clarence would have locked doors inside the boat.

I tapped gently on the door. There was movement inside the cabin. I imagined an ear pressed close against the door listening for any giveaway sound.

I put my mouth close to the door and whispered: "Shirley, it's me, Colin. Is that you?"

"Yes, Colin, it's me."

I said: "I've come to rescue you."

There was a spluttering sound behind the door. Then Shirley said: "And I thought it couldn't get any worse."

I said: "Are you alright?"

"You mean, apart from being kidnapped and locked up by a lunatic?"

"Are you hurt?"

"Only my pride."

"Can you move freely?"

"Yes, the fat old bozo untied me. Made it sound like he was doing me a favour."

"Have you told him who you are?"

"Yes. But the guy is living on another planet. Thinks I'm some ladyship character."

"Lady Frances Mountebank," I said.

"That's the one."

"I've got her with me."

"Jeez," Shirley said. "What is this? A kidnap victims' convention?"

I said: "I'll explain everything later. I've got a plan."

"You need a key to get me out."

"I'm going to get it."

"Colin, the guy's got a gun. That's how he took me."

"I know."

"And he's a fruitcake. He's dangerous."

"Yes. I can handle him. I'm going to do it now. Be ready to move."

Shirley gave a tiny tap on the door. "Colin."

"Yes."

"If this doesn't work out… I came back."

"I know. Thank you."

I walked towards the door at the far end of the corridor. I opened it and stepped into the day cabin.

Chapter 23

Clarence was lying on a couch covered with cushions.

He had his back to me. He hadn't heard me step into the room. Which was no surprise. The music was blasting from a battery radio. *Götterdämmerung*. The twilight of the gods. He was waving his arms conducting the orchestra.

While Clarence preoccupied himself bringing in the second violins, I rapidly scanned the cabin. His couch, an ancient affair with horsehair bursting from splits in its fabric, was over to the left. Cabinets, chairs, tables were stacked around the walls. Heaps of boxes littered the floor. Behind me, by the door, shelves were loaded with books, old newspapers and nautical charts.

No sign of the gun.

At the far end of the cabin, a companionway led up to the top deck. Presumably to the hatch I couldn't open from the outside. Near to the companionway, a table overflowed with books and papers. Behind it, a novelty key rack in the shape of the Titanic hung with half a dozen keys. I hoped one would open the door to Shirley's prison.

To my right, a small galley contained a hob fuelled by a large gas canister. A frying pan full of sausages and bacon sizzled noisily. The place smelt like the breakfast shift in a transport caff.

On the radio, the strings throttled back in a *diminuendo*. Clarence sensed my presence as I advanced into the room. He turned and his eyes glazed with confusion.

I nodded at the frying pan and said: "Gourmet night, is it?"

Clarence's brain, slow as a slug, lumbered into life. He scowled. Then he shifted his bulk. Tossed the cushions aside. It was like watching a prehistoric monster emerge from a swamp. He put a foot to the ground.

I took four rapid steps across the room. And as he began to rise, I thumped him hard in the chest.

Oooooooof!

The air rushed out of him like a punctured balloon.

He flopped back on the couch.

On the radio, the trumpets obliged with a little *ta-ra, ta-ra*.

I said: "Don't get up on my account."

He said: "Why are you here? I didn't invite you."

"Put it down to my bad manners. So why don't you have a nice lie down while I ask some questions?"

He stared at the ceiling as though it might provide some kind of answer. "Questions, questions. You shouldn't be here. Not asking questions. 'That is the question, whether 'tis nobler in the mind to suffer the slings and arrows of outrageous fortune...'," he rambled.

If I hadn't already met him, I'd have said that he was on something. I've seen journos who make friends with a whisky bottle in their twenties turn into rambling buffoons by their thirties. But Clarence's problems didn't pour from a bottle. They'd been drip-fed into him by his mother. A lifetime of fantasy. Of pretending he was someone he wasn't. Of playing a part instead of living a life. Of learning lines instead of speaking spontaneous words. Clarence was a hopeless case. A lost cause. But somehow I had to drag him back to the real world and make him confront his crime. It was the only way I was going to force him to free Shirley.

I said: "All right, Hamlet. I already know you're a walking dictionary of quotations. Let's have some answers in your own words for a change."

Clarence shifted on the couch. His lips twisted into a grimace somewhere between winsome and loathsome. With his chubby face and wisps of hair, he looked like a baby who'd decided to eat his nanny.

On the radio, Brunhilde hit a high C that had the portholes rattling.

I said: "You've got a young woman locked in the cabin. Where

Peter Bartram

is the key?"

"'The keys of the Kingdom of Heaven...'" Clarence babbled.

"No, the key to the cabin."

"'Lawyers have taken away the key of knowledge.'"

"Forget that, man. Give me the key."

He tried to rise again. I pushed him back. He giggled.

I said: "The woman you've taken isn't Lady Frances."

"You'll be telling me next she's the Lady of Shallot." He snickered. Saliva dribbled down his chin.

He reached in his pocket for a handkerchief to wipe it away.

And pulled out the gun.

He snarled. Now he looked like the baby who'd eaten his nanny.

And planned to feast on the nursery maid for afters.

He said: "'Guns will make us powerful...'"

"'... Butter will only make us fat.'" I completed the quotation. "And that old fatso Hermann Goering should've known. But that gun won't make you powerful. It will only make you dead."

"Make you dead first."

He put his feet to the ground. "Not pushing me back now, are you?" he said. "Not brave now. 'None but the brave deserves the fair.' And I have the fair Lady Frances."

"You don't have the fair Lady Frances. You have the fair Shirley Goldsmith, you fool."

"No. You're wrong. She's Frances and I'm getting ten thousand pounds."

"You're getting Sweet Fanny Adams. Except free board and lodging in Lewes Prison. Trouble is heading your way."

"'Forget your troubles, come on get happy...'" Clarence sang.

He waved the gun about like it was party favour on New Year's Eve. The clown could kill me by accident if I didn't watch out.

I edged away from him to the other end of the cabin. Nudged up against the table overflowing with papers.

I said: "Let Shirley go and you become an innocent man. We'll forget about this charade. Pretend it didn't happen."

Of course, we wouldn't. But when push comes to shove, I can lie with the best of them.

"'It is better that ten guilty persons escape than that one innocent suffer,'" Clarence giggled. "But I think it is better that ten innocent people suffer so that one guilty can escape."

I said: "Put the gun down. Give me the key to release Shirley and this problem goes away."

I moved towards the table near the companionway. Glanced at the contents. My heart lurched. My mouth went dry. I had a sensation like a frozen knife being drawn down my spine.

In the middle of the table, among a litter of newspapers was a stack of dogged-eared, sepia-tinted photographs. The top one showed a young woman sitting in her bath. I reached out and lifted the top photo. The second one was nearly identical. There'd been just a slight movement in her head. Beside the pile lay the title card: *Milady's Bath Night*.

I'd been treating Clarence like a fool.

But my thumping heart confirmed that he had become a dangerous man, even before he seized Shirley.

I said: "Where did you get these?"

He moved closer. "Don't touch them," he said. "They're mine. Mama said they would be mine."

"But you took them from the amusement arcade on Palace Pier."

"Yes, but Mama was wrong."

"About what you'd find?"

The memory flashed back into my mind. Trish, the nurse – the one who worked in Accident and Emergency – had told me she'd overheard Marie's last words to Clarence: "Your fortune lies on the pier."

I said: "*Milady's Bath Night* is not going to make your fortune. It didn't even make Marie's."

"Mumsie never told me a lie," Clarence wailed. "I thought the pictures would give me a secret – lead me to a fortune."

He was becoming morose. The bravado was draining out of him.

"But they turned out to be just pictures," I said.

"I couldn't believe it. I looked at them. All of them. No fortune. Nothing."

"So you went back to the pier to see if you'd missed anything."

"I hid in the coconut shy when it was time to close the pier. Like I did the first time. You can't have seen me."

"I didn't. But it was logical that whoever stole *Milady's Bath Night* would be the person who returned two nights later for a second helping."

"I was only looking for something that was mine. Only right. Only fair. But the old man said I shouldn't be there. Said he'd call the police. But I had to look. My Mumsie couldn't be wrong. My fortune was on the pier. I had to find it."

"And the man was the night-watchman, Fred Snout," I said.

"Don't know his name. Didn't until it was in the newspapers," Clarence said. "And then the old man started pushing me. I told him to stop."

"But he wouldn't?"

"Said he knew I was a thief and he was going to prove it. But I wasn't a thief. I took what my Mumsie said I should have."

"So you killed him," I said.

"I had to. Mumsie would have wanted it."

"No, she wouldn't."

"You're wrong," Clarence said.

"But why take Shirley?"

"She's Lady Frances…"

"Then why take Lady Frances?"

"Because I need money now. Must have money now that the man with the limp knows."

He meant Jim Houghton of the *Evening Argus*. With the aid of snitch Pinker, Houghton would have finally tracked Clarence down, despite my efforts to keep them apart.

"What does the man with the limp know," I said.

"What I did on the pier."

"Jim Houghton – the man with the limp – doesn't know that."

"He said in his newspaper that he does. He wrote: 'Police are close to arresting the man who killed Fred Snout.'"

So Jim's latest story – the one about the police planning a new arrest after releasing Tom Belcher – had triggered Clarence's final breakdown. But Jim was flying a kite based, no doubt, on a boozy boast from Tomkins.

I said: "Reporters sometimes write things they hope will happen rather than know for sure. I've done it myself."

Clarence curled his lip at that. He said: "Then you're no better than the rest of them."

He raised the gun. Held it with both hands and pointed it straight at me. I knew he was going to fire it and I knew that I couldn't stop him.

I watched his eyes. They looked like hard little marbles. I sensed his arms tensing. Watched his finger tighten on the trigger.

I threw myself to one side.

Half a second later, he fired. And missed. He'd committed to the shot and couldn't stop himself.

The bullet hit a metal stanchion, ricocheted and smashed a porthole. Cool night air wafted in.

The *Götterdämmerung* orchestra ramped up the tension with some dark chords from the cellos and a couple of ominous blasts from the trombones.

Berrrrum, berrrrum.

I sprawled on the floor. I gasped for air.

In the storeroom Fanny screamed.

Shirley shouted: "What's happening?"

Poppy barked.

Then Fanny shrieked: "Come back."

Clarence, confused, cried: "A dog? No dogs!"

And then Poppy raced into the day cabin.

I yelled: "Fanny, stay back."

Clarence stumbled into the table. Raised the gun. Fired another shot.

It missed Poppy and buried itself in the wall. Poppy bounded across the cabin. The shot hadn't troubled her.

I scrambled to my feet. Clarence aimed the gun at me again. I shoulder-charged him.

He dropped the gun. Swung round to hit me. I ducked. Charged in like a rugby back stopping a prop forward.

Clarence grabbed at me. Poppy jumped up at him. He lashed out with his legs. Missed the dog.

The trumpets blasted away like foghorns and the fat lady started into her big number.

Clarence and I grabbed at each other. He got his fleshy arms around me. I jabbed a fist hard into his kidney.

One. Two. Three.

Clarence yelled in pain and let me go. He stepped back. Flicked a grey tongue over his lips. Heaved up his shoulders and aimed a haymaker at my head.

He was a big man, but slow. I ducked. His swing carried him round. I darted forward and punched him in the kidneys again.

One. Two. Three.

Poppy snarled.

Brunhilde hit some high notes. The drums set up a rumble like thunder.

Poppy lunged at Clarence's legs.

Clarence stepped back. Crashed into the hob. Sent the frying pan with the sausages and bacon over.

The hot fat splashed into the lighted hob.

Whuuuuuuumph!

The fat flared into flame.

I cried: "Fire! You've set the place on fire, you idiot."

But Clarence was a man possessed. He charged back across the room at me.

As he closed in, I turned my right shoulder and took him square the chest. His weight made me stumble back, but he lost the force of his charge.

Whoooooooooph!

A heap of greasy rags in the galley went up like a Roman candle.

Tongues of flame spread along the cupboards lining the walls. Reached the books and newspapers on the wooden shelves.

I said: "We need to get out."

Clarence said: "You're not leaving here."

He stepped forward. Aimed a big punch at my head. I swayed back. Clarence's fist sailed past my jaw.

I moved in close and delivered a volley of punches to his chest and stomach.

One. Two. Three.

Poppy barked her approval. Jumped on the couch and tried to bite Clarence's leg as he stumbled by.

We could feel the heat from the fire now. The caked-in grease on the furniture and fabrics had turned the place into a firebox.

I scanned the room looking for the gun.

It was on the floor under the table.

But Clarence, now on the opposite side of the room, saw it, too.

We started towards it together. I felt like I'd gone ten rounds with a heavyweight. But I knew that if I didn't reach the gun first, we'd all be finished.

I pushed myself forward, leapt a pile of boxes, took three big strides.

But Clarence was closer. He shouldered his way through debris.

I was six feet from the gun.

But he was three.

And then Poppy dashed beneath his feet.

He stumbled over her. Lost his balance. Regained it. Then tripped again. I heard the thump as his head crunched into the side of the table. He crashed to the floor and lay still.

I moved forward and grabbed the gun. Cracked it open and checked the ammunition, closed it and replaced the safety catch. I thrust it into my pocket.

Then I checked Clarence. He was breathing heavily. He snorted like a sleeping pig.

I shouted: "Fanny, I'm getting the key to release Shirley. Stay where you are – I'm bringing it through."

I crossed to the Titanic key rack on the wall. Took the key labelled "Fore cabin". Called for Poppy and headed for the door.

With Shirley free, we'd be able to haul Clarence's unconscious body on deck and get off the boat.

And then the breeze from the broken porthole accelerated the fire.

Kerrruuuuumph!

The flames roared. Shelves by the door collapsed and a burning cupboard toppled over.

A bonfire of wood and books and papers blocked the doorway.

I moved towards the inferno, but the heat drove me back.

The fire had closed off all but a small space in the middle of the doorframe. If I tried to scramble through I'd be flambéed before I'd even reached halfway.

Behind the flames I could see Fanny heaving on the door handle which locked in Shirley.

I shouted: "Fanny, I've got the key but I can't get through."

"Throw it through the fire," she screamed.

"I can't get near enough to aim accurately. The gap is too

small."

"Just throw it."

"If it falls into the flames, we've lost completely," I shouted.

Then Shirley started beating on the door.

Even above the crackle of the fire, I heard her yell: "Get me out. The cabin's filling with smoke."

Frantically, I hunted for anything I could use to bulldoze the burning shelves and cupboard to one side. But everything was either too large or already smouldering.

And then Professor Pettigrew's words came into my mind. "She may look like a softy but that Poppy is the most fearless dog I've ever known." She leapt through fire on stage every day.

Poppy was scampering up and down the cabin. She was in a frenzy of excitement.

I knelt down. Coaxed her towards me. Rubbed the sides of her head as I'd seen Fanny do. She licked my hand.

I said: "Poppy, you've got to do it."

I felt a fool as I said it. I knew she couldn't understand me. Or could she? She barked. Did that thing where she stands up on her hind legs and turns round.

Then her furry face snuffled in my hands. I was holding the key. I put it in her mouth. She shook her head from side to side as I'd seen her do on the stage at the Hippodrome.

And then she turned and ran to the far end of the cabin.

I pointed at the fire and said: "Jump, Poppy. Make it the greatest jump you've ever done."

But she settled down and pretended to sleep.

I said: "Poppy take the key to Fanny. Go, now."

She nuzzled her head on the floor, opened one eye and blinked. As if to say, if you're so keen on jumping through fire, you do it.

I shook my fists in frustration. I couldn't understand why Poppy wouldn't perform like she did for Pettigrew.

But I'd forgotten the whole point of his act. The dogs did the opposite of what he ordered them.

On the radio, the French horns jumped in with some perky arpeggios.

Dum-di-dum-di-dum.

"Poppy!" I shouted above the roar of the flames, the crescendo of the music. "Stay. Don't jump through the fire. Sit."

Poppy scrambled to her feet. Snuffled around for a moment.

Then she careened forwards towards the door, legs pounding. Her floppy ears flapped behind her like a pair of pennants.

Her hind legs bent to what seemed an impossible angle and she took off. She was fully three feet from the fire. For a second it looked as though she hung in the air like a fluffy puppet.

She reached the height of her jump, and then started to descend. But she'd misjudged. She would land in the pit of the fire, where the books and old maps were burning most fiercely. But then she thrust out her front legs. It seemed to propel her forward. She sailed through the gap in the fire.

On the other side, I heard Fanny shriek. "My God, she's smoking."

"And her still under sixteen," I yelled back. I was so relieved Poppy hadn't fallen into the flames I just couldn't stop myself.

Fanny shouted: "No, she's fine. It's just sweat. I've got the key. I'm letting Shirley out."

Through the flames, I could see Fanny attack the door. Saw it open and Shirley race out. She was coughing like a stoker but seemed otherwise unharmed.

"Make for the wheelhouse and climb up the ladder to the deck," I yelled. "Get into the row boat and head for the riverbank. Take Poppy with you."

I saw them turn and race towards the escape hatch in the storeroom – and safety.

I breathed a heavy sigh of relief.

To celebrate, Brunhilde warbled a few high notes and gave her coloratura a workout.

And then a fleshy arm locked around my neck. I felt my windpipe close up.

Clarence whispered in my ear. "I hurt my head. That ruddy dog tripped me. I'll finish it. But I'll finish you first."

With the drama of the key I'd not realised that Clarence had regained consciousness.

"Let me go," I croaked. "Can't you see the place is burning."

The arm tightened around my neck. Little stars of light flashed in my eyes. My brain felt so light I thought it would float away. Ten more seconds and the lights would go out.

I rammed my elbow backwards as hard as it would go. I caught Clarence right in the bread basket.

Ooooooomph!

The flesh of his belly caved inwards and the air went out of him.

I repeated the manoeuvre. And again.

One. Two. Three.

On the third thump I felt something harder. What little was left of the muscles around his solar plexus. His arm came free of my neck and he staggered backwards. I gulped a mouthful of air.

I swung round to face him. He was bent double gasping for air.

I said: "We have to get on deck or we die."

And then the couch exploded into flame.

I dashed forward, grabbed Clarence and pulled him towards the companionway. It was like dragging a sack of coal. The earlier blow to the head and my thumps in his stomach had done for him.

I got him on the lower steps of the companionway. Tried to push him up one at a time.

First step.

Second step.

Third step.

He was going to make it. But he had a last reserve of strength in him. He lashed back with his left leg. Caught me in the chest. Sent me sprawling on the floor. I scrambled to my feet. But Clarence had already clambered back down and dashed back into the cabin.

"My pictures," he screamed. "My fortune lay on the pier."

He headed towards the table with *Milady's Bath Night*. But the main stack of photos was already alight.

I turned back, ready to heave him out again.

And then the gas canister exploded.

Kerrrrrrrrpow!

The force of the blast blew out the portholes, blasted through the ceiling. I dived behind the cover of the companionway. A ball of flame roared past me like a devil's thunderbolt.

My ears popped as the oxygen was sucked out of the room. I gasped for breath. But the air in my nostrils felt like fire.

I scrambled out from behind the companionway. The flames in the cabin were now roaring white with fury. The heat forced me back. Beyond the wreckage, I could see the lifeless body of Clarence on the floor. His dead hand had clamped like a claw around *Milady's Bath Night*. The old pictures were burning with a bright orange flame.

But not all of them.

The blast had sent the title card through the air. It had landed near me. I grabbed it and thrust it into my pocket.

I turned and pounded up the companionway to the deck.

Behind me the fat lady hit a final top C. The orchestra pounded out three crashing chords. And then the radio died.

It should have been over because the fat lady had sung.

But it wasn't.

It was very far from being over.

Chapter 24

"I have to say I'm a smidgeon disappointed," said Frank Figgis.

"About what?" I asked.

"I'd have liked a picture of the interior of the boat on fire."

"Sorry to disappoint," I said. "Next time I'm in a raging inferno I'll hang around with my Box Brownie while the flames lick up my inside leg."

We were in Figgis's office. It was the morning after – and for me, at least, felt like it. A proof of the front page had just come up from the compositors. The headline screamed in the largest type the paper owned:

PIER KILLER DIES IN BOAT BLAZE

My report was accompanied by a picture of the smoking remains of the *Marie*. I'd batted out the piece on my old Remington at six o'clock that morning when I'd eventually made it back to the office.

The final events of the previous night still played through my mind like a nightmare newsreel.

The *Marie* had burned like one of those fire ships Sir Francis Drake sent in among the Spanish Armada. I'd scrambled up the companionway with the inferno roasting my backside every sweating step. As I'd made it to the footpath – by jumping across three feet of water onto the adjacent houseboat – Shirley and Fanny were guiding the tender into the riverbank. Poppy had barked exultantly. I'd helped them all ashore.

If we'd thought the drama was over, we were wrong. The explosion of the gas canister had woken everybody who lived on the nearby houseboats. They'd crowded out onto the footpath. By the time the fire brigade arrived on the scene – they'd been called by a neighbour – there was nothing they could do to save the

Marie.

Then the police turned up. Shirley, Fanny and I – with Poppy in tow – were hauled off to Shoreham Police Station to make statements. When the cops realised that Fanny was the daughter of a government minister, they'd arranged for a police car to drive her back to Piddinghoe Grange. Shirley and I – with Poppy – were left to make our own way back to Brighton in the MGB.

During the journey, I'd tried to ask Shirley about how the kidnap had happened. But she'd replied that she didn't want to talk about it and all she needed was to get some shuteye. I'd offered to put Shirley up at my flat – despite what the Widow would say – but she'd insisted on checking into a small hotel where she'd made a reservation. As I dropped her off, I'd said I would contact her as soon as I'd finished at the paper.

She said: "I guess, for you, missing a deadline is worse than missing a girlfriend." Then she'd shuffled wearily up the steps into the hotel. I'd watched her go, cursing the day I'd first encountered Clarence Bulstrode.

Poppy had bounded into the now-empty front seat of the MGB. "What do you think? Is it finally over for us?" I'd asked the mutt.

I must've been too tired to think. I'd been asking a poodle for advice on my love life. I'd shrugged. "Let's get you back to the worthy professor," I'd said. Poppy licked my ear.

After I'd delivered Poppy to Pettigrew's digs, I'd snatched a couple of hours' sleep at the flat before heading into the office for an early start.

And, I had to admit, there was nothing like the sight of a front-page splash to raise a journalist's spirits. I picked up the proof from Figgis's desk and read the headline again.

"We've beaten the *Argus* hands down on this story," Figgis said. "But we need to keep running so they don't catch us."

I said: "We're so far ahead even Roger Bannister couldn't catch us."

"You say that, but the *Argus* could still outsmart us on follow-up pieces if we're not quick on our feet. It's a pity you let those pictures of *Milady's Bath Night* go up in flames."

"I didn't have a fire-and-rescue squad with me at the time."

"Even so, we could have built a great picture spread around them."

"Not if you didn't want every clergyman and the Clean Up Brighton campaign on your back."

"I'm sure there was nothing more offensive in them than you see on the front page of *Reveille* every week. Anyway, as they're now ashes washing out to sea the question doesn't arise."

"Yes, and taking whatever clues to this mystery they may have held," I said.

Figgis nodded thoughtfully.

I reflected on a story lost. The content of the film would have made good copy.

Instead, I said: "I'm planning a feature on Poppy. If she hadn't leapt through the fire, Shirley would have died."

"Good idea," Figgis said. "And we need an exclusive interview with Miss Goldsmith. We want to know everything from the moment Clarence burst into Mrs Gribble's house to the time she was released from the *Marie*."

"Shirley didn't look like a woman willing to give an exclusive interview last night," I said.

"I'm relying on you to make sure she speaks to us and nobody else," Figgis said. "I don't want rival papers muscling in on our story. The nationals with their fat cheque books will be after this one."

I had an idea. It could keep Shirley away from the tabloid hounds – and give me a chance of repairing my relationship with her. Everyone a winner!

I said: "Shirley is putting up in a grotty B&B off the seafront. We could move her somewhere more comfortable – and secure. Then the nationals won't be able to interview her."

Figgis scratched his forehead. "Where had you in mind?"

"A suite at the Grand Hotel. We could get one of those gorillas that work in the circulation department – the muscle-bound blokes who load the papers onto the vans – to stand guard outside the door to prevent other journalists getting to her."

"Good idea – but what about the other hacks calling her on the dog and bone?"

"As the *Chronicle* will be picking up the bill, we can have a quiet word with hotel reception to ensure no incoming calls are switched through to the room unless they come from us. It wouldn't affect Shirley making outgoing calls, so she wouldn't know."

"And how do we stop her leaving the room?" Figgis asked.

"After all she's been through, if I know Shirley, she'll be only too happy to sample life on room service for a while."

Figgis reached for a Woodbine and lit up. Took a thoughtful drag. "Okay. Leave that with me. I'll set it up from here. You concentrate on getting the interview."

I stood up and moved to the door. Turned back to Figgis.

"I have an uneasy feeling this story isn't over yet," I said.

Figgis blew a smoke ring and grinned. "For the sake of our circulation, I do hope so."

I walked back into the frenzy of a newsroom chasing a story in all directions and not quite knowing where it would lead next.

Mark Hodges had been on the phone to the West Sussex Fire Brigade. He collared me as I passed his desk.

"They still haven't got the body out," he said.

"What's left of it," I said.

Phil Bailey barged into the office and made straight for me. "Just been round to Clarence's flat."

"His former flat," I said.

Phil nodded. "The cops are round there. Wouldn't let me in, but I sneaked round the back and looked through a window by standing on a wall. They're taking the place apart."

Sally Martin, who'd been taken off the woman's page to join the team working on the story, called across the office: "Just tried to get a comment from Lady Piddinghoe on the death of her nephew. She put the phone down on me."

Susan Wheatcroft, the business reporter, folded up her *Financial Times*, and ambled over. "You look tired, honeybunch."

"I've had a restless night," I said.

"Well, if you ever want a restful one, you know where to come. But not too restful, eh?" And she left me with one her saucy winks.

I sat down at my desk wondering what I should do next. It was true. I felt as tired as an old nag. The adrenalin of last night had drained out of me. I'd nailed the story about the murder of poor Fred Snout – and beaten the competition hands down. But I couldn't shake off the feeling that I'd only uncovered part of the tale.

Why had Clarence thought he'd make his fortune from an old What the Butler saw film? In fact, why had Marie told him his fortune waited for him on the pier? Had that just been the incoherent rambling of a dying woman? Or was there a deeper meaning behind it? Whatever the answer, it had produced tragic consequences.

Then there was the puzzle over why Venetia was being blackmailed. She'd told me a story which I knew was false. But why was she hiding the real reason? Could it be that what the blackmailer had on her was something even worse? And who was the mysterious blackmailer that got a cocker spaniel to do his dirty work?

There were too many questions. Not enough answers. Worse, I couldn't think of any way of finding the answers. I'd already interviewed everyone who knew anything. Some had been evasive. Some had lied. I was used to that. I could usually pick my way towards the truth. In the past, I'd been able to call on the odd tip from Ted Wilson. But even he wasn't speaking to me now. It seemed that I just had nowhere to turn.

My old captain's chair creaked as I leaned back in it and surveyed the newsroom.

I smacked my forehead with my hand.

Of course! There was one source of information I hadn't yet investigated.

Marie's scrapbook.

I'd liberated it from Clarence's flat and stuffed it into my desk draw when I'd arrived back in the office shortly after dawn. Since then, I'd been so busy, I'd forgotten it. I yanked open the drawer and pulled out the book. The old paper crackled as I flipped through the pages.

Most of the newspaper clippings in the book came from the nineteen-thirties, particularly around 1936, the time of the big fall-out between Marie and Venetia. It was almost as though Marie had known that she would never return to Piddinghoe but somehow wanted to retain a link to it. Perhaps keeping the scrapbook was a kind of therapy – her way of dealing with the pain of rejection by her sister and the decline of her career.

The scrapbook was packed with ephemera about Piddinghoe life. There must have been eighty or ninety pages of it. I read one or two of the articles that caught my eye. A fire had burnt a cottage in the village and a cowman and his family were now homeless. The council was planning a new road to bypass Piddinghoe. A Mrs Tomkinson had chaired the annual parish meeting where the main item on the agenda was whether to install a street light.

A longer cutting detailed the events of the annual Piddinghoe carnival in 1935. It had been opened by Lady Piddinghoe who'd been presented with a bouquet by ten-year-old Henrietta Houndstooth. A Mr Bert Entwhistle had won the bowling for a pig competition. And he and his wife and gone on to win the three-legged race. Miss Enid Pinchbeck, a kennel maid from

Jumpers Town, had won the prize for the best-trained dog. And Mrs Gorringe from Newhaven had rounded off what the writer called "a perfectly spiffing afternoon" – where did they find reporters in those days? – by playing a selection from Ivor Novello on her piano-accordion.

I turned the pages. There was more in the same vein. Parish council meetings. Flower shows. Weddings at the church. Vegetable growing competitions. Children's parties at the village hall. Page after page of it. The tedium of village life.

On the later pages, there were some cuttings about the erection of the statue to the first Marquess of Piddinghoe in Victoria Gardens. There were profiles of the sculptor – a member of the Royal Academy (no doubt the Piddinghoes would settle for nothing less) – and the engraver who'd made the plaque. He'd previously been a calligrapher who'd written the intertitles for silent films and retrained when the talkies made his task redundant. There was a photo – printed on photographic paper, so not a newspaper cutting – of him and Marie standing beside the plaque. He had his hand around her waist. She was gazing at the plaque with the kind of self-satisfied look she'd no doubt worn when taking a curtain call. She'd captioned the photo in her own hand: "Archie Cobbold and self. Job done."

I closed the scrapbook wondering what it all meant.

And then a thought struck me.

Surely there was one cutting missing? The most important cutting of all. The biggest story in the *Sussex Express* in 1936 would have been the apparent suicide of Susan Houndstooth. The paper would have covered the police investigation and carried a big report on the coroner's inquest. Swiftly, I turned the pages to check that I'd not missed the pieces. Marie's scissors had been busy but they'd clipped no news of Susan's death.

What a fool I'd been. I thumped my old Remington so hard I made the end-of-line bell ring.

If the *Sussex Express* had carried a report on Susan's inquest so would the *Chronicle*. In fact, I knew the paper had done so – because it was the very cutting I'd discovered Henrietta weeping over in the morgue. She'd told me about it when I visited her flat. Yet, such had been the pace of events, I hadn't read it.

I shoved the scrapbook back in my desk drawer, hurried across the newsroom and headed for the morgue.

Henrietta was stacking some buff files on the shelf behind her desk.

She turned as I entered and said: "And not a scorch mark in sight."

At the table, the Clipping Cousins put down their scissors and goggled.

I said: "What were you expecting? Colin Crampton grilled medium-rare?"

Henrietta said: "I'm sorry. I shouldn't have said that. The experience must have been mortifying."

"Only for Clarence," I said. "And he probably had a quotation or two to while away his final moments."

"Like 'Oh, death, where is thy string?'," said Mabel.

"It's 'sting'," said Elsie. "What would death be doing with a piece of string?"

"Are you sure it isn't 'sling'," said Freda. "After all, dead bodies would need something to hold them up."

As the Cousins started on one of their pointless squabbles, I pulled Henrietta to one side.

"I need to see a cutting," I said.

"That cutting?" she asked. "Originally, filed under Piddinghoe? Now correctly filed under Houndstooth, Susan?"

"Yes," I said. "But I don't want to upset you again."

"It's all right now. It was the disrespect more than anything that upset me – not to file a report on my mother's inquest under her own name. It was like carving the wrong name on her tombstone."

"I understand," I said.

"Wait here." Henrietta disappeared into the filing-cabinet stacks. She was back within thirty seconds carrying a brand new folder. She handed it to me.

I looked at the label on the outside. Neat in Henrietta's own handwriting. Houndstooth, Susan.

"It's right that she's in the proper place," I said.

"It helps," Henrietta said.

"A little?"

"Just a little."

"But not much?"

"The pain will never go away until I know how Mummy really died," she said.

I took the file back to my desk in the newsroom.

It was half an hour to the Midday Special deadline and the sound of typewriters hammering out copy was reaching its crescendo. Some people like to study in silence. Not me. Give me a newsroom nearing deadline any time. It sharpens the senses, focuses the mind.

I opened the file. There was a single cutting. A long one. The paper's report of Susan's inquest had run to several columns of small type. I began reading. Evidence had started with Dr Peasemould who'd conducted the post-mortem. He explained that death had been caused by the strangulation of the rope around the deceased's neck.

The coroner – a Dr Goodbody – had questioned why the neck had not been broken as was normal with hanging. Peasemould explained that the noose had not been tied the way a hangman would have done, with a knot that would have tightened and broken the neck on the fall. Therefore, the deceased had dangled on the rope and suffocated.

I could see why Henrietta had been upset by the cutting. I admired her courage for refiling it.

There had been some evidence of a prescription sedative in Mrs Houndstooth's bloodstream, but no drug of that kind had been found in the cottage. In any event, the trace in the blood was consistent with Mrs Houndstooth having taken a normal dose. Goodbody asked what the effect of the sedative would have been. Peasemould said it would make the taker sleepy.

There was some evidence about how the scaffolding and pulley came to be at the back of Susan's cottage. I already knew that from what Henrietta had told me when I'd visited her flat.

Next Inspector Roundhay from Lewes police described his investigation. He could find no evidence of foul play. The conclusion he'd reached was that the deceased had tied off the rope to the pulley on the top of the scaffolding in such a way that it could not reach the ground. She had fastened the other end of the rope around her neck and jumped.

Lady Piddinghoe was then called to give evidence. (There were apparently gasps in the courtroom when she entered wearing a costume in brilliant blue instead of the expected black at such proceedings). Lady Piddinghoe said she had noticed nothing unusual in her maid's demeanour in the days leading up to the sad event. Susan's death was, she said, a tragedy as she would now have to hire another lady's maid for The Season.

Mr Pinchbeck, an under-footman – so Lord Snooty had risen high since those far-off days – was called. He gave his evidence in a quiet voice and was told to speak up several times by the coroner. He'd complained that he was nervous. He'd admitted that Susan had recently become withdrawn. Cross-examined by Goodbody, he finally admitted that Susan's change of mood dated to the afternoon when she had helped him serve tea to Lady Piddinghoe and her sister, Marie Richmond. Shortly after, both Susan and Pinchbeck had heard shouting from the drawing room and then two crashes as crockery was broken. Susan had been first into the room, Pinchbeck said. He'd followed a few moments later and seen the confusion, turned to clear the broken tea things and briefly noticed a photograph lying among them.

He described what Henrietta had told me during my visit to her flat – how Marie had rushed from the house, Susan had helped Lady Piddinghoe to her room, and order was restored. When next he looked, the photograph had been removed. Pinchbeck went on to describe how Susan's character had changed in the days following the incident. She became withdrawn, hardly spoke and walked around with a permanent frown on her face. He put it down to an after-reaction to the unpleasant incident at the tea.

Pinchbeck described how, on the day of her death, Susan had complained that a migraine was coming on. Pinchbeck had taken it on his own authority to mention it to Lady Piddinghoe. Her ladyship had called Susan and given her some aspirin to help and sent her back to the cottage to rest.

Goodbody recalled Lady Piddinghoe to the stand. He pointed out that if Pinchbeck had noticed Susan was not herself, was she sure that she hadn't noticed anything? "In the best houses, one does not notice one's servants," she had told Goodbody.

"But," said Goodbody, "you noticed your lady's maid, even helped her, when she complained of migraine."

"One likes to think one has at least a few drops of the milk of human kindness," Lady Piddinghoe had replied.

After that, there didn't seem to be much else to say. Two more servants were called and corroborated Pinchbeck's evidence that Susan had become withdrawn and worried in the days following the incident. Goodbody summarised the evidence for the jury. It took them less than half an hour to return a verdict of suicide while the balance of the mind was disturbed.

I closed the file. Leant back in my chair and surveyed the newsroom. Cedric was touring the desks, collecting final copy for the Midday Special which would carry my sensational splash about Clarence's death. But there was an itch at the back of my mind that wouldn't go away. There was more to this story.

Henrietta had told me at her flat that she'd remembered her mother being snappy and bad tempered in the days before her death. She'd pestered her mother, as ten-year-old girls will, to tell her what was wrong. But all Susan would say was that she'd seen a photograph she'd rather not. Presumably the same photo Pinchbeck had noticed. But a photograph of what? Or whom? It couldn't have been the strange photograph of Marie standing next to the statue of Lord Piddinghoe which was pasted into the scrapbook, because that was taken after Susan's death.

And was it linked to the obsession which had finally sent Clarence over the edge?

"Any more copy for the subs, Mr Crampton?" Cedric broke in on my reverie.

"Not at the moment, Cedric. I'm just trying to understand the bizarre mind of Clarence Bulstrode, the man who was willing to kill because he thought his fortune lay on the pier."

"Yeah, read your copy on that one. A cracker of a story." He moved off, said over his shoulder: "I reckon that Clarence must have had a screw loose."

A screw loose.

Of course, Clarence had had a screw loose.

But there was another screw loose, wasn't there? Not a metaphorical one either. A real screw. I'd seen it with my own eyes. The screw that held the plaque on the statue of Lord Piddinghoe in Victoria Gardens. After years of neglect, it had worked itself free.

In her dying moments, Clarence had believed Marie – barely conscious – was trying to tell him that his fortune was hidden on the pier.

But that was wrong.

There was never anything for Clarence on the pier.

Not the Palace Pier.

Not the West Pier.

Not any pier anywhere.

What Marie – confused and delirious – was trying to tell her son was that his fortune was hidden on the peer.

On the statue of Lord Piddinghoe.

A peer of the realm.

I sat in my captain's chair feeling very cold. The raucous noise of the newsroom on deadline faded to a distant hum.

I put my left hand on the scrapbook, my right hand on the inquest report. I tried to absorb the salient facts from both. To understand what they meant. To make the links between them. Slowly, those facts started to make connections in my mind. And they told a new story. A shocking story. Of a secret kept at any cost. And a cold-hearted murder.

My mouth was dry and I'm not so sure my hands didn't tremble.

For if I was right, Clarence had not been the only killer.

And the other still walked free.

Chapter 25

I was standing next to Bill Compton, chief engineer at the *Chronicle*, staring up at the statue of the first Marquess of Piddinghoe in Victoria Gardens.

We were about to commit an outrage on the old gentleman.

Or at least an offence against Brighton Corporation's byelaws. They were posted on a large board close by.

Half an hour earlier, I'd been sitting at my desk horrified by the thought there was another killer on the loose. I'd had a suspicion but no proof. Now I was determined to find it.

I'd left my desk and descended to the *Chronicle*'s machine room where huge rotary presses rolled off the paper at thirty thousand copies an hour. The presses were already printing the Midday Special. The cavernous place sounded like there was a permanent thunderstorm rumbling through it.

I'd found Bill in the cubbyhole he called his office. I'd explained I needed his help on an "outside mission". I knew Bill was keen on "outside missions" because when the business was completed, the mission would be rounded off with a pint in the Wagon and Horses.

"Bring a screwdriver," I'd told him.

"Phillips?" he'd asked.

"Peter's, Paul's, Percy's – I don't care whose as long as it takes out screws."

Bill rolled his eyes. "I'll bring my toolbox."

He was standing by me now, holding it as we surveyed the statue.

"If I had that much pigeon poop on my head, I'd ask for an umbrella," Bill said.

"It's not his head we're interested in," I said.

"So is what we're going to do illegal?"

"Only slightly," I said. "But, don't worry."

When you're pulling off a scam in public, the trick is to look as though you're entitled to be doing it. Bill was wearing the green overalls he always sported in the machine room. He'd be taken for a council workman by any casual passer-by.

I'd equipped myself with a clipboard and a pencil. I looked like the junior official telling the workman what to do. I strutted about a bit in that bantam-cock walk which minor officials put on to make themselves look important.

I said: "I'd like you to take that plaque off. I'll have a look at what's behind it and then you can put the plaque back. Even tighten the loose screw."

Bill selected a screwdriver from his toolbox and went to work.

"I've read your stories about the pier murder. So how does this malarkey fit in?" he said as he worked away.

"There's a picture in Marie Richmond's scrapbook of her standing in front of this statue with the engraver – one Archie Cobbold – who made the plaque."

"Happy snap, then."

"More than that. It looked as though the pair knew one another well. He had is arm around her waist. And he'd a history of lettering those intertitle cards they used in the silent movies."

I pulled the title card of *Milady's Bath Night* out of my pocket. "I managed to salvage this from the ruin of the *Marie* last night," I told Bill. "Look at the whirls on the S – identical to those on the plaque. And there are several similarities among other letters."

"So written by the same hand," said Bill.

"I believe Marie knew Archie well from her silent-movie days. In her scrapbook, she'd captioned the picture: 'Job done'. That suggested to me they'd been doing something with the statue. If my hunch is right, I think we'll find something hidden behind the plaque."

Bill took out the last screw and lifted the plaque away. We both stared at a recess in the stonework about six inches by four inches. I peered in. It was about a foot deep. Although the recess had been sealed by the plaque, there was a thick layer of dust. A couple of spiders, alarmed by the light, scurried for safety. I reached in my hand. It closed around a small package. I pulled it out. The package was wrapped in a thick oilskin and tied with string. The oilskin had turned green with age.

"This is what I came for," I said. "You can put the plaque back now."

Bill had the sense not to ask what was in the package.

I dropped Bill off at the Wagon and Horses for his post "outside mission" pint, then headed for Prinny's Pleasure.

I had a special reason for not opening the package in the office. I wouldn't be able to do it without attracting an audience of thirty gawping reporters. I needed to study the contents closely. And in private. There would be no one in Prinny's Pleasure – and even landlord Jeff would probably be asleep behind the bar.

But as it turned out, he wasn't. I ordered a G and T – and asked for the loan of a pair of scissors. I seated myself at the corner table at the back of the bar and cut the string around the package. Over the years, the oilskin had become hard and I had to prise it open with care.

Inside I found a roll of film and a small blue envelope. The envelope had been addressed in a feminine hand with one word: Clarence. It felt damp but the seal had held over the years. Gently, I opened it and extracted a single sheet of paper. I unfolded it and read:

My dearest, darlingest Clarence,
By the time you read this, I will have left you. I do not believe it will be for ever, for one day we will be reunited and will live together in a Land of Milk and Honey.

But until that time, you will need money. I have provided for us as best I can. I am not ashamed of what I have done for I believe that

all of us must pay for the consequences of what we do. In this
package, you will find a roll of film. It was made many years ago,
before you were born. Later, for reasons I will not distress you with,
I had it – except for the last seconds – made into pictures for a What
the Butler Saw machine on Palace Pier. As long as you have this
film, there is one who will pay you well. Look at the pictures in it
closely – particularly in the last four seconds – and you will see why.
     Your loving Mumsie.

I picked up the film carefully. A little eddy of grey dust landed on
the table. The film felt as fragile as an autumn leaf.

I unspooled the first few frames and held them up to the light
to get a better view. They showed the title card – *Milady's Bath*
Night – the one I'd taken from the houseboat. Unrolling the film
was delicate work but slowly I spooled through it. It broke every
few feet and I ended up with several pieces scattered across the
table.

By the time, I reached the final frames, my fingers were sore.
I took a gulp of G and T.

I held the last couple of feet of the film up to the light. It
showed a half-length shot of Marie. I followed the action frame
by frame. She turns to the right and begins to raise her left arm.

I spooled the film further on.

The arm was fully up now. And she was waving, her hand
rotating in a haughty circular motion.

I gasped. Felt sweat break out on my forehead. I swallowed
hard.

Those last few frames explained everything.

A secret had travelled across half a century and lay before me
in these mouldering pieces of celluloid on a bar-room table. It
was the evidence I needed.

I carefully rewound the pieces of film and replaced them with
the letter in the oilskin.

Then I thought about my next move. I couldn't make it

without involving the police. But not Tomkins. I wondered whether Ted Wilson was still mad at me for quoting his comments about the Snout murder case. I'd sensed Ted hadn't been pleased Tomkins had frozen him out of the case. But if my deductions were right, what I'd discovered was even bigger. It would make Ted's name as a top 'tec in every police force in the country – and that would mean he'd owe me a favour or two in the future.

I walked over to the bar. Jeff was stacking beer bottles on a shelf.

"Need to use your phone," I said.

"Cost you four pence."

"I'll give you a quid."

"What's the catch?"

"I get privacy for my call."

Jeff frowned while he thought about that. Decided he wasn't likely to make nineteen shillings and eight pence profit so easily any other way and said: "I'll be in the back, stocktaking."

I waited for Jeff to close the door to the stockroom before dialling a number at Brighton police station.

The phone was answered after three rings. "Ted Wilson."

I said: "Don't put the phone down."

"Why shouldn't I?"

"Because if you do you'll kick yourself from here to the Kent border for not making the arrest I'm about to offer you."

There was a moment's silence at the other end of the line while Ted thought about that. "Tell me more," he said.

I spoke for three minutes. Ted listened in silence.

"So what do you want out of this?"

"An opportunity to interview the suspect before you make the arrest."

"Why doesn't that surprise me?"

"So no jangling bells and uniformed plods breaking down doors," I said.

"Very well. But I'll need to bring my new detective sergeant – Graham Toole-Mackson."

"So have we a deal?"

"We have a deal."

"One more point," I said. "Bring two sets of handcuffs."

I replaced the receiver before Ted had time to ask why.

An hour later at Piddinghoe Grange, Pinchbeck showed us into the blue drawing room.

I led the way. Ted Wilson followed with his new oppo Graham Toole-Mackson, a tall man with a shock of dark hair and an infectious sense of fun. He was going to need it.

Venetia was sitting on the divan. She put aside a copy of *Country Life* and stared at us. Hostility burnt in her eyes. Fanny was at the writing table on the far side of the room. She turned in surprise as we entered.

Lord Piddinghoe rose from his wing chair. His moustache bristled over pouting lips. He took a couple of steps towards me. Punched his fists on his hips in a petulant gesture. "What the hell are you doing here?" he said.

He pointed at Ted and Graham: "And who are these Johnnies?"

"These 'Johnnies', as you so graciously put it, are Detective Inspector Ted Wilson and Detective Sergeant Graham Toole-Mackson from Brighton police station. And their presence here will become clear when you've heard what I've got to tell you."

"There's nothing you can tell me I want to hear," Piddinghoe said.

"Let him speak." Venetia had risen and crossed the room. She rested a gentle hand on her son's shoulder. "Why don't you sit down again?"

Like a little boy who'd been told off, he returned to his seat.

"You can go, Pinchbeck," he said.

"I'd rather he stayed," I said.

Piddinghoe snorted. "Damned fellow's giving orders to my servants now."

Pinchbeck shifted uneasily from one foot to the other. "Should I go or stay, my lord?" he asked.

"Better stay," Piddinghoe said. "Let's get it over with."

I said: "Frances will have told you about our adventure last night – about the fire on the houseboat and how Clarence Bulstrode died."

"No great loss from what I hear," Piddinghoe said. "The fellow was a bit weak up top. Couple of candles in the chandelier had burnt out years ago, from what I've heard."

"Clarence had been devoted to his mother," I said. "To be frank, she'd smothered him, worshipped him to the point where he'd developed a distorted view of himself. He found it difficult to deal with other people. Even to develop his own thoughts. That's why he fell back all the time on quotations. And it's also, in my opinion, why he took his mother's dying words too literally."

"What dying words?" Venetia said.

"When Marie was close to death in the Royal Sussex County hospital, she mumbled something about Clarence finding his fortune on the pier. He took it to mean Palace Pier."

Venetia turned to Fanny. "Did you know about this?"

Fanny's cheeks coloured. "Not until last night, Grandmama."

I intervened swiftly. "Without Frances's brave help, I might not be here now," I said.

"That's the trouble with good deeds," Piddinghoe grunted. "Cads and bounders get the benefit."

I ignored him and said: "In searching for his fortune on the pier, all Clarence found was an old What the Butler Saw film called *Milady's Bath Night*. He stole it, examined the pictures closely frame by frame, but couldn't find anything in it that would make him a penny, let alone a fortune. And, in any event, all the pictures Clarence had stolen perished in last night's fire.

All except the title card."

For the first time since I'd known her, Venetia gave a smile that looked as though it contained genuine pleasure. "So those disgusting pictures are gone for ever," she said.

"Good riddance to bad rubbish," Piddinghoe added.

"But it wasn't the end of the story for Clarence," I said. "Two nights after he'd stolen *Milady's Bath Night*, he returned to the pier. He had convinced himself that there must be something else that would make his fortune. While he was hiding in the coconut shy, he was surprised by the pier's night-watchman, Fred Snout. There was a struggle and Fred was killed."

"I'm sorry for poor Mr Snout," Venetia said. "But I can't see what this has to do with me." Her hand swept expansively around the room. "With any of us."

"But you know that's not true, Lady Piddinghoe," I said. "Because the root of all this trouble is *Milady's Bath Night*. And the star of the film is not your twin sister Marie Richmond."

I paused.

"It is you, Lady Piddinghoe."

The colour drained from Venetia's face. Her hands shook. When she spoke, her voice was little more than a whisper. "That's ridiculous."

"More than ridiculous!" roared Piddinghoe. "It's an actionable slander. Pinchbeck, throw this gutter journalist out."

Wilson stepped forward. "I don't think that would be advisable."

Toole-Mackson moved to block the door.

Fanny had risen from the writing desk and crossed the room. Now she sunk into an armchair. Her eyes had filled with tears. She looked at Venetia: "Can this be true?"

Venetia ignored her. Put the evil eye on me. "You dare to smear my name without a shred of proof. You've just said the pictures burnt to ashes. I'll sue you and that rag you work for until your bank accounts run as dry as the desert."

"Don't call your lawyer just yet," I said. "The What the Butler Saw pictures certainly burnt, but they'd been made from a sixteen-millimetre celluloid film. I have seen a copy of that film. I was surprised to discover that the final four seconds of it hadn't been included in *Milady's Bath Night*. In the early years of the century, silent films were usually shot at sixteen frames a second. So that means there are sixty-four individual frames – you could call them still photographs – of the actress in those last four seconds."

"I've had enough." Venetia stood and headed for the door.

"Stay."

The room fell silent. The cry had come from Fanny. Her face was stricken. "Please stay. I need to hear the truth," she said. "Please, Grandmama. No more secrets. No more lies. Tell me the truth. Whatever it is."

Venetia paused. Returned to the divan. Sat down again.

I said: "As well as the original film from which *Milady's Bath Night* was made, I've also seen a letter which your sister wrote to her son Clarence. Marie had intended that Clarence should read the letter after her death. In the event, he died before he could do so. In the letter, Marie tells Clarence to pay particular attention to the last four seconds of the film. At first, I hadn't been able to understand why the last four seconds hadn't been included in *Milady's Bath Night*. Especially as the model gives a charming little wave to say farewell. I thought it was because there wasn't room on the What the Butler Saw machine for all the individual photographs that had to be made from the film. But that wasn't the reason was it, Lady Piddinghoe?"

"No," she said.

"It was because the last four seconds gave away who the actress really was. Your left hand hadn't been visible in the rest of the film. It was either in the bath water, hidden by a towel, or tucked seductively behind your back. In fact, not visible until you raised your left hand to wave."

"Call that proof," Piddinghoe grunted. "Millions wave with their left hand. Even women," he added, as if that proved the matter beyond doubt.

"True," I said. "But no other left hand bears a distinctive engagement ring." I pointed across the room. "The same ring Lady Piddinghoe proudly shows off in the Orpen portrait above the fireplace."

Venetia's elegant shoulders slumped. Her eyelids drooped. Her mouth dropped open. For the first time since I'd met her, she looked fully her seventy-nine years. Slowly, she looked around the room at each of us. At me last. She stiffened her back. Pulled herself together.

She held the room in silence. Then she said: "Yes, I appeared in the film."

"Grandmama, you didn't!" Fanny's eyes brimmed with unshed tears.

"Cavorting in a bathroom like a common strumpet." Piddinghoe's face flushed. "And watched by a fellow with a film camera."

Venetia looked sadly at Piddinghoe. "Charles, I'm so sorry."

I said: "Why didn't you remove the ring while the film was being shot?"

Venetia sank back on the divan's cushions. "It's a question I've asked myself a thousand times over the years. Partly I think it was because I had no idea what the filming would involve. It never occurred to me that viewers would be able to identify a ring. But mainly it was because the ring had become part of me from the moment Algernon slipped it on my finger. Something that would never leave me until the day I died – and, perhaps, not even then."

I said: "The story you told us yesterday – about a liaison – with Edward the Seventh was a lie, wasn't it?"

"Strictly speaking, yes," Venetia said.

"But it was a very subtle lie, one that is based on truth. You told us that Marie took your place for a liaison with King Edward. In fact, it was you who took Marie's place in the film. That was a clever inversion of the truth. But you never had a romantic liaison with the King. You were already in love with Algernon, your future husband."

"Yes. It seemed like a dream. The draper's daughter marrying into one of the finest of England's aristocratic families. I lived every moment to the full. I toured the salons of London and Paris buying the finest gowns. I was determined that everywhere Algernon took me as his fiancée, I would dress to make him proud. Ascot, Henley, Goodwood – shooting parties in Scotland, yachting at Cowes – the summer of 1908 seemed endless. Everywhere I went I dressed to show I was worthy of being an earl's fiancée – and one who would, in the fullness of time, have every reason to expect she would become a marchioness."

"And these fine clothes from Worth and Givenchy and the like would have cost many hundreds of pounds."

"Thousands. If you include the hats. The boots and shoes. The gloves. The evening bags. The riding clothes. I had a wardrobe fit for a princess."

"But not the bank balance to pay for it," I said.

"No. In due course, I planned to approach my father. He'd always been generous in the past. I truly believed he would help me to meet my financial obligations. I'd have explained that my allowance was inadequate. That I needed to make an impression in the right circles. And that because I was to make such a good marriage, he would have no further financial responsibility for me."

"But then, shortly after your engagement, your father went bankrupt. No doubt he'd been hiding his financial problems in the way proud men do. Much worse, he killed himself."

Venetia raised a surprised eyebrow. "You know about that?"

"I've done my research," I said. I didn't mention Toupée Terry.

"Research? Snooping I call it," Piddinghoe said.

"Be quiet, Charles," Venetia snapped.

"So you agreed to appear in *Milady's Bath Night* for money."

"How did you know?" Venetia asked.

"Because it's the main reason why women agree to take their clothes off on film."

"But that's close to being a…a harlot," Fanny said.

Venetia swung round towards her, eyes blazing: "How dare you!" she screamed. "Don't presume to judge me from the comfort of your pampered upbringing. Good home. Good family. Expensive education. You've had everything. I had to fight for every tiny advantage. Don't ever think you know what it was like for me."

Fanny collapsed in tears. She leapt from her chair and rushed from the room. I moved to follow her. Then checked myself. Time to console Fanny later. My business here wasn't finished.

I moved closer to Venetia and said quietly: "Tell us what it was like."

She shrugged. "I was facing ruin. I owed seven hundred pounds, had little income and no way of repaying my debts. Unwisely, I had taken out loans from certain gentlemen in the City of London who specialised in lending money to young women in the kind of position I found myself."

"With expectations," I said.

"You have my point, Mr Crampton. But with my father bankrupt – and dead – no allowance, and my marriage still several months off, these gentlemen became very pressing in their demands."

"Could you not have asked your future husband for help?"

"I considered the possibility. He would have seen my plight, but his father was a man of Victorian rectitude and thrift. I knew that he would disapprove of my financial folly. And if he withdrew his consent to the marriage… I dismissed the prospect of borrowing from my future in-laws out of hand. And then Sybil

– Marie as she was then universally known – came to see me."

I said: "She was already a successful music-hall star and siren of the silent-movie screen. Surely she would have money she could've lent you?"

"My sister and I had reached a position where we tolerated one another," Venetia said. "It was a position that was to worsen as the years rolled by, but at the time, we did no more than accept one another's company. I knew that if I borrowed from her, she would hold an obligation over me for life. She was that kind of woman.

"But, as it was, Marie came to me with a proposition which seemed, at first, as fortuitous as it was outrageous. It is true that it was she rather than I who attracted the favourable attentions of a certain royal personage. I had already heard the tittle-tattle. In those days, society gossip transmitted rumours faster than Mr Marconi's wireless apparatus.

"What I didn't know was that Marie had also developed a scheme which made money at a rate faster than I foolishly spent it. It transpired that some wealthy gentlemen were prepared to pay for private films to be made for their personal enjoyment."

"Films? You mean indecent films that would be seized by the police?" Piddinghoe said.

"Yes. Films that would put a rise in the Old Bill's truncheons," I said.

Venetia sniffed as though the whole thing was beneath her. "In any event, Marie had developed a profitable trade in these…entertainments. She had been commissioned by a mill owner from Bradford to make a film of her bathing. The arrangement was always that the film would be made on the strict understanding that it would be viewed by no one other than the gentleman who commissioned it.

"Arrangements had been made with a film-maker from Paris who specialised in this discreet work to come to London. But on the day the filming was due to take place, Marie received an urgent command to accompany her royal mentor to a house party in Scotland. She was beside herself. On the one hand, she could not refuse the King – not without being banished from his circle for ever. On the other, she had taken the advance payment of seven hundred and fifty pounds from her client.

"She bluntly proposed that I should take her place in the film. We were identical twins. She had never met the Parisian film-maker before. And the mill owner had only ever seen her at a distance on the music-hall stage. She proposed to give me five hundred pounds of the fee. Naturally, I argued for all of it. But Marie was as tough as she was capricious. We finally settled on six hundred pounds. It was enough to settle my most pressing debts and see me through until my marriage. It went against every fibre of my being, but what was the alternative? And, in any event, the film would always purport to be of Marie. The buyer had promised totally secrecy. And Marie herself vowed she would never mention it to a soul."

"So you became a star of the silver screen?"

"Reluctantly, yes, Mr Crampton."

"But the film did not remain secret?"

"No. Although I have every reason to believe the mill owner was as good as his word."

I said: "But when Marie's career collapsed, she revealed that she had kept a copy of the film herself. And that unless you were prepared to pay her 'a pension', as she no doubt called it, the film and your part in it would become public."

I barely heard Venetia's whispered: "Yes."

"And, initially, you refused," I said. "But then Marie demonstrated how serious she was. She piled pressure on you by having a What the Butler Saw version of the film displayed on Palace Pier. But she left out the final frames which identified you."

I looked around the room. Pinchbeck was twitching from foot to foot by the drinks table. Piddinghoe, in his wing chair, stroked his moustache nervously. Venetia sat pale and composed on the divan. Wilson had taken up a position by a bureau where he could watch all of them. Toole-Mackson blocked the door.

I said: "And it was at this point, Lady Piddinghoe, that *Milady's Bath Night* led you to murder."

Chapter 26

Lord Piddinghoe shot out of his chair and wagged his finger at me. "The fellow should be put down like a mangy mongrel."

The whisky veins in his cheek strobed like neon lights. A bead of spittle appeared at the side of his mouth. "I'll be in the library." He moved towards the door.

Venetia rose from the divan. "I'll deal with this, Charles." She turned to me. "Mr Crampton, your presence is no longer required. Get out of my house and never return."

I frowned: "Not just yet. I'm the guest who won't leave until he's had his say."

Wilson stepped forward: "Everyone will stay where they are."

Piddinghoe subsided into his chair. Venetia sat on the divan, composed her hands on her lap and studied her nails. Pinchbeck fidgeted from foot to foot by the drinks table.

I said: "Your reluctant decision to appear in *Milady's Bath Night* rescued you from your debts, Lady Piddinghoe, but it came back to haunt you. And, as you saw it, threaten everything you held dear – the love of your husband, the respect of your family, your place in society."

I had Venetia's attention again. Her nails could, apparently, wait. "The fact of the matter is that I couldn't bear my late husband to know what I'd done," she said. "I'd hidden it from him before our marriage. I couldn't face telling him after. I felt ashamed about appearing in the film. I had to save my husband from sharing in that shame. That's why I paid Marie for so many years. And that is the truth."

"But it is not the whole truth, Lady Piddinghoe. Back in 1936, you had two meetings with Marie, didn't you?"

"I seem to recall that is so."

"The evidence I have is that the first meeting was cool but civilised. I infer that Marie laid out her financial predicament, mentioned the fact that she held a copy of *Milady's Bath Night*, and made a polite request for her 'pension'. You would have been shocked to learn that Marie had a copy of the film. But you would have wanted time to consider the implications of that news. Most importantly, to consider what you could do about it. From what I've seen of you, Lady Piddinghoe, you are a woman who calculates carefully before making a move."

Venetia bowed her head slightly to accept the compliment.

"But you had forgotten that identical twins don't only look alike," I said. "Sometimes they think alike. And Marie was a calculator, too. I expect she worried that now you knew about the existence of a second copy of *Milady's Bath Night*, you would make an attempt to steal it. I learnt from the late Clarence that it was a few years before the last war when Marie arranged for the locks to be changed at her flat and bars put over some of the windows."

"I may have done many things, Mr Crampton, but I am not a thief."

"No, you realised that stealing the film would not work. But you had angered Marie by dismissing her request for financial help out of hand. And your hope that the problem would go away was shattered when Marie visited the Grange the second time."

"Yes."

"She brought a photograph from the film – one of the frames that showed you with your engagement ring. They say a picture is worth a thousand words. That photo must have been like a thousand threats to your hopes of a happy future."

"Yes."

"And you were furious. There was a row. Crockery was smashed."

"Yes. I was at the end of my tether. Paying what Marie wanted would reduce me close to penury – but not paying would bring disgrace to me and my husband. In my anger, I attacked Marie."

"But afterwards, in cold reflection, you realised you had no choice but to pay her," I said.

"Reluctantly, yes. I faced a lifetime of penny pinching."

"But the alternative was worse," I said.

"I exchanged a number of letters with Marie as we haggled over how the arrangement would work. By this time, I no longer trusted my sister to keep any promise she made. Eventually, we agreed she would hand over the original sixteen-millimetre film from which *Milady's Bath Night* had been made – including the vital final four seconds. In return, I would write a letter instructing my bank to make monthly payments to Marie until her death and provide her with a copy of the letter."

"So if you stopped paying the money, Marie would at least have evidence to back up any allegations she made," I said. "You would've had to explain why you were making monthly payments to her."

"You are correct, Mr Crampton. Marie sent me the sixteen-millimetre film which I burnt in the fireplace in my boudoir. I sent her the letter. No doubt if you search hard enough, you will find it among her private papers."

"And, of course, Marie could also claim that the *Milady's Bath Night* on Palace Pier was also you. The payments would have supported her story."

Venetia sighed. "It was too late to do anything about that. Trying to remove it from the pier would just have raised suspicions. In any event, it did not contain the final four seconds which positively identified me. If it came to the matter, I would deny it. I was confident that the word of a marchioness would trump that of a faded film star."

"But why stop the payments now – after all these years?" I asked.

"Because the cupboard is bare, Mr Crampton. More than bare – mortgaged to the hilt and in hock to money lenders. Only Charles's ministerial salary is keeping us afloat. And even he has to shoot and sell rabbits to pay for his brandy."

Piddinghoe piped up: "Good God, she knows, blast it."

For a moment, the sharp lines on Venetia's face softened as she looked at her son. "I've always known, Charles."

"But all of those payments for nothing, Lady Piddinghoe," I said. "Because, beside the prints of *Milady's Bath Night* used in the What the Butler Saw machine, Marie also had a second copy of the sixteen-millimetre film made. The one I discovered today."

"Duplicitous bitch."

"And because she didn't trust you, she wanted to hide it somewhere completely safe. Then she had a piece of luck. The engraver your family hired to make and fix the plaque on the statue of the first Marquess of Piddinghoe was an old friend from her silent-film days. He'd originally lettered the intertitle cards. With his help, she hid the film in the very last place any member of your family would think of looking – in a recess behind the plaque on the statue. I imagine it gave her an extra thrill to know that every time you looked at the statue you were close to the film that could destroy you."

"Odious weasel woman."

"It's a little late for name calling now, Lady Piddinghoe. In any event, Marie wasn't the only person who realised it was you who appeared in the film."

Venetia glared at me. "I don't know what you mean."

I said: "When the crockery was smashed at that second tea party, your lady's maid Susan Houndstooth rushed into the room to see what had happened. She found you unconscious on the floor and Marie screaming at you. But she also saw something else. She saw the photograph Marie had brought to threaten you with. It was, according to evidence given at Susan's inquest, lying on the table among the ruin of the tea cups. Susan immediately recognised the ring on your finger. How could she not? She saw it every day as she manicured your nails. She realised the enormity of this to your position. So while you were being carried to your room, she quietly took the photo and placed it in a private place in your boudoir. You would've known that only Susan could have done that."

"This is pure invention," Venetia snapped.

I ignored her and said: "In the days after the tea party, Susan recognised the full implications of what she had seen. Of course, there would be a scandal that could destroy your family. But worse, if that happened, all the other families, like hers, that relied on the Piddinghoe estate, would suffer, too. They could lose their livelihoods and their homes. Her daughter has told me how Susan withdrew into herself. If a child noticed that, you would certainly have done so. You'd reluctantly decided to pay Marie – but if the secret were to leak from another source, those payments would have been like throwing money into the River Ouse. Worse, from your point of view, it was a servant who knew – and you had no respect for the ability of servants to keep secrets."

"That is rubbish. I trusted Susan implicitly."

"At Susan's inquest, you said that servants weren't noticed in the best houses."

Venetia waved away the remark. "I was under pressure at the time."

"Maybe. But you could see that Susan was under greater pressure – and you were afraid that eventually the pressure would explode and she would tell someone what she'd seen. And your life, as you imagined it, would be ruined."

"I was confident Susan would never breathe a word of it."

"But that isn't the case. In fact, Susan's daughter believes her mother would have carried the secret to her grave. Except, Lady Piddinghoe, you'd decided the secret would not be safe until she was in her grave."

"What are you suggesting?" Venetia snapped.

"I admit that I now move from fact to speculation. However,

my theory ties in with all the evidence I've collected. I imagine that the knowledge that Susan knew your secret must've preyed on your mind. You wanted to kill her, but could think of no way to do it without risking your own freedom.

"And then fate played into your hands. Repairs were needed to Susan's cottage. Builders erected scaffolding and installed a rope and pulley to hoist building materials onto the roof. What if you could stage Susan's death to look like suicide – that she had hung herself from the scaffolding? You knew that it was becoming common talk among other servants that she had become depressed – what better backstory to give your plan credibility?

"But you still faced the problem of how to overpower Susan and hang her from the scaffolding. I've been told by a witness – Susan's daughter – that you spent an unusual amount of time watching the building work. No doubt you were observing how the rope-and-pulley system operated. Then, a day or two later – it was Good Friday, 1936 – you heard that Susan had been complaining to the other servants about suffering from a migraine. And you saw your opportunity. You gave her two tablets to take. You told her they contained aspirin. In fact, as the post-mortem revealed, they were powerful sedatives. You told Susan to return to her cottage and rest. You knew there would be no workmen at the cottage because it was a bank holiday. And Susan's daughter had been taken to the Stations of the Cross service at the local church by another family.

"You went to the cottage where Susan was drowsy, perhaps even asleep, from the effects of the sedative. You strangled her – and here, I accept, I'm guessing – using rope similar to that on the pulley so that the marks on her neck would be consistent. Then you hauled her body outside, tied a noose from the pulley's rope around her neck, hauled her up and tied off the rope to make it look as though Susan had jumped."

Venetia leant back on the divan. Her lips curled into an

indulgent smile. "I had low expectations of you, Mr Crampton. And you have not met even those. If you publish a word of that fiction in the scandal sheet you call a newspaper, I will sue you through every court in the land. You have not a shred of proof."

I turned towards Lord Snooty. "Oh, but we do, don't we, Mr Pinchbeck."

Lord Snooty had edged towards the door. He shifted uncomfortably from one foot to another. His eyes darted from side to side like a cornered fox.

He turned to Lord Piddinghoe. "I don't know what this gentleman is suggesting, my lord."

"Damned if I do myself," Piddinghoe said. "This whole business has left my mind spinning."

"Then let me explain," I said. "A few days ago, Lady Piddinghoe wrote to Marie to say that she could no longer make the monthly payments. Marie telephoned Lady Piddinghoe from a call box – it was the last thing she did in her life. I believe that during the conversation she begged Lady Piddinghoe to continue making the payments. When Lady Piddinghoe tried to explain that there was no money left, I suspect Marie, herself desperate, turned to threats. I imagine the conversation became heated, as it did during the crockery-smashing tea party. And, you, Pinchbeck overheard some of that conversation. Perhaps an incriminating comment or two. In any event, it was enough to make you realise the truth of something you'd long wondered about. Whether Susan Houndstooth really had killed herself – or whether she had been helped on her way."

"I do not listen at keyholes," Pinchbeck said with forced dignity.

"You wouldn't be the first butler to do so. I was telling some colleagues only the other day about the late Lord Colin Campbell's butler, who was another keyhole spy. But you already had other reasons for wondering whether Susan's death had been suicide, didn't you?"

"I don't know what you mean."

"Earlier today, I read a report of the coroner's inquest into Susan's death. I hadn't realised that you were an under-footman in those days. You gave evidence that you entered the drawing room after Susan when the crockery went flying. In your evidence you said you'd seen a photograph on the tea-table."

Pinchbeck fidgeted with buttons on his jacket. "Doesn't mean I saw what was in the photograph."

"It was the photograph of a naked woman, wasn't it?"

"It might have been."

"I'm not suggesting the significance of the photograph immediately hit you as it did with Susan. You didn't have the woman's eye for detail. When a man sees a picture of a naked woman, his eyes are not naturally drawn to the fingers. But as the tragedy developed, I suspect you pondered on it and developed your suspicions. You have harboured those suspicions for many years. I believe they started at the inquest when you learnt that Susan had traces of a sedative in her blood, rather than the aspirin Lady Piddinghoe claimed to have given her. And they turned to fact when you overheard Lady Piddinghoe's row on the telephone a few days ago."

Pinchbeck stood stiffly to attention. "I can assure you, my lady, that I have never entertained the thoughts which this…this person has ascribed to me."

"In that case, you will be able to explain why you sent a blackmail threat to Lady Piddinghoe and arranged for the money to be collected from behind a telephone box in Ashdown Forest two nights ago."

Piddinghoe exploded. "Is this true, Pinchbeck?"

"I have never collected money from behind a telephone box in Ashdown Forest," Pinchbeck wailed.

"That I am prepared to accept. Instead, you arranged for a trained dog to do your dirty work for you. I watched it snaffle the loot in its jaws."

"Where would I get a dog?" Pinchbeck said.

"Earlier today, I read a press cutting about the village fête in Piddinghoe in 1935. A Miss Enid Pinchbeck won the prize for the best-trained dog. Pinchbeck is an unusual name and it would be a reasonable assumption that she was your sister – or at least a close relative. The cutting included the detail that Enid was a kennel maid and lived at Jumpers Town. The place is in Ashdown Forest and less than a mile from where Lady Piddinghoe left the pay-off money behind the telephone box. Too much of a coincidence. I suspect Enid still lives in Jumpers Town and still trains dogs. Besides, you would have needed an accomplice to make the phone call which Lady Piddinghoe took in the phone box – a voice she wouldn't recognise."

Pinchbeck stood stiffly erect. "I wish to state this is all conjecture," he said.

I said: "I took a picture of the dog. It was a cocker spaniel. It had distinctive markings which will be easy to identify. I think Detective Inspector Wilson's colleagues will find it at your sister's kennels when they call shortly. I doubt whether Enid will be able to provide an adequate explanation for what the dog was doing in Ashdown Forest in the middle of the night. The officers may also find the package when they search your sister's house. I'm betting you haven't had time to retrieve it from her yet."

I looked at Pinchbeck. Pink blotches had appeared on his cheeks. Snot ran down his nose. His hands shook. A wet stain appeared in his trouser crotch. Lord Snooty would confess everything he knew to save his own skin.

The butler was a broken man.

Venetia's eyes stared ahead at some unseen point in the distance. A vein throbbed in the side of her neck. A nervous tongue flicked over her dry lips.

I turned to Wilson. He nodded at Toole-Mackson who pulled handcuffs from his pocket and moved towards Pinchbeck.

Wilson crossed the room to Lady Piddinghoe. As he passed

me he whispered from the side of his mouth: "Forget what I said the other day. Normal service is resumed."

Wilson placed a hand gently on Venetia's shoulder. He said: "Lady Piddinghoe, I am arresting you for the murder of Susan Houndstooth. You do not have to say anything, but anything you do say may be taken down and given in evidence."

Venetia turned her head slowly towards him. A single tear welled in her eye. It hovered for a moment on her lower lid. And then she blinked. The tear dropped free. It glided, like a lonely raindrop, down her cheek.

She didn't brush it away.

I left Toole-Mackson arresting Pinchbeck, stepped through the door into the hall – and came face-to-face with Fanny.

Her eyes were swollen from crying. But there were no tears now.

"It's bad, isn't it?" she said.

"The worst," I said. "Your grandmother has been arrested for murdering Susan Houndstooth, her former lady's maid. Pinchbeck is being charged with blackmail. He'd suspected for years that Susan's death wasn't suicide. Then he heard Venetia incriminate herself during a phone call with Marie a few days ago. I expect he will turn Queen's evidence in Venetia's trial to gain a lower sentence for himself."

We walked toward the door and stepped out onto the terrace which ran along the front of the house.

"This is my fault. I should never have agreed to spy on you," Fanny said.

"You were sent on a false mission," I said. "Venetia wasn't honest with you about what was at stake."

"If only I'd said no to Grandmama, but I've never been able to refuse her."

"You shouldn't blame yourself. It wasn't your idea to lift the lid on this snake pit."

"But I helped to. And now I expect Daddy will have to resign."

"Yes. After the Profumo affair, Prime Minister Macmillan won't want another member of the government tainted by a scandal."

"Daddy doesn't say much, but I think it's only his government salary which keeps the Grange afloat. He might have to sell up."

"I don't know," I said. "Perhaps he could open the place to the public at half-a-crown a head – like the Duke of Bedford at Woburn Abbey."

"Daddy would never agree to that. He hates ordinary people."

"Especially reporter Johnnies," I said.

Outside we looked over the countryside towards the River Ouse. The sun had come out and the woods and fields sparkled with that brilliant green the way they do in June when the leaves are freshly out of bud.

"Perhaps I'll get a job," Fanny said.

"At the knicker factory?"

"Starting at the bottom – like you said." She tried a laugh, but it didn't work. "What will happen to Grandmama?"

"I don't know. There will be a trial, certainly. It depends what further information comes to light."

"Everyone will know," she said.

"The truth should never be hidden," I said. "And whatever happens, never forget this started years ago when Venetia decided to appear in a risqué film because she desperately needed some money. She created her own nightmare because she was never able to live with the consequences of what she'd done."

Fanny gazed wistfully over the countryside. The shadow of a lone cloud chased across the landscape.

"I just can't understand why two sisters – identical twins – should hate each other so much," she said.

"I think it started with envy – and then just got out of control. Marie envied the fact that Venetia had found true love while she only had affairs – and a sad marriage of convenience. Venetia envied Marie because she evoked warmth and happiness in everyone who knew her – and because she attracted the admiration of the King. Envy is just one of the seven deadly sins, but it encourages the other six."

"And their envy eventually destroyed one another," Fanny said sadly.

"But all his happened long before you picked me up in Marcello's," I said.

Fanny pulled her shoulders back and stared defiantly at me. "Let's be clear. You picked me up."

"Yes, I've wondered about that. You didn't even know what I looked like."

Fanny gave a sly smile. "That wasn't difficult. You leave eighty thousand copies of your picture lying around every Saturday."

"Of course. My round-up column in the paper on the week's crime stories. I have a photo byline."

"But the job advertisement was real."

"I found it in Daddy's copy of the *Chronicle*."

"And what about the job-agency card?" I asked.

"The kitchen maid has been given notice and is looking for a new job. She'd been round several agencies in Brighton. She gave me the card and I wrote my own appointment on the back of it."

"I still don't understand how you tracked me to Marcello's."

"I got up early and waited in a shop doorway across the street from the *Chronicle* offices for you to arrive. But you must've already been in the building. You keep early hours."

"Not always."

"Fortunately, you then left again and went to Marcello's. That made it so much easier – especially as the place was full and I had a ready excuse to share your table."

"Where you played your little-girl-lost act to perfection."

Fanny shrugged. "And if I get lost again, will you help to find me?"

"If I can. I owe you a lot – more than you realise. Without your help, we'd have never saved Shirley."

"I'm not sure that other people will see it that way. Not when they find out about Grandmama."

I took Fanny's hand.

I said: "Last night, you showed the kind of courage which lies in the hearts of only one in a million people. Use that in the days ahead. You've plenty more of it to draw on. Use it to do the right thing whatever the consequences. Use it to carve out the life you want to live. Use it to stare the future in the face and take it on your terms."

Fanny squeezed my hand gently. She leaned towards me. Kissed me lightly on the lips.

"Thank you," she said.

She turned and walked into the house. Her back was straight. Her step was confident. She held her head high.

She didn't look back.

Chapter 27

"Couldn't you have managed more than a five-line news-in-brief for the stop press?" Frank Figgis asked.

We were in his office. Figgis was on his third packet of Woodbines for the day. The atmosphere in the place was so thick you could have smoked kippers in it.

I said: "It was already twenty minutes past the Afternoon Extra deadline when I reached the phone box in Piddinghoe village. Much too late to remake the front page for a story this big. So I dictated a nib for the fudge and raced back to the office to write the full story for the Night Final."

It was just after five o'clock in the afternoon. The Night Final – which also carried a thousand-word backgrounder I'd rattled out at turbo-charged speed on the Remington – had hit the streets. Figgis picked up a copy from his desk and studied the splash headline:

MINISTER'S MOTHER ON MURDER CHARGE

"This trumps anything the nationals have had on the Profumo affair," he said.

"Did you know the Piddinghoe family motto is *Cave latet anguis in herba*?" I said.

"Your fancy university education doesn't impress me, young Crampton."

I said nothing. Let silence hang in the air. Figgis took an embarrassed drag on his fag. "Well, what does it mean?" he said.

"Beware the snake in the grass," I translated. "Who'd have thought the snake would turn out to be Lady Piddinghoe?"

Figgis pointed at the front page. "But what I can't understand is why you've included the copy boy in the byline. This was your story."

I reached over for the paper. The byline read: by Colin Crampton and Cedric Tubbs.

I said: "It was Cedric's chance remark – about Clarence having a screw loose – that provided the clue which led me to discover the hidden copy of the sixteen-millimetre film. Besides, the lad's been aching to get his name on a story. You should give him a chance."

Figgis stroked his chin. "I'll think about it. Maybe he can give you a hand following up this other story."

He pointed at the second screamer headline further down the page:

BUTLER FACES BLACKMAIL RAP

"We haven't had such a good run of headlines since the Trunk Murders back in 1934, the year I joined the paper as a tyro reporter," Figgis said. "But I want more."

"I assume that means I won't be getting the day off I so richly deserve."

"Pleased to see you're keeping up. Now, I want two pieces tomorrow. The first is the interview with Miss Goldsmith I mentioned to you this morning. Let's get a graphic account of her ordeal. Something to tug at the heartstrings."

"And what if she doesn't want to talk?"

"I thought you pair used to walk out together."

"Actually, we preferred to lie in together. But that was before she went on her trip to India. Before she suffered the ordeal of being kidnapped at gunpoint. I don't know whether she'll even speak to me – let alone give the kind of interview you want."

Figgis stubbed out his Woodie and reached for another. "Use those legendary powers of persuasion I keep hearing about. You could finagle a vicar into reading the *Kama Sutra* to a congregation of nuns."

"Actually, that could prove easier than persuading Shirley to spill the beans on her night of terror."

"Night of terror." Figgis made a note on his blotter. "We may use that as a headline."

"If she's prepared to talk."

"I've installed her in a luxury suite at the Grand. Everything on expenses. And I've got a muscle-man from the circulation room guarding the door so no hacks can get near her."

"Except me, apparently," I said.

"That's the spirit. Anyway, that brings me to the second story I want from you. And it should be a peach."

"More fruity copy, then."

"I want a scene-by-scene description of *Milady's Bath Night*. Tell it raw, like it really is."

"The What the Butler Saw pictures all burnt in the houseboat fire," I said.

"But you've recovered a copy of the original film."

"Yes, but it's old and flaky. I'd need special viewing equipment to see the frames properly."

"Arrange it with Freddie Barkworth," Figgis said. "There must be something in that photographic department of his which will do the job. We spend enough money on it."

"I'll do what I can, but some of the frames have faded. They're just a sepia blur."

"Well, look at what's left and imagine the bits that are missing. With your experience of women, you shouldn't find that too difficult."

"So this is going to be a trip down a naughty memory lane," I said.

"I'm running this as the story of a woman who pretended to be something she wasn't. She posed as an aristocrat but performed as a stripper."

I said: "Only once – and she wasn't an aristocrat then. Only hoping to be one. Which is, incidentally, why she did it."

Figgis grinned. "I shall headline the story: THE LADY IS A

TRAMP."

"Then I shan't write it."

"What?" Figgis's mouth opened so fast, his fag dropped into his lap. He rummaged furiously in his crotch for the errant ciggie.

"Don't worry," I said. "I don't suppose there's anything flammable down there these days."

Figgis retrieved the gasper and stuck it back on his lower lip. "Are you refusing to take on an assignment?"

"Only with that headline. It's unfair to Lady Piddinghoe – and probably a source of legal trouble to. If we defame her ladyship, her legal counsel will claim we've prejudiced a fair trial. If the judge agrees, you'll be the one standing in the dock on a contempt charge."

Figgis stroked his chin. "Okay. I'll change the headline. But I still want the story."

"If you insist." I stood up and headed for the door. "But just because I'm writing about naughty pictures, I don't want you calling me a porn broker."

Cedric saw me as soon as I stepped into the newsroom.

He'd obviously been hovering around my desk waiting for me to put in an appearance. He rushed over. He waved the Night Final at me. Pointed at his byline.

"Can't thank you enough for this, Mr Crampton. It's my big break."

"Don't mention it, Cedric." I decided I'd take Figgis at his word and let the lad work with me on the Pinchbeck blackmail follow-ups. "Tomorrow you can help me on a story that will unravel the background to another mystery."

"What's that?"

"I'll tell you more in the morning. Except that, in this case, we already know that the butler did it."

Cedric bounded off to spread the news that he was now an ace reporter.

I made my way towards the morgue. I needed to speak to Henrietta Houndstooth quietly – but most definitely away from the flapping ears of the Clipping Cousins.

So when I strode into the room, I said to Henrietta: "That Polish musician who gave a concert at the Dome last year – Zakiewicz I think his name was – do we have a file on him?" I added a conspiratorial wink only she could see.

Henrietta looked puzzled. Then she caught on to my ruse and returned the wink.

"Yes," she said. "I'll show you the file. It's right at the far end of the stacks."

At the cuttings table, Elsie said: "I don't remember clipping an item about a Polish musician."

Freda said: "I see they're selling stuff for getting rid of Polish people."

Mabel said: "What's that?"

Freda said: "Polish remover. You can buy it in Boots."

Elsie said: "Don't be stupid. That's polish remover. For removing your nail polish."

I followed Henrietta swiftly into the filing stacks. We walked down a long corridor towards the back of the cabinets – where the letter Z cuttings were kept.

I said: "I wanted to get you as far away as possible from those crazy women to tell you this. You deserve some privacy to hear it."

Henrietta reached forward and squeezed my shoulder. "Thank you."

"As you'll have seen from tonight's paper, your suspicions about your mother's death were correct. She was murdered by Lady Piddinghoe. I wanted to tell you more than I could include in my report."

Henrietta broke down and sobbed. I put my arms around her while a quarter century of grief flooded out. It was several minutes before she spoke.

"Tell me everything," she said.

I did. As gently as I could, but I felt she had a right to know every detail. Besides, she would be reading about it in newspapers – not least the *Chronicle* – for weeks to come. She would be handling clippings about the story.

She listened intently, with no more tears. Her grief was spent. When I'd finished, she said: "I've often thought that if I got the truth about my mother's death it would be the end of the matter. But it's not. It's the beginning of it again."

"I'm sorry," I said. "I thought you would want to hear about it. I'll need to get a comment from you, but that can wait until tomorrow. But, in the meantime, I'd appreciate it if you didn't talk to any other reporters."

A thin smile passed over Henrietta's lips. "And spoil your exclusive? Don't worry. I won't. And that wasn't a criticism."

"If it was a reproof, I'd accept it," I said. "Sometimes we reporters forget that our stories are about real people. With genuine hopes and fears. Not just fodder to fill up a column or two."

Henrietta said: "I know this story has been personal for you, too. That must've been hard."

"You mean Shirley's kidnap?"

"Yes."

"There were times when I didn't know whether I was a reporter or her rescuer or her lover."

"But you were all three."

I leaned against a filing cabinet. "The first two, certainly. I'm not sure now about the third. I think the shock of it all has made Shirley think I'm too much like Lord Byron."

"A poet?"

I grinned. "No. 'Mad, bad and dangerous to know.'"

"I'd forgotten Lady Caroline Lamb's comment about her lover," Henrietta said.

"And now Frank Figgis wants me to interview Shirley – the

full inside story. He's moved her into a luxury suite at the Grand. He thinks it will soften her up. He'd have more luck softening granite with soap flakes."

"You think it will be difficult to get the interview?"

"I don't even know whether she'll want to speak to me."

"I see." Henrietta looked thoughtful for a moment. "We better get back to the Cousins. They'll think we're having a secret romance."

We threaded our way back through the corridors and the filing-cabinet stacks.

As we stepped into the clippings room Mabel said to Elsie: "I've been thinking about what you said earlier. If they sell polish remover in boots, doesn't it leak out of the lace-holes?"

I looked at Henrietta. Her lips twitched uncertainly into a smile. After a moment, her eyes sparkled with fun. Then she threw back her head. And she hooted with laughter.

The Grand Hotel sparkled in the sun. It looked like a multi-tiered wedding cake.

I stood on the prom and stared up at it. I wondered which room Shirley occupied. Whether she was, even now, looking at me from behind a discreet curtain.

It was a balmy summer's evening by the beach. Couples ambled by. Some arm-in-arm. Some holding hands. A perfect time to relax. To enjoy life. To find romance.

Or, in my case, to find a story. And, perhaps, romance. Or maybe neither. But there was no point standing around thinking about it. Action, I'd always found, was the best antidote to worry.

Not that, until now, I'd had much time for anxiety. After my talk with Henrietta, I'd hurried back to my desk and spent nearly two hours writing the piece about *Milady's Bath Night* that Figgis had asked for.

And now I had to discover what Shirley had in store for me.

I dodged between a bus and a couple of taxis and ran up the

steps into the hotel. Toby Baldwin, one of the *Chronicle*'s general reporters, was hanging around the lobby. He spotted me as I barged through the door and made his way over.

"What are you doing here?" I asked.

"Keeping an eye on that lot." He pointed to the bar. "There's half of Fleet Street in there and a couple of television crews. They've been trying to get into Miss Goldsmith's suite all afternoon."

"And you've stopped them?"

"Not alone. Harry Boggs is outside her door on the third floor."

Harry was a nineteen-stone monster from the circulation room. Rumour had it that he'd once been an all-in wrestler but had been blacklisted because he was never willing to throw a fight. The man was said to have never lost one – in or out of the ring. And I believed that.

I said: "I'll try my luck with Shirley. Let's hope it's in. If not, you'll be standing me a G and T with the other hacks. A very large one."

The lift doors on the third floor opened with a hiss.

I stepped out. Halfway down the corridor, Harry's bulk blocked out the light from a window.

My shoes sunk into the carpet with little squidgy sounds as I made my way towards him.

He nodded a greeting as I approached. "Thought you'd turn up sooner or later."

"Is she in?" I asked.

"Wouldn't let her out," he said.

"In a good mood?"

"Couldn't say."

"Is she expecting me?"

"I didn't ask."

"Anything sent up to the room?"

"Coffee and sandwiches."

"That's promising," I said.

"For one," Harry said.

"Not so good."

Harry nodded at the door. "Want to risk it?"

"I've got no choice."

I felt my heart quicken a beat as I opened the door and stepped into the room.

The place was just what I'd expected from a suite in Brighton's swankiest hotel. The walls were decorated in cream and red regency stripes and hung with landscapes of the Sussex countryside. Devil's Dyke, the Seven Sisters, Ditchling Beacon. A huge four-poster bed with damask drapes dominated one end of the room. A two-seater sofa and an easy chair were arranged so that guests could sit and look out to sea. A writing desk with an upright chair stood against the far wall.

Everything was as it should be in the best suite of a luxury hotel.

Except there was no Shirley.

Her backpack lay on the bed.

Beside it, her Australian passport looked creased and travel worn.

I moved further into the room. I took another look around. Off to the right was a door which led to the bathroom.

I walked over to it. A sign had been handwritten on a sheet of the hotel's notepaper. It was stuck to the door with a piece of chewing gum.

The sign read: *Milady's Bath Night.*

The bathroom door was ajar. From inside came the sound of splashing water.

I pushed the door open and stepped into the bathroom.

Shirley was lying in a bath big enough to hold a water-polo tournament. Steam floated up from the water. Soapy bubbles covered the surface – but not enough to spoil the view.

The bath oil filled the room with a seductive musk – the kind which hints that cleanliness is not always next to godliness.

Shirley read the question on my face before I spoke.

"Henrietta came half an hour ago," she said. "She explained everything."

I said: "Everything?"

"Yes. About her childhood. About her mother's murder. And what you've done to find the truth and bring the killer to justice. She thinks you're the kangaroo's cobblers."

"And what marsupial body part have you marked me down as?"

"Wouldn't you just love to know?"

Heat radiated off the bath water. Sweat was pricking at my pores. I felt hotter than I thought I should. I was breathing too fast. My heart had raced into overdrive.

Shirley grinned. It was that grin she does when her lips widen and part ever so slightly, her eyes shine with a tease – and a promise – and you just know that it's all come from her giant Aussie heart.

That grin answered all the questions I wanted to ask.

Shirley raised her hand and curled her little finger a couple of times towards me in a come-hither gesture.

"Well, Big Boy, are you just going to stand there?" she said. "Come on in. The water's lovely."

Read more Crampton of the Chronicle stories free at:

www.colincrampton.com

About Peter Bartram

Peter Bartram brings years of experience as a journalist to his Crampton of the Chronicle crime mystery series. Peter began his career as a reporter on the *Worthing Herald* newspaper before working as journalist and editor in London and finally becoming freelance. He has done most things in journalism from door-stepping for quotes to writing serious editorials. He's interviewed thousands of people from cabinet ministers to cabinet makers. He's pursued stories in locations as diverse as 700 feet down a coal mine and a courtier's chambers at Buckingham Palace. Peter wrote 21 non-fiction books, including five ghost-written, in areas such as biography, current affairs and how-to titles, before turning to crime – and penning *Headline Murder*, the first novel in the Crampton series. There is a free novella, Murder in Capital Letters, on the Crampton of the Chronicle website (address above).

Follow Peter Bartram on Facebook at:
www.facebook.com/peterbartramauthor

A message from Peter Bartram

Thank you for reading *Stop Press Murder*. I hope you have enjoyed reading it as much as I enjoyed writing it. If you have a few moments to add a short review on Amazon, GoodReads or Apple iTunes Store, I would be very grateful. Reviews are very important feedback for authors and I truly appreciate every one. If you would like news of further Crampton of the Chronicle stories, please visit my website – the address is at the top of this page.

Acknowledgements

It's not just the author, you know. Many people have helped to make the *Crampton of the Chronicle* series a success.

First, there is the fantastic team at Roundfire Books who've helped to bring out this book as well as *Headline Murder*, the first in the series. Special mention must go to publishing manager Dominic James as well as Catherine Harris, Maria Moloney, Mary Flatt, Nick Welch, Stuart Davies, Krystina Kellingley and Maria Barry.

Barney Skinner is the web genius behind the Colin Crampton website at www.colincrampton.com. The brilliant Caroline Duffy created the caricatures of Colin Crampton and his colleagues, including the redoubtable Shirley Goldsmith, on the website, in the books and on my Facebook page.

Paul and Inge Sweetman from City Books in Brighton & Hove provided invaluable help and advice on running the launch party for the first Crampton mystery. That talented and versatile actor Peter F. Gardiner brought Colin Crampton to life with a lively performed reading. I must include a special thank you for Graham Toole-Mackson who won the launch party's competition to be a character in *Stop Press Murder*. I hope he's enjoyed being a detective sergeant!

Then there are the book bloggers in the United Kingdom and the United States who have featured Crampton on their blogs. (Just Google *"Headline Murder* Peter Bartram" and your search results will light up with their contributions). Their help in spreading the word is invaluable for a new crime series and I greatly appreciate it.

Finally, and most important of all, as with *Headline Murder*, my family has been a constant source of love and encouragement during the long hours it takes to write a book.

Headline Murder

A Crampton of the Chronicle mystery

Murder, he reported... Colin Crampton faces dangers they never mentioned at journalism school when he hunts down a secret killer.

It's August 1962, and Colin Crampton, the *Brighton Evening Chronicle*'s crime reporter, is desperate for a front-page story. But it's the silly season for news – and the only tip-off Crampton has is about the disappearance of the seafront's crazy-golf proprietor, Arnold Trumper. Crampton thinks the story is about as useful as a set of concrete water-wings. But when he learns that Trumper's vanishing act is linked to an unsolved murder, he scents a front-page scoop.

Powerful people are determined Crampton must not discover the truth. But he is quite prepared to use every newspaper scam in the book to land his exclusive. The trouble is it's his girlfriend, feisty Australian Shirley, who too often ends up on the wrong end when a scam misfires.

Crampton has to overcome dangers they never mentioned at journalism school before he writes his story. *Headline Murder* will keep you guessing – and smiling – right to the last page.

Available in paperback and ebook format

At Roundfire we publish great stories. We lean towards the spiritual and thought-provoking. But whether it's literary or popular, a gentle tale or a pulsating thriller, the connecting theme in all Roundfire fiction titles is that once you pick them up you won't want to put them down.